CONTRACT OF BETRAYAL

SPECTRAS ARISE
BOOK 2

TAMMY SALYER

CONTRACT OF BETRAYAL

INTRODUCTION

Hello and thank you for being here! Should you enjoy the words on these pages (and I hope you do!), I encourage you to join my Book Club and visit me at:

www.tammysalyer.com

I occasionally send newsletters to my Book Club with new releases, special offers, and other bits of news. As a special thanks to new members, please enjoy a handful of novellas and short stories from my many and sundry universes FOR FREE.

ONE

I'm rushing over the hot desert skin of the planet, pushing the Rover at top speed just for the fun of it, hitting sandbars and bouncing high off the ground at times. It's good to get out of the mine, and late fall on Spectra 6 has come in with enough of a cool breeze blowing through the brown hills to keep me from sweating rivers every time I step outside. I'm moving too fast to really accomplish what I'm out here for—Bodie asked me to gather some samples of a newly engineered species of brush at the base of these eastern hills—but at the moment, I'm enjoying myself too much to care.

The sand is compacting into hard earth as it rises into the baked hillsides, so I steer the Rover south to flank them and give myself a few more minutes of fast-moving freedom. I come up over a finger of the closest hill, the front tires rising vertically for a moment before falling flat back to the earth—and I see it. A transport ship is sitting on the flat plain two hundred and fifty meters from my position. Immediately, I lay off the accelerator and pray that the sound of the Rover's engine doesn't echo against the hills and give me away. The ship could belong to anybody, including people it would be best to avoid.

A culvert at the base of the nearest hillock provides me plenty of cover to be hidden from the ship's view and I coast into it, kill the engine, and switch on my wrist VDU to contact the control room at Agate Beach, where someone is always listening.

"Beach control, this is Aly. Do you copy?"

"Erikson, it's Mason. What's up?"

"I've got a ship I've never seen before out here by the Torarua Range. Can you get me V?"

"Wait one."

Vitruzzi's image comes into focus on my VDU within seconds. "What's going on?"

"I'm about thirty klicks east of the Beach, at the base of the Torarua Range. We've got some company. Looks like a transport ship. Admin manufactured. Did they contact you?"

"We haven't been hailed and"—she turns to confer with Mason—"there's nothing on radar. Have they seen you?"

"Negative, as far as I can tell."

"What's their status? Does it look like a crash? Can you see any registration marks?"

"No, I just got a quick look before I got out of sight. It doesn't look like a crash. No smoke, no burns, no runners. But they're pretty far from Hell's Gate."

"We've been expecting a delivery from an old friend. It could be him. I'm on the way. Do me a favor and just hang tight. Don't let them see you. But if you can keep them from going anywhere, try. We don't want anyone unexpected flying around the Beach."

"Affirmative."

"We have your grid. Be there in twenty." There's a click as she breaks the link and my VDU screen fades to black.

Cautiously pushing the Rover's clamshell hatch open, I decide to climb to the top of the culvert to keep eyes on the stray. If they decide to launch, I'm not exactly sure how Vitruzzi expects me to keep them from going anywhere, but I'll cross that bridge if I come to it. There's no movement around the ship. From my vantage point, only the stern is visible, and I'm looking straight into the engine outflow chambers. They look clear and operational, and the inner coils have a slight reddish glow. Still hot; they haven't been here long. The fact that our radars at the Beach didn't pick them up indicates that they'd entered the atmosphere from another part of the planet and flown in the direction of the settlement below radar. Whether they intended to use stealth or if it was only coincidence is impossible to know, and it makes me nervous.

Five minutes pass and hot, stagnant air pools in the deep depression, baking my skin as if I were in a convection oven and sending streams of sweat dribbling from my hairline to the tip of my nose. Keeping my movements to a minimum, I switch on my carbine's scope, ratchet up the magnification, and peer through. A light breeze blows a welcome puff of cooler air on my face but also carries the noise of hydraulics. Panning to the left and right helps me pinpoint the cause of the noise, and I finally make out a ramp lowering from the ship's bow, the wind grabbing up a flurry of dust when it hits the ground.

That's all I need to see. Leaping back into the Rover, I yank the hatch shut, slam on the ignition, and jump it out of the culvert at top speed. I don't want whoever is on that ship to get aboard a land trans and head for Agate Beach. It's easier to hold them here than chase them down. Of course, they may be harmless. Maybe lost citizens with broken communication equipment, who knows? Better to find out now, while they're locked down, than after they've reached the settlement.

Pushing the Rover hard, I cover the distance in a few seconds and skid to a stop behind the engines. The smell of super-heated metal and burnt dust fills my nostrils as I run from the Rover to the front of the ship and take a firing position next to the lowered ramp. Raising my carbine barrel, I line up the sight with the center of the opening, ready for anything. Sounds of movement come from inside.

With a raised but steady voice, I order, "Come out slowly. You're covered in every direction."

The movement stops cold and, after a second, a voice carries down the open hatchway. "We're not armed. Coming out. Just keep cool."

That voice . . .

The first thing to emerge from the sloping ramp is a pair of military-issue boots, old and scuffed, made of a dingy pseudo-leather material that's at least five years past a military polish. Their owner jumps to the deck, kicking up wisps of desert dirt. He's about midthirties, close-cropped brown hair, hands exactly where they should be—shoulder height and empty. He's followed by a woman and two more men, all dressed in similar civilian clothing. The last one exits and takes a few short steps forward. Still a couple of meters from the opening, I keep my barrel trained at chest level, but when the man moves forward, I'm dazzled by the sunlight slanting through the ramp struts. My eyes squeeze shut involuntarily at the sudden brightness, and a tiny warning dose of adrenaline shoots into my veins at the realization that I've momentarily given up the advantage.

"I'll be goddamned! Aly Erikson!"

It can't be. The silhouette moves closer, blocking the piercing light, and I'm finally able to focus on him.

"Sergeant Cross?"

"Oh, come on, Aly. You know me better than that! I don't believe what I'm seeing!"

There are hundreds of rocks in this solar system, and the likelihood of running into someone from my past on this one had, until now, seemed like a complete impossibility. It would be like finding a bullet from your own gun tumbling through the floating debris of a long-since-concluded interstellar battle.

Impossible or not, I'm staring at proof that it can happen. Rob Cross. Munitions team platoon leader from the 808th Ground Division. I last saw him a year before the Soldier's Rebellion, when David's and my flight patrol unit stopped dropping troops into hot zones. His detachment was reassigned to another ship. We hadn't kept in touch.

Nearly stuttering with surprise, I ask, "Wh-what are you doing out here?"

"Is that happiness to see me? It's hard to tell." He's standing less than a meter in front of me, smiling in a cavalier way I remember too well. But his eyebrows are raised in a hint of concern—a natural response to the fact that my carbine is still leveled at his heart.

Regardless, it's been eight years since I've seen him, and I'm not that trusting. "I don't believe this is a coincidence."

Before he can respond, the ground around us begins to gyrate as the *Sphynx*'s shuttle descends. No one speaks, the craft's engines too loud to be heard over. I cover my eyes with one hand and let the carbine sag. Vitruzzi's coming in close, not showing the kind of concern she would for someone she doesn't know. Could Cross be the person she's expecting?

When they hit the dirt, the shuttle's door slides open and she steps out, Karl and David following behind. "Cross, it's good to see you. Why didn't you signal us when you got in our orbit? You're three days early."

He turns toward them with a renewed smile, and I finally lower my weapon. "Good to see you again, Eleanor. Her reversals went haywire and caused a wiring issue that sucked all the power from my com system *and* my engine backups. We were hoping to get a little closer to Agate Beach before we had to set her down, but . . ." He shrugs.

"No backup power? I'm *glad* you didn't get any closer." Vitruzzi steps aside, letting me get a better look at David, who stares at Cross with a gape-mouthed mixture of shock and disbelief. I can't help but grin at his incredulity, though my own expression moments ago must not have been so different.

"Rob Cross?" David takes a step forward and peers at Rob, as if questioning his own eyesight.

"I don't believe this. This day just gets better and better!"

The two men embrace in a hearty man-hug like brothers, slapping each other on the back. David asks, "What the hell are you doing out here on the fringes? And with your own transport ship? I didn't think the Corps would ever trust you among civilians." I haven't seen him so pleased in quite a while. The three of us had some good times together, back when we all still belonged to the Corps.

"I take it you know each other," Vitruzzi comments, surprised.

"Know each other? Eagle Eye Erikson's the only man in the system who could keep up with me back in the old days." A huge smile spreads across Cross's face, causing a fan of crow's feet to sweep out in a winning arc. He has the kind of smile that makes a person feel like they've just been reunited with a twin brother or best friend after years of being apart. There's no sign of sarcasm or irony in his face; his expression is complete and genuine openness and enthusiasm. All of a sudden, I feel like I did a few years ago when I woke up to that same smile nearly every off-duty morning. My mind summons the mildly sharp smell of his skin, and I remember too clearly how his body felt next to mine. It throws me off balance for a minute, and I realize I'm blushing.

I pull my eyes away from his face and catch Karl looking at me strangely. Blushing twice as hard, I turn back to the ship, which at this moment is the only safe thing to look at.

"Let's get you guys back to Agate Beach. When was the last time you ate anything fresh? We can talk over some lunch," Vitruzzi says.

"Sounds terrific. And can you spare any viridian heat rods? If we can get those in, we'll be able to get the *Red Horizon* to your mine. I hate leaving her out in the open. You never know what kind of scavengers may find their way out here."

Vitruzzi gets on her com and locates Bodie. A moment later she says, "Bodie and Venus will be here in a few minutes to get you squared away. Were you able to get everything we talked about?"

"Have I ever let you down, Eleanor? Yeah, come on in and check things out. There's at least ninety kilos of scrap steel and enough wire to build yourself a new ship."

"What about the comlink switches? And the seeds?"

"And those."

"Thanks, Rob. It's good to have someone we can rely on."

He smiles again, not quite gloating but close, and focuses his attention back on me. "So what do you say, Aly? You're too quiet. That's nothing like I remember."

I have to clear my throat before I can speak. I woke up this morning thinking I'd be helping Bodie collect specimens from the local plants. Nothing prepared me to be standing face-to-face with an ex-lover, the first man in my life that ever meant more to me than just a pleasant way to kill a couple of hours. "I'm just really surprised. I never expected to see you again." I'm at such a loss for words that I'm nearly mumbling.

"I know! It's amazing, isn't it? You're as beautiful as I remember." One of his crewmen, a tough-looking hatchet of a man, walks between us to get back on the ship, finally breaking through my paralysis.

Time to escape this awkward situation. "Vitruzzi, I'll take the Rover back to the Beach. It looks like you have things handled here."

She shrugs and I turn to climb aboard. Before I can pull the clamshell cover closed, Karl steps over and motions toward the seat. "Mind if I drive?"

I shrug and push over to the passenger side. Before the hatch closes, I hear Rob ask, presumably speaking to David, "So what's that about? She's not angry with me is she?"

"It's a little . . . uh . . . complicated."

TWO

Karl accelerates back to the settlement, and I lean back in the seat, feeling a strange sense of time-vertigo, as if I'm stuck in a black hole's event horizon. My life up to now is in redshift, simultaneously standing still and blurring away at the edges. What the hell had just happened? For a second, it had seemed as if my real life was back in the Corps—fresh out of the Academy and aboard my first duty ship with my older brother and the charming squad leader, Tech 1 Sergeant Cross, who'd caught my full attention the first time I'd seen him.

My swirling thoughts turn sour as they mix with guilt and I glance sideways at Karl. We're a team now, lovers, friends, together as much as we can be—partners. If you had told me six months ago that I'd find someone, besides my brother, that I cared about more than myself, I would have thought you were sadly sentimental and possibly delusional. What Karl and I had been through—the Fortress, the rescue mission to save David, Zeta, Mason, and Jade, and the fact that Karl had risked his life more than once to save mine —had affected me, changed me to my core. His selflessness and perseverance brought me back to life when I should have been dead, and resuscitated the part of me that understood that there was more to being alive than just breathing and making it to the next day. With all that's passed, Karl and the settlers at Agate Beach have become more than friends; they're all my family now.

He drives as if he'd seen me doing more than blushing over Rob, in some kind of fury that I only half register as I silently struggle with the realization that things that had only recently begun to grow stable and steady—both life in the Beach and between Karl and I— may have just become complicated again. When Cross's unit had been reassigned, it was hard on me. The dread I had about the Corps and its master puppeteer the Admin was already rooted deep in my psyche. The loathing I felt for the way they wore out lives—the same way machines wear out gears—for their convenience and greed was taking its toll on me, and my allies were getting fewer and fewer. Even David was telling me I sounded paranoid and needed to keep my mouth shut before the Corps put me on the mentally incapacitated chit and locked me up. Cross's departure left me with no more distractions and no one else to lean on. By that point, I had lost both my lover and my convictions, and my life changed completely.

Karl hits a sandbar going too fast and I jolt back into the present. "Careful, kamikaze, or we're going to have to replace the rear axle again." He remains sullenly silent without even a glance in my direction. "Hey, you okay?"

"Yeah, just didn't see that." He reaches into his vest and pulls out his pack of homemade cigarettes, clamps one between his teeth, and lights it with one hand. He takes a deep pull from the smoke, squinting until the color of his eyes is hidden, and keeps his gaze locked on the baked earth outside the Rover's cockpit.

Yeah, something is bothering him, but I know him well enough by now to know that he won't breathe a word about what it might be until he's either ready to hash it out at full volume or decides to let it go forever. There is no in between with him, and he never hesitates to point out that I'm exactly the same way. He'll tell me what's on his mind when he's ready for me to know.

We're still ten kilometers from the settlement when a shadow quickly overtakes us from behind. I raise my head to see what's going on just as the *Red Horizon* buzzes past in a low bank no more than fifty meters above our heads on its way to Agate Beach. Vitruzzi transmits to Karl's wrist VDU. "We're all getting together at Pat's and my place at 1900 hours for dinner. Can you two make it?"

Karl glances at me before answering, and I don't miss the reluctance stretching the skin around his mouth too tight. "Want to go?"

"Why not?" I try to sound neutral, but the pitch of my voice raises a notch, completely betraying me.

He depresses the transmit button and replies, "See you tonight, V."

THREE

Unable to find Bodie to explain why I hadn't gathered any of his samples earlier, I ditch the mine early and walk to Vitruzzi's. As I enter, I find her and Bodie side by side, hunched over the main room's central table and raptly focused on the fleximesh monitor covering it. They both nod a quick *hello* and return their attention to the meshmo, as Bodie calls it. Like an overprotective librarian, he has assumed control over the variety of scientific and monitoring equipment stored within the mine's control room and this delicate readout device rarely leaves it. Most of the equipment has been painstakingly "acquired" from Admin ships or cities and now makes up the Beach's technical hub. Besides the *Sphynx*, this equipment is the only thing that differentiates the Beach from the kind of anachronistic settlement people must have lived in on old Earth before such "high-tech" advancements as electricity and indoor plumbing.

All right, maybe a slight embellishment, but no one can deny that the Beach is just about as primitive as colonies come in the Spectras —which, surprisingly, suits me fine.

"You see the numbers, V. It can't work," Bodie says as he taps a stream of text and images slowly descending the screen's surface. "It's the same exact problem they documented in the reports we took from the Fortress. If we'd only had fifteen more minutes, I could have taken a complete copy of the data. It was right in my damn hands."

"I know, I know. But fifteen more minutes and we would have been vaporized right along with it. Either way, we don't know what their final developments were. We don't even know if they were successful," Vitruzzi answers.

Brady and Vitruzzi's residence serves as the crew's de facto meeting center during the cooler evenings. Few people bother to knock when they know they're expected, and I'm no exception. Glancing around, it doesn't look like Brady is here, causing me an involuntary twitch of relief. The amount of time we can tolerate each other is inversely proportional with the amount of time we share oxygen molecules, and our fragile truce is strongest when we're miles apart. With him out of the picture for now, I can relax and pay attention to Vitruzzi and Bodie's conversation.

Bodie sighs, and then seeing something on the screen, taps the command to stop its flow. "But look here. This is the thing that really grabs my interest." He points.

The data Bodie has is a by-product of our mission to the Fortress. While the crew waited for Karl and Desto to bring in my brother and I, Bodie had the time to retrieve files from the laboratory computers that had been left unguarded after the prisoners we'd set loose went on attack. I considered it morbid curiosity at first—not realizing those so-called scientists had been working on projects outside of whatever evil shit they could invent to inflict suffering on people— but Bodie had mentioned that most of the information had something to do with soil alteration experiments. "Growing better food, Aly," he'd tried to explain, which naturally reduced my interest from marginal to extinct. I've lived on ship and field rations for more than half my life, having long since given up the ambitious expectation of actually enjoying my meals. So when it comes to food production, it's not an exaggeration to say I know more about the workings of a pulse carbine or interstellar system map and can't be bothered to care much about where my food comes from as long as I have some when I need it.

Still, Vitruzzi's next question yanks my attention to front and center. "Now what the hell would they have been doing on Keum Libre?"

As I step up to the table to get a look at whatever Bodie's pointing at, they move closer together to allow me to see it better.

The advanced developmental formula being tested on Keum Libre has shown favorable results. Potential increased production is anticipated to be approved and commence within 30-60 days. Director T'Kai has reiterated that no commercialization foci will be pursued.

"Do you think that means what I think it means?" I ask in a voice gritty with anger and disgust. The penal colony is inhabited by only the worst of the worst criminals, the ones the Admin has deemed incapable of rehabilitation and readmission into society. After what we'd heard from the twisted Admin doctor Kellen Vilbrandt and then seen them doing to people on the Fortress, it's no stretch to imagine they'd be doing the same to the inmates of Keum Libre.

"Yeah, it seems like the logical conclusion to assume they're testing stuff on KL's population, but I don't think that's what it is, Aly," Bodie answers. "I think they had a more complete version of this soil application that was working, and they were maybe testing it there. It's a natural environment that no one cares about, so it would make sense to do field tests where results would be more reliable than they would in lab research."

"Sure."

He arches one bushy eyebrow in annoyance at my scorn. "I guess the only way to know would be to make a trip to KL. But that statement about a commercialization focus makes it pretty clear, at least to me, that it wasn't something that would be considered a hazard."

He has a point, and this time I keep my mouth shut.

"What did you say about going to Keum Libre?" Brady steps inside carrying a box full of food, presumably for dinner. He lays it on the counter at the far side of the room, then walks to Vitruzzi and kisses her cheek. With the barest glance at me in greeting, he leans over the table to examine the meshmo.

"I was saying that I think they may have completed the research they needed to do to make this soil enhancement formula work and were probably testing it on KL. If I had even just a sample of the ground from there—"

"Forget it," Brady says. "You know how crazy that sounds? It's a least a week of flying, probably more like two, and there has to be a solid force of Corps or Admin security surrounding the rock. Especially if this formula, or whatever it is, is as valuable as you've been saying. Anyway, we have what we need to keep the settlement running. This 'soil enhancement formula' sounds too good to be true."

Scowling, Bodie folds the meshmo, his frustration evident in his slow and deliberate movements.

"WE'RE FLOATING FIFTY meters off the bow of this frigate with its engine completely locked thanks to the EM pulse we shot it with. I'm thinking that we fried at least half of the thruster grid and maybe their coms, so it wasn't going anywhere on its own. Erikson's crew searched it top to bottom using both eyes-on and scanners, but there wasn't anything. Their CO—you remember that guy, David? Captain Hobins or Hogans, something like that. What a bastard. Anyway, he was pissed because he swore the intel on these smugglers was right. My squad's in the airlock ready to escort their crew to lockdown when David's team brought them back on board. They came in and Hobins instantly starts chewing Erikson a new one. Why didn't you find anything? Why was the search ineffective? Did you use the scanners? Et cetera, et cetera. Erikson's just standing there, staring out of the airlock hatch, and then he blurts out, like the captain isn't even there, 'Doesn't this class of frigate have a concave forward hull?' Hobins starts to steam at being interrupted, but one of the other crewman says that's correct and Erikson says, 'Then why is this one's convex?'

"Hobins hadn't ordered a hull scan, and he gets so worked up about Erikson drawing attention to the fact that he makes him suit up and go check it out. Sure enough, the whole shipment of missing mining core-bits is there. One thing you can say about Eagle Eye, he never misses the obvious."

We're all seated around the main room in the center of Vitruzzi and Brady's hexagonal dwelling. Dinner is over and Cross and David are reminiscing about the days when the three of us were stationed on the Corps long-range enforcement ship the PCA *Thor's Hammer*. I glance around the room noting how everyone listens raptly to Cross's story. He's always liked attention.

David picks it up. "The funniest part about it was that the smugglers had left one of their men with the stolen equipment. When I broke into the compartment, he looked pretty surprised to see me. I think he was even more surprised when he realized his whole crew had been arrested and left him out there with no way to get back on the frigate. Since the controls were burnt out, he wouldn't have been able to open the airlock hatch from the outside. And his buddies weren't talking. Honor among thieves, right, Twig?"

He winks at me, no doubt thinking, as I am, about the way we'd been betrayed by our own former smuggling crew. I can only hope the attachments we're developing here won't turn out the way those had. Part of me still struggles against an ingrained reluctance to get too close to the settlers, people I hardly know, but Karl helps me keep from giving in to my old habits. Cutting bait and running every time things get tough is no way to live.

The thought makes me look over at Karl sitting next to Venus. He's been quiet this evening, his forehead crumpled in a brooding scowl. Every so often, he walks outside by himself to smoke, but I'm starting to wonder if he just doesn't want to be around Cross. Ever since the *Red Horizon* landed, Karl's been edgy. Is it because he can tell that Cross and I have a history—though he hasn't asked me about it —or is it something else?

"Man, I though Hobins was going to come apart," Cross says, chuckling over the way our old CO had reacted about being upstaged by his subordinates. "He'd already reported that we hadn't found anything, and then you come back with the entire missing cargo. That guy was your typical company commander—promoted beyond his capacity to be effective, but short of his capacity to realize it."

Everyone laughs, even those who hadn't been in the Corps. A pompous jerkoff too busy stroking his own ego to know when he's wrong is a universal character.

"Aly, do you remember that time he busted us in the armory?" Before I can respond, Cross launches into another tale from our past. "Aly and I were getting in some off-duty 'recreation' in the *Hammer*'s portable arms storage when Hobins comes in and scares the shit out of us. I stood up too fast, trying to get dressed, and ran into one of the arms-locker doors. It latched with Aly's shirt stuck inside and locked, of course. So she grabs her rifle and slings it over her chest just as the captain walks around the corner. We did what we were supposed to —came to attention and saluted. Me with only one leg of my pants on and Aly using her carbine to cover her top, and both of us nearly having a stroke from trying not to laugh. He freaked! Damn, we were so in for it."

I catch myself simultaneously wanting to smile and wanting to run Cross through with my dinner knife. How could he tell a story like that? Here? Desto and Bodie are practically falling off their chairs with laughter. In fact, everyone is getting a good guffaw at my expense. Everyone, that is, except Karl. He rockets from his seat like he'd been stung by it and strides out the door. His sandbike rumbles to life, the noise of its engine fading as he drives away.

The chuckles subside, and Cross asks, innocently, "What did I say?" But he's looking at me knowingly, and I feel hot blood rush to my cheeks for the second time today.

I have to say something in my defense, but David beats me to it, "So Rob, now that you've done the impossible and made Aly speechless, I guess you probably know to sleep with one eye open tonight." He's trying to lighten the mood, but his eyes shift toward me with concern. He knows the deal between Karl and I, everyone here does. If the tables were turned, I'd probably be just as pissed off hearing Karl's old flames talk so openly about their prior excursions. But dammit, this is all out of nowhere and I don't really know what I'm supposed to say. I had not planned on crossing paths with Cross today—or ever—and I'm not sure how to respond to the whole situation.

"Actually, that kind of brings me to a question I wanted to ask." Cross changes the subject, finally, and addresses Brady and Vitruzzi. "With the changes to Admin contracts coming down, we've found ourselves with a few less clients than normal and time on our hands until we can line up another job. I thought we might stick around the Beach for a while. Take a minivacation."

He stops, taking in the silence and quizzical looks that surround him. "I mean, we can make ourselves useful, and we have all the provisions we need. We won't put any strain on your food or other supplies."

"Hell yeah! Give me a chance to win that pile of money back you fleeced from me last time you were here," Desto responds.

Vitruzzi pulls up closer to the table and lays her hands flat against it, as if bracing herself. "What changes to Admin contracts, Rob?"

Sudden understanding settles on Rob's face and his olive skin loses a shade of color. "You haven't heard," he states.

"Heard what?" Brady asks.

Before answering, Rob walks over to the counter and pours himself another glass of water. Turning, he says, almost to himself, "That makes sense. You wouldn't know if you hadn't traveled to the Obals lately." He pauses, taking a long drink. "The Admin started rescinding all of their contracts with non-cit crews or crews with non-cits in them. They're basically closing all Obal space to anyone who isn't an Admin citizen. Some are saying it's a matter of time before they even let anyone leave, citizen or not. There's been so much upheaval, and that facility that was destroyed a few months ago . . . they're on serious crackdown, doing a bigger policing job of the system than I"—he glances at me—"or any of us, have ever seen.

They're serious about catching whoever blew up their—whatever it was. The rumor is that an important research facility was destroyed. What kind of research is anyone's guess," he adds as an afterthought, finishing the water and setting the glass down.

My eyes find Vitruzzi's face. If what Cross is saying is true, Agate Beach could be in real trouble. Much of our equipment, a good portion of our food, and all of our medical supplies are brought in from citizen ports. Ports that Vitruzzi and Karl have easy access to given their citizen status and Admin contracts. If they can't leave the Spectras or run cargo for the Admin, this settlement could just dry up and blow away.

"Why don't you want to head back to Obal 10? Isn't that your usual port-of-call?" Brady asks, apparently deciding the subject isn't to be discussed now. Brady and I may have our differences, but the man has shown me in these last couple of months that there is nothing he won't do to keep himself, and the people he feels responsible for, safe. I often wonder what the system would be like if men like him were running it instead of the scum serving as members of the Admin Cabinet of Directorates.

"Yeah, it is. But what's the harm? It would be great to catch up with David and Aly. Eight years is a lot of water under the bridge, and by the look of those raccoon rings Erikson's sporting, I suspect they've got some interesting stories to tell. Am I right, Eagle Eye?" Cross is referring to a residual pinkish discoloration of the skin encircling David's eye sockets. A happy little reminder of the shit the Admin had put in them on the Fortress to test whatever god-awful chemicals they had concocted for whatever unspeakable purpose. David's sight has returned as acutely as ever, but the skin around them seems burned, and it's uncertain if it will ever look normal again.

David says, "I don't see any harm in it, Brady. I'll vouch for Rob."

"I don't have any objections." Vitruzzi adds her piece. "If the material he just brought isn't exactly what we need, maybe he can do another run for us before his next job. Save us some time and trouble, at the least." *Especially if we can't get them ourselves*, she doesn't have to add.

"That would be no problem. Happy to help," Cross responds.

After a few more seconds of quiet deliberation, Brady finally says, "Yeah, okay, fine. Desto or Bodie could probably find room for you and—"

"Don't even worry about it. We're fine sleeping on the *'Rize*. She's really home anyway."

Cross's three companions have said very little all evening, accepting food and drink with reserved politeness and melting into the edges of the group. I notice that even Cross rarely addresses them, and I wonder how long they've flown together.

"The night's young. Why don't you all come over to our place and pony up some of that hard-earned cash in a rematch? I feel like revenge may be mine tonight. Anyone else want to get spanked?" Desto's poker tactics are a local phenomenon. I've learned that the only way to keep from losing money to him is not to play. David and Bodie, however, aren't resigned to their collective losses and get ready to go.

Cross stands up and beams a winning smile at Vitruzzi and Brady. "Thanks again for the hospitality. Agate Beach has become my oasis from the Admin's BS these last couple of years. Tomorrow, whatever you need help with, the crew and I at your disposal."

"Thanks, Rob. I have some ideas," Vitruzzi responds.

Cross looks over at me. "How about you, Aly? Care to join us?"

"No, I've got some things I need to take care of." In reality, if Karl's gone back to the dwelling he shares with Desto and Doug Mason, I'm not sure it would be a good idea for me to show up there with Cross. I'll see Karl tomorrow and maybe find a way to smooth out whatever's going on between us. That, or he and Cross will "smooth" it out tonight. Either way, I'd rather avoid being around if the two of them decide to beat their chests in a testosterone-soaked dick-measuring contest.

"Suit yourself. In any case, it's good to see you again." He walks out with his crew, leaving me to wonder how he could possibly sound so sincere.

When the sound of Bodie and Desto's sandbikes and Cross's

team's land transport fades off, I turn my attention back to Vitruzzi and Brady.

"You've known Cross for a while?"

Vitruzzi is collecting plates and piling them in their sanitizing system. "Since I was still on Obal 10. He was already a contractor and helped Karl and I find the *Sphynx*. He's a good man, but it sounds like you know that." Even she can't avoid joking about my obvious embarrassment.

I manage to keep the blush at bay this time. "What about the rest of his crew: Baker, Montoya, Sims? Who are they?"

A crease slides down between her black brows like the drop of rain that precludes a thunderstorm, but it's Brady who responds, "We don't know them."

"V, do you think it's a good idea to have a bunch of strangers hanging around while we're building the transceiver? I mean, yeah, you trust Rob, but these others? They do work for the Admin, you know."

"Jesus, you two are more paranoid than rats in a storm drain during monsoon season. Look, the fact is, the transceiver will be ready for testing soon, and we could really use another ship in the sky to tell us if it's working. I think we should ask Cross. With him and the *Sphynx* and . . ."—her eyes shift away from me and her jaw tightens for a split second—"and a lot of luck, we'll know if our plan is a go, or if it's just wishful thinking."

The plan she's talking about, she and Brady are thinking of it as the best insurance policy money can buy, but I'm not so sure.

She continues, "Rob's loyalty to the Admin only extends up to a point. We can trust *him* if we can trust anyone. I'll talk to him about it tomorrow."

Neither Brady nor I say anything more. At least in this one thing we're united: neither of us likes to show our cards unless we know we have nothing to lose.

Reading the doubt in our eyes, she adds, "If it makes you feel better, I'll ask him to keep it quiet and leave his crew out of it."

"I think that's the best option. Cross is reliable, but that doesn't make him one of us, Eleanor. You know I trust your instincts, but we can't risk too much," Brady says.

I'm not convinced that it's a good idea to let anyone else in on the transceiver. The thing itself might be a harmless communication device, but the way we plan to use it is a one-way trip to the Admin's version of hell if we're caught—but arguing with her isn't going to change her mind. "I'd like to be there when you tell him about the transceiver."

Vitruzzi levels her hard almost black eyes on me in a stare that would make most people uncomfortable, but I'm used to it. "Sure," she says flatly. "See you at work tomorrow."

As I walk out the door, I feel a strange discontinuity turning knots in my stomach. Besides David, I know Cross better than anyone here, and eight years ago I wouldn't have thought twice before trusting him, even with my life. But people change. Things grow unstable, unpredictable. Sometimes, people can be pushed, or they take risks that are too big. And before they even realize what happened, their backs are against the wall and they're doing dangerous, unexpected things just to survive. Sometimes that means sacrifice, sometimes it means betrayal. I can't help but wonder, what has Cross been doing since I saw him last? What kinds of risks has he taken?

It's a subject I know a lot about. In the six years since David and I deserted the Corps, I've made compromises and taken risks that seem insane. That *were* insane. Risks that eventually culminated in being betrayed by Rajcik, nearly losing my brother, and almost dying on the Fortress. The wound has fully healed and I no longer walk listing to one side to compensate for the nerve damage caused by Rajcik's bullet—the only thing he ever gave me—but it could have gone another way. For a while, every decision I made, even the ones that seemed firmly rooted in self-preservation, was the wrong one. My recklessness may or may not have been wise, but David and I are still alive and I've learned a hard lesson. Cross had never been reckless in the same way, at least not when I knew him. But, just as Vitruzzi had said, his loyalty has its limits. Always has.

. . .

KARL AND I had gone to Vitruzzi and Brady's for dinner together and his abrupt departure earlier leaves me on foot, but I'm content to walk. Venus had dragged me out of my bunk on the *Sphynx* a month ago, telling me that living underground wasn't healthy, and it's only a short distance to the dwelling we now share. The cool night air of the desert will be a perfect balm to my overheated brain.

At the time, I thought Venus was doing me a favor, but as the weeks have passed, I realize she needs me more than I needed somewhere besides the *Sphynx* to go. Her constant frenzy makes managing routine tasks, such as cooking without burning the place down, a challenge. The only time I've seen her truly calm is when she's at the helm of a ship, and almost as a matter of survival, I've embraced the challenge of ensuring she doesn't kill herself, or me, out of pure absentmindedness. Besides the bathroom and main room, we each have our own room for racking out, but unless we're sleeping, we're never there. The settlement, despite its isolation and limited resources, keeps me busy and there isn't much slack time. It's better that way. The routines I've carved out here bring me a kind of satisfaction smuggling never could.

The western horizon is a deep shade of red where Algol B spins, only fully setting for a few short hours each night. As I approach the dwelling, lights and laughter twine together in an inviting stream that spills from the doorway. Jeremy La Mer—a prisoner from the MCACS we'd hijacked to infiltrate the Fortress—is here. I stand outside for a minute, hesitant to enter for some reason. Hearing Venus and La Mer, their happiness and carefree youth, sends a pang of . . . what? sadness? . . . through me. Karl and I have our fights, *loud* ones, but since the first night we'd spent together—lying out under the shadow of the cliffs to the west of the settlement, the scent of night and desert grasses making me giddy, his hands moving in delicious exploration over my body in a way that left my skin thirsty for more—I haven't considered the possibility that such fulfillment may be temporary. But his coolness since Cross had landed today and the way he'd reacted tonight at hearing Cross's story jams that possibility into my gut in a way that hurts more than any bullet ever could.

There's a crash inside followed by immediate silence. Seconds later, Venus's explosive laughter splinters the air. I take a deep breath and walk in.

"Hey."

"Aly! Jer was just showing me how to convert these broken-down com monitors into signal magnifiers."

The sharp smell of burnt electrical components stings my nose and a full-sized VDU lies shattered at Venus's feet. She sees me looking and says, "I got a little carried away with the testing, but you should see what the sound of radio feedback looks like! It's the craziest wave pattern you can imagine."

"It carried a little more vibration than I expected, but these monitors definitely aren't junk yet," La Mer tells me, a lopsided grin on his face. Wearing that expression, he looks like a kid barely old enough to shave, and I laugh at myself for how much of a battle-hardened harpy I'm starting to sound like—at only thirty.

La Mer is tall, taller than anyone else in the Beach except Desto. His skin is the sable, silky hue of strong black tea, always seeming to glow with a moonlit sheen, even in the day. His eyelashes are long and flirtatious, arrayed around his tranquil green eyes like a corona. It's not in the least difficult to see why Venus fell for him the instant he'd suggested a recode of the *Sphynx*'s engine sequencers to help increase reaction speed. His quiet yet contagious enthusiasm is an excellent counterpoint to her nonstop energy, and his Cimmerian tone is an elegant backdrop to her colorless, nearly transparent paleness. The only surface similarities they share, in fact, are their youth and their brilliant green eyes.

Mason had found La Mer stowing away aboard the *Sphynx* after we'd escaped the Fortress, and his story is an interesting one—which is fortunate for him. It had to be to keep Desto from throwing him out of the airlock. I'm still not certain I believe it, but I have to admit, the sheer unlikelihood of why he'd been taken prisoner is what makes it plausible.

The Corps picked him up on Eruo Pium, one of Spectra 3's habitable moons, and arrested him for treason two weeks before we'd hijacked his prisoner transport. He'd been on the run for six years, and in that time they'd identified him as a member of a network of programming techs and citizen wire-rats who had worked together before the Soldier's Rebellion of 2719, developing, testing, and, eventually, unleashing the software virus that completely wiped out the primary records database for all Corps personnel, then hunted down and erased more than half the data backup logs before the Admin had stopped it. The system-wide manhunt started right after the Soldier's Rebellion and had been going on since. In the Admin's eyes, wire-rats like La Mer are the single biggest threat the government has ever encountered.

They're both smiling at me and I realize I've been standing in the doorway silently for several seconds thinking about all the things that have happened since I'd deserted the Corps. In a way, I have this shy, boyish wire-rat to thank for most of it. If the Corps's records hadn't been destroyed, they'd have probably tracked David and I down a long time ago. La Mer and Venus don't seem to be concerned at my awkward entrance and merely wait for me to come in. I guess they've gotten used to the way I disengage, easily distracted by my own thoughts. It's been this way since Rajcik shot me—surviving a death sentence tends to make a person more thoughtful than they once were. Sometimes I wonder if I'm getting soft.

"Desto radioed us. Said there's a poker game at his and Karl's place. Rob's there. He's an old friend of yours, right, Aly?" Venus asks as she carefully toes the shards of the VDU screen aside.

I walk around the mess toward my bedroom door. "You could say that."

"You're not interested in a hand? I know Desto's insanely competitive, but he really sucks at poker." Venus is the only person in the system who could think Desto isn't a savant at poker. Her ability to read people is almost preternatural. It's a good thing for the rest of us she's too high-strung to play. "You'd probably be able to win a couple hundred dollars, or at least make him take some of your shifts in the grow rooms." My dislike for gardening is well-known throughout the settlement.

"Nah, I'm a little tired. Just going to turn in early tonight."

La Mer's thoughtful eyes are pinned to my face and I catch his gaze. He does me a favor by changing the subject. "Bodie and I should be able to wire in the last pieces of the transceiver in the next couple of days. If Vitruzzi and Brady say it's a go, we could test it by the end of the week. Pretty exciting, huh?"

"That's great news." With my concern over Vitruzzi's plan to ask Cross to help test, I can't quite summon the enthusiasm I know he's feeling.

"Using Admin tooders to transmit to and from the *Sphynx*? It's not just exciting." Venus takes an almost condescending school-marmish tone that is comical coming from someone who's too guileless to be anything but puppy-dog friendly. "It's *brilliant*! They'll never know, and our link ups will be almost instantaneous! No more days of lag between the Beach and the rest of the system. We'll finally be able to communicate and coordinate in real time. Just what they don't want."

Tooders, aka TDRSs, or Tracking and Data Relay satellites. The Admin builds and controls the only reliable satellite network in the system. Therefore, they control the air-to-ground communication throughout. If you control coms, you control everything. Private individuals, mostly citizens, have built and dispersed a handful of open-link satellites in out-of-the-way pockets of space, but they're so distant that messages take from hours to days to get from sender to receiver, and if either party is on the move, it takes even longer.

La Mer's expression is somber. "*If* it works. We can't be sure—I still don't know if my programming will override their lockouts until we test it." He bends down and slowly begins collecting some of the broken hardware on the floor. "It's actually a big risk. If they catch us trying to boost their coms . . . you know, it could be bad."

"Don't worry! You're a genius, Jer. I know it will work," Venus says.

"V is thinking about using Cross to help us run the test," I comment, hoping they'll come up with a reason it would be a bad idea, maybe something that can help me convince Vitruzzi of it.

La Mer turns sharply to face me. "What? Why?" he asks. "I mean, we could use another ship in orbit to test the transmission, but he's not, not really—I mean he's *Admin*."

Finally, another person who gets my concerns. "That's what I told V, but she thinks he's trustworthy." I sigh.

"She wouldn't take any risks she hasn't already calculated. Rob and V go back a few years," Venus muses. "Seems like you and he have too, Aly. You really think he'd turn us in for something like this?"

"I don't know. It's just—shit, never mind. I'm going to turn in. See you in the morning." It's a done deal. Worrying about it isn't going to change Vitruzzi's mind, and La Mer is right. The thing needs to be tested. It doesn't do us any good if we don't know if it works reliably.

"Night, Aly! We'll try and keep the noise down."

To Venus, keeping the noise down means trying not to make anything explode, and I lie awake for another couple of hours while they continue their experimentation. It's not a problem. I have a lot on my mind.

FOUR

In the morning, I run four laps around the settlement, about nine kilometers, grab a quick, tasteless breakfast of watery fortified grains, and head directly to the mine. It's still early—Algol A is draped along the crest of the Torarua Range, not quite high enough yet to beat the planet into smelt-hot submission, and the glittering debris belt around the distant red dwarf that comprises the third star in our system, Algol C, can still be faintly seen in the southern sky—but there is no shortage of early risers in Agate Beach. People here seem to naturally sleep less, having grown accustomed to the five short hours of complete darkness at night during the fall, and less in the summer.

I'm supposed to be working underground with Desto in the weapons vault today, doing overhaul and maintenance. Even in the fall, it gets hot out there, and being underground is usually a respite welcomed by all. A quick ride down the mine tunnel on my sandbike takes me into the main cavern, ready to get busy. The mine's central room is gigantic and the *Red Horizon* sits neatly on its tripod landing gear beside the *Sphynx*. Built for long hauls transporting heavy-volume loads, the *'Rize* is a bigger ship by a factor of about two. Next to it, the *Sphynx* looks barely fit for cross-continent hops.

The *'Rize*'s cargo-hold ramp is down, leaving the ship open to anyone who might want to wander aboard. Curious, I stop my sandbike in front of it and try to get a look inside. No lights on, just a dark hold, even after I pull off my thick, tinted riding goggles. Oh well. I throw the goggles in my back carrier and reach out to kill the bike's engine and park.

"Hey, good morning!" Cross calls, coming down the dark ramp.

My first instinct is to keep going, but there's no reason to be rude. Could I still be harboring some resentment for the way he'd just dropped off the map when his unit was reassigned? After eight years? Being this uncomfortable around him is starting to get on my nerves and I make an effort to answer amiably. "How are you? Sleep well?"

He runs his hand through his tousled black hair, leaving thick sheaves of it standing on end. "Honestly, I always sleep better on the ground than when I'm in the sky."

"You're probably in the wrong profession then."

He looks at me oddly for long enough that I think he must have misunderstood me. Then he says, "Yeah, but the money's good in what I do."

"Which is?"

The crooked grin that spreads across his face embarrasses me slightly. I'm giving him the third degree and I don't know why.

"Same sweet Aly. You've never let anyone off the hook, have you?"

"Sorry," I answer, tossing my leg over the sandbike saddle and dismounting.

Footsteps clang off the ramp and we both turn to see who it is. Baker—I hadn't caught her first name—the ship's navigator, is approaching. She's taller than me, and lean in a featherweight boxer's way. Her long brown hair is tied back and she wears a utilitarian sleeveless shirt that shows off her wiry arms. The straight-legged pants tucked into her high black boots give away her former Corps status as clearly as if she were wearing rank. Her unflinching blue eyes weigh down on me as she addresses Cross. "We still have some work to do on the reversals." She says it flatly, like a command.

"Yeah. Get started. I'll be right there."

She hesitates for another second, still trying to stare me down and fronting a distinct attitude of dislike. I don't drop my eyes, far too used to this game. Finally, she reverses and heads back into the belly of the ship.

Cross turns back to me with a slight *what can you do?* lift of his eyebrows.

"So, you and Baker?" I ask.

"What? Nah. We just work together."

"We just worked together too, back on the *Hammer*."

"Yeah, but that was completely different."

In what way, I want to ask, but leave it alone. It's none of my business. In any case, if she wants to be jealous of something that doesn't exist, that's her own problem.

"I've got work to do. I'll see you later."

"Okay." I feel his eyes follow me as I push the bike over to a paddock where several others are parked.

Before I make for the vault and a day guaranteed to leave me sooty, oily, dirty, and tired, I do a quick search inside the *Sphynx*, hoping to find Karl. He's not around, so I wander into the control room and find Bodie standing by a table-sized electron microscope that is known, for reasons I've never been able to put my finger on, as Medusa. His eyes are pressed firmly against the viewing lenses, probably indulging in his favorite hobby, i.e., analyzing anything he can fit under a lens or in front of a reader. His recent obsession is trying to splice the staple crops the settlement usually grows in underground greenhouses and grow rooms with the hardier local plants that are adapted to the harsh dry environment of Spectra 6. If we can do a better job of acclimating ourselves and our food sources to the local environment, there's a better chance of the settlement remaining a viable and independent long-term home. He doesn't look up when I come in, totally absorbed in whatever he's staring at, until I get his attention with a gentle tap on his shoulder.

"Oh, hey, Aly. You looking for Desto?"

"No, actually, I was wondering if you've seen Karl? I thought he might be working on the *Sphynx* with Venus today, but neither of them are there."

"He and Doug left on the Rover awhile ago. I think they're taking some of the new parts out to the transceiver."

A brick of disappointment lodges in my stomach. Until I moved in with Venus, Karl was at my infirmary room first thing every day to wish me good morning. Since I've recovered, we've kept up the tradition, always getting together for breakfast or to exchange a few quick words before the day's work takes over. So what's changed with him? Is he really jealous of someone I haven't seen since I was twenty-two years old? He's always been a hothead but this is just irrational. Between him and Baker, it's almost hard to believe there *isn't* something going on between Rob and me. The idea is absurd, and my disappointment starts to morph into a feeling I'm much more used to: anger.

"Want me to send him to the vault when they get back?" Bodie is staring at me the way he'd just been looking through the scope lens, and I wonder what he's seeing in my expression.

"No, I'll catch up with him some other time. Thanks."

"No problem."

I don't have time for this hassle; I have work to do. If Karl wants to sort this out, he knows where to find me.

When I pass by the *'Rize* this time, no one's outside. There's a hydraulic lift built to handle bigger pieces of cargo at the far end of the cavern where it finally dead ends at the heart of the mountain. I take it down past the midlevel subfloor and its network of grow rooms to the lowest subfloor. The lift is a wall-less platform and it settles to the floor at the bottom of the shaft into a dusty, barely lit room no bigger than a closet. The original miners who'd dug up this mountain to extract whatever the Admin was looking for had blasted one last shaft down here before giving up and going home— or dying off, whatever happened to them. Maybe they'd found something, maybe not, but this room is only an antechamber to a tunnel that was once about twenty meters long and five or so wide. Now, all a person standing where I am can see is a rock wall three meters in front of them. It feels uncomfortably like being inside a grave.

There's no sound down here but that doesn't mean I'm alone. The electronic door hiding our ammunition vault—an airlock hatch salvaged from a derelict that a hawker had been piecing out in Hell's Gate—is thick. Any sound on the other side would have to be as loud as a symphony for a person on this side of it to hear. It's controlled remotely by a twelve-digit code, transmitted via the wrist VDUs we all wear. I enter the sequence and watch as the rock in front of me splits along a left seam and begins to slide to the right. Small puffs of pulverized dust shake from the ceiling and rain into the lighted opening.

Rectangular overhead lights hang in meter intervals along the chamber's ceiling. When they're all functioning, they flood the room with blazing white light, sucking a lot of juice from one of the generators in the mine's main chamber. Most of the settlement's power is derived from an array of photovoltaic heliostats that cover an acre of hard desert nearby, and with our three stars, they're never in danger of going dry. Two of the ten light rigs are down right now, but the chamber still incandesces like the center of a fusion bomb, making the cold surfaces of rows of missiles, rifles, thrown projectiles, and assorted electronic surveillance and explosive devices gleam. It's a tomb for contraband military hardware. Vitruzzi thinks of the transceiver as an insurance policy against surprises, but to me, this room holds the real insurance.

"Twig, how are ya?" Desto calls, standing before the open housing of a Glower missile, where he's testing its navigation mechanism.

I move over to the gun racks and start pulling down rags and cleaning compound. "Please don't call me that."

"Why not? It's perfect! You're short, skinny"—a devious smile replaces the frown he'd adopted to feign insult—"and sometimes a little sharp."

"Forget it, okay? That's what my mom use to call me."

"Yeah? Why'd she call you that?"

Irritated, my voice gives off sparks as I answer. "I don't know. She took off when I was a kid." The past is over and I don't like to think about it.

"All right, all right. But if even half those stories Cross was telling us last night are true, you haven't been a kid in a long time."

"Jesus, Desto! Can you just drop it?" I'm a little shocked that Cross would have much to say about our shared past, but then, what else do men have to talk about when they're drinking and playing cards?

"Don't freak, babe, I'm not talking about anything naughty. I'd prefer you showed me that yourself." He winks. "Cross and David were talking about some of the work you all did for the Corps. Back before you grew an unauthorized conscience."

Feeling foolish, I try to ignore him, but Desto's directness and total lack of tact are all part of his appeal. That and the fact that he can quote you exactly what kind of blade, firearm, bomb, or tactical missile you'll need to get the job done to specification for any, and I mean *any*, situation.

"We've all done shit we wished we hadn't, huh?" He doesn't respond, doesn't need to. Desto's had his own taste of the Corps and its explicit antimercy policy. I'd like to get on with work so I can stop wondering about Karl's strange behavior and forget about Cross's unexpected reintroduction into my life. "So, what's on the agenda?"

He hands me a small receiver. "Today, you get to be the target." Meaning, he'll be checking the missile calibrations as I move around to make sure they're tracking.

To keep perspective on the utter dullness of the next couple of hours, I keep telling myself I could be stuck outside in the 35 C heat, working on the transceiver. That isn't enough though, and soon I'm thinking about last's night's conversation again and what Cross said about the Admin rescinding its contracts with non-citizen crews.

We've tested about half of the missiles when I bring it up. "Things are going to get rough out here if Vitruzzi loses her Admin contracts."

Grunting, Desto squats and reseats a Glower in its cargo box, a job that usually requires two men. Straightening up, he answers, "Nah. There's always the black market." Waving me away, he opens the crate for the next one.

"Sure. That's true. But the risks are higher."

Connecting the test rig, he gives me a count of three on his fingers. After confirming that the coordinates locked, he answers, "The stakes aren't high enough stealing from the Admin? Damn. Besides, we already have mostly everything we need. Far as I'm concerned, the less we tango with them, the better."

"And what if they close the Obals to non-cits? Are you ready to be cut off from . . . ?" I let the sentence hang.

"Civilization?" He laughs. "Aly, we may be on the fringes out here, but if that means I don't take orders from anyone, I'm good. Besides, did you book a vacation to Tunis City or something? And, oh yeah, I hear the weather on Keum Libre is fucking great this time of year." Chuckling harder, he wrestles the next box down from its shelf.

Frowning, I wait for him to set the test rig. Desto has a point, but I'm somehow not finding it as easy as him to let go of the idea of never being able to travel to an Admin city. Banished from law and order for good. How do you get used to that?

FIVE

Two hours later, the back of my throat tastes like an oil slick and my hands are a uniform black from carbon dust. Desto suggests we take a break and go topside for some food and sunshine, and I can hardly contain my eagerness. Whatever Venus's reasons for wanting me as a roommate, she was certainly right about people not being built to live underground. Though it makes me wonder why I don't feel this cooped up when in flight for months at a time. It's darker in space than any cave, and there isn't much room on a ship. Still, being in the sky has always felt right to me. There's no explaining it, not even to myself.

When the lift reaches topside, Vitruzzi sees it and walks toward us. "I was just about to come and get you. Cross is free and I'm going to take him out to the transceiver. Do you still want to come, Aly?"

I nod. "And his crew?"

"They're occupied with the *Horizon*. It'll just be him. Desto, join us?"

"My pleasure."

We walk past the *Sphynx* and I notice the Rover parked alongside its loading ramp, but still no Karl. Brady and Cross stand beside it chatting amiably, as if they've been friends for years. Rob's always been the kind of guy that people take an instant liking to, both charming and funny and rarely anything but polite. He's probably been doing pretty well for himself as an Admin contractor. Besides being likable, I remember him as being efficient and reliable, and he'd risen through the ranks back in the Corps at a speed that would ordinarily make people mutter about bribes and blackmail. But it was just Cross's personality and rock-solid capabilities that got him so far. Now as a citizen, his ship, a newer model with solar amalgam-powered engines, reflects at least some measure of the same success, broken reversals aside. Sitting next the *Sphynx*, whose hull is pocked and scraped to raw metal in more than a few places, the *Red Horizon* epitomizes the difference between citizens and non-citizens, those living on the Obals and those living on the Spectras.

Brady gets into the driver's seat and Vitruzzi, Cross, and I load up and roll outside the mine's tunnel, Desto following on his bike. The day is hot already and we extend a shade flap along either side of the Rover's clamshell spine to block the driving sun. Vents along the base of the sideboards let air circulate through the vehicle's cab, but no one would describe it as a cool and comfortable ride. The best way to drive the Rover on this planet to keep from getting broiled is *fast*.

The transceiver sits north of the mine about five klicks, planted atop the first high ridge of the complex canyon system extending between Agate Beach and Hell's Gate. I'd passed through that labyrinth during my first visit to the Beach, trying to get back to Rajcik and my old smuggling crew. Now I know the area as Mecca Flats. Having explored every circuitous crag and peak since settling here, I know how easy it would be to get lost in there, or lose someone else, plus it provides excellent cover from airborne spies.

The top of the ridge sits a couple hundred meters from the valley floor, and there's a vehicle-wide path carved and graded up the gradual slope. The device itself is only about the size of a standard radar dish, oblong and convex, and mounted on top of a metal base that also serves as a battery housing. The batteries can be rotated from a supply we keep at the Beach, or juiced up directly from our generators via a long cable. The entire apparatus lies hidden beneath a scavenged military net colored in desert camouflage and wired with radar jamming sensors. The only way to see the device from the sky is when it's uncovered.

La Mer glances over as we drive up. A panel he's removed from the base lies next to him and he sits on the hard-packed earth, elbow deep in wiring that bursts from within. The transceiver dish is still covered by its camouflage netting, giving him a hint of shade, but sweat streaks down the sides of his face anyway. Brady pulls the Rover up and we all climb out.

"So what is this, Eleanor? It sounded like you were going to make me swear over the life of my firstborn not to tell anyone about it before you brought me up here. But I have to admit, it doesn't look like much," Rob says, grinning crookedly.

Brady begins circling the dish, untying the netting from stakes in the ground. When they're all loose, he motions to me to take one side while he grabs the other. With a yank, the netting slides into the dirt at our feet.

"Rob, we've built a transceiver that sends and receives in real time using satellites." Vitruzzi explains. "We'll be able to talk to you or anyone else we want outside of our orbit now with no lag. La Mer's been helping us build it, but we'd like your help to test it."

"Brilliant! Yeah, I'll help. Definitely. But"—his forehead furrows in skepticism—"did you build yourselves a satellite network, too? The Admin is a little stingy with theirs, which you know."

There's a quick pause and he understands immediately what's not being said. "Oh. You figured out a way to hijack Admin tooders."

"Now you see why we've kept it under wraps," Brady responds.

"Okaaayyy." He draws the word out, then stays silent for a minute, considering what he's agreeing to. I watch him closely, trying to read what he's thinking. Finally, he continues, his voice tight but sincere, "Sure, I can help you test it. But first you have to be honest with me, what kind of safeguards do you have in place so they won't be able to either detect a hack, or trace it if they do? No offense, but I'm not sure it's worth my ship, or jail time, if you're not a hundred percent it'll work. I'd be out more than just a few contracts."

"You've got nothing to worry about," La Mer answers. "You'll just be picking up the signal. No harm in that. We'll use the *Sphynx* to transmit back to the Beach, which is the only way the Admin could trace it. But I know their systems, and they aren't going to know a thing."

"Yeah? How could you know their systems?"

La Mer is, as always, reluctant to talk about himself. The fact that he'd managed to stay hidden from the Admin for six years can be attributed to his tight-lipped style. "It's a specialty of mine," is his short reply.

"Okay, man. Just asking." Cross walks over to the dish and gazes up into his reflection in the steel bowl. Without turning around, he asks, "When's the test?"

Vitruzzi and Brady exchange a glance and I read uncertainty in their eyes. We've just put the Beach and every settlers' freedom on the line on a bet that Cross, citizen or not, friend or not, won't find a reason to turn us in. Paranoia once again bristles along my skin like a rash and I find myself wondering just where he got the funds to buy such a nice ship, but I throttle the thought before it can dig in.

Vitruzzi answers him. "The parts you brought us yesterday are the last ones we needed. Bodie and La Mer should be done putting it together . . . when?" She raises her eyebrows and looks at La Mer.

"Tomorrow maybe. Definitely the next day if not." He's still looking at Cross, his face neutral. I can't say why, but I get the impression he doesn't like Rob.

Cross turns around and asks, "Is there anything I can help with?" The calm sincerity in his voice instantly shuts down the voice in my head that keeps questioning his reliability. What's my problem? He's just a guy, an old friend. Trusting people has never been my style, but being betrayed by Rajcik must have affected me deeper than I realized.

"This is handled," Brady answers. "But you and your crew could help us move some equipment in the mine. It'll only take an hour or so."

"Sure. Anything you need."

"One more thing, Rob," Vitruzzi says, "we think it's best if you don't mention this to the rest of your crew."

"Of course, don't even worry about it." He flashes another winning grin, then looks over at me. "You know you can rely on me."

IT'S LATE AFTERNOON and still no Karl. After finishing the day off in the vault with Desto, I grab a quick dry-shower in the mine's lavatory to blast the grit and carbon off my skin, then hop on my bike to head to Venus's. As I drive past the *Red Horizon*, the only thing on my mind is food, but I spot two of Cross's crewmembers—Sims and Montoya—standing atop their left engine housing, struggling to keep solid footing while they work inside the engine compartment.

Stopping, I shout up at them, "Hey, you guys want a better platform? I can drive the airstairs out here for you."

They both glance down at me and quickly decline with a short "no thanks." Shrugging, I keep going. On my way out, my VDU vibrates as David buzzes me.

"Hey Aly. Come by Bodie's and my place. Rob's coming over for some chow and to catch up on more old times."

I've already decided to have a quickie dinner and then track Karl down, having grown both irritated and concerned over his no-show all day. "No thanks. I'm beat. I'm just going to call it a night."

"Don't give me that. You get your ass over here—that's an order." His smile fills the VDU screen, punting my resolve aside like a deflated ball, and I can't help but react to the challenge in his voice. He'd laugh at me if I told him my concerns about Karl, and I can't have my big brother giving me shit. Besides, if I don't find Karl, what am I going to do? Sit around Venus's like a heartbroken teenager?

"Fine. Be there in five."

SIX

Bodie and David are more like an old married couple than roommates—an old married couple who specialize in gourmet cooking—and put on an excellent feast of fresh vegetables and spice-enhanced protein concentrate that tastes almost *better* than a steak. I can't believe I almost didn't come. To top off the delicious meal, Rob has brought along several bottles of contraband wine that he says he keeps in its own secret stash room on the *'Rize*. The settlement only has enough room to grow foods for their nutritional value with nothing being wasted on fermentable grains and fruits. Consequently, we rarely see booze, and it isn't long into the evening before I'm feeling as relaxed and boneless as a drunk amoeba.

We're all lounging on a deck Bodie and David built from broken crates and spare hardware, feeling the night drop its pleasant breeze over us like a cool sheet. David takes a sip of his wine and comments, "I never had it this good, even before I joined the Corps. You know, being a citizen had its perks but there wasn't any adventure in it. It's like your life was a book that you read when you were a kid. Too simple, no surprises. Rob, I don't know how you stand it."

Rob chuckles, not offended. "It's not that bad. There are surprises, especially when you're a transport contractor like me. There are plenty of days when I don't know exactly what to expect. Take yesterday for example—who would have ever suspected I'd run into the two of you? Besides, nothing I do is routine. Running down illegal goods for folks like Eleanor and Brady isn't the stuff of a mundanity. And some of the things you've asked for, Bodie— sometimes I almost need a planetary engineer to tell me what they are before I even know where to look."

David chuckles, "Yeah, I see what you mean."

"Rob, you always seemed pretty content with life in the Corps, what made you give it up and become a citizen?" I ask.

He thinks about it for a minute before answering. "To be honest, a lot of it has to do with some of the things you talked about when we were still on the *Hammer*. You know, things about how we were being used, not having real freedom, the lies—however you put it. I don't know what I thought of it then, but I started to believe it after the Rebellion."

I turn to look at him, surprised. He's looking back at me frankly and the fading daylight casts deep shadows around his eyes, leaving just a wink of light reflecting from them. "That, and I'd finally had enough of being pushed around. The Soldier's Rebellion changed everything, for everyone. It got tough in the ranks after that; everyone was suspected of being complicit with the rebels, always monitored and scrutinized. My unit was tasked with hunting down deserters, and that's when it really came to a head for me. It was one thing to hunt down criminals who were legitimately dangerous, but some of the men and women we had to pick up were people we'd served with. *Good* people. And we knew they were as good as dead." His voice grows thicker and he pauses for a long moment. "So when my enlistment came up, I took the out." He flashes me a sad smile and takes a long drink from his cup.

"What about your crew? Did you serve with any of them?" Sims, Montoya, and Baker aren't here tonight. Curious.

"You can tell they're former Corps, huh? It's hard to shake off all that training. But no, I didn't know any of them before, uh, before I hired them. Baker and Montoya started working with me about six months ago, and Sims about four. Met them all in Tunis City."

I'm about to ask more questions, wanting a clear picture of his life since leaving the Corps, but Bodie stands up and stretches, letting out a ratcheting belch that would make a bullfrog proud. "Kids, La Mer and I are heading up to the dish early tomorrow before it gets too hot, so I'm going to leave you to your reminiscing. But I have to tell you, you sound like a bunch of grumpy old vets whose only pleasure comes from rehashing their glory days together."

We laugh and say good night. I stand up to leave as well, not wanting to be a nuisance to Bodie, and have to put a hand out on the building's wall to steady myself. Rob jumps up with me. "Aly, would you mind giving me a ride back to my ship?"

The question comes out awkwardly, like he's asking me to do something mildly indecent. Before answering, I catch David's eye and read a hint of both amusement and interest in them. I can't think of a reason to say no and don't even know why I want to. "Sure. Come on."

It takes us less than ten minutes to get back to the mine entrance. I switch off the engine and Rob lets go of my waist and jumps off.

"Almost like old times," he says, smiling, his body close to mine.

"In what way?" The cooler night air washed away some of my dizziness, but looking into his dark eyes brings it back, and for a moment, I'm lightheaded.

"Okay, you're right. Nothing like old times, really. But I want you to know that I meant it when I told you how good it is to see you again. I missed you."

I know he's not intentionally making me uncomfortable, but I feel a very strong urge to peel out and speed away as fast as I can. Instead, I try to deflect, "Look Rob, that was a long time ago. I have a new life here. I've put the Corps and everything else behind me."

"I completely understand that. I, you know, I just didn't realize . . . I mean, until I saw you yesterday, I had almost forgotten what things were like when we were together. That's what I mean when I say it's good to see you. It's good to see you happy. You're doing well here, and that's what I always wanted for you. The way things were in the

Corps, before the Rebellion . . . and then when we lost touch. I was afraid you were dead, and that was hard for me."

I know I shouldn't say anything, should let sleeping dogs lie, but the world is so quiet, the binary suns' scorching light muted for the night—this moment seems to exist outside of time and may be the only chance I get for answers I've wanted since he stepped out of my life. "When you were reassigned, why didn't you keep in contact? If I meant *so much* to you."

He looks away from me and takes the tiniest step backward. I know that no matter what he says next, no matter how sincerely he believes it, the truth will always be that back then we were still too young to know what we wanted, or to appreciate what we had. It wouldn't have been hard for me to find Rob, if I'd really wanted to. Just as easy as it would have been for him to find me.

"I don't really know. I guess I took too much for granted." He sighs as if he's trying to decide if he should tell me something, but the rasping click of a sandbike as it downshifts echoes throughout the mine tunnel, cutting him off. We both look toward the entrance and see Karl emerging. He sees us too and looks like he might drive past us for a second before pulling up.

I haven't done anything wrong, but suddenly I feel unaccountably guilty and catch myself glance at Rob. Out of the corner of my eye, I see Karl's expression turn sour.

Not sure what to say, I finally break the silence: "You're working late."

"Yeah," he replies curtly, then shifts his gaze toward Rob and nods in a manner that borders on unfriendly. "Cross."

"Strahan."

"I've been wondering where you were all day."

"Busy. Working. We've got a lot to finish up before the transceiver's operational."

"I know, but . . ." I stop myself. I'm not going to get into this with him here. "Tomorrow should be just as busy. I should get going."

I haven't left the saddle of the sandbike and a flick of the engine switch brings it purring to life.

"Good night, Aly," Rob says as I roll forward.

I nod at him and turn the bike around as I approach Karl. Stopping in front of him, I ask, "Do you want to ride together?"

He gives me a noncommittal shrug and restarts his bike. Within seconds, we're clear of the mine and riding beneath the not-quite-black night sky toward his place. Once we arrive, he pulls around to the back and parks next to Desto's assault motorcycle, its huge faring and projecting rifle barrels giving it the look of a monstrous insect in the starlight. I stop next to him and kill the engine.

Stepping off, I stand squarely in front of him. "Karl, what's going on? Something's bothering you. Why don't you just tell me what it is so I don't have to guess."

Avoiding my eyes, he lights up a smoke and says nothing for a few seconds. Long enough to frustrate me. Then: "Look, Aly. I realize you've got a history that I don't really know much about. There're things in my own past you probably wouldn't care to hear about. But it's not easy when—"

I cut him off, "Karl, Cross is someone I knew in another lifetime. What he said at Vitruzzi's last night, and whatever he may have said when he was over here playing cards, that's all history. It has nothing to do with . . . with us." I almost said, *It has nothing to do with how I feel about you,* but something stopped me. It's never come naturally for me to talk about my feelings; for soldiers, emotions don't factor it to how we operate. I'd been in the Academy and then the Corps since I was fourteen and become a person of actions, not words. Talking things out doesn't give me the instant resolve that I'm used to. Maybe I've never learned how to express myself, but so far, Karl has seemed to understand me just fine. What's changed?

He stamps out the cigarette and puts the butt in a container sitting next to his dwelling's adobe walls. Standing there with his arms at his sides, his back straight, he looks almost like the mien of some primeval ruler about to pass judgment. At times, that immobile stance makes me feel safe, protected, like I have someone solid to rely on when things get tough. Other times, like now, his way of looming silently, almost stonewalling me, infuriates me to the point that I want to shake him.

"How are things between us, Aly?"

The question hits me like an unexpected backhand and I wince, knowing Karl sees it. Immediately, I want to explain myself, to tell him that it's only surprise that makes me react in that way. But I can't do that. Don't even know how. What could I say to him that he doesn't already know? How can I tell him my feelings for him without it sounding awkward and insincere, or worse, like a lie?

So, instead of telling him the truth—that I would die for him if necessary, that since meeting him, I've learned what it means to actually live, what it's like to share everything that matters with another person in a completely selfless way—I say, "You tell me." Because I need to hear it before I can say it. I need to know that if I go out on a limb and leave myself naked and vulnerable, I won't be out there alone.

There's a subtle shift in his expression, something more felt than seen, and I know I've stung him. If only he would understand that I can't expose myself like that no matter how bad I want to. I can't let myself get hurt.

He looks away over my shoulder and sighs. "I'm not sure I even know. Good night." Then he walks inside, leaving me standing alone in the night.

SEVEN

The next day begins the same as the one before, and every one before that during these past few months. Bodie and La Mer ask me out to the dish for a couple of hours—my petite hands make it easier to fit together some of the smaller components—and after I've done what I can to help them, I head out to the firing range with Desto to test some weapons. I don't bother lying to myself that mostly what I'm doing is finding ways to avoid Karl this time, wanting to drown with distractions the panicked feeling that had started the minute he'd closed the door on me last night.

Avoiding the thoughts rolling around my head like loose cannon-balls on a ship's deck anytime I'm not busy is priority—so I stay busy. While Desto and I practice until we've sweat through every fiber of our clothes on the range, we get word that they've finished wiring the final pieces to the transceiver. The test will be tonight and Karl, Vitruzzi, and Venus take the *Sphynx* off-world toward Spectra 4, preparing to wait for the transmission scheduled to be sent at 2030 hours. Less than five minutes after hearing this, Mason pings us both simultaneously.

"What now?" Desto wonders, cueing the go button on his VDU.

"You two, we were just hailed by an Admin security ship. They're landing in less than ten minutes. Get your asses to the mine on the double."

We drop the rifles we'd brought into a crate and cover it with a tarp, hoping no one bothers to come out here and take a look. Scrambling onto the back of Desto's bike, I grip his waist as he guns it. We jump onto the dirt track leading to the Beach too fast and the front wheel starts to skid off the edge of a brief incline, spraying rocks and pebbles behind us and guaranteeing us a more than a few abrasions if we go down. In a synchronous movement that would seem graceful if the stakes weren't so high, we lean together to regain a balanced center of gravity and the wheel rights itself.

We reach the mine where the settlers inside are working in a frenzied but orderly burst. There are plenty of items littering the cavern that a destitute group of non-cits can't easily justify having, and tucking them away or making them appear more derelict than they are is top priority. Admin security never travels out this far, so we've been surprisingly lax about keeping things that might be suspicious under lock and key. It's much too late now, but the realization of how incredibly stupid we've all been is drilling into my skull. More than stupid, we've been *crazy* not to take better precautions. Yet the reality is that there is *no* reason for Admin security to be here. They only handle civilian centers. Anything criminal or suspected of being criminal on the Spectras gets automatically dished out to the Capital Military Corps.

Vitruzzi, Bodie, and Karl are loping from the *Sphynx*'s hold as a blast of air wafts down the tunnel from the mine entrance. It can only be one thing—a ship landing. Spotting us, Vitruzzi says, "Desto, get the vault squared away and hide. Take them with you." She waves a hand toward David and La Mer—just pulling their sandbikes in after having come from the transceiver—and I.

Desto breaks into a trot, slapping La Mer on the shoulder as he goes by in a manner that says *follow me*. David turns to go after them, but I stand beside Bodie.

"What do you have in the control room that we need to do something about?" His deep-set blue eyes widen for second, and he glances at Vitruzzi as if wondering if she knows why I'd be crazy enough not to get out of sight. "Bodie! What's in there that could tip them off about the security worm or the transceiver?"

Finally realizing what I'm getting at, he grasps my forearm, saying to Vitruzzi, "Com room. You have to scramble the last day's outgoing transmissions," and starts to pull me along as he makes for the control room.

"There's a safe-box dug into the floor beneath the holodisc reader. We need to throw in some of the terminals Jeremy and I used to track and crack the satellite programs. Most of the other equipment doesn't matter; they can't prove what's stolen and what's not."

He sounds as if he really thinks that matters, but I keep my mouth shut and run along beside him. The noise of a large vehicle echoes from the mouth of the tunnel as I pull the control room doors shut behind us. Not much time.

Doug Mason sits at the monitoring station and jumps to his feet as we enter. "What are you doing here, Erikson? They're right outside, for God's sake."

Neither of us answer as Bodie runs toward the central bank of computers lining the far wall and starts pulling datablocks from their connectors. "Keep an eye outside, Aly. Let me know if they're coming in. Doug, help me out with these. We need to cover all the evidence of the satellite hack."

I press up against the door and stare through the shatterproof window. My Derg is in my hand, though I don't remember reaching for it. Hard to see outside through the thick, nearly translucent material. People look like wavering ghosts as they hustle about and the *Sphynx* and *Red Horizon* are large gray beasts taking up the cavern's bulk.

A track–propelled transport vehicle rolls into my limited field of view and stops about ten meters outside of the control room. "Hurry it up, Bodie," I whisper. "They are right outside." He curses, then grunts as he shoves the holodisc reader aside.

The mechanical sound of an electric motor hums through the air as the hatch to the safe-box opens—I hadn't even known the thing was there. A quick glance over my shoulder catches him tossing the datablocks inside hastily, then clicking a button on the remote in his hand to close the hatch again. Pushing the disc reader back, he tucks the remote inside a storage drawer and grins. "We're good."

Appraising him calmly, I ask, "Any other handy nooks where a person my size might fit?"

His grin fades like chalk in a rainstorm. "Maybe they won't—"

"Shh!" I hush him with a sharp chop of my hand. Four security personnel have emerged from the interior of the transport and stand a few meters away. The control room doors are thick, but I don't want to chance anything drawing their attention to us. Bodie steps up beside me and activates the door's electronic lock.

Brady walks into view outside, his gait fast and aggressive. I glimpse him run his hand over his VDU and it gives me an idea. Moving the Derg into my left hand, I unlatch the tiny earpiece housed along the edge of my own VDU and insert it into my ear. Then I turn the unit on, already set to the channel the regular *Sphynx* crewmembers use.

Brady's voice comes through clearly. "What are you doing here?" Not the warmest greeting I've ever heard.

A member of the security team steps forward. It's difficult to make out her rank or features, but her voice carries through Brady's VDU with authority. "Are you in charge here?"

"This is a free settlement. There's nobody in charge." The officer who'd spoken stiffens. Brady continues, "Why's an Admin security team here?"

"The Political and Capital Administration is undertaking a census of all the primarily non-citizen settlements and colonies on the Spectra planets. Your cooperation, or lack of it, will be noted."

Bodie and Doug have pressed in next to me to watch through the window. At the officer's words, we exchange a brief, troubled glance.

"A census? Why?"

"Sir, that information is relevant to neither our mission nor to you. Now, is there any population accounting or tracking system here that we can look at, or will we need to do a walk-through of the settlement and take count ourselves?" The way her voice drops at the last part makes it clear that if the Admin team is forced to do a head count, it won't be fun. For anyone.

Brady stands in obstinate silence, staring her down. After a few seconds, he says flatly, "There are 125 people in Agate Beach."

"And do you have a list of their names, ages, and citizen status?" Her response is quick and nearly as toneless as Brady's. She's been doing this for a while and has probably dealt with worse hostility than his.

I can almost hear Brady's thoughts. His detestation for the Admin is part of his physical being; when the subject of the Obals-based government comes up, it's nearly as visible as a malignant growth would be. He'd probably like nothing better than to reach out for the officer's handgun and use it to pummel her self-important face to the other side of her head. Of course, that wouldn't do much good for him or for the larger goal of getting the Admin crew well and away from Agate Beach. He says, "Wait here." Giving them a list of the settlers is the quickest means of making them disappear.

His figure moves out of view and the officer turns to the other three personnel standing behind her. Only a faint murmur of their voices passes through the thick divider between us and we can't tell what's being said. Two of the security team crew set off deeper into the mine, apparently sent on some kind of reconnoitering mission. The officer and the remaining crewmember begin walking toward the control room.

We all lean away from the window instinctively but there's no way to see in. The room is much dimmer than the cavern and the window is too thick and mottled for visibility from their side.

"If they come in, Aly, you hide inside one of the equipment lockers. You'll fit," Mason growls in my ear.

I'd rather throw myself into the engine housing of an MCACS—being stuck in small spaces makes me feel like I'm napping in my own coffin—but I keep calm by telling myself they won't be able to get in.

The officer reaches the door and tugs against the handle. Her face is centimeters from the window and I peek through. The insignia on her uniform shows she's a Chief Class II from the Obal 8 Security Squadron. They're a long way away from home. What the hell could the Admin be doing a census for anyway?

She tries tugging the outer handle first left then right to open the door, but it's not moving. She puts her face up against the window and the three of us withdraw quickly. Her voice is faint but clear as she says to her subordinate, "Locked. We may want to take a look inside here when that Spectre comes back."

"Chief," another crewmember says, approaching the door. "We just received a message from headquarters."

"What's the gist, Corporal?"

"An Obal 5 security crew has taken casualties due to an uprising of prisoners they were transporting to Keum Libre. They want us to reinforce that crew and help neutralize the prisoners."

"They want us to aid a prisoner transport crew?" The officer sounds about as happy as if she'd just heard she'd be mopping up sewage spills with a hankie for her next mission. "Don't they have anyone closer?"

The corporal instinctively remains silent.

The chief continues, "It can't be any worse than leapfrogging around the Spectras dealing with a bunch of backward primitives. We'll get that list from the local honcho and head out. Shouldn't be more than twenty minutes from now. Corporal, send headquarters our ETA to rendezvous with Obal 5's crew."

"What about checking this room, Chief?"

"Forget it. By the look of that transport ship and this Eleanor Vitruzzi's contracting status, they have plenty of things in there that they shouldn't, but that isn't our problem. We'll ping HQ, let them figure out what to do about it. Maybe send a Corps squad down to clean up."

"Roger, Chief."

As we wait behind the control room door, it occurs to me to wonder if David and La Mer had had time to cover the transceiver. What better piece of equipment for drawing *very* unwanted attention? The three security personnel turn and walk back around the far side of the transport vehicle, causing us to lose visibility. I take a breath of relief as Brady returns and hands the officer a small disc.

Without even a nod of thanks, she motions her team to load the transport and climbs aboard last. The transport executes a six-point turn to pull headfirst out of the mine. When the sound of its engine has faded to a dull growl, I push through the control room door and jog up to Brady.

"What the hell was *that* about?" I ask.

His eyes don't waver from the retreating vehicle as he says, "Something is very wrong."

It's late evening by the time everyone is back at the Beach, and we all meet in the main cavern so La Mer and Bodie can fill us in on the transceiver's status. The entire population of the settlement has maneuvered their way into the subterranean hanger, a hundred-plus warm bodies barely making a dent in the vast space. Rob has taken the *'Rize* up ostensibly on a test flight to check out their patch job on the broken reversals. They should be in orbit somewhere near the southern pole of the planet and outside of regular communication range waiting to hear from the Beach.

With so much going on, the crew hadn't had a chance to regroup and speculate on why the Admin would be taking a census of the Beach and other settlements like it. Vitruzzi and Brady had been AWOL since the security team left.

The crowd is restless; most of the people here have marginal interest in the transceiver and the effort it took to build it. They have little to do with the other planets and don't crave any connection, especially at the risk of Admin retaliation. But they also see the benefits of having people like Vitruzzi with her Admin connections and Bodie with his in-depth scientific background to help keep the colony afloat and healthy. They grudgingly accept the transceiver as a necessary means to ensure their continuity. They know only too well that if you live outside the law, you still have to be prepared for it to find you.

As I look over the group, I don't see in them many similarities to me—I'm the outsider here. Most of these people have never experienced the benefits of citizenship. The majority were born in non-cit colonies on the Spectras or their moons and have never set foot on a planet with clean air or organized development. Some are miners that were either abandoned when their mines ran dry or escaped Admin conscription, having been forced into labor on planets too harsh for softer citizens to inhabit, much less tame. A handful are like Vitruzzi and Bodie—citizens who found life under the Admin's thumb even less appealing than the hardships that come with being out here on the fringes. And then there are Desto, David, La Mer, and I—the only deserters in the bunch. We share an intimate familiarity of the costs of citizenship with the other citizens or former citizens here but have lived our lives on a tangent far removed from those who'd suffered since the day they were born. I've always thought of myself as tough, but I've never had to fight the very elements of the planet I live on for the sake of basic survival. The people here have taught me what it really means to be strong, and how to not only survive, but to thrive, without the Admin pulling my strings. It's made me realize that the years I spent with Rajcik may have gained me some coin, but they cost me nearly as much as if I'd stayed in the Corps.

Brady, back from whatever brainstorming he'd been doing with Vitruzzi, stands up on a cargo box and asks people to quiet down. He says a few words, thanking the settlers for the help they all provided in getting the dish built, recognizes La Mer and Bodie specifically for their contribution, and comments about the success and independence of Agate Beach and the example it sets as an alternative to the Admin's special brand of control. I feel an inadvertent swelling of pride in our accomplishment, reminding me of the way I used to respond to these kinds of motivational speeches from the high-ranking leaders I'd admired when I first enlisted at the Academy. I stifle the feeling quickly, my cynicism warning me not to get too wrapped up in minor successes that ultimately don't mean much.

When he's said everything he intends to, he steps onto the lift to the communication room where Desto and Bodie are already waiting. At the last minute, he motions to David and me. I'm a bit surprised that Brady would want to include me, with our endless disagreements, but don't hesitate to join them. When we enter the small room, La Mer already sits in front of main com console, a set of earphones clamped around his head, testing various relays and switches. He looks as if he's concentrating intensely and bites reflexively on his lower lip. He's not the only one feeling a case of nerves. We all know that his programming—the key to the entire experiment—will do one of three things: fail completely, work enough to hijack the Admin satellites but not enough to hide our pirated use of their system, or be a success.

The room is barely big enough to hold all of us and we wedge ourselves uncomfortably around the console. "Ready to go, La Mer?" Brady asks.

He clears his throat, brightens the resolution of the central VDU, and says, "It all seems ready."

His apprehensiveness is not reassuring, but I clamp my mouth shut against the question: *Are you sure this is going to work?* If La Mer is as good as he says he is—and if what he'd done with the Corps personnel database before the Rebellion is any indication, he is—this kind of job is routine.

"The satellites we're using are all operational. One minute until transmission. Bodie, you're up."

Bodie takes a seat next to La Mer and turns on a speaker channel. All our eyes are on the countdown, and as soon as it says 2030, Bodie depresses the comlink and says, "This is central hailing the flightline. Do you read?" The transmission was planned so no specific names or locations would be used—a precautionary measure, though the most damning breach will be if the Admin detects La Mer's security bypass.

The seconds seem to draw out too long, then finally, Vitruzzi's voice: "This is Orbiter One. We hear you loud and clear." Followed by: "Orbiter 2. That's a copy. Congratulations!" Rob had decided to transmit after all, despite the risk.

La Mer and Bodie turn to each other, grinning so widely their lips seem to have stretched halfway around their heads. David gives Brady an enthusiastic slap on the back, and Desto puts a hand on La Mer's shoulder, saying, "Never had a doubt, brother."

"Central, I think—" but Vitruzzi's voice suddenly cuts out as if it's been chopped in half.

"What the hell?" Bodie ask, then a light on the console begins to flash ominously.

La Mer looks confused, then cries, "It's the sensor on the dish. Something's wrong!"

The two of them bullet from their seats and race to the lift, followed by Desto and Brady. David and I barely get on before it starts descending at full speed, the ratchets on the cable clanking ferociously. Once at the bottom, they rush for the Rover and David and I jump on our bikes, speeding past the settlers' confused faces to the dish.

From the outside, nothing seems to be wrong with the device. La Mer and Bodie attack one of the housing panels at the base with screwdrivers, and as they yank it off, a thick balloon of gray smoke wafts out. "Shit, dammit, come on, shit . . ." Bodie intones, a mantra of disgust.

Brady brings an extinguisher into action and douses the inner compartment until it vomits foam. The smoke disappears and we all stand by silently, held rapt with disappointment. Bodie shakes his head, his face a volatile mix of anger and dismay.

"It was the goddamn relay capacitor. It was too small for the juice we sent through it. That's got to be what happened. It's fried and who knows what else in there is fucked." He stands with his shoulders hunched, speaking to the ground, looking like a defeated Pamplona bull.

"Don't worry, man. It's fixable. The damn thing works and that's the good news." Desto tries to console him.

The rest of us stand mute, feelings that crested in excitement moments before now ebbing in frustration. It might be months before we can reassemble the parts needed to repair it. Brady scans the sky thoughtfully and I guess what he is thinking: Did it really work, or is the Corps on the way to arrest us right now?

He turns back to the group. "There's nothing we can do until the fire retardant dries out and we get a better look inside. Let's get back to the mine and let everyone know what happened."

Bodie paces back and forth in front of the opened panel, each footfall hammering down like he means to hurt the ground. "I'm going to stick around for a while, see if I can do anything. You all go ahead."

Brady shrugs, letting him brood. I leave him my bike and catch a ride back on the Rover.

EIGHT

On watch in the control room the next morning, my eyes stay glued to the radar screens and cameras we have surrounding the Beach to alert us of unexpected company. I'm more than a little anxious, wondering if we'll have any unwelcome visitors.

At close to 1200 hours, when my shift is almost over, the walls of the control room begin to vibrate in a familiar way, announcing an incoming ship. Cross had radioed in a few minutes ago to get clearance, so I switch to the video-link inside the mine and see the *'Rize* settling smoothly into place on the rock floor. Hydraulic shocks on the landing tripod vent pressurized air in a high-pitched whistle, and the engines reduce speed in a cyclic hum. It's been a tense morning. I'm anxious for Mason to come and replace me, but it's Rob who enters the control room.

"I have to hand it to your crew, Aly. That was some piece of work to get that transceiver going."

"It was only partly successful."

"I know. I heard. Vitruzzi buzzed me when we got back into radio range and told me there was a fire."

He comes up beside me and leans over, placing one hand on my shoulder and one on the counter, getting a closer view of the monitors. His proximity doesn't seem casual; I get the feeling that he's trying to be near me without it being obvious, and surprisingly, it doesn't bother me. Heat from his palm radiates through the light fabric of my shirt. Inadvertently, I'm reminded of the way the rest of his body used to feel, naked and pressed against mine like a second skin. A new heat rises, flushing my cheeks.

"Looks like the *Sphynx* is here," he says, jolting me.

We watch the internal feed as Venus floats the ship into the mine as gracefully as a hawk riding a thermal and sets it down. His hand is still on my shoulder when the control room door opens and Karl and Mason step inside. Rob straightens and lets his arm fall away as I swivel my chair around quickly. I hadn't been doing anything wrong, but there's a residual blush creeping up from the neck of my shirt that implies otherwise.

Karl immediately turns and jets from the room. Mason walks up to the consoles and examines them, completely ignoring Rob. "I'm all set, Aly. Anything I need to know?"

I shake my head, already off my seat and heading toward the door to catch Karl. He's kicking up the balancer on his sandbike, which is parked among a group of them near the end of the tunnel, before I reach him.

"Hey, wait a minute." I reach a hand out to take hold of the handlebar, not letting him run from me.

"For what?" His voice echoes loudly inside the cavern, and I see the flash burn of fury in his sepia eyes.

"What are you doing?" It's such a simple question on the surface, but what I'm asking is so much deeper.

His jaw clenches until the striations of his masseter are clearly defined, then: "What are *you* doing?"

Instantly defensive, I counter, "What did it look like I was doing? Watching out for the goddamn colony!" *Calm down, Aly, don't let this get out of hand.* I take a deep breath, trying to make it clear that I'm interested in talking, not fighting. "Look, I can see that having Cross here is upsetting you, but I haven't done anything wrong."

My tactic has no effect and it's clear that he's experiencing some sort of misguided jealous hemorrhage. His sparking eyes bore into my face like an auger. I've seen him enraged before but never directed at me. It catches me off guard, so unexpected and undeserved, but I meet his rage with implacability. I *haven't* done anything wrong. Finally, he responds, his voice almost drowning in his chaotic emotions, "You're free to do whatever you like. I don't control you, and you don't owe me anything."

I feel his words like a fist to the stomach. "What are you talking about?"

"Since he's been here, you and Cross have been like fucking Siamese twins." I start to interrupt, getting angry now myself, but he keeps going, "You've never been happy at the Beach with us lowly non-cits and Admin goose-stepping contractors. Your life's not flash anymore and you don't get to be a hotshot thief, sticking it to the Admin with every take. You're bored, and Cross is living the life that you had before you got stuck with us small timers. If you want to go back to that, do it. I'm not going to stop you."

I'm completely floored by his accusations and presumptions, unable to argue or even speak. Where did he get such bullshit ideas? I'm at a complete loss and stare at him like I've never seen him before. He doesn't wait for me to figure out how to respond and drives off much too fast, leaving me standing in the mine like so much discarded rubbish.

Feeling numb, I turn around and find David behind me, looking at me with a mixture of bafflement and sympathy. "You didn't deserve that."

The muscles in my throat are contracting spasmodically, but I'm not sure if I'm about to scream, vomit, or cry. I look over his shoulder and see a few other people scattered within earshot, their faces reflecting David's surprise, and I feel an acute need to get the hell out of here. I turn, jump on my bike—much the way Karl just had—and switch it on. I hear David say my name, but I speed off, not wanting sympathy or anything else.

NINE

The silence of nighttime in the cool desert has become an ambient cocoon by the time I roll back into the Beach, wrapping me in a fragile, but blissfully detached, bubble. The suns will begin to rise in a couple of hours, but with most people asleep, for now the settlement is quiet. I am alone, free of obligation, connection, or direction. The things I deny craving the most.

The bike's quiet engine barely disturbs the stillness as I drive into the mine. The *Horizon* is docked as before with its ramp down, but this time lights from inside spill into the night. For no reason I care to ponder, I park the bike and walk aboard.

I haven't been inside this model before and find myself on the bottom level of a two-story cargo hold. The space is huge, its size emphasized by the lack of any shipment to fill it. The ceiling is segmented and looks as if it can be retracted, opening up the hold to make room for bigger machinery, possibly even small inter-atmospheric ships.

"Hello? Rob?" *Don't do this, Aly,* I tell myself. *If you need someone to talk to, go wake up David.* But it's too late, the hatchway across the hold is opening and Montoya steps out.

"What are you doing in here?" His question is blunt, almost aggressive. He doesn't appear to be armed, but the angry set of his face shows that doesn't mean he's not ready to fight. I, however, never go anywhere without the Derg strapped to my calf, hidden inside the material of my pants, and wonder if I'm actually going to have to reach for it.

"If you didn't want visitors, you shouldn't have left the ramp down."

"Relax, Montoya. It's fine. Aly is a guest." Rob enters the space and walks up beside Montoya, facing him with a stern expression that doesn't invite argument.

Montoya turns and scowls at Rob, then hunches from the hold. The exchange surprises me; I've never seen anyone react to Rob with such obvious animosity before.

Rob crosses the hold and I meet him in the middle. "Hey, it's good to see you. How are you doing?" It's clear from his concern that he'd seen, or at least heard, the altercation between Karl and I.

"Fine. Friendly crew you have."

"Yeah, well, they're not happy with me right now. I'm their captain. I'm supposed to be looking for new jobs so we can make some money, not taking a holiday on a non-cit planet so I can catch up with old friends. You know, some people just have a hard time sitting still."

"Yeah." I pause, not really sure what else to say, or even why I'm here. Finally: "Do you have anything to drink?"

He smiles, pleased to be able to help. "Right this way. I've got more of that quality claret we were drinking last night, but if you're more in the mood for some stronger hooch, I've got that too. Come on." He begins walking back through the hold and I follow. His unquestioning easiness makes me feel better about having come in the first place.

Beyond the hold's hatchway, we enter a wide corridor with large reinforced walls and access tunnels extending horizontally in both directions. The design is common enough for me to know without needing to see a structural schematic that the steering engine harnesses are attached at the ends of each tunnel, and that we're standing midship, the nexus of the structure and strongest section of hull. Beyond the access tunnels, the corridor is lined with smaller doorways, probably leading to various elements of the craft infrastructure and control: the dual emergency shuttles, avionics, propulsion controls, guidance and attitude sensors, life support, et cetera. As we make our way to the end of the corridor, he eventually stops in front of an open doorway to our right. There's nothing securing the door and no locking mechanism besides the regular airlock hatch, but it's what's inside that draws my attention.

"You don't leave those in there when you're in the Obals do you?"

Crates of contraband sit in organized boxes along shelves that fill an entire wall of the small room. Cigarettes, liquor, small arms, medical supplies—luxury items most average people desire but no one is allowed to own.

Cross smiles like a cream-drunk cat. "Yeah, actually, we do."

I hesitate, certain that I must be missing something, and he continues, "Watch this."

He squats down in front of the open door and removes a small metal panel from the floor, revealing a dark niche. A moment after he reaches inside, the doorway completely disappears. The metal wall of the corridor suddenly seems to grow right over the top of it, like a flap of skin that heals instantly and leaves no scar. It looks as if there had never been any doorway at all.

I take a sharp step back. "What did you do?"

"A buddy of mine who works in the Ministry of Security R&D Division needed a quick—and discreet—transport job. He traded me this little magic-maker for it." His smile grows as he explains this, apparently enjoying my disbelief. Leaning over again, he reaches back into the small compartment and pulls free a radio-sized tubular device with a liquid plasma display along the body and a crystalline projector emitting from one end. As he draws it out, the fake wall wavers like radar interference on a VDU.

"It's a holographic imaging device. You can take an image of anything you want, say a cargo hold wall, and then project the holograph onto a solid object—or even just empty space. Its internal processor will analyze whatever you're projecting onto and re-pixelate the holo to make it look like it's part of the object."

Impressed, I take hold of the device. It's heavier than it looks, due to the crystal projector, but compact. As I swing it slowly around, the image of the wall moves to wherever the projector is aimed. "Can it hide anything?"

"The technology can—anything that's stationary that is. It doesn't have enough processor power to replicate something that's moving. This particular device will only cloak about ten square meters. It's called a *cloak*, by the way. It's been a lot of fun to have around." He reaches for it and replaces it in the floor compartment. "About that drink."

We walk through the fake wall and he pulls a box containing a variety of clear plastic containers from the center of a shelf. Gripping the neck of one, he pulls out a bottle holding a dark blue liquid almost the color of antifreeze. "Should do us nicely. There are glasses in the galley."

The corridor ends in a teardrop shaped alcove with an elevator at the far end. We take it up to the second level where it opens out into a round galley with several chairs and small round tables arranged throughout a dining room. The right side of the room is dominated by the basic appliances needed to cook and clean more than simple traveling food and a walk-in that contains most of the ship's perishables.

As he looks for glasses, I comment, "You have a nice ship here, Rob. Looks like you have room for quite a few more crewmembers."

"That would mean less of a split. No, we do fine. It's usually the deliveree who gets to unload the cargo. We just transport the goods."

He pulls out a metal chair, spins it around backward, and sits at one of the small tables. As I follow suit, he pours us out two full glasses of the peculiar liquid. "I'm just going to come right out and say it—here's to us. Old friends. Let's not lose touch again." He tips the glass in my direction, then belts the drink down.

"To old friends," I say and swallow mine. The liquid is both spicy and sweet, running down my throat smoothly. "Not bad."

"Agreed. This is probably the best hooch you can get. A friend of mine makes it on her cruiser. She won't divulge the secret ingredients, but that doesn't stop me from trying to charm it out of her."

I refill our glasses and we drink amiably for a few minutes. "You're up late. I didn't expect to find anyone around."

"Clients on Obal 10 sent me a wave that just came in—a job—so I was just doing the research on that. Still adjusting to Spectra 6 time, too."

"What kind of job?"

He hesitates before replying. "Oh, just a quick pick-up and delivery from one of the Spectras. Nothing too exciting." *Then why the need for a lot of research?* "How about you, are you always out and about this time of night?"

It's my turn to hesitate. "Just having trouble sleeping. It was a long day."

"Lots on your mind, right?" His eyebrows rise sympathetically. It makes me uncomfortable, but also makes me want to spill it—to just say what's bothering me, to talk to someone. But that would be too awkward. Cross is the reason for Karl's behavior and accusations. What would be the point?

He seems to pick up on my reluctance. "Hey, no problem. You've never been one to spend a lot of time talking about yourself. If you change your mind, I'm happy to listen, okay?"

There's something reassuring in his familiarity, the way he talks about me as if he's known me for years. He still remembers so much about the person I was back in the Corps, and it makes me realize that, despite the Rebellion, the years of smuggling, and all the shit that's happened since the last time we spoke, I still am the same person, deep down.

He refills my glass and I slug it down. Letting impulse take control, I stand up and walk around the table. Taking Rob by the sleeve of his shirt, I pull him toward me and he gives no resistance, as if he'd been waiting for this very thing. Our lips connect and it feels the same as it had eight years ago. His mouth is soft, warm, inviting—so different than Karl's strong, urgent kiss. Not better, just different. Rob lets the kiss linger, and I force myself to stop comparing them and just let the moment sweep me away—from myself, from my fears. From my guilt.

TEN

Waking up in Rob's bunk is like getting a glass of cold water in the face. I had not expected to stay—or to fall sleep—and when an abrupt buzzing sound jerks open my eyelids, I'm disoriented by the unfamiliar room.

Rob leans over and presses a button on the com console next to his bed. "Yeah." His voice is rough and throaty from being woken up.

"Message in from Obal 10."

"Roger that. I'll be down in a minute." He lies back and the sheet crumples at his waist, leaving his chest bare.

The darkness of the room is illuminated only by a faint red glow from the clock on the com console display, showing 0730. I stir, ready to leave and feeling foolish and out of place. I refuse to let my mind jump to the day ahead or what people seeing me leave Rob's ship might think. The mine is a busy place and it'll already be populated with early morning crews starting their daily work. As I lean forward, Rob reaches up and turns on a soft light.

"Good morning, beautiful."

I look down at him, and he beams a smile at me that could melt the ice core of an asteroid. His body hasn't changed much. The galaxy of small scars that he'd received from the shrapnel spray of a cluster bomb still trail down his right side in a scattershot pattern. Their intense pinkness has faded to a paler hue and they've flattened out some. He's just as muscular as ever, and his olive skin has not lost any of its rich, sun-loving hue.

"I have to get going," I mutter. The bunk is wider than those aboard the *Sphynx*—another example of his flushness—but still built against the wall, forcing me to stretch over the top of him to get up. He doesn't reach out to stop me. I put my feet on the cold floor and gather up my clothes, first replacing the Derg, followed by my pants. My back is to him, but I can feel him watching me. As I pull on my shirt, I feel his fingers trace lightly along my skin and linger on the ten-centimeter scar midway down my right side—Rajcik's parting memento.

"This is recent. Looks like it was bad. What happened?"

"A goodbye gift from my former boss." I slip the shirt over my head and follow it up with my jacket.

"Jesus, Aly. What kind of people did you work with?"

"The wrong kind. Smugglers. It was a mistake, but I didn't have a better plan after I deserted." My boots are the last thing I put on. Buckles tight, I stand up, preparing to go.

"Hey," Rob gets out of bed, pulling the sheet around his waist, and stands close. He's taller than me by a head and a half, lean in the hips and broad in the shoulders. I fit in his shadow when he's close. "I know you have to rush off, but can I get you breakfast first? Coffee, at least?"

"I have to go," I say again, reflexively, wanting to make my exit as quickly as possible. This time he does reach out, brushing the back of his hand against my cheek, then cupping it around the back of my head. He leans forward to kiss me, but I step back, gently releasing myself from his arm. "I'm sorry, I just have to go, okay. It's nothing personal. I'll see you later." I don't rush from the room, but I don't linger either. Rob has been good to me. I don't want to leave him with the impression that I don't care, but right now I need space, time to think.

As I pass through the galley, his three crewmembers are seated, eating breakfast. They all stare at me, their faces clamped in expressions of practiced neutrality. Except for Baker, whose scowl could peel paint. I don't avoid their looks, but continue to the hold and down the ramp without stopping.

At the bottom, the tightness in my chest begins to relax and I breathe deeply, hoping for a quiet day. My plan is to find La Mer or Bodie and see if there's any work I can do on the transceiver. At least that's one place I'm unlikely to see Karl and have to cope with the wreckage that meeting will bring.

I'm not watching where I'm going and step sharply off the ramp, straight in front of a sandbike. "Aly!" I jump back and Bodie swerves and comes to a stop, fortunately going slow enough that he's able to react before smashing into me. At first, surprise is etched on his face. "What are you—?" Then, realization of what I must be doing here strikes and he cuts himself off, having enough tact not to ask.

"Shit, sorry about that, Bodie."

"You okay?" He glances up the *Horizon*'s ramp, a troubled look on his face.

"Yeah, fine." Bodie and Karl are close, nearly as tight as brothers. I can imagine what he's thinking right now, the kinds of questions he must have, and decide it's time to channel the conversation into the day ahead. "What's the status on the transceiver? What can I do to help get it fixed?"

His eyes snap back to my face and his lips are tight, but he seems relieved to have something else to focus on. "There's not much left. Fortunately, it's only the main capacitor that needs to be replaced and some rewiring. We could use your help on that, like before. Vitruzzi is taking the *Sphynx* to Hell's Gate today to see if any locals or off-world traders are around that have the component we need. If they do, we'll be up again tomorrow."

There's a noise from inside the *Horizon*'s hold and I glance back over my shoulder nervously. It's time to get out of here. "That's fantastic news. When should I get up there?"

"You could get started right away. I think La Mer's already there."

"Sounds good. See you later."

When I arrive at Venus's, she is on her way out. "There you are! Karl came by this morning looking for you. Told him you probably crashed on the *Sphynx*. Heard you two had a row. Hope you're okay. Did Karl find you?" Her monologue crashes into me at a hundred miles an hour, almost too fast for my mind to grasp all at once.

"Did you say Karl was here?"

"Yeah, 'bout an hour ago. Didn't he—?"

"Did he say what he wanted?"

"I don't know. No, I mean. I think he was going to apologize. You know, for what he said. I heard about that! He's just a hothead. You know that. Karl's just Karl, always ready to boil over the rim. Want to come with me? He's riding along to Hell's Gate this morning, to get new parts for the transceiver. Isn't it great? It works!"

Shit, what did I do? The temptation to go with Venus and confront Karl is strong—who knows what conclusions he's drawn? Then I realize that the worse conclusion he could draw is true. I'm not prepared to face the brute force of his accusations again, even though I'll be forced to eventually. "No thanks, Venus. I'll stay back today and help La Mer and Bodie out. Let us know if things pan out at Hell's Gate."

"You got it. See ya!"

ELEVEN

It's noon and the twin Algols blaze on us like God's judgment. We've staked the transceiver's netting out in a makeshift awning over the open side of the housing assembly for some relief, but the temps are at least in the 40-degree Celsius range.

"Do you see that capacitor?"

Inside the box, where the upper half of my body is jammed, flashlight in mouth and sweat pouring from my face and neck in streams, it's even hotter. "Yeah, it looks like it's cooked."

"Can you get it free?"

Grunting, "One sec," I have a moment to think that La Mer had better be grateful for the luxury of not being inside this oven. They'd done most of the original wiring before mounting the dish and hadn't had to perform this kind of jack-in-the-box contortion act. I finally get my right hand on the crisped capacitor and yank, banging my elbow on a corner of metal in the process. "Goddammit!"

"Get it?"

I squirm my way backward and take a deep breath, showing them the damaged piece. It had smelled like overcooked plasterine in there. "I know how important this dish is, but if I have to go back in there to put in the new—"

Sand starts kicking up in a frenzied wind from the side of the hill, and a second later a shuttle I've never seen suddenly rises silently over the rim as if it bounced off the valley floor. David, who'd come up with me, has his rifle at the ready almost before any of us realize what it is, pointing it toward the cockpit screen. Like an idiot, I'd left all my hardware except the Derg behind in the *Sphynx*.

The shuttle comes to rest on the slope leading away from the dish toward the Flats, but the engine stays hot. The three of us stand still, not knowing what to expect but seeing no point in trying to run. It's a Speeder model with a center-hung gyroscopic fuselage that links to long, planed jets optimized for minimal air resistance on both sides. The fuel cell engine is mounted on a crossbeam between the two jets at the rear of the fuselage, and the entire shuttle, minus the retractable landing gear, is no taller than a seated man. There's no running from something that fast.

As we watch, the cockpit screen slides backward, opening the fuselage to reveal the pilot's controls and six passenger seats. Rob sits at the controls.

"You all need to come with me quick!" The urgency in his voice is unmistakable and even more alarming than the unexpected shuttle's appearance.

"Rob, what the hell—?" David begins, but Rob cuts him off.

"Don't argue, just get in. You've got Corps landing in the Beach!"

It's like being touched with a live wire, and I'm instantly galvanized by a surge of adrenalin and fear. "Jesus, we gotta get back there."

"Forget it, there are too many. They've got a least one gun ship and a transport. If you go in there fighting, you'll just be killed. Vitruzzi and the others are still at Hell's Gate. We'll regroup with them later, when there's a chance. But right now, we have to get you out of here. Move!"

La Mer is already hoisting his long body up the mounting rungs embedded along the fuselage. David breaks and is up next, pulling me in. Rob immediately accelerates and we speed south, staying low.

"What do you know, Rob? What's the Corps doing here and why didn't the Beach warn us? How did you know they were here?" David bombards him with questions the second the screen closes.

"Look, all I know is we took the *'Rize* up into atmo to check the modifications we've been doing on our backflow valves, and we picked up two ships on radar coming in too low for the Beach's systems to track."

Just like Rob did a few days ago. It's a weakness in the Beach's tracking, another issue that could be resolved with the transceiver functioning as it should.

"I told my crew to keep the *'Rize* in orbit so I could come pick you up. Maybe it's routine, I don't know. But none of you are legal and neither is that dish. I figured I'd get you out of there before they found you."

It takes less than an hour to rendezvous with the *Red Horizon*. I contact Vitruzzi en route to tell her what had happened, and she and the crew with her leave Hell's Gate immediately. Vitruzzi is legally contracted with the Admin, and no other Beacher besides us deserters have any outstanding warrants. Why the Admin would send Corps—with a gunship—to the settlement is anyone's guess, but if there's a way to smooth things out, Vitruzzi is the one to do it. While we wait to hear back from her, we congregate on the *Horizon*'s flight deck where Sims is at the helm. Rob says his record is clean, and if the Corps detains him, he can hide us.

I get antsy waiting and lift my VDU to contact Vitruzzi for an update. Just as I do, both my and David's devices buzz to life and I take a quick, relieved breath, expecting it to be Vitruzzi. Instead, Bodie's face, panic-stricken and fervent, fills our screens.

"We're in deep shit here. The Corps landed about fifteen minutes ago and they're arresting everyone. Repeat, they're arresting the entire settlement. I've locked myself in the mine's control room, but it's only a matter of time. V, Brady, if you're reading this, get the hell off world. They're—"

A teeth-rattling thud rips through the room, and the image on my

VDU shifts wildly as Bodie swings his arms, trying to cover his face from flying debris. Dust fills the screen for a moment, and David and I exchange alarmed glances, both of us holding our breath. I start to depress the transmission key when Baker violently yanks my hand back. "Don't do that, they'll trace the signal."

"Goddammit that's my friend in there!" I holler, yanking my arm free.

"No, Aly, she's right. There's nothing you can do," Rob says.

Before I can argue, another voice comes through the device.

"This is Major Stanford of the Capital Military Corps. You are under arrest. Lay down any weapons you have and walk forward with your hands visible. If you do not comply in ten seconds, you will be forcibly taken."

My eyes are fixed to the screen.

"You have no reason to arrest anyone. We're an independent settlement." We can hear Bodie's voice, but the image on his screen has changed. He must have tossed the unit under a desk or chair with the transmit button locked on; all we see is a fragment of counter and ceiling.

"Don't try to resist. Step out." The same commanding voice as before.

"By whose orders? What authority do you have?"

There's a pause, and then: "By order of Director Kurosawa T'Kai of the Ministry of Science and Engineering. This unauthorized colony has been implicated and found guilty of high treason. All non-citizens found on site will be immediately moved to the prisoner settlement on Keum Libre for sentencing. This is your last opportunity to surrender."

All of us stare transfixed at my VDU, listening to Bodie's deep breathing, sounding almost as if he's sleeping. David suddenly grabs both of my hands, and I realize they'd been shaking from a mixture of fury and fear for Bodie.

Bodie's voice: "V, Karl, if you're hearing this, you can't let these bastards get away with this."

"What's he—?" I start, but I'm cut off sharply by the blunt sound of guns firing, at least three automatics opening up. Gasping, I feel myself coming apart at the seams as I listen to the barrage, knowing that Bodie had fired first, knowing that he would rather die than be taken captive. "No, Bodie, no, no . . ." The words echo through my head, *no no no*, but it's all over in seconds. More dust rains down on the VDU he'd left, then clears. At the screen's rounded edge a few meters distant, Bodie lies still, his blond hair filled with dirt and blood. In a few seconds, we hear the gritty sound of boots stepping into the room.

"Bag that body. See if you can find ID but don't spend much time. We need to hit that other cesspool west of here today. Get a team in here to catalogue this equipment. These non-cits were doing more than growing vegetables."

"Should we bring any of the equipment with us, sir?"

"Not at this time. We'll leave a squad behind to secure it and come back once we transfer the prisoners to the fleet for disposal on Keum Libre."

"Yes, sir."

The room grows still at the sound of the soldier retreating. I want to stop watching but can't tear my eyes from the screen. As long as there's something to see it feels like Bodie is still there, still communicating. A pair of military-issue boots moves into visibility and the man standing in them leans over the counter above the VDU, presumably looking over the equipment lying there.

"Sir—"

At the sound of his voice, the officer turns around and one foot stomps down on top of the device, killing the transmission.

I look up into David's face and see my own horror and sadness reflected in his wide eyes and downward-curling mouth. "Those murdering fucks," he says and falls heavily into the wall behind him, shaking with shock and rage.

"Cross, we got issues." Sims is staring at a console, the bluish light reflecting off the whites of his narrowed eyes. "We need to get ourselves the fuck outta here immediately."

I turn, ready to argue—David and I have to get to the *Sphynx,* talk to Vitruzzi. I know that at least Brady, Venus, Desto, and Karl are all with her, and David, La Mer, and I are here with Rob, but that still leaves about 125 people—124 without Bodie—who are being rounded up like sheep as we speak. We'd planned for a lot of possible scenarios after we'd done what we had on the Fortress, but never something as horrific as this. I suspect I know what Vitruzzi will want to do, the same as what I want to do, but the first thing we *have* to do is regroup. Rounding on Cross, I say, "You can't go anywhere until you get us to the *Sphynx*."

"You don't tell us—" Baker growls, standing close to me like she's going to swing.

Facing her, more than ready to take this to the next level, the muscles in my arms and back tense. *Do it, Baker. Push me just a little bit more. Give me a reason to unleash this horrible rage before it poisons me to death.*

Rob chimes in before that happens. "Bodie was a good man. I don't know what the hell the Admin would want to do this for but I'll do what I can to help." Montoya, Sims, and Baker stiffen, ready to protest, but he continues, "Within *reason*. We have to be careful but we'll get you back to your crew."

La Mer remains standing to the side, quietly, fading into the background, but the despondency in his face shows how hard it's hitting him. I don't know what I can say to help him, but I do know that the Admin and the Corps are going to pay for this.

David says, "Rob, you don't have to do this. Just put us down in the Flats and leave. You don't need to be part of the shit storm that's coming."

I twist around and glare at David, furious with him for letting Rob off the hook, but he gives me a look that convinces me to drop it for now.

"Erickson, are you there?" It's Vitruzzi. I jump a little at the unexpected transmission and hold my VDU up. Her face is a mask of pain.

"Here."

"You saw?"

My throat feels like it's filled with dirt, dry as dust, and I have to swallow before I can speak again. "Yeah."

"What's your status? Has the Corps made contact with Rob?" She's already thinking ahead, trying to figure out what happens next, and her deliberate response helps me get back on track.

"No. We're clear for now. He's going to bring us to you. Where should we rendezvous?"

Vitruzzi is silent for a moment and I wonder if I failed to transmit. Then she says, "Let me talk to Rob."

I hold my arm up so the screen faces him. He reaches out and holds the transmit button. "Eleanor, I'm really sorry."

"Thanks." Lines around her eyes show she's suffering, but she controls it with granite resolve. "Look, we can't go near the Beach. How far are you willing to take the three of them?"

"What do you have in mind?"

"We're planning to make for R'Kadia."

Rob considers it for a moment. R'Kadia is a little more than a day away, and that's if we can fly straight to it without having to evade pursuit by Corps ships. Every decision he makes from now until he cuts us loose is overshadowed by one major complication: he's harboring wanted fugitives. He, and his crew, are in jeopardy until that's no longer the case. If I were him, I'd hesitate before agreeing to Vitruzzi's proposal.

"We can do that," he replies, and I feel a touch of the tension in my shoulders let go.

His three crewmembers respond with surprising restraint. Whatever their history together, this crew has shown that it regards the rule of unquestioned loyalty to their captain as a trifling inconvenience at best and an outright joke at worst. But no one protests.

Vitruzzi sounds relieved. "You have our thanks once again. I'm sending coordinates for a rendezvous point. We hope to be there within thirty-eight hours if things go well. Let us know if you have any trouble. We'll do the same."

Rob turns to the navigator. "Baker, set our course. We'll see you soon, Eleanor." My VDU darkens as she cuts the transmission.

"Rob, are you sure you want to do this?" David asks.

"Yeah. It's fine. We'll get you there. Don't worry, man." Even as he says this, wrinkles of anxiety settle across his forehead and convert the laugh lines around his eyes into something much less whimsical. "Sims, Montoya, find them somewhere comfortable to stay for the next few hours." He turns to us. "In case you want to catch a nap . . . or something."

TWELVE

Only six hours pass before a Corps scout ship catches up to us. David, La Mer, and I sit morosely in the galley, sipping food supplement mixes and not saying much, wondering how things could have gone so wrong so fast. The craving for one of Rob's illicit cocktail mixes is strong, and I struggle to keep myself from finding the contraband room and drinking myself comatose. When Rob said Bodie was a good man, he couldn't know the half of it. Bodie was more than that; he was a friend. Despite our first inauspicious meeting, what we'd been through together—the rescue mission on the Fortress, the way he made me laugh and brought me freshly grown fruits during my recovery after Rajcik shot me, and the way he brought a sense of calm and serenity to every situation—had made him more like family, nearly as close to me as David. Thinking about a day passing in the grow rooms without seeing his wide, welcoming smile and laughing blue eyes makes tears sting my eyes, but I force them back. This isn't the time for sorrow. The Corps—vile, murdering animals that they are—ruthlessly killed one of the best men I'd ever known. And they will answer for it.

David and La Mer sit in silence battling their own pain. Despite the fragile quiet, none of us let our guard down, and no one is surprised when Rob enters the galley—not exactly running, but definitely not doddering.

Rising to his feet, David asks, "What's going on?"

"Corps-security patrol ship. They're demanding to board for a routine contraband search. Come with me. We can stash you in the swag room."

"Are you crazy? You want us to hide behind a holo?" There's no way in hell I'm going to hide in a place where the only thing between me and armed soldiers out for blood is a fragile electronic fakeout."

"Do you have a better idea?"

"You're a smuggler for fuck's sake. Don't you have a *real* hiding place?"

"Sure, if you can shrink yourself down to half a cubic meter, I've got just the place for you."

"Aly, we don't have time to argue," La Mer says, not realizing what he's in for.

To punctuate Rob's point, Montoya's voice comes through the intercom. "Cross, they're linked and engaging the airlock." Cross cocks an eyebrow at us, and with a sinking feeling in my stomach, we all sprint to the room where his illegal cache of goods are stored. In plain sight.

He activates the holographic deflector and the false wall materializes in front of us. "Keep it quiet. This always works."

"Just get rid of them," David growls.

He begins walking back up the corridor just as we hear the leader of the security squad step out of the cargo bay.

A woman's voice comes down the corridor. "You must be Captain Cross."

"That's right, Major. What's this about?"

"Under Admin authority code six-zero-six, we have the legal imperative to search your ship, and that includes seeing your identity registrations. We'll ask for them one by one. Your full cooperation is required and expected."

The voice clangs off the corridor walls, sounding full of bloated self-worth. David and I look at each other and his lips pull back in an infuriated snarl, the strange inner luminescence of the holo-wall giving his teeth a silvery cast. I hadn't thought what it would be like to be on this side of it, but the fact that we can't see through the wall—as if it were actually real and solid—does nothing to improve my confidence.

"Yes, ma'am. You're aware that I'm legally contracted to be in this quadrant. My contract is current, granted by the Ministry of S&E."

"Yes we are, Captain Cross. There have been activities in the area that have necessitated tightened security measures."

"Well, if you could hurry it up. We're on our way back to the Obals and most clients aren't very understanding when they're contractors are late. You understand."

There's no response as their footsteps echo past us toward the bow end of the corridor. None of us look at each other. We're all staring at the fake wall fervently, as if concentrating on it will make it more real, more *solid*.

Forty-five minutes pass before the sound of people returning echoes toward us. We all tense, counting their steps until the go by and back into the cargo hold. A few minutes later, we hear the airlock engage and a hollow sound as the outer airlock opens, releasing our uninvited Corps guests. Rob returns and shuts down the projector.

"You're in the clear. They're already outside of visual range. No worries. Just routine, like they said."

La Mer is visibly relieved and David takes a deep breath. "Nice one," he comments. "Now if you don't mind telling me what the hell that thing is . . ."

THIRTEEN

The *'Rize* settles onto the dusty landscape of R'Kadia with the fluid grace of luxury cruiser-class engines. My only other visit to this desolate Spectra 5 moon was shortly after meeting Vitruzzi and her crew—if you can call being kidnapped *meeting*. She'd recruited me to help ensure a smuggling exchange arranged with a local band of brigands went down smoothly. It hadn't, and our scramble out of the abandoned mine that served as their hideout had not been bloodless. Still, we'd taken what we'd gone for—a significant payload of solar amalgam seeds that will serve to keep the *Sphynx* powered long after we're all dead. Thinking back on that confrontation now, I realize Vitruzzi had been testing me to see just how far I could be trusted. That decision was a huge gamble, but she and her crew had been desperate. So had I. The irony that the situation this time is practically interchangeable does nothing to lift my spirits.

La Mer, David, and I stand in the cargo hold listening for the hydraulic landing tripod to lockout and give us clearance to open the port door. The *Sphynx* is already here, sitting silently in the dirt with her landing ramp open. We walk aboard, anxious to hear what Vitruzzi has in mind.

The rest of the crew await us in the open cargo hold, the compartment seeming small and outmoded after the last few hours spent aboard the newer and grander *Red Horizon*. I meet Karl's eyes as we approach and he holds my gaze. So much has happened since our argument two days ago that it's impossible to guess what he's feeling. Or what I am, for that matter.

Vitruzzi begins to speak, but Venus suddenly runs to La Mer and grasps him in an embrace that nearly knocks the wind out of him. They hold each other in silence, the rest of us taking some vicarious comfort in their relief.

After a few seconds, Vitruzzi says, "We're glad to see you're all safe."

David responds, "We were lucky Rob picked us up. Otherwise . . ." He trails off. At the mention of Rob, Karl finally drops my eyes, lines deepening on his forehead.

We're standing at the rear of the hold in a group. The *Sphynx* had not been stocked for a long excursion before last leaving Agate Beach and the only thing occupying the compartment right now is the Rover. No one seems to know what else to say, but a look I can't read passes between Vitruzzi and David. Something about it is unsettling.

"Okay," Vitruzzi says and swallows like she has something in her throat. "The reason I wanted to regroup on R'Kadia—"

Before she finishes, her eyes drift over my shoulder as someone else climbs the ramp.

"I didn't think I'd be seeing you people again so soon."

I swing around in a smooth, liquid turn, right hand already drawing my Mini-Derg from my calf holster.

Rajcik.

His voice vibrates nerves deep inside my core like a shockwave, triggering reflexes that come from a dark place, a place where the worst things a person is capable of come from. As I pull the trigger, an arm sweeps down and knocks my wrist aside, forcing the cutting beam of the laser to streak across the floor, its silence punctuating my furious rage. I turn, instinctively raising my other arm to strike my assailant.

"Aly, hold up!" Karl yells into my face, but it's like he's speaking another language. I swore I'd kill Rajcik if he ever crossed my path again . . . and what the fuck is he doing here now?

"Let go of me!"

"No, wait, just hold it a sec. He's working for us. Hear me?"

I hear him, but I simply can't believe it. I yank hard, trying to get him to release my arm, but his grip doesn't loosen. I'm about to strike him with my free arm, but Rajcik speaks again, freezing me.

"You don't seem to have expected me, Aly." The last time I looked into that malevolent face was while he leaned over my broken, helpless body and threatened to murder David and the crew. I almost can't believe my eyes as I run them over his swarthy features, trying to make sense of something that can't possibly be happening. He gives Vitruzzi a disgusted look. "You didn't tell her our deal?"

"Tell me what? What the fuck is going on here, Vitruzzi?" I whirl on her and the rest of the crew, my voice shrill. This time when I pull, Karl releases my arm.

"Erikson, you need to calm down until you understand the situation." Her voice is cool, placating, but with a hard steel edge.

I've gone mute, struck dumb by what I'm hearing. But fury quickly burns through my paralysis. "Understand what situation? You cut a deal? With *him*!" My voice cracks and my stomach clenches involuntarily as if the wind has been knocked out of me. "Do I have to remind you people that he's the reason every one of us nearly died out there? He betrayed everyone in this room, some of us more than once, and now you've cut a fucking deal? Are you nuts?"

The more I speak, witnessing the careful neutrality in their faces, the more the reality hits home. Of the six people standing in front of me, La Mer is the only one who seems slightly confused, his glance bouncing to Rajcik, to the crew, to me, and back to Rajcik as he tries to piece together a connection he knows nothing about. A new thought floats into my mind like a dead and bloated thing. *David knew about this.* My own brother. The blood drains from my face and my limbs go slack. Turning back to face Rajcik, I feel my hand still holding the Derg begin to rise again on its own. His lips curl back in a snarl, then David's voice stops me.

"Aly, don't." My eyes snap to his face and I see his guilt. He betrayed me. All of them had.

Without another word, I drop my arm and careen past them through the airlock and into the passageway leading to the crew quarters. My only thought is to take what's mine and get the fuck out of here.

FOURTEEN

"I can pay you. I've got cash, I just need your help getting it. Will you do it?" I'm sitting on the *'Rize*'s flight deck proposing a deal to Rob. I need a ride off of R'Kadia. If he can take me as far as the moon Kai Lum that orbits Spectra 4, I'll cut him in on a third of the money David and I have stashed over the last few years—our own insurance policy. If Rajcik hasn't gotten to it first, that is.

"Yeah, of course I'll take you. But, Aly, you're clearly pissed about something. I think you should tell me what's going on before I agree." He puts a reassuring hand on my shoulder.

"I wish I could." His hand slips from my shoulder as I begin pacing. His hesitancy makes it apparent that my decision to abandon the crew, brash as it is, is going to require some careful negotiation. The irony in the whole fucked-up situation is enough to make me want to scream. I'm forced to rely on Rob to get me gone, despite the fact that relying on others is what got me here in the first place. How could they do this? They *knew* Rajcik was alive. The *knew* it, and even worse, they forged some sort of arrangement, some sort of fucking contract with him. *With Rajcik!* Their decision compromises every-thing we'd fought together for. Why would they do it? Desperation? Ignorance? Necessity? I don't care. My brother, even Karl, betrayed me. It shakes me more than seeing Rajcik again in the first place has. What else are they hiding from me? Why didn't they tell me? Were they trying to spare me this rage, this disbelief? Does it matter? No. Whatever their reasons were, they still betrayed to me.

I can't explain all that to Rob, there's no time. "You just have to trust me. It's better for you and your crew if we get the hell off this rock ASAP. I'll explain on the way."

He regards me with a distant consideration that I'm not used to. "And what about David? Is he coming?"

"No, I'm not."

We both turn, surprised to see him standing in the galley's doorway. Before he tries to speak, I cut in, "Whatever you have to say, you can choke on it."

"Aly, come on. You need to just listen to this."

"Listen to what, David? That lunatic tries to kill you, and you, what? Ask him to be part of your crew?"

"It's not what you think—"

"You're my fucking brother! I'm supposed to be able to trust you!"

He's also getting angry now. Redness only slightly darker than his hair creeps out of his shirt collar and up his neck. "Dammit, Aly. Look at the way you're reacting. Are you surprised we didn't tell you? You probably would have tried to fly up here and kill him yourself like some kind of goddamn merc."

"You're damn right I would have! And so would you if you were thinking straight."

"Do either of you want to tell me what this is about?" Rob speaks quietly, leaving the request optional.

Taking a deep breath to calm himself, David continues, "Look, I know we should have told you, but this wasn't supposed to happen. Working with Rajcik was supposed to be a last chance option, a backup contingency. There was never any need to tell you because we —I—knew you wouldn't understand."

"Wait a minute," Rob cuts in. "Are you talking about János Rajcik? The arms smuggler?"

The urgency in his tone derails our argument and we both turn to him. His usual warm tan has gone the color of off milk and his brown eyes are wide. "Do either of you realize what kind of trouble working with him can get you into? The Admin has dedicated patrols looking for him system-wide—he's basically considered the antichrist."

"Which is why we need to get out of here."

"No, listen, both of you. Aly, just shut up for a minute." The hard set of David's jaw tells me what I know all too well; he's past the point of arguing. Pinning me to the spot with eyes as ferocious as a pouncing lion's, he forces me to listen to his explanation. "Rajcik came to Vitruzzi a couple of weeks after the Fortress. He was injured in the explosion and the *Temptation* was damaged, and they made a deal. He'd leave the Beach alone if she gave him the aid he needed."

"And you believed him—" I start to interrupt, but he doesn't let me get far.

"Vitruzzi didn't just say yes without thinking it through. She had us strip the *Temptation* of its weapons and most of its fuel and strand Rajcik out here on R'Kadia."

"Why? Why not just kill him? After what he did to us—"

"There's more. He's been helping get some of the stuff the Beach needs through his old contacts—Chisolm, Howard, the Spectre Triad. And this is the part you need to pay attention to. Rajcik had something to barter with, something we thought we might need. We assumed we could use it to keep the Admin and the Corps off our backs if they ever pieced together what happened at the Fortress."

I fall into a chair, still angry, but also intrigued enough to hold my tongue for a few minutes. Rob remains standing resolutely beside me, his sinewy frame tensed in anticipation of where David's story will lead.

"What is it, David?" he asks.

"It better be good," I add.

He tries to wither me with an exasperated look and continues, "He recorded all of the communications he had with T'Kai. And Aly, this is going to be hard to hear, but their deal was never even about stealing the Nova. T'Kai hired Rajcik to detonate it and *destroy* the Fortress. That's what the payoff was for. Rajcik lied to us. He made up the story about blackmailing the Admin so we'd help him get the Nova for himself."

"Are you saying that you two were involved with that space station? That Rajcik is your old boss?" The look on Rob's face is perfect incredulity. "I can't believe what I'm hearing."

My brain is reeling, too much unexpected news all at once, too many surprises. Plotting. Scheming. It's like being in the Corps again. I thought I'd left that world behind, thought I was in a place where I could trust the people I was with, believe in what they stood for. I should know better by now.

David's eyes feel heavy on my face as he examines it, preparing for what I might do. For the time being, I'm frozen to my seat, unable to react. He turns to Rob to explain, "There wasn't much time for planning. Neither of us was prepared for life outside the Corps. We just fell in with Rajcik by chance."

"Do you have any idea how many deaths he's responsible for?"

There's a subtle change in Rob's tone, no longer simple disbelief but moving toward something closer to anger. The hair on my arms stirs and I glance toward David, seeing the same apprehension settling over him.

"Rob, you know we wouldn't be part of something like that." David faces Rob, toe-to-toe, only taller by one or two centimeters. "But if you knew what the Admin was doing on that space station, you may not think it was such a bad thing that Rajcik blew it up. You see what they did to my fucking eyes. And what they did to Bodie. This shit needs to stop. It *has* to stop."

Rob turns around and moves toward the pilot's console, putting it between him and David. David and I look at each other, sharing a sudden realization that we may have underestimated his loyalty to the Admin. We're allies again, at least for the moment, and wondering what the hell we're going to do if that's the case. Rob leans forward on his hands, staring absently at the screen, keeping his thoughts to himself.

I should say something. "Look, Rob. This isn't your fight."

He takes a long breath before answering. "No, forget it. As hard as it is to believe what you're telling me, I guess I do."

"Then you'll still take me to Kai Lum?"

"Aly—" David starts to protest, but Rob cuts him off.

"It's not that simple anymore."

The wills of two soldiers start fighting inside me, one trying to tell me to just shoot Rob and stop him from making the mistake I'm afraid he's about to, the other not wanting to jump to conclusions. "What do you mean?"

"János Rajcik is worth a lot of money."

"Wait a minute, Rob. You can't turn him in. We need him."

I whirl on David. "Why?"

"He's the only person we know with information about Keum Libre. He can help us get to the Beachers, maybe get them out of there."

"He'll never help us."

"He doesn't have a choice."

"He'll never help us, David, and if I see him again, I swear to God I'll kill him."

"Just try to be rational, Aly. You've got friends that are being held in prison for no other reason than that they were trying to live their lives. You have to start caring about more than yourself." He hovers over me, trying to intimidate me, but we've been siblings too long and it doesn't work anymore. Despite the impatience growing in his own eyes, I don't drop mine, letting the fury there speak for itself. He stares back for a moment, then turns around and walks a few steps away, running his hand through his overly long hair in distress. "Did you really think what we had at the Beach was going to last? You were so caught up with the idea of things being normal, you and Karl living some fantasy happily-ever-after story, you forgot what was really going on. We're *deserters*, little sis. As far as the Admin is concerned, we're their number one problem, and they're not going to forget about us."

My eyes jerk guiltily toward Rob at the mention of Karl, but his face is stern, lines of agitation forming deep furrows around his mouth and narrowed eyes. David is studying my face with increasing intensity, but I say nothing. What else can I say? It's the truth. I wanted to forget about the control the Admin has over us, over our lives. I'd let creature comforts and a façade of freedom take the place of the more practical side of me, the side that's always ready for trouble and always running from it.

Taking my silence for agreement, David turns to Rob. "Look, I understand the dilemma this creates for you. You didn't expect to get caught up with something like this when you brought us those parts for the transceiver, and you couldn't have known what we were involved in. But"—he sighs exasperatedly, glancing back at me—"I'd almost be willing to drop the Nova on the Admin myself for what they did to Bodie. If getting justice for him means working with Rajcik, at least I'll be able to sleep at night. I don't care about anything else."

Rob says, "I understand. I do. But if I just walk away and forget that I know Rajcik is here, I stand to lose a lot more than my ship."

Neither of us respond. Finally David says, "It's not too late, Rob. If you left now, no one would ever know."

He sighs. "I need a little while. I have to think this through." Looking at me, eyebrows arched in worry and uncertainty, he says, "I'm sorry, Aly."

"There isn't much time, Rob," David warns.

"I know that," he answers sharply. Then continues more calmly, "Just give me a couple of hours." His eyes shift toward the flight deck hatch in a request that we leave.

I hesitate, wanting to press Rob into a decision, but stop myself. He has to decide this on his own.

Following my brother off the flight deck, we only get a few steps down the corridor before he grabs my arm above the elbow, pulling me to a stop. "Look, Aly, I'm sorry. I didn't know how to tell you."

I want to accuse him, yell at him, continue the battle until he's bruised and beaten, but what good would it do? The fight has finally gone out of me. Rob was my only chance of getting out of here and he has his own agenda. Where would I go anyway? The realization that

I'm involved in circumstances I'm powerless to control holds me in check. If I killed Rajcik now, who would benefit and who would lose? The answer to that is not as clear as I'd imagined it would be before today. The settlers have given me more than I can ever repay. If Rajcik can help us free them, don't I owe them that? David and the crew betrayed me, yet I have no other choice than to come to terms with it.

"You know we have to watch him every second," I finally say, giving in completely. "He'll tell us what we want to hear, but you can bet your life that he has plans of his own. Oh right—you already have bet your life, *our* lives." My last statement wilts as soon as it hits the air, resignation making it toneless.

He looks me over, relieved that I'm dropping it. "You know Vitruzzi won't leave anything to chance. Rajcik is bugged, just like the rest of us are. We can keep tabs on him."

"That'll be a huge comfort when he does something like turn us over to the Admin."

His head bows and his chest expands in a deep sigh. "We owe it to Bodie."

For the first time, I realize how much he's suffering over what has happened. I've been too self-absorbed to realize I'm not the only one. Bodie meant a lot to all of us. I reach out to put a hand on his shoulder and he grabs me, drawing me into a hug. With my face pressed against his chest, I whisper, "We're all going to miss him." Tears are close, but I smother them with a promise—Bodie's death will be avenged.

We embrace for a minute, then David drops his arms. "The crew is waiting for us. And there's one more thing, Aly. I promise you, no more surprises. But you should know . . . Thompson is still with Rajcik."

Fuller Thompson. Rajcik's sadistic shadow. A man who hates me almost as much as I hate him.

"Jesus, what have we gotten into?"

FIFTEEN

"Right now we have two imperatives: get our people off Keum Libre, and do whatever it takes to stop T'Kai." Brady stands next to the *Sphynx*'s galley doorway, addressing the crew and Rajcik. "We all agree that the Admin is dangerous and forces its rule too far, but it's T'Kai, and others like him, that are pushing the buttons. We'll never get any peace until he's brought down. And we have what we need to do it."

"You're talking about blackmail," David states. He looks around at the rest of the crew, then continues, "We were only building the transceiver in case the Admin got too close. If we change the plan and go after T'Kai, I mean actively, that will push things a lot further. Maybe too far."

Venus stands near the cabinets next to La Mer. She holds a tube of food in one hand and methodically squeezes the contents from one end to the other. The pressure she exerts is just enough to make the end of the tube bulge with each squeeze, barely short of popping it and spraying orange goo all over the room. I have to force myself not to take it away from her as she speaks. "But why does he have to know about us at all? Won't the Ministry of S&E come after us if we threaten T'Kai? We can't fight the whole Corps."

Rajcik makes a disgusted sound, and Venus, looking shaken, glances around the room, hoping to see some sign of agreement from any of us. But the crew's certainty that we're on a collision course with the director of the Ministry of Science and Engineering, and the Admin in general, is unanimous. No one will meet her eyes except La Mer, who gives her a small reassuring smile. Whatever happens in the days ahead, they'll still have each other. But for how long? The thought nearly makes me shudder.

"I don't need to tell anyone how dire the situation is," Vitruzzi says. "We need to agree just how far we're willing to go, how much we're willing to risk, to get justice for Bodie and get our people safe."

"What I want to know is why the Admin did this? Did they know about the transceiver? How did they find out?" La Mer is spooked. Not being able to identify how, or even if, his programming was detected tears at the core of his confidence, but no one has an answer for him.

"Even if we can rescue the settlers, we can't go back to the Beach," Brady states. Hearing it said aloud brings it home. To all of us. Our lives aren't just changed, they've been turned upside down, ruined. What difference does it even make if we can rescue the settlers? Where can any of us go now and not be hunted as fugitives? Just like that, the Admin completely destroyed the tenuous peace we'd managed to carve out of nothing.

Looking around, I see the same fear on everyone's faces. Everyone except Rajcik. Like an animal, he has learned the law of the jungle. Hunt or be hunted. Kill or be killed. He's not afraid of losing anything, because he has nothing to lose. Just another non-cit lowlife scum with a life story that was written before he was born, and he plays the role with perfect, even serene, ease.

"We can't leave them there," says Mason, his voice thick.

"No. We're not going to," Vitruzzi answers.

"Then we do whatever it takes." His nutmeg eyes gaze fiercely into everyone's faces, and the heavy wrinkles spanning his forehead add to his serious, not-to-be-fucked-with gravitas. Mason, as a rule, is usually quiet and brooding, and when he does have something to say, everyone listens.

"All right, so what's the plan?" David's tone is all practicality.

No one has said a word to me about earlier. When I look at Vitruzzi, she meets my eyes with stoic resoluteness, not a shred of guilt or apology about having hidden Rajcik's whereabouts from me. It's exactly the kind of reaction I'd expect from her. If Vitruzzi has any weakness, it remains as invisible to me as the day we'd met.

Rajcik sits across the galley opposite me, near the exit. His presence alone makes my stomach churn, but knowing it's my choice to be here—and let him live—ignites bile in a rancid torrent. Every time his black eyes slide toward me, I want to gag and go for my gun. Reminding myself of the reasons to let him live only makes it worse. If this is what pure hate feels like, it must only be one step short of total madness.

Brady leans against the wall near me with his arms folded. "With the data we took from the Fortress and Rajcik's recordings, we have enough leverage to make T'Kai pay attention. If it gets out to the public and the right people in the Directorate, he'll never be able to refute it. It may be enough of a bargaining chip for him to let the settlers go, maybe even leave the Beach alone for good."

I wrap my hands around the back of a chair and lean toward Vitruzzi and Brady. "But the transceiver's not fixed and the Corps has the Beach secured, probably even under surveillance. We don't have a way to wavecast it. T'Kai will know that. And there's no way we can just send a copy to the Directorate and hope they'll do something about it—except silence us. It's their job to protect the Admin's image and maintain control." My words may sound harsh and unproductive, but they are the truth.

Without raising his eyes from where he stares at the floor, La Mer responds, "Well, the transceiver's just a device. It's the programming I did that makes it useful. The security worm hijacks the TDRSs and allows us to boost their waves."

This grabs Vitruzzi's attention, "You mean you could send from any transceiver, as long as it was powerful enough to transmit to a satellite?"

"Basically, yeah."

Brady says, "So we could get the message to T'Kai—the Beachers go free or we bring him down—and find a transceiver that can carry out our threat if he doesn't."

"What's our insurance?" Desto asks. "Even if he releases them, it won't be long until he decides to shut us up for good."

It's Rajcik who responds, "So we bring T'Kai down anyway." He rises from his seat and regards the crew with wicked earnestness. My hand immediately reaches for my 'Bad, but the warning does nothing to deter him. "You all know that it's only a matter of time before he completely obliterates your little settlement and every person who can tie him to the Fortress. You're already living on borrowed time. Your choices are either to go all the way, or go cower in your hole and wait for him to find you." His speech elicits frowns from everyone, but no arguments. Scowling, he finishes, "Captain Vitruzzi, your friends don't have long. I suggest you make a decision soon. You know where to find me."

"Where do you think you're going?" The sound of my pistol being drawn stops him.

Instead of answering, he turns, raising an eyebrow as he looks toward Vitruzzi. "Let him go, Aly," she commands.

Arguing is pointless. It's like they've all lost their memories. Do they really believe he's not planning to double cross us again while we stand here and argue about plans for our own funeral?

"So what do we do?" Karl picks up the thread.

Vitruzzi responds, "We should consider Venus's suggestion. If there's any way to get the Beachers off of Keum Libre without drawing the Admin's eye, our chances will be much better."

"Assuming everyone is still alive, that's 125 people." Several of us wince at Brady's statement. "The *Sphynx* can carry them, but it might be better to separate, use two ships."

"What about the *Temptation*?" David asks.

"We shouldn't consider anything of Rajcik's an asset," I comment, glaring at David. "He's a tool with limited usefulness."

"We can't use the *Temptation* anyway; it's compromised," Vitruzzi continues. "Anyone flying on it is a target, and we can't put the Beachers in that kind of jeopardy."

"Can we buy another ship?" Karl asks.

"I don't know what with. Most of our assets have been seized."

"So we go back to the Beach and wipe out the security squad guarding it. We have to get supplies and weapons, anyway."

"What about Cross? Would he help us?" Desto asks.

"No way, he's Admin, and he's not part of this crew," Karl responds, animosity curdling his voice.

"He's still a friend," David says, defensively.

"He has nothing to gain. Why would he put himself at risk? He already knows enough to—to have us arrested," Karl says.

Startled by what he's implying, I say, "It's thanks to Rob that the three of us got out before the Corps could catch us. What more reason do you need to trust him?"

"Why do you feel like you have to defend him?" he spits back.

"Both of you drop it," Brady orders, his impatience sparking like a loose wire. "We can't ask Cross to help us. We're in this on our own. But we do have to get him out of here. We're a liability for him, and the longer he sticks around, the more of a liability he becomes to us."

David and I exchange a dark look. "It may not be that easy."

Everyone turns to my brother. "He knows about Rajcik and . . . shit, he may want to turn him in."

"Well he can't do that," Venus says, distress making her voice flat and winded, like she's been running.

Brady slowly straightens, his accusatory stare igniting the air between him and I. "How the fuck does he know about Rajcik?"

I feel hot blood rushing through my veins, threatening to bubble over. "Don't kid yourself. I'm not the problem. You're the ones who involved that sonofabitch in the first place."

He speaks slowly at first, but his words gain momentum as his anger starts to get loose. "Your goddamn vendetta is going to get people killed. Damn you, Erikson, is that what you want?"

"Stop." Vitruzzi steps up next to Brady and slaps her palm loudly against a table. She turns to me, her eyes strangely kind. "We have enough problems to deal with right now. Rajcik isn't anyone's favorite option, and if we had any choice, he'd never factor into this. But that's not reality." She scans the room with a commanding gaze. "We're going to get our friends off that prison rock, whether that means taking T'Kai down or not. But the first thing we have to do is get our assets in order, and Aly's right, that means a trip to the Beach."

SIXTEEN

A set of military-issue leg sheaths with built-in kneepads fits perfectly over my pants and zips around the lip of my combat boots. Their lightweight plating is almost as adept at repelling low-caliber bullets as the body armor I wear over my torso, but more importantly, they provide stellar soft-tissue protection in high-impact activities—perfect for an assault on the Beach. I finish gearing up inside the cramped passenger cabin of the *Sphynx*'s shuttle while Doug Mason and Desto do the same beside me.

Almost four days have passed since Bodie's death. After our conversation aboard the *Sphynx,* the crew roughed together a sketchy plan for gathering the supplies we'll need from the Beach, and now Karl lowers the shuttle into the labyrinthine canyons of Mecca Flats, carefully picking his way through sharply twisting spires and gullies. We do a final gear and weapons check before we land, the three of us preparing to jump out and sneak quietly into the settlement on foot in order to recon the security squad's position and find their vulnerabilities.

"Karl, we're in position. What's your status?" Vitruzzi checks in from a low-orbit holding pattern. The *Sphynx* did a sweep for other Corps ships in the area and is ready to back us up if we need it.

"We're almost at the drop point." Karl turns around from the pilot's seat and draws a circle in the air with his index finger pointing toward the ceiling, our signal to get ready to land.

Desto stands by the shuttle hatch, ready to slide it open. Karl eases us down while I watch the rusty sand walls, no more than a couple meters distant, rising up through the porthole window. The canyon is deep enough that we descend beyond where the suns' rays are able to penetrate and the walls are cast in deep shadows that serve to conceal points where the large, ratlike rodents living in Mecca Flats hide. Even though they are mammals, they're covered in scales, and they brandish retractable claws like a cat's, only several centimeters longer and as hard as petrified wood. When walking on all fours, their bullet-shaped heads, with jaws containing rows of long, sharp teeth, reach about midthigh on a person my height, slightly more than one and a half meters. Instead of ears, they have highly perceptive auditory organs that form ridges of concentric circles of flesh that taper toward the base of their skulls, an occasional wiry hair sprouting here and there. Like radars, they can pick up sounds several kilometers distant. The noise made by a ship is usually loud enough to scatter them and send them hiding in their caves, but the shuttle is much quieter. We'll have to be extremely cautious as we pick our way over the last couple kilometers to the Beach. These ugly beasts are meat eaters, and they'll be eager for an easy lunch.

The shuttle rises a few centimeters as the reverse thrusters activate and then drops to the ground with a thud. We waste no time getting outside and I take point. Mason and Desto fan out behind me, the three of us moving rapidly as a single unit through the canyon that eventually feeds out into a half-kilometer flat plain south of the Beach. That will be our longest sprint with no cover, but we timed our landing so the noon sunlight will be beating directly down and heat shimmers will help camouflage us from naked eyes. At least, that's the plan.

My breathing and footsteps beat a dull and persistent pattern in my ears as we run, and my eyes move ceaselessly over the top of my raised carbine, picking out shadows ahead of me that mean a blind corner or crack in the walls. The air is cool this far below the tops of the canyon walls, and the run would be pleasant if circumstances were different.

A sound catches my attention, and I pivot my eyes to the right where small pebbles tumble down the sloping wall. Jerking my head up, I catch just a glimpse of a Flat Rat's tail as it runs along a horizontal off-width a few meters up and disappears from sight. With a quick hand gesture, I make Desto and Mason aware of it.

Two kilometers later, we're almost to the edge of the canyon. I round the final bend, feeling the heat from the plains already beginning to push into the shadows. There's a clicking noise that my body reacts to before I realize I'd heard anything. A remote sentry, either motion or noise activated. But we've been *so* quiet! I fling myself back behind the edge of the wall and the others respond immediately by finding cover of their own. It's a flying mechanical device about the size and shape of a human head; its job is to provide surveillance in areas that aren't patrolled by ground troops and deliver our coordinates, capabilities, and numbers to a response squad. If it sees us, our cover and surprise advantage are blown.

It buzzes just barely within auditory range, moving slowly around the corner of the wall, seeking us. Even if we destroy the unit, any malfunction will alert responders. We need a diversion so we can pass by unnoticed. As I contemplate options, pellets of dirt rain down on me, and I feel a warm droplet of something land on my cheek. My head tips back in time to see two Flat Rats descending in leaps down the nearly vertical wall, their black lips drawn back and yellowed monster teeth revealed in ferocious grimaces. The closest is already in midair, its thirty kilos of predatory malevolence moments from crashing into me as I drop to a crouch and pull my knife free from my utility vest. Swinging almost wildly, I stab the blade into its side as it hits me, its weight flattening me to the ground. Wounded, it shrieks madly in my ear as its head lunges for my vulnerable neck.

Before it can clamp down, the other rat smashes down on top of us both, the smell of its wounded compatriot's blood already driving it into a voracious frenzy. Their combined weight and chaotic scrabbling is impossible to fight, and I know that I am seconds from being shredded to pieces. My arm is pinned to my chest; I can't get it free to stab again. Screaming for help will bring the sentry on us in seconds, but panic is beginning to replace my reason. Before I start shrieking, I draw my knees into my chest, hoping to protect my vital organs, and also hoping Desto or Mason gets to me before it's too late.

Suddenly one of the rats quits squirming and rises up on its haunches, hissing and baring its teeth. Mason runs toward me and kicks the rodent squarely in the ribs, sending it flying into the opening in the canyon wall. The wounded one is still on top of me but its strength is quickly ebbing. Deep lacerations caused by the other rat and a severed artery from my knife have mortally wounded it, and its life is leaking out all over me. The smell of its blood is a sickly sweet combination of rotten meat and carnivore viscera, making me gag. Mason grabs one of my arms and pulls me to my feet, letting the wounded rat fall. At the same time, we hear the remote sentry buzzing around the corner and we both freeze, pressed against the wall. The rat he kicked also sees it and picks itself up, limping off in a furious trot back toward the darkness and safety of the inner canyon. The sentry locks onto its movement and follows, unable to tell an actual threat from a random animal.

Mason steps back and looks me over with raised eyebrows. A quick mental self-scan reveals that I'm not badly hurt; my body armor and the durable material of my long-sleeved jacket protected me from any deep gouges, and a small scratch on the left side of my head has already stopped bleeding. I give him a thumbs-up, wishing I could take a few extra seconds to catch my breath, but this is the chance we need to get out of the canyon without being detected, and we move out at top speed. We reach the plains in a couple of minutes —our timing perfect. The only signs of Agate Beach through the shimmering haze are darker spots that might be the shadows of the settlement's squat buildings. Half a kilometer to the north stands the hillside outcropping that houses the mine. More remote sentries will be emplaced amid the dwellings, but the security force is probably inside the mine itself. If there's anything we haven't thought of, we'll know in less than four minutes.

We move in fast, low lunges and Desto reaches the settlement first. Despite the weight of his Thresher M-2209, his long, pistonlike legs never seem to get tired. Heaving himself onto the flat roof of Venus's outlying dwelling and dropping into a prone position, he provides perimeter coverage from the west while Mason takes the same position on another dwelling a hundred meters to the east. My job is to be the bait. Slinging my carbine onto my back and slowing to a walk, I head straight into the settlement's center.

Three sentries are on me within seconds, hovering at head level with their glistening camera lenses protruding in a ring around their centers like insectile eyestalks. A message from their internal transmitters plays in sync.

"You are under arrest. Stop immediately and place your hands on top of your head. You are under arrest. Shoot authority is granted if you attempt to run. You are under arrest . . ." Repeat.

The metallic taste of adrenalin coats the inside of my mouth as I comply. Five, four, three, two . . . the security force personnel don't disappoint. A heavily armored vehicle rolls nimbly across the packed earth and comes to a stop five meters in front of me. The base of its troop hold sits waist high above the ground, balanced over all-terrain tires covered by armor-plate shields. It takes a few seconds before the doors open. They're probably analyzing the sentries' video feeds, making sure I'm not hiding any surprises. Finally, the door opens and three soldiers jump down and surround me, weapons aimed at my chest.

"You are in a quarantined area. Let's see some ID and your authorization to be armed," the corporal in charge says, his voice resonating with a metal tininess through his helmet and breathing apparatus. I still wear the nostril filter Venus had given me the first day I'd set foot on Spectra 6, having grown enough used to it that I no longer even notice the soft pressure inside my alar sidewall.

"I don't have any."

"Ansen, relieve her of those guns."

The soldier to my right approaches me, his steps light and quick and his posture betraying a nonchalant casualness that will be his downfall. "Turn around and keep your hands on your head."

I do as he says and feel him grab the buckle of my carbine strap, preparing to remove it. Big mistake. He should have taken my Sinbad first. As I feel the carbine come loose, I drop to a crouch and draw the pistol from my left hip holster. Five shots split the air above me, dropping the other two soldiers and the sentries, and I spin around and press the pistol into the man's chin and pull the trigger. The inside of his helmet explodes in a red gush, but the bullet doesn't exit. Corps armor is tough, the best.

Before his body hits the ground, I sprint into the troop carrier hold. Thankfully, it's empty. The driver engages the partition that divides the cab from the hold but it's too slow. I'm able to fire through three times before it shuts, and his body folds forward over the steering wheel. Within seconds, Desto and Mason have joined me and Desto frantically works at the keypad that will reopen the partition, hoping to short it. We need the vehicle; it's our best way inside the mine.

"Should we call in the *Sphynx*?" I ask.

"No, not yet," Mason says. "If they're detected, the security force will call for backup and we'll have more than we can deal with."

Which means it's three of us against approximately seven. The inside of the mine serves as an excellent stronghold to counter a siege by three people or thirty. The settlers engineered it that way, which had been a smart decision when they were the mine's occupiers. Now that we're the ones laying siege, I can only wish it weren't so damn secure.

Still fighting the hatch mechanism, Desto finally gives up on shorting it when we hear the voice of their squad leader calling for a SITREP. Desto jumps out and runs to the passenger side of the cab, which is, except for the doors, a seamless bubble of bulletproof resin. After sticking a ball of E-10 wax about the size of a rifle scope lens on the bubble, he lets it cook for a few seconds, then fires a shot from the

2209 into the middle of the wax. The entire shell fractures instantly, crashing inside the cabin and leaving a jagged ring around the rim.

"Aly, put on that uniform and be our driver."

Desto and I yank the body from the cab. Fortunately, my point-blank shots had been enough to pierce his uniform and body armor, but didn't penetrate all the way through. Only the back of his jacket shows obvious damage. I strip off my own, bloody and shredded from the rats, and put his on, followed by the helmet, first smashing one side of it against a rock to damage the com system, making it appear as if the driver couldn't hear the SITREP request. As I dress, the other two haul the dead soldiers into the troop van. The light-colored uniform for soldiers in this quadrant of the system are close enough to the color of my own aged and faded pants that I don't bother trading up. Finally, I belt on the dead man's sidearm holster but sheathe my own 'Bad. His assault rifle is still locked in its cradle, and I place mine out of sight but within quick reach next to me. "Let's go!"

We've lost a precious five minutes but no one's emerged to check on the doomed group. Our plan is developing as we go along, and Mason fills me in on why they loaded the bodies. I need to draw as many of their remaining security squad to the vehicle as I can once we get inside by signaling that the dead soldiers need urgent medical aid. They'll be using a portable transceiver to communicate with their airborne commander and we'll have to take that out ASAP. Once Corps command realizes there's a problem it will be an estimated fifteen hours maximum before help will arrive, if their nearest battle cruiser is within the quadrant. However, if they have a shorter range QRF ship on standby, like the one that had boarded Rob's ship on the way to R'Kadia, our time will be considerably compressed. We'll have no more than four or five hours to get the *Sphynx* in, loaded, and back out. But first, we have to settle the immediate problem.

I drive through the lead-in tunnel faster than safety dictates, but I have to make the situation appear life or death. Of course, the risk is that they'll shoot me as soon as I clear the tunnel. The thought makes sweat drip from my brow line, stinging my eyes. Why can't the Admin develop helmets with better ventilation?

Hardly slowing as I exit the tunnel mouth into the vast inner chamber, a quick look around confirms what I'd expected—the Corps has been busy organizing and separating all the settlement's equipment and belongings into easily wrapped, transport-ready piles. Even as I notice this, I spot two rifle barrels trained toward us from behind a section of earthmoving equipment and another pointing out from behind the tunnel branch leading to the infirmary rooms. I hit the brakes a little too hard and hear a loud thump as someone is thrown against the inside of the transport's hold. Immediately, I raise my arms to where the soldiers can see my empty hands, and then start waving frantically toward the back of the transport.

"McMillan, what is your situation? Why aren't you responding to your coms?" someone yells, presumably at me. I can't answer verbally without giving away that I'm not McMillan, so I do as I'd planned and point exaggeratedly at my helmet, then back toward the rear.

No one moves. Shit!

There's a scrape as Desto or Mason pulls open the transport door, and I prepare to take cover underneath the steering column inside the cab, then Mason shouts, "Riordan and Chin are down! We need a medic back here!"

Somehow the authority in his voice, with the help of catching sight of the dead men's bodies, galvanizes the other soldiers. Four of them break cover—the three I'd already spotted and another from inside the tunnel mouth—and run toward the vehicle. As they approach, I jump from the cab, AK-80 in tow. They converge as a group on the transport's hatch and the first one begins climbing the ladder welded to the side.

"Hey!" he has enough time to yell before Mason shoots him dead in the chest. His body whips around backward before he falls from the ladder, and I see the shock that will forever be stamped on his face. The other three respond immediately, diving beneath the vehicle before Mason can fire again. Sprinting in the opposite direc- tion, I'm able to reach the cover of the earthmoving equipment that they'd recently vacated. The firing stops, but my nerves don't cease dancing like an electrocution victim. The others could be calling for backup at this moment.

The mine goes quiet. Desto and Mason are safe inside the transport thanks to its full-shell armor designed to protect the troops from bullets and buried explosives, but I have no vantage on the soldiers hiding beneath it. The brain bucket has become constricting and is no longer serving the purpose of hiding my identity, so I ditch it and try scaring them out.

"Soldiers under the truck, you're surrounded. If you come out, we won't kill you." I fully intend to kill them, but they don't need to know that.

There's no response for several seconds, then one of them yells, "You won't get away with this."

Asshole. "I'm giving you to the count of ten."

"We've already got backup on the—"

Before he finishes the sentence, several shots ring out overhead from the direction of the communication room. Instinctively, I duck down before I can zero on exactly where they came from. Then Karl's voice echoes against the walls, "Two down up here, and their coms are destroyed."

I barely believe it. He was supposed to stay with the shuttle in the canyon until we secured the site. Obviously, he decided to take matters into his own hands. He must have crawled down from the airshaft that leads to the upper lookout and taken the personnel positioned in the com room by surprise. His initiative probably saved all of us.

"Karl," I yell, "do you know if they were able to call out?"

"Don't think so. I'm contacting the *Sphynx* now."

"You hear that? You're cooked. Throw out your weapons and get your asses out from under this truck." Desto's voice is thick with menace.

We'd hit four soldiers outside, Mason killed one trying to climb into the truck, three remain beneath it, and Karl says he's shot two others. Typical security squad size is ten troops, so it's probable we've neutralized the full threat. Still, I'm not going to take the chance that there's a rogue we haven't spotted and stay covered behind the equipment. The noise of the lift descending draws my attention and I peer around a 'dozer's corner to see Karl coming down. He doesn't share my concern apparently. The lift stops half a meter short of the floor, enough gap that the soldiers under the truck won't be able to get a shot at him without exposing themselves to me.

Desto drops the cap of a grenade over the edge of the truck as a warning. "We're not going to ask you again. Move out now, or they'll be picking your teeth out of the engine block."

Rifles scrape along the dry concrete of the mine floor as the trapped soldiers give in to their fate. As they drag themselves out and stand up, I move out from behind the equipment, my carbine level to my shoulder, ready to dispatch them. They stand in front of the open door of the vehicle, hands locked on top of their heads. Karl stays in the lift, keeping an eye on things.

Mason places the barrel of his rifle against the base of the middle soldier's helmet and asks, "How many Corps are on site?"

The solider answers quickly, "There are—were—ten of us."

"When is your relief scheduled to arrive?"

"We just got here this morning. There isn't another rotation for a week."

"You sure?" He jabs hard with the barrel, causing the man's head to jerk forward.

"Yeah! We're it. Just don't shoot us."

I flick my gaze up, look into Mason's eyes briefly, and settle the carbine's barrel firmly against my shoulder. Training the sight on the man farthest to the left, I start to squeeze the trigger.

"Aly, stop!" Karl yells. I turn to look at him, the insistence in his tone catching my attention. He's loping across the cavern toward me. "You can't do that."

I'm surprised, thinking I must have misunderstood him, but his expression makes it clear; he's not going to let me shoot them.

"Karl, don't be ridiculous. These guys killed Bodie. They deserve what they're about to get."

"We aren't going to get anything out of killing them. Doug, let's tie them up. We can lock them in the com room when we leave."

"Karl! What's your problem? What about Bodie? Who's going to pay for that?" My strained tone echoes against the walls, eliciting concerned stares from Mason and Desto.

Karl turns around and steps up closer to me, laying a warm and callused hand on my shoulder. His gaze is unwavering, but there is a gentleness that I rarely see hidden behind the hard shine of his pupils. "Do you really want their blood on your hands? Killing them won't make any of us feel better. It won't change anything."

Slowly, I lower my barrel and take a deep breath that turns into a tremble. It's hard to look at him, and my eyes fall to his chest. I want to press myself against him and let this all be over, but he turns away and starts walking toward the prisoners, leaving me feeling empty and defeated.

"Let's get these men secured and start moving supplies out," Desto says. "V and the crew should be here in half an hour."

SEVENTEEN

The remaining security squad are locked down in the disabled troop carrier, and Desto waits on the observation platform for the crew to arrive. The rest of us divide up and begin collecting the supplies we'll need for an extended trip.

I take the control room. Inside, the lingering signs of a gunfight exhibit themselves through broken equipment, and dirt and gravel from the rock walls lie in blasted chunks everywhere. There's a grit-flecked mahogany smear on the floor near the main bank of monitors that must have been where Bodie had fallen. My eyeballs feel over-heated and coated in tears as thick as motor oil as I go through the room. The Corps had taken his body somewhere, but that only makes the impact of losing him harder. How dare they? It wasn't enough to murder him, but they also took him from us. There can be no funeral, no lasting gravestone in his honor. Just that red stain and our memories.

Once the *Sphynx* arrives, the crew moves with calibrated quick-ness, making certain that nothing of potential use is left behind. The *Sphynx* is crammed full, floor to ceiling and wall to wall. Contraband, weapons, and stolen Admin supplies lie everywhere, with no way to conceal them. It's not important. If the Admin comes after us, the only thing we can do is run.

The last items we go after are the settlers' personal belongings, things we know of that are important to them, but there's no way we can sort through everything. With limited time and space aboard the ship, we don't bring much. Going through the dwellings shows how busy the Corps has been in the last few days sanitizing the settlement of anything valuable or potentially dangerous. Everything of use has been collected and brought to the mine to be sorted and hauled off. With a mixture of relief and uncertainty, we find no bodies or graves. If anyone besides Bodie had been harmed, the Corps didn't leave behind any clues.

Eight hours later, I watch Spectra 6 fall away like a particle of dust through the *Sphynx*'s nav-system's local display grid. And it hits me. A dropping in my stomach, like the bottom of everything is falling loose. Will I ever see the Beach again? Will I ever know what it feels like to belong somewhere again? My last sight of the mine cavern was a mess of plundered, nonessential items scattered haphazardly around like discarded junk. But it had been our home, and I'm blindsided by a sense of plummeting sadness. I never expected to become so attached. Now that the strings are being severed, I finally understand what it really meant to me.

Once we've broken out of atmosphere and our coordinates are set, I leave the flight deck. Neither Vitruzzi or Venus meets my eyes as I excuse myself. I head to my bunk to be alone, but as soon as I lie down, there's a knock on my door.

"It's open."

Karl steps through the doorway and I sit up. Our eyes lock for a moment, his serene brown and mine sapphire blue. "Hey," he finally says.

"Hey."

"Mind if I come in?"

I shake my head, indicating it's okay.

He sits on the bench that doubles as a storage locker across from my bunk, the space so narrow that his knees nearly touch the bed. He leans on his elbows, looking at the floor for a minute, and my senses are flooded with him: his smell, cinnamon and leather; his countenance, stern, deeply engraved with sadness; and his presence, solid, determined, unyielding. That feeling of coming undone begins to fade instantly as I realize, without a shred of uncertainty, that he is my home.

"Look, Aly—"

"I want—"

We both stop and I wait for him to go on. "This is hard for me," he continues after a second. "I think you know how I feel about you. It was a mistake to keep our collaboration with Rajcik a secret. But you have to believe me when I say that it wasn't meant to hurt you. I didn't want to lie to you, no one did. I think, maybe . . . I *thought* that I was protecting you." He waits for a second before continuing, hoping I'll make it easy for him, but I keep my silence. That wound still gapes, raw and hot. "You have to realize we're only working with him because it is, or was, the best thing for the settlement."

Was it? I consider asking, but bottle it.

"We really need you behind us on this one. You and David are part of this crew, and we shouldn't have left you in the dark. I know that. I'm sorry." He slides forward on the bench and wraps both of my hands in his, drawing me closer to him. "And I don't want to lose you."

My skin absorbs the warmth from his palms like a desiccated flower finally being given water. The sorrow in his eyes is clear, devoid of any masked accusations or machismo. Is my return silence just me being stubborn and unreasonable, some kind of punishment for the things he said? The argument we had in the mine was bad, his explosion hurtful and unnecessary, but what good does it do me at this point to hold onto my anger? If I let it go, we may have a chance at working things out.

He looks into my face, and whatever he sees there seems to encourage him. His mouth wrinkles to one side in a half grin. "Why don't you say something?"

I consider for only a moment, then say, "I'm sorry about what happened with Rob."

Apparently that was not what he was expecting to hear. Though his expression doesn't change, the muscles holding his smile twitch. "What do you mean?"

And it hits me. He doesn't know about the night I'd spent with Rob. How stupid can I be? "I thought you didn't care, Karl. The things you said . . . I was hurt."

Clenching his jaw, he drops my hands and leans back, his torso becoming as straight and rigid as a plinth. "So you fucked your old boyfriend?"

I wince. "Isn't that what you were accusing me of? What did you think? You can't treat me like that and not expect me to—" I stop myself. What I was about to say is *get even*, but is that what sleeping with Rob had been about? No. It's time to start being honest. I won't lie to Karl, and I'm done lying to myself. I slept with Rob because it was easier than trying to explain my feelings or make myself vulnerable. But I'm tired of this combat, both with myself and with Karl.

Leaning toward him, trying to take one of his hands, I continue, "Karl, I can't keep doing this with you. I—" *love you*. But it's too late. He stands up and charges from the room, nearly running.

For a minute, I forget to breathe. When I start again, my chest convulses violently, like it's being crushed under hundreds of pounds of stone, like I'm being buried alive. I fall back onto my bunk, the leaden mass of my loss pushing me against the mat like a tombstone. I'm too empty to resist. Whatever happens now hardly matters. Rescuing the settlers will be the end for me. The Beach is gone, Karl's gone, and everything that matters—gone. There's no reason left to run. And nothing left to run to.

EIGHTEEN

"Rob's agreed to help us," Vitruzzi announces while standing in the *Sphynx*'s galley, where she'd called us all. We're five hours out from landing back on R'Kadia and moving into the next, and most crucial, phase of our plan to rescue the settlers from Keum Libre. "He's going to smuggle La Mer and a couple more of us into Tunis City, and then go on his way. The risks for him are minimal and Tunis is his next stop anyway."

Our heads all turn to La Mer, none of us yet understanding why he'd sign up to go to Tunis, the most unlikely place in the system to hide. He begins to explain, but his eyes are on Venus, as if trying to make her understand. "I know people, other wire-rats, on Obal 10, who can help us access the Admin satellites. If I can get back there—without getting caught—we can provide the cover the rest of you will need to get to Keum Libre and save the Beachers. We can call in the threat to T'Kai and show him what we've got. Maybe create enough of a distraction."

So that's it—keep one of the Hydra's three heads busy while the rest of the crew slips past. That still leaves the Corps and whatever security exists on Keum Libre. I glance at the others, seeing the same thoughtful look on all of their faces. La Mer's newness to the crew and the Beach should be enough to ensure his plan is automatically regarded with skepticism. Yet somehow Venus's devotion and his total absence of guile have endeared La Mer to all of us quickly and thoroughly. I still have to work to convince some of the crew, mostly Brady, that I can be counted on, but La Mer has fit in with ease since almost the beginning.

"These wire-rats—why would they help? It would be crazy for anyone else to volunteer to get involved in this," Karl says.

La Mer looks away from Venus for the first time, and I catch the glow of fear behind his eyes. He's well aware of the risks in what he's proposing. "I know. And they know it, too. But this is a network that has been working against the Admin in secrecy for years. Their goal is to change the system, to erode the Admin's power any way they can. Once I talk to them and explain what we've got, they'll help us."

"What will they want in return?" I ask.

"If we can expose the corruption in even one of the Ministries, that'll be reward enough. And if not"—he shrugs—"we may have to write them an IOU."

With no one else prepared to offer up a better idea, there's a pause in the discussion. Eventually Desto breaks the silence: "Sounds shaky, but it's all we've got right now. V, how do you want to divide up?"

"I'm going with Jeremy," Venus states.

I don't miss the way Vitruzzi winces, as if slapped. She says, "Venus, we need you to fly the *Sphynx*."

Venus's already pale skin becomes nearly translucent as the blood drains from it. "Karl or Doug can fly it just fine. I'm not going to be separated from him." She reaches out and grasps one of La Mer's hands hard enough to make her fragile blue veins stand out.

Vitruzzi's voice becomes very quiet, a tone that would be soothing under normal circumstances. "Yeah, they can, but what if we get into trouble? No one can make the *Sphynx* fly the way you can. The Beachers need you. Jeremy can handle things on Obal 10, and he won't be alone."

"I'll be keeping you safe, love," he says, staring into Venus's frightened green eyes.

She looks around at the rest of us, searching our faces, and I know I'm not the only one who has trouble meeting her gaze. Her voice tremors at the realization that the decision isn't hers. "After you send the transmission, how are you going to get off of Obal 10?"

"Don't worry about that yet. Eleanor is right, you'll be helping more people if you go to Keum Libre," Brady says, trying to soothe her, but his words have the opposite effect.

"I don't care about that!"

"Venus . . ." La Mer says.

She whirls around without releasing his hand and sweeps her bulging, phosphorescent eyes over the crew. "They're going to wipe us out. You all know it. What's the point? They'll just keep coming until they kill all of us. Like Bodie! Like my parents!"

This time my glance drops to the floor. I can't help feeling guilty and I don't know why. She's probably right. It feels like a lie to try and convince her otherwise.

La Mer wraps her in a hug, folding his long arms around her petite form like a cape. She stands stiffly in his embrace for several seconds but she doesn't cry. Like the rest of us, she's been too hardened by a life that's already seen too much loss to waste any more tears. After a few seconds, she steps back and says in a husky voice, "I'll be in the cockpit."

The galley is quiet for several seconds after she leaves. Each of us contemplate her outburst, the words like a shroud threatening to suffocate our resolve.

Finally, Vitruzzi says, "We only need to send one or two others with La Mer. Think about it and decide for yourselves who'll go. I've already transmitted the plan to Rajcik. We'll pick him up and leave for Keum Libre at first light tomorrow."

NINETEEN

Venus plants the *Sphynx* like a lawn dart outside the mine entrance where Rajcik has taken up residence. Unlike her normal, floating descents, the haphazard way she ratchets the ship between the canyon walls feels like we're descending on a broken elevator whose cables snap and catch. One second we're dropping much too fast, the next she's opening up the reverse thrusters with maximum torque, effectively braking us with the force of a crashing tidal wave. I have to grab the handrail of the galley stairs to keep from breaking my neck, and there's a crashing sound somewhere inside the ship as unsecured cargo topples. Brady curses in the galley behind me.

Vitruzzi transmitted Rob the coordinates and asked him to move the *'Rize* to as near the cave entrance as possible. Two ships the sizes of the *Sphynx* and the *Horizon* docked together on this stripped moon will quickly attract any scout ships in the quadrant, so we plan to keep the stop short and to the point. La Mer and the crew going with Rob will load weapons and the equipment they'll need on Obal 10 aboard the *Horizon* right after meeting with Rajcik and depart immediately. Everyone else will board the *Sphynx* and should be back in the air and on the way to Keum Libre early tomorrow morning.

The crew's been too busy to discuss who'll go with La Mer, but I've already decided to put in my ticket. Karl has moved around the ship like a ghost since our last encounter, confirming my grim fear that anything we had is over. I'm certain Vitruzzi will want him to stay with Venus and be her backup, and getting as far away from him as I can is the only way I can cope with his anger and my own feelings of betrayal. I can still aid the settlers and give him what he wants by taking the trip to Obal 10. Everyone wins.

The cargo hold ramp lowers and the rest of the crew disembarks while I hang back to gather a few extra magazines and clips for my carbine and 'Bad. As I pry the lid off a case of ammunition, David walks up behind me.

"You're going with Rob." He doesn't have to ask.

I acknowledge the statement with a quick nod and shove as many magazines for my AK-80 into my duffel as it can hold. He watches me quietly for a minute and then sighs. "All right, me too then."

I pause, feeling both relieved and touched—and slightly embarrassed about it. "You don't have to do that."

"Yeah I do, Twig."

There's a familiar vibration in the air. I zip up the duffel and we step out into the shifting sand-colored haze of the R'Kadian evening to watch the *Horizon* settle onto a flat plateau above the mine's entrance. Everyone else has already gone underground, but David and I wait for Rob. He, Baker, and Montoya drive sandbikes down a narrow trail that twines its way into the canyon between boulders and spires, finally reaching us at the base within a few short minutes.

Rob stops beside us and David asks, "You ready for this?"

Apprehension ripples across Rob's face for a second, then it's gone. "Ready for anything, brother. Just another job. Maybe a tiny bit more, uh, interesting."

He smiles and asks Baker and Montoya to double-up on one bike so David and I can take the other. As our group enters the mine tunnel, the bikes' low-watt headlights are barely powerful enough to illuminate our path. The mine has been out of commission for a long time, and none of the original fixtures mounted along the tunnel's high ceiling still work. There's a dry, desiccated smell to the air as if nothing has lived inside for years. As we approach the central cavern, a dull yellow glow creeps along the walls toward us. At least one generator must be running, but the air is so full of floating dust and dirt from the Rover and sandbikes that it's hard to just make out the tunnel corridor, much less gauge distance.

We reach the end and the walls rise at precise right angles ten meters above our heads to the ceiling. Sitting on one side and filling half the cave is the *Temptation*, safely docked under millions of tons of rock and earth where no Corps scanning system can detect it. As soon as I see it, my guts do a nauseating flip-flop and my palms grow slick as a combustible mix of fury and revulsion begin seeping from my pores in a feral sweat—a poisonous biochemical reminder of my hate for the Admin and what they'd taken from us and for Rajcik for what he'd nearly taken from me. We made the wrong decision, I know it. I *feel* it in the way my stomach clenches and my skin leaks a layer of oily dampness. Counting on Rajcik to help us is a mistake, the biggest mistake any of us will ever make. And if Venus is right, none of us will get a chance to make another one.

Dismounting the bike, David catches me staring at the ship and nudges me forward with his elbow. "Hey, they're over there. Come on."

It takes an effort to pull my eyes from the *Temptation*. "David," I warn, "this can't end well."

"It will. We just have to stay together, little sis." He gives me a smile that's supposed to be reassuring, and we move to catch up with the others.

Everyone is gathered in a circle near the freight elevator. The hole Desto had punched with grenades into the nearby wall during my first visit to this rock has a fresh scar of blocks and mortar plugging it, but it's the man standing next to it that draws my stare. The vulpine, brown-stubbled face of Fuller Thompson evokes as much disgust in me now as it always has. He stares back at me, our mutual animosity eliciting the same reaction in both. He's grown thinner, as has Rajcik, but neither are any less menacing, like a pair of sharpened axes dangling over us by the thinnest of threads.

Vitruzzi sees us approaching and says, "Now that we're all here—"

Nobody expects the way Karl spins around and leaps at Rob, one fist balled and swinging through the air in a precise trajectory directly into Rob's chin. It's a sucker punch, and Rob is as surprised as everyone else. His head jerks backward, snapping to a stop as his neck catches, his body following. Staggering, he still somehow deflects a second blow coming from Karl, and by then everyone is jumping in to stop him. Desto and Mason race to Karl's side, each of them taking hold of an arm as he strains forward, looking as if he wants to tear Rob's heart out. To my surprise, both Baker and Montoya have drawn small handguns like my own Mini-Derg, aiming them directly at Karl's chest, their mutual expressions of detached alertness almost an exact match.

"Karl!" I yell, but his attention stays on Rob, who quickly regains his footing.

Rubbing his bruised chin, Rob's eyes contract into wounded, watering slits. He's not badly hurt, and the fury radiating from him almost heats the air around us. "What the fuck do you think you're doing, Strahan?"

Karl acts like hasn't even heard him. He jerks against Desto and Mason, but the two men hold on like plow oxen, solid and unyielding.

Brady steps between them and leans toward Karl so their chins are centimeters apart. "Dammit, Karl, we don't have time for this."

Finally, Karl shifts his gaze to Brady, and a battle of wills is fought between their locked eyes. After a few more seconds, he relaxes his shoulders, letting his balled fists drop to his sides. Mason and Desto exchange a glance, then release Karl's arms, but don't move away in case he erupts again. The fire stanched for now, Brady turns away from Karl and abrades me with a look of exasperation and frustration. "The same goes for everyone here. Whatever petty bullshit you're holding against each other, it doesn't matter anymore. There are lives at stake, and not just the settlers'. Every one of us is in the Admin's crosshairs. We've all lost people we care about, and it's time to stop fucking around and start working together."

His eyes land on me once again during his last statement, infuriating me, then he turns to Rob. "Cross?"

Rob's attention is still on Karl, both wary and furious, but he waves a hand toward Baker and Montoya, who sheathe their pistols inside their jackets. I don't like the way they reacted to the fight, like fixers who will clean up whatever mess inconveniences them. Rob I can, if not trust, at least understand, but his crew is another story. In the days ahead, something tells me I better pay close attention to them.

Rajcik clears his throat with a guttural flourish and says, "Are we ready to get on with business? Vitruzzi, I thought you had better control of your crew." His callousness is typical—Rajcik isn't concerned with making new friends.

Vitruzzi lets his statement slide, the familiar vein pulsing prominently between her eyebrows giving the only indication that she's having to work to control her anger. Walking into the center of the group, she lays the plan out.

"This is how things will go down. Rajcik, you'll fly with the crew on the *Sphynx* and take them to KL. La Mer, me, and . . ." She pauses, looking around to see who's decided to go to Obal 10. I can't look at Karl and witness the expression on his face as I step forward, David right next to me. Vitruzzi nods and continues, "Aly and David will go with Cross to Tunis City. We'll contact La Mer's sources and set up the security worm, then we'll send a warning shot to T'Kai. The *Sphynx* will stay in a holding pattern, either within safe distance of KL or on the rock itself, until we confirm we've succeeded—"

Rajcik cuts her off, "And if you don't succeed?"

"We still go after the settlers," Brady answers.

"With your one ship? You people really are suicidal," Thompson grunts.

Vitruzzi looks Rajcik and Thompson over, gauging their dubious commitment to this mission. Her eyes flick to Rob, then fix on Rajcik.

"I'm sure it's occurred to you that we may already have all we need to bargain with T'Kai for the settler's freedom."

I'm reminded of just how relentless, grim even, she can be, and my admiration for her swells again as she implies that we could exchange Rajcik for the settlers.

"The only thing I can't figure out is why we haven't already done it," I blurt out.

Thompson's hate-filled stare burns like two hot coins laid on the skin of my face.

Vitruzzi continues, ignoring my comment, "But we already have a deal, Rajcik. And we intend to uphold our end of it. As long as we think you'll uphold yours."

"I'm as trustworthy as you," he says, and it's my turn to grunt in disgust.

"Fine. How long do you expect it to take to reach KL?"

"No more than fifteen days, provided we avoid any patrols."

"And Rob, it should take you approximately ten days to reach Obal 10. Is there any way you can shave that time?"

"The best we can do is about eight." Since recovering from Karl's attack, Rob hasn't taken his eyes off of Rajcik. I'm sure he's thinking the same thing Vitruzzi had threatened, and Vitruzzi's glance a few seconds ago tells me she knows it. Rajcik is worth a lot of money to the Admin. The gamble is tremendous; all sides but ours have more to gain by following their own agenda instead of the one she's laying out. For Rajcik, this operation is a plot to get even with T'Kai for reneging on their deal, and it's only a matter of time before he does something unlooked for that could help him do that. Whatever it is, it's certain to jeopardize the rest of us. For Rob, the only thing that's stopping him from apprehending Rajcik, or at least leading a Corps security patrol to his doorstep, is a sense of loyalty to Vitruzzi and the crew, maybe even to me. The question is: What would it take for that loyalty to expire? The *Red Horizon* is a nice piece of machinery, advanced, expensive. Maybe all it would take for Rob to switch sides is money. How much is anyone's guess.

It's a dark thought, but the kind of thought that's kept me alive this along. *You're just being paranoid*, I tell myself. But looking at Montoya and Baker, I wonder if that's true. They've been standoffish, even outright hostile, toward the crew since coming to the Beach. Even if Rob is on board with our plan, what's going to keep them in check?

"When do we leave?" Rajcik wants to know.

"First thing in the morning. Pack your gear aboard the *Sphynx* tonight."

He nods, then says, "One final thing, Vitruzzi. I have interests to protect. Thompson goes with you to Tunis."

TWENTY

As if stage directions have been given, the group breaks up, everyone jumping onto their respective transportation and heading to the ships to prepare. I'm already packed and deliberate about staying behind to keep tabs on Rajcik and Thompson. If they have plans to jam us up, this is the best opportunity to put an end to them. I know as certainly as I know that I'll never taste squash as good as Bodie's again that they're operating from an alternative agenda, and it will most likely come into play when it's least looked for and most damaging. But Rajcik is much too shrewd to be caught off guard this early in the game. He and Thompson loiter around the cargo bins where we'd met, their nonchalance seeming to mock my paranoid hypervigilance, and reluctantly, I jump on the bike with David and follow the rest of the crew to the *Sphynx.*

Low clouds, tinted a sickly grayish-red like festering flesh, drape heavily over the landscape and along the horizon. Compared to the relatively clear and sunny atmosphere of Spectra 6, evening here is dim and oppressive, and I look forward to getting off this rock as soon as possible.

Hanging back outside the ship's opened cargo bay ramp, I wait for David and Vitruzzi to collect their weapons, supplies, and sundries, and I have time to think over the plan we've discussed. We have enough food for the duration we expect to be on Obal 10—around a week, two at the most—and we'll be relying on La Mer and Vitruzzi's familiarity with Tunis City to find a place to hide and set up the security-override worm. Despite how direct and simple the plan is, a deep, foreboding gloom clings to me. I wonder if this will be the last time I ever see the *Sphynx* and the crew.

Squatting at the edge of one of the landing legs, I draw bored circles in the sand with my index finger, anxiously awaiting our mobilization. This is the hard part, the anticipation of what's coming. The sound of a motor catches my attention, and I look up as Rajcik approaches on a bike. Knots of tension cinch tightly around my muscles as I jump to my feet, surprised that he's arrived so quickly. The prospect of a one-on-one encounter with him makes me feel like an overpressurized oxygen tank next to a lit torch. Before I can do more than draw my Sinbad and glance down the sight in a reflexive check, he pulls up to an idle a short distance away, remaining astride the bike. Temptation to put a bullet through his forehead shakes my reason, but my gun hand remains steady and straight.

Letting the engine rumble in a synchronous thump, he stares at me. "We have some past business to put behind us."

I let the words hang in the air for a few seconds, trying to get my snarl of emotions under control. Finally, I spit out, "Why would you help us, Rajcik? What are you planning to get out of this?"

"I have my reasons." The words thrum from his tattooed throat like a slow-burning fuse.

"I know, and you better tell me what they are or I swear I'll kill you where you stand."

Laughing, he replies, "Maybe this is my idea of atonement for betraying you. What? You don't think I'm capable of remorse?"

"You're no more capable of remorse than I am of believing you. I know you, Rajcik." The words come out slowly, deliberately. "I find out whatever you're hiding on my own, it's not going to go half as well for you as you're expecting."

A dangerous look dances behind the dark sheen of his pupils. "I'd be more careful about making idle threats, Aly. You never know when someone will take you seriously." Engaging the bike's tripod, he slowly dismounts and steps into a more conversational range. He's not wearing a jacket, and for the first time I notice a long, still-red and puffy scar emerging from the outside of his right sleeve and curving down to the back of his arm, nearly to his elbow. The depth of the gash is wicked, showing that whatever had caused it had bitten deep, probably to the bone. He's lucky not to have lost the arm.

So, that's what had made him desperate enough to call on Vitruzzi.

"But you want an answer, here it is. T'Kai fucked me. It's time to pay him back. I know you, of all people, can understand that." Coming even closer, he leans forward, carefully ensuring his hands remain visible. "You know what I'm talking about. You felt that bitter hatred worming its way through your guts when I betrayed you. Treachery, like a poison, working itself deep. And it will stay there, cooking you from inside until you have your revenge. That's what you live for." He draws back and looks at me candidly, holding my unwavering blue eyes with his cave-black ones, and the savagery lurking in them makes me almost pity T'Kai.

I finally look away, repelled by the intensity of his hate. "I'm just trying to help the settlers." But is that true? The memory of my intention to kill the defeated soldiers at the Beach, and how Karl had had to stop me, bobs to the surface of my brain. That had been pure darkness, bloodlust. A demon of revenge, as insidious as Rajcik just described. Was the look in my eyes then the same as his now? No. I won't believe that. "Whatever your sick reasons," I say, trying to cover my unease, "just make sure you stick to the plan. You'll get your chance, but we're all in this together this time. If any one of us fucks up, we're all going to die."

"There are worse things than dying."

"What do you mean—"

He turns away and begins untying a bag from his bike, cutting me off. "Aly, you're such an idealist. That's what I used to find interesting about you. But you still haven't learned that idealism means nothing unless you're willing to take action. You and your brother were only content to run from the Admin, hide in a hole like scared rodents. You never had enough guts to do anything that mattered."

His tone grates my nerve endings raw. I should turn around right now and walk back aboard the *Sphynx* before one of us does something that will endanger the mission. Instead, I counter, "You're talking about conviction, János, and we have more than enough of that. We just knew better than to inflict our 'idealism' on innocent people. All you believe in is murdering for profit. You aren't fooling me—you're just as demented as T'Kai and people like him."

As soon as the words leave my mouth, I realize they're a mistake. He's on me too quickly for my eyes to register, spinning me around and wrenching my right arm behind my back, forcing the Sinbad to fall uselessly into the sand. He slams me face down against the ramp, and I feel his weight come down on me, pinning me to the spot.

"Get off me!" I manage to grunt, immediately wishing I could get the air back as his heft compresses my lungs.

"Step the fuck back!" Desto yells, and two sets of booted feet run down the ramp toward us. Rajcik is off me instantly.

"Just discussing the plan," he says, as if that truly is all that we've been doing.

I roll over, sucking in a deep breath. His face looms just above me, his expression calm and implacable, barely seeming to notice Desto and Mason. It's almost as if Rajcik is somewhere else, the people around him not even present, and I realize that, in a way, he's *not* here; his interests have nothing to do with me, with the settlers, or with the crew. For the first time, I'm really seeing who Rajcik is, what drives him. He's not moved by petty feelings or interests the way normal people are. He doesn't feel a sense of attachment or concern for the mundane humdrum of typical lives and can't be distracted by things that don't move him toward achieving his purpose, no matter how sociopathic and twisted that purpose is. Until he resolves his issue with T'Kai, nothing else will factor in. The realization that he feels nothing toward me or about what he did to me, one way or another, completely sucks away any satisfaction I might have had in getting even with him. What good is killing a ghost? He has no more interest in my selfish, vengeful hatred than he had in my loyalty.

"You okay?" Desto helps me up with one hand, pointing a modified Bhishma pistol the size of my forearm at Rajcik's chest with the other.

"Fine." As I brush the sand from my clothes, the need to confront Rajcik and make him suffer for what he'd done fades like a carcass washed off a beach, pulled away by the tide. I'm beginning to understand David's perspective, how he'd been able to move beyond Rajcik's betrayal and get to the point where he can see him as an asset instead of an enemy. "I'm fine. Let him be."

Desto stares at me for a few seconds, surprised at my quick forgiveness, then holsters the Bhishma and says to Rajcik, "Come on. I'll show you where you're bunking."

Mason starts an inspection of the ramp hydraulics as Rajcik unloads his belongings and follows Desto inside—to my old bunk. The place I'd called home on many nights for the last three months is now Rajcik's, another rude slap symbolizing just how dire and desperate things have become. Lending Mason a hand helps pass the time, and a short while later David emerges, soon followed by Vitruzzi and Brady, their hands held tight. I can only imagine what the doc is feeling at this moment. She's already lost one husband to the Admin. How can she be so calm and resolute, knowing that the chances of reuniting with Brady again are so small? A knot rises in my throat, realizing that the same is true of Karl and I. Hopelessly, I wait for him to come out, at least to say goodbye.

La Mer and Venus are the last to join us, Venus's eyes and nose red from crying, and La Mer seems unable to quit wiping his own eyes with his sleeve.

"I'm going to tell you one last time, I wish you'd let me go to Obal 10 instead of you, Eleanor." Brady's face, usually ruddy anyway, has hectic patches of red on the checks, making his scar stand out starkly. There's no doubting the distress he's feeling, though he's trying, like the rest of us, to keep it together.

"I know you do," she replies, and brushes a kiss across one of his cheeks. "Someone has to negotiate with T'Kai, and I'm better at it."

He grabs her in a tight hug and I hear her whisper, "The Sphynx is yours now. Take care of it. I love you." When he lets her go, water threatens to break over his lower eyelids, and for the first time, I see softness in Brady.

"You be safe," he says and shakes David's and La Mer's hands. When he turns to me, that same softness is still there. "You too, Aly."

His gentleness hits me like a soft blow, driving home more than anything else the possibility that this may be the last time the crew will ever be together. My voice is tight as I respond, "You all be careful, too."

The rest of us say our goodbyes, Desto nearly squeezing me lifeless in a farewell hug, and we make ridiculous promises to be seeing each other again soon. Then the three of us going with Rob mount sandbikes and trace our way up the canyon walls. I look back one more time before boarding the *Horizon*, but Karl is nowhere to be seen.

TWENTY-ONE

"Stay off the bridge," Montoya says, backing me through the doorway. He towers over me, his brick-shaped jaw only centimeters from my forehead. His face tilts down as he enters the door code, his hostility emphasized by the deep, oversized pores running along his cheek and nose as he promptly seals me out.

I've been walking around the ship, taking in its design and layout in case the need for a quick evacuation or disappearance comes around, laboring valiantly to keep my thoughts strictly on the mission ahead. Most of the doors inside the main hull are locked, and the ones that aren't lead to insignificant storage rooms and empty berths. Besides our quick flight to R'Kadia, I haven't been aboard a ship this size since the Corps and find its roominess a little disconcerting. The beauty of these long-haul cargo carriers is their self-sufficient handling. It's easy for Rob to run a skeleton crew with the ship's advanced piloting functions. Besides handling takeoffs and landings, the only essential functions to fulfill are setting the coordinates and fixing anything that breaks. Even so, I bet Venus could make it dance like a ballerina if she had a chance to bump it off auto.

After my sweep, I came to the bridge looking for Rob. The moment I entered the flight deck's open hatch, Montoya shut me down, jumping from his seat and letting me know in no uncertain terms that the bridge is now off-limits. What are they afraid I'll do? We're all headed to the same place. So maybe it's not what I'm doing that's of concern, but what *they're* doing. Montoya's behavior is just another example of their odd behavior, and nothing about the crew has put my mind at ease since they landed at the Beach.

Jesus, has it already been over a week?

I'd gotten just enough of a glimpse onto the flight deck to see that Rob isn't there, but it's time to track him down and get some answers, so I head straight to his cabin. When my knock is answered, I find both him and David inside, sitting at a table and talking.

"Pull up a seat. I've been wondering what you're up to," Rob says.

I sit down. "Why aren't we allowed on the bridge?"

There's a slight blue tinge to his jaw where Karl had struck him, almost lost in the shadow of a day and a half's growth of dark beard. "Just trying to keep things as under control as possible, Aly. My crew isn't exactly celebrating the fact that I've agreed to help out on this mission—"

"And why are you helping us? You said yourself that you stand to lose a hell of a lot if it comes out that you're involved in anything that happens in the next few weeks."

Rob hesitates before answering, thinking about his words carefully. His eyes search my face, as if picking out a bottle of Bordeaux. David leans back on two legs of the chair and remains diplomatically quiet, knowing that it's better for me to get my questions answered now, regardless of my own lack of tact, than to leave me guessing.

"The Admin went too far. The settlers at the Beach are peaceful people. They shouldn't be treated like this." There's nothing in his dark brown eyes but calm sincerity as Rob continues, "Besides, hundreds of ships go in and out of Tunis City every day. Mine will be just another entry in the dock logs, and no one will be able to connect whatever happens to me."

"So that's it? You just want to help?" I'm not that easily convinced. "What about the money you could make by turning Rajcik in?"

A worried shadow passes over his features, then it's gone. "If your crew needs him as much as it sounds like, I'd be doing more harm than good by turning him in." His glance jumps between David and me. "You know, I'm more than a little curious about this footage you say Rajcik has. I mean, information that could implicate Kurosawa T'Kai—that's heavy. Any chance I could see it?"

"*I* haven't even seen it," I comment caustically.

Changing the subject, David asks, "What about your crew? How did you get them to agree to this?"

Rob cocks one eyebrow in an expression I can't read. "They'll do as they're told. They're citizens, but they're also ambitious enough. If they think there's a payoff, they won't question too much."

"Rob, there's no payoff in this deal."

"Yeah, but they don't know that." His mischievous grin is tired, and he sighs. "I've thought of something to keep them off your backs. Leave that to me."

"Look, Rob, I wish this didn't have to involve you. You realize that, right?" David says, his face drawn. "Old friends or not, you've got more at stake here than we do. If there was any other way, we wouldn't have asked for your help." My brother the peacemaker. He didn't get my temper, which is a surprise. It was David's father who was always the angry one, the guy who'd jump off the handle if you said anything disrespectful or sarcastic. David's father, not mine. We only had the same mother, and David tells me she was always more passive, docile even, before she split.

"After the shit we've been through together, brother? This is nothing. You'd do the same for me." Rob seems to relax a little, and his charismatic grin returns.

We fall silent for a minute, then David pushes back from the table and stands up. "I'm going to get something to eat. Anyone else hungry?"

Neither of us are, and David drops a teasing wink at me before heading toward the galley.

Rob leans forward and lays a hand on my leg. "So how are you holding up?"

I have to think about that for a second, but thinking makes me worried, and worry makes me feel helpless. I answer stonily. "I really don't know. How would you be doing in this kind of situation?"

"Yeah, I hear you."

Our eyes stay locked. "I'm sorry about Karl . . ." I trail off, not really knowing how to apologize for something like that.

Anger flashes behind his pupils, but he shrugs. "Yeah, well, I'll live. But your boyfriend better not try that again. It could get messy."

His comment strikes a painful chord, and I look away, letting the conversation lull. Rob leans back on his chair and takes his hand off my leg. After a few seconds, I start to stand up to leave but am stopped by his muffled chuckle, as if I'd said something mildly amusing. "Look, Aly, it's obvious that you're in love with him. So why don't you just tell him—go and be with him? I mean, I know I have my appeal"—he smirks a little—"but what are you doing with me?"

"I don't know."

"Come on, give me a real answer."

Tearing my eyes away from the table and looking into his face is harder than it should be, but I'd made a deal with myself to start being honest. So I answer with the truth. "Being with you—it's just easier. You seem like a better alternative."

He stares at me blankly for a second, then his lips wrinkle back in a cynical smile. "I'm an *alternative*. Alternative to what? Forgive me for sounding like an asshole, Aly, but that's exactly what you just sounded like." He chuckles again, like an exhalation. "You're still so much like that kid you were a few years ago. I have to admit, I'm a little surprised."

I want to be angry at him, but I just don't I have the energy. In fact, more than anything, I feel tired. Depressed. Like I lost something I should have fought for much, much harder. He must sense the way my mood is spiraling because he stands up and puts his arms around me tightly, almost protectively. "Hey, sorry. You'll be all right. You just have to quit worrying about it, you know. Things will work out the way they're supposed to. 'Cause look, it's not hard to tell he feels the same way about you. You both just have to relax long enough to tell each other the truth."

I pull away, not liking the way he's lecturing at me, as if to a child. "What do you know, Rob? You're not exactly an expert on relationships. You want to talk about honesty? Do you really think I believe there's nothing going on between you and Baker? And back in the Corps, when your detachment got reassigned, what happened there? Did you even try to keep in touch?"

Instead of biting at my hotheaded bait, he walks away and sits down on the bunk. "Yeah, I noticed the waves pouring in from you."

Ouch. Nothing like pointing out someone's hypocrisy to douse whatever self-righteous fire they were starting to whip up. Instead of getting pissed off and storming out of his cabin, I'm back to feeling the same empty sadness that's begun to take up permanent residence in the pit of my stomach. "Yeah, well, I was still a kid. Like you said."

Before I can walk out, he comes up behind me and gently takes hold of one of my wrists. "Come on, don't be like that. We have too much happening to start fighting over old news." The sincerity in his face is enough to melt through some of the frost starting to form between us. "I'm sorry, okay? We're good, right?"

"Yeah. We're good." My eyes are pinned to the ground, and I start to speak before I realize what I'm going to say. He's always had this kind of effect on me, made me feel like it's safe to talk to him. "It's really not as easy as you think it is, though. Karl and I are through. And once this job is over, once we get the settlers free, I can't go back to the Beach. I don't know what I'm going to do."

He's silent and I begin to feel a little foolish. It's not like me to be so forthcoming.

"You could become a citizen."

There's no need to tell him how crazy I think he is; the expression on my face makes that clear enough.

"I mean it. You said you had money—it's not that hard to buy an identity. You know? Your records were destroyed in the Rebellion, right? And you haven't been arrested and IDed since you deserted, right?"

"That's right."

"I know people who could make you a real person, fabricate an entire life history for you, and get you back on the Admin registry. It could be a fresh start for you."

"And what would I do?"

"You could come work for me."

I say nothing.

"Okay, okay. Whatever you want. That's my point, though. You can start over and do anything you want."

Before I can even think of how to respond, Sims comes through on Rob's wrist VDU. "Captain, you need to get up in the flight deck. There's some trouble with one of the, uh, passengers, the one that works with the smuggler."

"What kind of trouble? You were supposed to be watching him!" Rob answers while reaching inside his closet to retrieve a handgun, instantly transformed into the no-nonsense platoon sergeant I remember from the Corps.

"He's a sneaky sonofabitch. Slipped out of the galley while I was eating. Montoya says he bypassed the code somehow and just walked on deck. He's under control now."

I follow Rob out of the cabin during Sims's explanation, and we move out at a good clip toward the flight deck. I'm not in the least surprised Thompson pulled this kind of maneuver; he isn't one to stand by meekly and do what he's told, unless Rajcik is doing the telling. Halfway down the crew quarters corridor, Rob stops at the elevator and uses a personal code to open the door. It puts us one story up, directly onto the flight deck. When the doors open, we're staring into a wall of streaked blackness. The observation shields are open and the entire front surface gives us a view into nothingness as we cruise through hyperspace.

Thompson sits stiffly in a seat near the door with his lower lip split and bleeding. Montoya stands nearby shaking one fist limply, letting the sting in his knuckles diminish, and pointing a pistol at Thompson with the other hand.

Rob turns to Sims, who stands just on the other side of the main entryway working with a set of dangling wires extruding from a missing panel where the entry keypad belongs. "Damn it, Sims. How hard can watching one guy be?"

Sims glares back. He's taller than Rob by a few centimeters, but lanky and long limbed and closer to my age. His frosted blue eyes rest on Rob angrily, obviously resentful of the criticism, but he keeps his mouth shut.

"Captain, he used this to get through the door. And I took this from him," Baker informs Rob, handing him a portable electronics board with various leads hanging from it and a pistol. "He wanted our client's name and clearance codes for Tunis."

Scowling at Thompson, Rob says, "Who our clients are is not your problem. You're just a passenger on this trip and you either follow the rules, or you'll have to deal with the consequences."

"I'm just making sure you aren't flying us straight into an Admin security station." Thompson's angular face and crooked, jack-o-lantern eyebrows always make him appear to be sneering. The expression is more pronounced with Montoya's pistol pointed at him.

"Even if we were, there's not a goddamn thing you can do about it," Baker says.

The look on Thompson's face makes it clear that Montoya's pistol is the only thing keeping him from leaping at her. "Fuck you, bitch."

"Quiet. We've got a few days to go. Everyone here needs to keep their mouths shut and stay where they belong." Rob sweeps the crew, Thompson, and me with a hard stare. "Thompson, you're just going to have to take it on faith that we're doing exactly what we promised Vitruzzi we'd do. Since that doesn't seem to be easy for you, you'll stay in your bunk until we get there."

"Try it," he mutters, but not loud enough for Rob to have to do anything about it.

"Montoya, put him and his gear in twelve," he waves the bypass board at the crewman, "and double-check that there's nothing in there he can use to short out the lock."

"I can take him," I volunteer. This is a good opportunity for me to make it crystal clear to Thompson what will happen to him and Rajcik if they fuck this operation up.

"No way," Baker instantly says.

"It's fine," Rob jumps in. "Go ahead, Aly. You know where it is?"

"Captain—" Baker continues to argue.

"It's *fine*." He turns and faces her, his stance rigid and irritated. She holds his eyes for a few seconds, then turns angrily back to the navigator console.

Putting my hand on my Sinbad, I jerk my eyes toward the exit to get Thompson moving. He does it with a last scathing look at the crew.

When we've walked too far from the bridge to be overheard, he says, "That crew is Corps."

"Don't be an idiot." He stops and turns to face me, prompting me to pull out my 'Bad. His long figure and wide shoulders create a barrier directly in front of me, but the corridor is plenty wide enough to dodge if he lunges. "Keep moving."

"What? Are you blind? Living on that rock made you stupid, Erikson. You used to be able to smell Corps coming before they were in atmo."

"Listen to me, Thompson. I know you and Rajcik are planning something, but you're not going to distract me with accusations about Rob's crew being Corps. I'm warning you now, and it's the only time I'm going to do it, David and I will be watching you like a germ under a microscope. If you do *anything* I don't like, you know it won't bother me to kill you. I might even enjoy it."

"Stupid cunt, wake up! They're *Corps*."

"*Move!*" This time I swing the pistol up and point the barrel at his stomach. This gets him turned around.

David meets me at the bunk where Thompson will be deposited, keeping watch over the smuggler while I sweep the small room and his gear for any objects that can be used to his advantage. By Rob's orders, Thompson's weapons have been locked up, and the rest of us keep ours only because of his heavy-handed dispatching of his crew's protests. There's no reason for Montoya, Sims, and Baker to distrust us as much as they do, but their survival is being gambled. I can understand their concerns about getting pinched by

Admin security, but Rob trusts us. That should be enough for his crew.

Once Thompson is secure, David and I walk back toward the cargo hold with a vague plan to re-inventory the equipment we'd brought from Agate Beach, but his statement, and his sincerity, worms through my brain. *They're Corps.* Why would he say that? Is it just paranoia, the result of living most of his life as a thief and a hood? They *were* Corps, yeah, I can see that much. But Rob had assured me that they were citizens he'd contracted as his crew. My instincts are usually good, but they aren't coming through as clearly or loudly on this one as they usually are. If we're being set up, how could Rob possibly sound so sincere?

Forget it. This is just the result of the past couple of weeks' insanity fucking with me. Anyone would be a little insecure, a little strung out, after what had gone down. The best thing to do is stay alert and come to my own conclusions. Hopefully, not too late.

Vitruzzi and La Mer are also in the hold, loitering in a convex extension of the main cargo area where most of our gear is stored. Our footfalls are quiet, but they notice us anyway, proving everyone's nerves are on high alert. Vitruzzi would at least be considering the possibility of Rob's crew being Corps if it were even remotely possible, and she hasn't said a word. Obviously just part of Thompson's gambit to keep us on edge.

She looks over and nods a welcome, but La Mer, sitting cross-legged inside a helter-skelter ring of parts, doesn't look up. The components are spread around him like the blast pattern of the world's strangest frag grenade, the frags in this case being wires, transistors, capacitors, electrical boards, levers, and assorted metal and plastic miscellany.

"What's up?" David asks as we approach, but his tone and the way one of his eyebrows rises suggest that what he's really asking is, *Has La Mer gone off the deep end?*

La Mer halfheartedly tosses a part back into the pile and says, "We should have brought some receiver plates. They're lightweight enough; we'd just need a transport. They break so easily, we may have a hard time finding extras."

"Why would we need any? Do you think we'll have to build a new transceiver?" I walk over and lean against a table next to Vitruzzi.

"I want to put together a prototype, something small that I can use to do some regression tests. I know most of the Admin protocols well enough to set up temporary barriers, I just want to make sure I'm not missing anything."

I'm anxious to pass Rob's suggestion about becoming a citizen by David, get his take on the idea, but don't want to do it now while La Mer and Vitruzzi are here. Neither of them could easily entertain the same option, and hearing it may be more demoralizing than hopeful. Vitruzzi's been calm and focused since the Corps assaulted the Beach, despite the fact that they'd killed Bodie. It's hard to say how she's taking it, the way she bottles everything. Even now, she's methodical as she inventories her medkit, the one she carries anytime she's on the job. Its contents lie spread across the table. Beyond the basics we all carry—bandages, antibiotics, skin glue, a retractable splint, and rehydration tablets—hers contains a variety of drugs in syringes, liquids, and pill form that serve not only to dull pain and inhibit fluid buildup in soft tissues, but, when mixed properly, can make even a mute whisper the contents of their soul.

She shared this with me one day back on Agate Beach while I was still recovering in the colony's sick bay. If she'd carried the specific drug cocktail at the time, she could have used them on the commander of the MCACS we'd hijacked to get to the Fortress when he'd refused to tell us the station's coordinates. She'd ordered his execution as incentive to make his XO talk, and it had worked like magic. I've never faulted her decision, but it seems to bother her.

Shifting my attention back to La Mer, I comment, "I thought you already tested it before we tried the first time."

"Yeah, I did. But they found us. I must have missed something."

"We don't really know if the Admin caught on to the satellite hijack," David says, attempting to pull La Mer out of his brooding. "They could have been tipped off about a smuggling job the crew pulled or even noticed discrepancies in some of the *Sphynx*'s contract manifests. Who knows?"

La Mer's shoulders are hunched, and he won't meet David's eyes. "Or maybe it's my fault."

David squats down to get his attention. "Look, don't beat yourself up. I don't think you should take the blame for something like this. We all knew there were risks. Everyone was behind it, and we still are." He glances at Vitruzzi and me for confirmation, and we dip our heads in agreement. "The important thing is to keep our focus and figure this out."

La Mer sighs heavily, then nods, looking moderately less beaten. It's not a good time, but it seems important to mention it anyway. "Thompson thinks Rob's crew is Corps."

"Did he say why?" Vitruzzi asks.

"I think it's just a guess, or maybe part of some alternate plan of his and Rajcik's, but he sounded pretty sure."

La Mer's response surprises me. "There's something . . . off about all of them. No offense, I know you two and Cross go back, but I don't trust him."

I can't easily dismiss La Mer's suspicions. His instincts are solid. After all, it took the Admin over six years to catch him. When they want someone as bad as they want him and the group responsible for destroying the Corps records, it isn't a simple matter of staying off the grid. Like every Corps deserter who still draws free breath, La Mer had to develop a sixth sense for danger. Still, the idea of Rob being an Admin sympathizer sounds absurd. Even when he was Corps, it was just his way of filling a need for adventure and direction. Yeah, he has his faults—his unnerving capacity to be simultaneously sincere and manipulative, well-meaning and self-serving, loving and licentious. But treacherous? I just can't see it.

Trying to deflect the insidious fear and paranoia beginning to sweep over us like a polar crosswind, I say in a voice that carries no farther than their ears, "We're going to have to stay sharp and not let our guards down. I know Cross isn't going to turn us in, but that doesn't mean we can afford to take it easy. His crew makes me nervous, too." Admitting this out loud finally brings it home to me, centering the weight of my suspicions like a heavy lead ball in my chest cavity. "And I—"

"What are you doing?" None of us heard Baker enter the hold. Her stealthy approach, intentional or not, and the accusatory note buzzing in her tone, increases my swelling apprehension. She stands just inside the entry to the main passenger section, her frame as rigid and challenging as a wolf's circling for a fight.

David stands up and turns toward her slowly, his deliberate movements announcing his irritation. "What does it look like?" he responds angrily, making it clear that he doesn't appreciate having to explain himself to her.

She squints, her icy blue eyes chilling the air between them a few degrees before traveling over the rest of us like a fly across a horse's flank. "You need to stay out of the hold. Your bunks or the galley are the only places you're allowed."

"Is that your captain's order?" I challenge.

"I'm part of the crew, you're just passengers. You do what we say, when we say it. Do you get me?"

I don't see what she stands to gain by provoking us, but her tone is jarring and my patience lacks the endurance it would take to ignore her. "Whatever you're trying to prove, you can put the fucking brakes on right now, Baker. You have zero authority over us."

She squints angrily and steps farther into the hold, closing the gap between us and reducing firing range. Her right hand goes inside her jacket. I can't see a weapon, but I read the movement as clearly as the page of a book. The fact that this citizen crew carries weapons is another of the many discrepancies about them that feeds my doubt, and I realize Thompson must have clued in on it as well.

"Baker, what's your position?" Rob's voice comes through the fabric of her jacket. She has to withdraw her hand to access her wrist VDU, but her weapon stays put.

"In the hold." Her eyes don't drop from us.

"Is Thompson secure?"

"Roger."

"Then why aren't you back on station?"

"The passengers are in here messing around with the cargo."

There's a long pause, then Rob responds, "And?" Then my own VDU pings. "Aly, everything all right?"

"Baker seems to think our access is restricted to the galley or our bunks."

There's another long pause, then he speaks to all of us. "Would the four of you mind meeting me in the galley? We've got some things we need to discuss." Then we hear his voice clearly from Baker's receiver. "Baker, get your ass back on the bridge. Now. Out."

Vitruzzi quickly repacks her med-kit, and we walk out together. Baker doesn't move and stands like a sentry at the door until we pass her. I'm the last one out, and she steps in my way before I can exit.

"You and I are going to have to work some things out before long." She has a few centimeters in height advantage, but otherwise, we're similar in size and shape.

"Let's work it out now."

Before either of us move, David steps around her and puts a hand on my back, gently pushing me forward. "Enough. Come on."

Neither she nor I move. My breathing and heartbeat are slow and steady, a subdued physiological state that years of danger have trained my body to assume before combat. Baker's hate for me is like a cloud of mustard gas. I can only assume that she's jealous of what's going on between Rob and I, but I feel no sense of guilt or remorse. Fucking your CO is never a good idea, and if Rob's chosen to break it off with her, it's not my problem, or my fault. She's dangerous, I can see that in her fluid, stealthy movements and taciturn threats. She isn't scared and nervous like someone who's reacting out of emotion, but calm and steady, like someone who's accustomed to carrying out her threats. With an implicit promise for more trouble, she finally turns abruptly around and strides toward the stairs leading up to the flight deck level.

"Probably shouldn't have hooked up with Rob again, Aly. It doesn't look like the natives are friendly," David quips.

I give him a disgusted look, and he leads the way to the galley with a chuckle.

"WE CAN'T LET YOU put yourself in that kind of danger. You've already done enough. Maybe too much," Vitruzzi says.

Rob stands by the galley's rear door with his back to it, but he keeps glancing into the hallway as if expecting someone. Vitruzzi is the first to recover her voice after what he's suggested, but the rest of us still can't believe it.

"Don't worry about it," he responds, throwing another glance outside. "Flying you off Obal 10 after you shake things up with T'Kai is all contingent on things going smoothly. If you all get into serious trouble . . ." He lets the statement hang. "But I can help out as a transport."

"Rob, you'd never be able to fly again if they suspect your ship of harboring fugees," David says.

"Believe me, I know. The *'Rize* has a reputation for being squeaky clean, and that hasn't been easy. But I've got another ship, an unregistered ship. Anonymous and fast enough for our needs." He looks around at us, and continues, "Who better to get you out of there? Have you even thought about how you're going to do that?"

No. At the moment, it's more expedient to keep our thoughts on what we know and what we can control. Figuring out the next part of the plan is being shelved until the first part is complete. But . . . but if we agree to let Rob join us, we'd have one of our many problems already solved. Looking around the room, I see expressions of careful neutrality on everyone's faces. No one wants to hope for that much good luck.

Seeing our hesitancy, he leans casually against the wall and holds his hands out in a gesture that's both generous and oddly contrived. "Look, I'm not the kind of guy who just turns their back on friends when things get heavy. I'm not doing this as a favor, I'm doing it because"—he glances in my direction—"I care about what happens to all of you. We've been in business for a while. David and Aly and I go way back. I don't think I could sleep if I left you hanging, you know?"

TWENTY-TWO

Streamers of steaming exhaust billow out from the pipes and turrets of the industrial complex surrounding us like a post-apocalyptic graveyard. The air glides slickly into my nostrils and down my throat, tasting more like a chemical vapor than oxygen, which is perfect. We all still wear our nostril-implanted air filters to protect our lungs, but no one else wants to come near an urban junk-yard where ragged and dangerous dregs of people mix like rotting vegetables with the toxic soup that stands in for the environment.

Tunis City, despite being located on the most populated Obal planet, still has its industrial blights. Once they outsourced dangerous manufacturing jobs to the already hazardous Spectras and smaller moons, these dilapidated factories were simply abandoned, one by one. Over time, they've been picked bare by vagabonds and skulkers looking for materials that can buy them a meal or a fix. The only thing left is the sludge and pollutants that were never cleaned out, slowly aging and festering like wounds and occasionally spewing out their noxious residue. Like I said—for a quiet, witness-free loca-tion, it's perfect.

Rob put us down two days ago on a busy resource shipping dock, and we'd gotten off the *Horizon* with almost unbelievable ease. Most of the transports in the area were older and bigger, beaten from traveling to and from the Spectras carrying heavy loads of metals, minerals, and ore, making the *Red Horizon* almost conspicuous in its newer, shinier state. Rob procured a small land transport and snuck us aboard while the dock controllers read the *'Rize's* manifest and checked his crew's IDs. Lying in back of the transport, I could smell smoke and hear shouting and alarms as the engines of a nearby ship went to shit. The airspace around was crowded and getting worse by the minute thanks to the grounded ship, and the controllers moved on without hesitation. With Rob at the wheel, we merged with the general din of road traffic and traveled quickly to this section of town, more a satellite district of Tunis than part of it. And the wait for La Mer to track down contacts from his past to aid us began.

Though it's dark inside the old factory, the gloom is still more inviting than the penetrating fog barely held at bay outside. The last forty-eight hours have ticked by with the painful slowness of waterboarding while La Mer sends out queries. If there is a bright side, it's Rob's assurance that he can get us off-world when the time comes. Maybe we'd accepted his help a little too fast, but without him here, Brady's tendency to painstakingly consider every option before making a call got dropped. If our choice was too brash, there's only one way we're going to find out.

It's almost my watch on the rooftop, and I glance at La Mer on the way up. He's been monitoring his netwave console almost constantly, barely leaving to sleep or eat, but he's not looking too worse for the wear. A few anonymous wire-rats have responded to his queries, and they keep a running conversation, speaking in a lingo that seems to be universally understood by their type but is basically indecipherable to me—quantum process transmogrifications this and transduction referrals that. I put enough effort into trying to make sense of their communications to make sure La Mer isn't giving anything away that could get us caught, but stay out of his way outside of that.

He's talked to some about the security worm, keeping the details of how it'll be used as ambiguous as possible, and refining things based on their recommendations and questions. One mobile console stays with him at all times, its screen filled with code that shifts and changes regularly as he makes minor tweaks. In many ways, the fewer changes he makes to the bypass program, the more relief I feel, and I'm guessing the same is true for the others. La Mer's code is good, at least good enough to deal with the Admin security he knows about. The question is: What if there are things he doesn't know about? Detection programs, tracking programs, new technology that's been deployed since the Soldier's Rebellion? It's all too easy to think something like one of these led to the discovery of our first test at the Beach and the subsequent invasion by the Corps. What else can we do though, besides take our chances?

On the *'Rize*, when La Mer'd copped to the fear that it was his fault the Corps found us and killed Bodie, I had worried he wouldn't be able to gain enough objectivity to keep working on the worm once we reached Tunis. Even now, I can't imagine the pressure he must be feeling. Despite what's at stake, his attitude is shifting slightly, and his confidence in the worm, and himself, is building. The heavy-hearted gloom he's carried since the Beach is lifting, incrementally being replaced by infectious optimism, and we've all started to share it to a degree. It helps make the passage of time more bearable, even as our fears for the *Sphynx* crew and the settlers grows stronger.

The shifting dark of our second night here wraps around me as I step onto the roof. David leans against the south lip of a half wall, gazing into a puzzle of thick, curdling fumes and fog. He looks deep in thought, his forehead wrinkled in frustration and that omnipresent feeling of impotence that we all loathe. His thoughts probably aren't far from mine: with so many lives depending on us, it's excruciating to have to find and rely on a group of unknown wire-rats to make our plan operational.

"My turn to watch the toxic waste bubble."

I move up beside him and he half turns his head, nodding an acknowledgement, but makes no move to go back inside. Leaning up against the wall next to him, I raise my AK-80 to the rim and settle it on its self-mounted tripod. The scope's dark eyepiece stares back at me, seeming to ask where its next target is. The rifle is short and compact with a built in scope and tracking light, yet still weighs less than its cousin, the Corps-issue CCIX-2655. The effective range is slightly less, approximately 550 meters with night-vision scope or 720 meters on a clear day, but when the bulky CCIX and its ammo weigh a soldier down too much, I'll still be firing up the night with my lighter extra magazines.

He rubs a hand along his jaw, the scruff of a new auburn beard scratching a whisper as he does. "Yeah, but there's nothing going on in there. La Mer's got it under control, and I hate just sitting there watching. I feel less than useless. V can keep an eye on Thompson. Mind if I just hang with you up here?"

I shrug, happy to have the company.

After a while he says, "What do you think of our chances, little sis?"

"Honestly, I think the best thing we can realistically hope for is to keep ourselves alive for a few months until T'Kai sics every last soldier in the system on us."

"Not very optimistic."

"Do you think otherwise?"

"I don't know. But if I didn't think we had any chance, I wouldn't be here."

We fall silent, listening to the sounds of decaying buildings settling around their bones. Eventually, I say it, letting the fog soak up my words. "David, I'm getting out."

He turns toward me, eyebrows raised.

"Rob knows people that can forge citizenship registration papers, create a fake history. He can get me back in the system as a new person."

"You really think you could go back to that life?"

"There's nothing else left. They'll catch up to us eventually, even if we succeed in bringing down T'Kai. But if we're not criminals, just regular people doing what regular people do, with real lives . . ." I pause, not ready to look into his face and read his reaction, then continue, "We can just buy them—new lives, new identities. Start off working for Rob, then set ourselves up with our own ship, or even live on one of the Obals, maybe here in Tunis City. You'd be crazy not to come with me."

Finally I face him, and I don't like the way his blue-green eyes peer into mine, as if trying to brand his disapproval on my brain.

"Aly, what about our friends? What about Karl?"

"He left me, David. He doesn't care about me. Our friends are probably dead already. What do we have to go back to if we live through this? Any of us?"

Holding back a response, he looks out into the night. I want to keep trying to convince him, argue the point until he agrees with me, but don't. Eventually he'll either come to the same conclusion, or he won't. He's always been the more thoughtful of the two of us, even-keeled and deliberate. He knows as well as I do that things will probably never be easy again. Neither one of us are martyrs, all we can do now is pick the path with the least exposure. Or Corps.

TWENTY-THREE

"Which one of you wants to go to the docks and get a read on Cross's ship?"

Before the sentence is out of Vitruzzi's mouth, David and I are both on our feet, the game of Pussers Bones we've been playing for the last four hours instantly forgotten. A hint of a grin lifts one side of her lips, but she says, "Just one."

This time, a game of Bear, Ninja, Cowboy resolves the issue, and David exits back up to the roof in disgust to keep watch both with and on Thompson.

"Rob sent me the location of the warehouse where he's storing his planet-hop, and I want someone to take a look around to get the lay of the land. Keep your eyes open for regular security patrols in the area, who's coming and going, and how likely it is we'll be noticed if we have to get out of here fast. Keep your face covered and don't, whatever you do, get out of the land trans." I'm nodding as she speaks, impatient at being told what I already know, but Vitruzzi is going to say it anyway. "Just look around and then turn around. Read me?"

"Loud and clear."

As I sling my carbine strap over my shoulder, she says, "You're not taking those." Her eyes drift between the AK-80 and my Sinbad pistol, then stare straight into mine. "And the Derg stays, too."

"What if there's trouble?" Surprise and irritation fight for control over my tone.

"Then handle it, but no shooting. You'll be dead before your rounds hit the target if you fire a weapon. This isn't a Spectra. Security teams are all over the place." She throws me my watch cap. "Be careful."

I hate that she's right, but I deposit the guns on the table next to La Mer's consoles. She and I walk into the warehouse's garage, and I jump in behind the beaten-up transport's driver console. The electric engine chugs unevenly as she raises the garage door for me to drive out. In a few minutes, the industrial complex fades from the cracked rearview display, and it takes another thirty before I get to the shipping docks where we'd parted ways with the *Horizon*.

The Uhr River, meandering thousands of kilometers down from the northern border of Obal 10's largest continent, spreads wide and deep on the western edge of Tunis City. It serves as an economic divider separating the city, with all its controlled cleanliness and orderly development, from the shipping and manufacturing operations. The river grows wider and fatter over the distance of several kilometers, leveling into a bloated estuary before rolling into Voltendar Bay. The bay is easily a half-day trip by boat from north to south and varies in width from east to west before it feeds into the Gemenez Ocean through the Strait of Ruiz.

Docking platforms and piers for water-capable craft line every grid of earth along the bay's western and southern banks. Where each ship is docked depends on what they're delivering and to whom, and less important clients or ships peddling unsought goods are more likely to be directed to the docks along the bank's southern stretch. Dock access is a mark of status, and those that can't pay or don't have something the Admin wants don't get any favors. The south bay docks are the cheapest and least regulated, and the security teams roving along them are often more corrupt than some of the privateers that frequent them. This opens the area up for more people like us: questionable, crooked, and, more often than the Admin finds it convenient to notice, criminal.

But the area is still monitored, and security forces still have all the authority they need to hold and question anyone that could be on their wanted lists, or who just pisses them off. If you're not paying a bribe, and sometimes even if you are, the rule is to keep your head down. A skill I've practiced to an art.

Once at the bay, I drive cautiously through the sprawl that's grown up to accommodate incoming and outgoing ships, the road made even more congested by off-loaded shipments from other planets that are waiting to be either hauled off or paid for. More than once, irate drivers in transports bigger than mine pass me, their scowling faces looming down as they go by. The need to avoid any ill-timed confrontation, or worse, a wreck, compels me to keep my speed steady, hoping not to draw too much attention.

I drive along the main road feeding into the line of docks until I reach a T-intersection snarled with traffic branching east and west along the bank. The location Rob had given us is west, so I wait for a gap and hang a left. As I pull into the milieu, gridlock quickly forces a standstill, wedging me between two larger transports with no room for escape. The stoppage is caused by a parade of haulers waiting for loads a few docking platforms down.

Time on these docks truly is money, and the traders exhibit very little patience at the inconvenient slowdown. Rude shouts and pounded-on horns signal their disgust. The ship most responsible for the delay is some kind of contractor-owned piecemeal conglomeration of a decommissioned Admin cargo carrier and private sector model. It's being guarded by tough-looking pirates planted strategically around the hold while others unload it. Their matching grimaces and bulldog statures indicate they can handle any trouble people decide to shove their way and do it without breaking a sweat.

The longer we sit, the more tangled the congestion becomes, and each additional vehicle piling up behind is like another brick piling on top of me until I'm nearly squirming from claustrophobia. There's no way to drive free of this mess, and if any security comes by and decides to kill time by checking IDs, I may as well have a target drawn on my forehead.

After five minutes of waiting, the situation goes from annoying to incendiary. A twelve-ton transport with a double trailer is attempting a wide turn that cuts through the full width of the road when a sizzling arc of electricity suddenly blazes through the cab, instantly turning the driver into a smoking husk of meat and leaving the hauler equally dead. Realization that no one is going anywhere for a while sweeps through the crowd of stalled transports like the scent of fire on the wind. People start to exit their vehicles and enter the street, some carrying crowbars and other tools. The warm day and mounting hostility over the delay gives the crowd a sharp, sweaty odor, like a cornered beast. No one acts in the least concerned about the dead trucker, instead converging like a hellish ant hive on the line of transports still being loaded. Security teams start signaling each other, preparing to close in and circumvent the looming brawl.

Goddammit, this is *not* what I want to be happening. Time to fade out of the scene. If I stay with the transport, I'm sure to get pinched. Abandoning it is the only way I'm getting out of this clusterfuck. I'll have to figure out another way to get back to basecamp later when things cool down.

A quick sweep of the cab unearths a bent metal rod about the length of my arm. It's thin but has some heft. Might come in handy. As I pull on the door handle to get out, a column of the dock security crew leapfrogging their way up between the line of stopped vehicles shows up in the rearview display. Shit, shit, *fuck.* They're working in pairs, one scanning each vehicle's cargo, and the other shoving hand-held ID scanners at the drivers. If I get out of my trans, they'll see me, and if I run, they'll chase me.

Pressing back into the seat, I force myself to calm down and plan an escape. Many of the stalled transports are bumper to bumper, so I can't run through them without scrambling over hoods and tailgates. No good. That will just slow me down and make me an excellent target. I'll have to run straight up the line and look for a break, try to get to the warehouses opposite the docks. The teams will see me if I try to run, but maybe I can lose them amid the buildings.

The nearest man is still about ten meters behind my truck. Using my shoulder to shove the door free of its warped frame, it swings open with a teeth-clenching squeal that makes me curse darkly. Sliding from the seat to the ground, metal rod hidden against my leg, I leave the door open to provide some cover to my rear and start walking casually up the line.

Two steps forward and I hear: "You in the black hat! Stop where you are!"

No, no, no, this *can't* be happening. It suddenly hits me that I hadn't called in the situation to Vitruzzi and David. Too late now.

Opening up my stride, I hurtle forward, increasing the gap quickly, praying no one opens their door to find out why dock security is going ballistic. A shot rings out, and heads inside the cabs drop behind their steering consoles, everyone having the same automatic reaction to the sound of a firing weapon. The bullet whips by me, embedding itself in the rear bumper of a hauler a few meters ahead. Thank dumb luck that they're not using seekers. Too many potential targets in the crowded street.

In moments, I reach the crowd, five or six people deep, that forms a semicircle around the stalled hauler and smoking driver. Up ahead and to my left, there's an alleyway passing between two warehouses. That's my opening. A quick look over my shoulder shows the squad closing the distance between us, their faces hidden behind black helmets and lowered face shields. Renewing my effort, I shove through the crowd, putting the full force of my shoulders and elbows into people. Most are too surprised to stop me, but one or two shove back. Doesn't matter, I'm getting closer to the edge near the warehouses. Another look back shows the security squad yelling at the crowd, forcing a hole by waving and pointing their weapons. People turn to find out what's going on and start dropping to their knees around me. No, dammit! I need cover!

With a final shove, I try pushing by two of the thugs guarding the cargo ship, but their combined mass is solid and unmoving. One grabs the meaty part of my arm to stop me, jerking me backward, probably thinking he can turn me in to the security team for a reward. I snap like a rubber band at the end of his yank and bring my metal bar up, using momentum to double my own strength. The bar connects with a chunky slap against his cheekbone, opening it up and whacking his head to the side. He releases me immediately and I squeeze past, sprinting into the alleyway.

My excitement evaporates instantly as I realize the end of the alley is completely blockaded by a wall, easily ten meters tall, all smooth concrete. No way to scale it. Panic starts to bubble like acid in my throat. Looking side to side for a way out—a door, a fire escape, fuck, I'd take a trampoline—reveals nothing but five or six stories of featureless walls. I start to turn around and go back the way I came with a hopeless goal of somehow getting lost in the throng, but a darker depression to one side of the barrier catches my eye. It looked like a shadow at first, but maybe it's something else. Maybe a doorway. I reach it in a few quick strides and yes! It *is* a doorway, with a heavy steel door. Locked, of course.

As I strike the handle hard with the bar, wicked pain reverberates through the bones of my hands and up my arms to my shoulders at the force of the blow. They go numb, almost making me lose my grip on the bar. Regardless, I raise it again and swing it hard—but the door opens on its own and I tumble into pitch-blackness. Spreading out my arms to catch myself, I end up face down on the ground, my knees and palms stinging, and the bar tumbles off somewhere ahead, clanking against the concrete floor. Before I can get up, someone has a grip on my arms and pulls them cruelly behind my back. Panicked now, I begin bucking, trying to flip myself over and get some leverage with my feet, but the assailant straddles me, his weight like a tank on my back. He binds my wrists quickly, expertly, and I hear the door pushed closed and locked. A rag is stuffed into my mouth as I try to yell, and then a bag is pulled over my head. Thrashing and kicking nets me nothing but bruises and at least two different voices cursing at me, but they have my legs also bound in seconds, trussing me like a turkey.

Helpless.

Someone starts banging on the door from the other side and muffled, indistinct voices demand it be opened. The words "security" and "violation" come through loud and clear, making me realize that whoever has me is *not* the security team that had been pursuing me. I am in deeper shit than I thought.

The voices on the other side of the door continue to yell as I'm lifted off the floor, none too gently, and carried away.

To where?

TWENTY-FOUR

The bag is yanked off my head, pulling my watch cap and a few errant hairs with it.

"You a merc? Or just popular."

A man stands in front of me arm's length away, looking at me flatly as if examining something he finds slightly objectionable. He has dark hair and dark eyes set into a flushed face that's oblong and squat, like a melon thrown against a wall. He's not very tall, about Doug Mason's height, stringier, with arms crossed, and wide, slightly hunched shoulders.

So this is my abductor. The latest in a string of them.

"Who. Are. You?" Things have to unfold a little more before I'll know how much danger I'm in, but the sound of a gun being cocked behind me is proof that it's enough.

"You can call me Quantum. And you are Aly." His arms open and he holds my VDU up in one hand. "Associate of David, Vitruzzi, and" —he pauses for a long second—"La Mer." Returning the device to the pocket of his cargo jacket and recrossing his arms, he finishes, "And who else?"

My team must have been calling me, trying to find out what's been going on. I take a minute to look around, letting him wait. The room is deep and long, several computer and equipment consoles lined up in neat rows filling the space. I've been their captive for over two hours at this point, but we only arrived in this location a few minutes ago. After I'd been gagged and hooded, they'd made me sweat it out in some sort of tiny burrow in the warehouse that had been barely big enough to lie lengthwise in. Something thick had been lowered over the space, and I'd been left trapped underneath for a long, cramped hour. Panicked claustrophobia had me nearly screaming to be let out, but somehow my rational mind had held it in check, knowing that I'd be beyond help if the Admin security team found me. They'd finally pulled me out, and with no explanation, driven me to this place. Saying that I'm angry and frightened enough to kill someone right now is like calling a bullet hole in the stomach a minor annoyance.

Keeping my fury in check until I can suss out the situation, I ask, "Why should I tell you?"

He takes a sliding step forward and backhands me across the cheekbone. It stings, but it isn't hard enough to bruise. He's trying to scare me.

My cold stare is enough to make it clear that I'm not easily intimidated. He gives me another few seconds, then tries a new question.

"What are you doing on Obal 10?"

Recollection suddenly pierces through my anger like a shard of ice. Quantum—he said I can call him Quantum, and it's a name I've heard before. One of the wire-rats La Mer's been trying to reach—he'd called the guy our best chance. "Looking for you," I answer.

He reaches back inside his jacket. When it comes out, he's holding a very long, very sharp-looking knife. He steps forward and leans over me, pressing its needlepoint tip into my throat, just to the left of my windpipe. His other hand comes to rest on my thigh, its warmth oppressive through my pants.

"Toying with me will not make this easy for you." His teeth are jagged, like an animal's, fierce and feral. The knife tip presses deeply into the fragile skin of my neck, so sharp it almost doesn't hurt, but I reflexively try to draw away. "You have only this chance before I decide you're not worth my effort. How many people have you brought to Tunis City, and which one of them is Axone?"

La Mer hadn't mentioned anything about what kind of man Quantum would be. I assumed—wrongly—all these types were unprepossessing, noncombative punks who would run at the first sight of trouble. Not bring trouble *to* us.

"If you pull that blade out of my throat, I'll start talking." I need to swallow, but the knife has started to pierce. Swallowing will make it bite deeper.

He removes the point, but keeps the edge against my throat. I never thought I'd be the one negotiating for help from some wire-rats, and I try to imagine what approach Vitruzzi would take. Unfortunately, my reactionary personality is nothing like her natural composure. It seems likely that what I come up with will barely scratch the surface of how she'd have chosen to handle this situation. So be it. I decide to proceed with my usual tactic—the forward assault. "We're going to blackmail the director of the Ministry of Science and Engineering, and we need your transceiver."

Without backing up, he laughs, his breath exploding against my face. When he does, his lips roll back to show his teeth have the same ragged sharpness all the way to his molars. "You're going to blackmail Kurosawa T'Kai? That is really funny. Please, tell me more, merc." He shifts backward and the knife is finally withdrawn.

I don't usually underestimate people, and I won't make that mistake with him again. But I have to give him something that shows we mean business. "You sound like you don't think we can do it. Believe me, T'Kai will take us seriously after what we did to the Fortress. And we're not mercs."

He stops laughing, the cold sincerity in my voice freezing his febrile humor, and studies me closely. "You are trying to tell me you had something to do with that biowarfare laboratory?"

"More than something—*I* destroyed it." His expression doesn't change, but I recognize the effort it takes to keep it that way. "You wouldn't find it so funny if you knew what we have on T'Kai."

He looks over my shoulder and nods his head at someone behind me. One of the other men pushes the end of a gun against the back of my head. I press my body tightly against the seat, using its stability to provide the leverage I'll need if I'm forced to lunge. Keeping my eyes on Quantum, not sure what I'm going to say, but knowing that I better say something fast or I'm going to be treated to something decidedly more painful than a slap on the cheek, I start to bargain. "Now look, Quantum, let me talk. I think you'll see—"

Before I can tell him what exactly it is he'll see, he leans forward again and takes hold of my left hand, pressing the knife through the skin of my palm and downward in a diagonal line. The pain is like fire, streaking up my arm, bursting into my elbow, and continuing until it dissipates at my shoulder. I cry out, the pain and fear of a bird caught in a net, and the knife is withdrawn. He leans close, putting his face centimeters from mine. "You are arrogant and fool-ish. To throw words at me like the Fortress. What does an Admin spy know of the Fortress? It's only a superstition made up by simpleton non-cits who think there is government conspiracy everywhere."

Now I'm a spy instead of a merc. It must be a trick, an attempt to manipulate me into giving up my cover—a cover I don't even have. It would be my turn to be amused if I weren't fairly certain that I'm about to be carved up like a whittling stick.

I stare directly into his face, unflinching and calm. "I'm not a spy and you know it. I'm a deserter. And a friend of Axone's. He's a wire-rat who helped destroy the Corps records database during the Soldier's Rebellion. The Admin sent him to become a test subject at the Fortress. My team intercepted the prisoner transport he was on, and he's been working with us since then."

"He was arrested?"

"Why else would he be on a prisoner transport?"

That comment gets me another backhand, this time across the other cheek. And this time, a lot harder. But he leans back away, giving me hope that he'd seen what I wanted him to see in my face—the truth. I take hold of my injured hand and hold it up and away from my body. Blood streams down my palm and forearm and begins dripping onto the floor. I wiggle my fingers. No tendon damage, not that deep, and—most importantly—not my primary firing hand.

"How much does the Admin know about the people that destroyed the database?"

"Nothing. La Mer—Axone—didn't tell them anything. They sent him to the Fortress to spill it, I guess, but according to him, everyone else is already dead."

"Everyone." He says the word in a peculiar flat way.

"Yeah. Dead."

"What do you have that will force T'Kai to cooperate?"

My whole world has become Quantum's unwavering eyes, their irises deep brown and flecked with hints of gold like glitter. I stay silent. It's turning out that he's more of a free agent than any of us had anticipated. The way he's strong-arming me and his focused, intent questions make me wonder if he's planning to try and take over the show. Maybe use me as a bargaining chip of his own to get the footage Rajcik had collected. He must have friends, a network he can rally to go after T'Kai. If he gets that footage, he won't keep us around, a bunch of non-cits and deserters. The fact that he's only asked me *what* we have that would impact T'Kai, and not *why* we'd want to go to such outrageous lengths, concerns me the most.

That, and how he'd found me in the first place.

He lets me hesitate for a few seconds, then grips my shirt in his fist and pulls me up. My nose comes to his chin, and there's still a gun pointed at my head. I'm pushed to a bank of monitors and he switches them on, saying casually, "Your friends will not be able to help you."

The monitors hum to life and focus on images of Vitruzzi, Rob, David, and Thompson scattered throughout a stairwell.

"They are outside, not far from us, but they cannot go anywhere. I've activated the firewalls and sealed the stairwell. It would be easy for me to gas them, or pull out all of the oxygen, whatever I choose. Do you finally understand what the stakes are?"

They must have found me using the tracker Vitruzzi implanted in my arm. The building is at least a few stories tall. When they'd brought me in, we'd descended three levels in an elevator and the lack of noise or windows makes me think we're underground. With the amount of equipment in here and the promise in Quantum's voice, I have no doubt that he can do exactly what he's threatening to. Through the monitors, I can see the words SUBLEVEL 1 painted on the wall behind Thompson and David, and SUBLEVEL 2 painted near Rob and Vitruzzi. They're spread out. How long have they been here? I can see on their faces that they know they've been barricaded in.

But I'm not ready to surrender or give him the satisfaction of believing he has the upper hand. Without turning, I warn, "Maybe *you* should consider your options. They're here, and they're not going to leave without me. Besides, what do you gain by killing us?"

Before I finish speaking, the monitors are suddenly filled with an explosion of white, then blank out in quick succession. There's a loud *bong* from outside of the room, and the window in the stairwell door is shattered. Everyone ducks instinctively. Immediately, the air is suffused by a fizzing sound, as if a steam pipe has broken, and moments later the heavy, garlicky-smelling smoke of a phosphorous device begins to fill the space.

The man with the gun yanks me backward by the shirt. This is my moment, while they're distracted. I leap forward, breaking out of his grasp easily, and dart past the equipment, grabbing a handheld radio as I divert behind a bank of tables and hit the deck.

"Hirota, get her!"

The overhead lights cast a yellow pall that barely penetrates the thick smoke. I pull my shirt over my nose and try not to breathe heavily, relying on my nasal filters to help protect my lungs. I can see the stairwell door at the end of the room. The man called Hirota is moving around nearby, and he'll be on me in a second. As he approaches, I crouch and wait until the moment I know he'll have to come around the desk's edge, hopefully with his gun held in front of him where I'll be able to knock it free.

My eyes grow teary, blurring my vision just as I start to lunge, but someone has come up behind me and grabs me by the hair, pulling me to my feet. I swing the radio like a hammer at his face and strike him in the chin. He curses loudly, and his grip comes loose enough for me to pull away, but Hirota is right here, a laser pistol pointed at my chest. Frantic, I glance behind me toward the stairwell opening, and my last hopes are dashed. It remains closed.

Blood is dripping from a deep gash along Quantum's jaw. I have a moment to savor the fact that I'd injured him in return before he walks in front of me and plugs his fist into my stomach, doubling me over and leaving me completely breathless.

"You should not have done that."

Water pours out of my eyes as my chest hitches for air. He glowers over me like an enraged dog, all snarling teeth and fierce eyes. "What are you going to do now?" I manage to gasp.

Before he answers, the sound of Vitruzzi's voice comes from his pocket. My VDU. "Aly, what's your status?"

I straighten up and feel the barrel of Hirota's pistol poke against my spine, just beneath my cervical vertebrae. Quantum looks thoughtful for a moment, then walks a short distance away, pulls the VDU out, and activates the screen.

"She is fine for the moment."

There's a pause, then Vitruzzi again. "Whom am I speaking to?"

"Enough games. Your friend has managed to put a bad taste in my mouth, and now I will tell you what is going to happen." As he speaks, he motions Hirota to push me into a chair and places my VDU on a desk, where he links it to a console. Vitruzzi's face comes up on the attached monitor. "She mentions that you have some very important plans for a very important man. You have some information that will convince this man to meet your terms. I want to see this information."

"There's no way."

Quantum looks over at me and a drop of blood falls from his chin, splashing onto the console. He turns back and says, "That's a rash decision. How much do you want to see this woman again?"

David breaks into the conversation and his face appears in another square on the monitor. "You should be careful who you threaten, whoever the fuck you are."

"Uh-huh. So, Vitruzzi, this information?"

"Let me speak to Aly."

Quantum nods and Hirota walks me over to the console. I pick up the VDU. "I'm okay, V."

"What's going on?"

Quantum nods at my questioning look and I reply, "I'm, um, with Quantum, the wire-rat La Mer's been trying to contact, and a couple of his friends. I don't know how they found me, but they picked me up on the docks."

"Tell us exactly what happened, Aly. Are we compromised?"

Compromised? That's not so easy to answer. I'm fairly certain the Admin security teams on the docks hadn't IDed me, and right now, they're a minor issue. Mainly because I'm feeling majorly fucking compromised by Quantum and his thugs. I'll just go with a simple response. "There was some trouble and I lost the truck, but I'm certain we're still clear of the Admin."

While we speak, the third man working with Quantum goes to a control box on one wall and triggers the ventilation system. The room begins to clear.

"What do they want?"

I glance at Quantum and answer, "You'll have to ask them that."

Quantum retrieves the VDU and pushes me back. "Vitruzzi. Your associate tells me that you have some means in which you intend to blackmail Director T'Kai, and that you need my transceiver to do so. This tells me that your information is digital, perhaps video." He pauses, assessing Vitruzzi's reaction.

"Continue," she replies.

"We have some common interests, but it doesn't matter to me if the Admin discovers your scheme and obliterates you. And they will. If you have any sense, you will leave something of worth, like this information, behind, where it can be leveraged effectively. Which I have the means to do. And I also have your friend."

Vitruzzi closes the connection and my VDU darkens for several seconds. Quantum quickly grows impatient and forces me to open a link to her. "I don't think you understand the urgency of this situation. Your tactics to get my attention lacked subtlety, and now that you have damaged the firewalls, maintenance will be coming. I'm sure you didn't fail to notice that we are in an Admin structure. When they get here and find you loitering in the stairwell—illegally armed —we will already be gone. And they will find your friend's body in the bay."

She responds this time. "If you let us use the transceiver, you can have our information after that. That's the deal." The edge in her voice is cool but frustrated.

"I must see it to make this deal. Is it with you?"

"Yes. But I won't show it to you over the com." There's no give in her voice, and Quantum's tight mouth curls at the edges, looking almost pleased. He walks to a console near the elevator and manages a series of switches and buttons, presumably retracting what remains of the fire barriers and unlocking the stairwell door.

The third man takes a position near the door and yells in an accent that sounds far-Obal, "Place your weapons down on the floor in front of you. Now turn and walk to the back wall. Put your hands on it. Stay there." He opens the door and he and Quantum quickly gather their guns.

Once the team's inside, excitement and relief flood my overly taut nerves, quenching some of the anticipation that's been burning through them for the last several hours. Seeing Rob here helping the crew gives rise to a complicated set of emotions: guilt for putting him back in danger, and a heavy and awkward jolt of relief that he's willing to take a risk—again—to come to our aid. To come to *my* aid.

"You okay?" David catches my eye and checks in.

"As good as can be with a pistol in my back."

"Your hand?"

Blood has soaked through the material I'd wrapped it in, but it's not leaking. Judging by how heavily it throbs with each heartbeat, my heart must be the size of a whale's. I nod to let him know it's not a concern at the moment. I can still shoot, provided I get my hand on a weapon.

Quantum looks them over like a scientist examining something new at the bottom of a lab petri dish. "None of you are the wire-rat she has called La Mer."

His sharpness exceeds his people skills, that's a given.

"He's keeping an eye on our basecamp," Vitruzzi responds.

"I see. I'd very much like to meet the *last man alive* who was responsible for bringing the Admin as close to its knees as it has ever come."

"You'll get your chance."

Quantum looks at her sharply and the corners of his mouth retract into a snarl as he realizes she's been playing him.

Vitruzzi continues, "You're going to have to take us back there to see the footage."

She drops her hands from her shoulders and the others follow. Quantum's men don't react. The tide has shifted.

"Look, your fucking game is as tiring to us as it is to you," she says. "You'll see the footage, but first we have to come to an understanding. You're not going to kill us or throw Aly in the bay. And you're not going to continue this pointless charade of yours. You're just a pretender, dicking around on jacked satlinks. Not some of kind of antigovernment subversive." There's a faint sheen of sweat on her forehead, so thin you might think it was just glare from the lights. But she keeps her cool. So cool I can almost see the air condensing around her breath, as if her lungs were made of the same frosty material as her composure. "If you want to step up and do it for real, this is your chance. We're going to bring T'Kai down. Either he's going to agree to our terms—which you don't need to worry about—or we're going to show the entire population of the system what our government is doing to people behind closed doors. We have the power. *We have* the leverage. We just need a goddamn transceiver and someone with enough balls to give us access to it."

One thing is clear, she's completely shed the last vestige of herself that was ever Admin. She sides with non-cits now. Anyone who hedges their bets by playing the Admin's game is nothing but a tool to her, or an impediment.

Quantum's face turns red. This is the first time he's been at a disadvantage since abducting me on the docks, and he doesn't like the situation. He points a small-caliber pistol with a silencing barrel at Vitruzzi. She and the other three have spread out at arm's length, blocking the stairwell and keeping them covered a few meters away from where Hirota holds me at gunpoint. If shooting starts, there's enough equipment in the room that at least David and Rob, who stand on the ends, may be able to dive under cover out of the line of fire. Quantum's third man stands behind them, right where he's most likely to get picked off by Quantum or Hirota's crossfire, so Vitruzzi and Thompson have a better than average chance of not dying if they duck in time. Still, I've had odds I liked a lot better.

Anticipation, fear, and anger mix with every breath taken and exhaled, making the air so dense I could choke on it. No one speaks. Several monitors still feed live footage from cameras placed in various parts of the building, and movement in one of them catches my eye. A municipal emergency truck is pulling into the garage above us and maintenance workers begin to disembark. They'll be here in minutes.

Turning to Quantum, I ask, "So how do you want to do this?"

TWENTY-FIVE

When we enter the warehouse, it's hard to tell if La Mer's nervousness has more to do with the fact that he's meeting Quantum in person or the fact that our group has nearly doubled—and all of us, including Quantum and his compatriots, carry weapons. When the impasse downtown had tilted in our favor, Vitruzzi had gambled they wouldn't be dumb enough to shoot us and expose themselves, so we hadn't disarmed them. If we'd been stopped by Admin security before getting back to the industrial district, this mission would have been over. We're in the middle of the hornet's nest where even the tiniest shake will cause the entire hive to erupt.

After Vitruzzi helped Quantum adjust his perspective, he and his men must have liked the odds less than I did. As the maintenance team descended the stairwell, Quantum led us out of the room through a service tunnel filled with banks of power-storage units serving the downtown area, out through a storage closet for the city's zip-rail line, and topside through the zip-rail station. Without citizen ID, none of us from Agate Beach could take the underground transportation, but Quantum and Rob were able to return to the garage and retrieve their vehicles, just as if they were average citizens on their way home after a day of work. The rest of us waited at a bench outside the station, sheathed in cold sweat and feeling completely naked. All of us but Vitruzzi have been criminals for too long to be at ease standing on the street corner of one of the settled planets, knowing that everyone around us has implicit or explicit authority to detain us, place us under arrest, or if they're security, outright shoot us. V appeared much calmer than I felt, and I couldn't tell what was going on inside her thoughts. I'm not really sure I would have wanted to. In less than half an hour, they returned with both vehicles, and we mixed our teams and drove back here to the decrepit factory.

While La Mer sets up the video feed with Rajcik's footage, I pull Rob aside and ask quietly, not wanting to draw the others' attention, "What are you doing here? You weren't supposed to get involved until we were ready for an outbound ship."

Basking me in a fawning smile, he answers, "Involved? Is that what I am?"

I stare at him blankly, knowing he's misinterpreting my reason for asking. After a pause, he says, "Yeah, I guess that's what I am. Vitruzzi pinged me and said you needed my help. What was I supposed to do?"

"We can't trust these wire-rats. They could turn you in." I don't add the fact that I'm relying on him to stay in the clear in order for David and I to get new identities. "I know you know that, so . . ."

His smile tightens as he realizes that what I'm really trying to figure out is his angle. What's he getting out of this?

"Losing you again would be worse than getting compromised, " he says. He catches the way I wince and continues, growing defensive, "Jesus, Aly, why are you still pushing me out? Don't you trust me?"

"Okay. I get it. I just . . . I just don't want to be responsible for what could happen." That came out wrong. "I mean to you," I add hastily.

With a derisive shake of the head, he walks past me, not bothering to respond. Dammit, I really have a way with people. I hadn't meant to . . . to what? Hurt his feelings? I'm too raw, still aching from Karl and the way things had ended. Whatever feelings I'd once had for Rob are part of the past. Right now, all I want is a clean break, a new life, and an escape.

La Mer has set up a monitor for viewing Rajcik's footage and Rob joins the others around it. Thompson is the only man absent, keeping watch on the roof. Night has fallen around us now, the darkness close and dangerous, more like the walls of a prison than a cloak of anonymity. I see David lean toward him and say something, and Rob responds with a sharp shrug. Feeling small and mean, like child who has cruelly pulled the wings off a butterfly, I stay where I am, keeping my distance.

"Aly, will you make sure all the window and door covers are tight?" La Mer asks. "We don't want any sound to carry outside and draw attention."

I make a circuit around the small room—once used as an office or file room—checking on the panels we'd placed over all the openings, then give La Mer a nod to let him know things are good to go.

He stares at the screen as he places a disc in the connected console. "T'Kai made the transmissions using digital blocking codes, but Rajcik recorded everything with a nonlinked camera disguised inside part of his ship's nav console housing." His tone is neutral, but the shake in his hands shows he's grappling with a bad case of nerves. He actions the video and the monitor switches to life, showing us an image of T'Kai's face staring out of the communication display in the *Temptation*'s cockpit. The camera's perspective is odd, capturing the scene from below and slightly to the side, turning T'Kai's tan features and narrow, almond-shaped eyes into a hatchet's profile. This is the first time I've seen the man, and though his skin is flawless, the rigid, distinguished posture and wash of gray in his eyebrows suggest he's an older man, maybe early seventies, but it's hard to know for sure.

The video plays.

T'Kai: "I want the entire place destroyed. You'll have entry access near the weapons labs, hangar zero-one. There will be plenty of items there that can accomplish this task."

Rajcik: "Is that where I'll find the Nova?"

T'Kai: "The Nova and any number of other useful pieces of equipment you can turn into profit. Just remember that your first directive is to destroy the Fortress. Concentrate on that or you'll see no reward. Understand?"

The camera never captures Rajcik's face, but the low-pitched growl in his voice makes his disgust of T'Kai clear. "What will it take to override the airlocks?"

"I have a man on the inside. Command Major Sydney. He'll be at the helm when you arrive to grant you access and open the airlocks. However, he specifically will need to be disposed of once his usefulness to you is complete. I assume that won't be an issue."

Rajcik doesn't bother to respond other than to say, "Send me his direct link." He pauses, and we can see T'Kai's hand moving to cut the transmission, but Rajcik halts him with another question. "This is more than we originally agreed on. I'll assume this replaces your claim to anything I make."

T'Kai: "Yes, you can assume that. The Fortress has become an unexpected liability. It's costing me too much to keep the personnel quiet and I have intelligence that there may be an attempt to expose the cause of the Soldier's Rebellion. Experimentation on our fine military was, perhaps, an overly ambitious enterprise. Three weeks, Rajcik. If you haven't completed the mission by then, you can also make the assumption that our deal is null and void."

The image on Rajcik's monitor flicks off and La Mer disengages the disc.

"Motherfuh . . ." Rob's voice fades out. Besides him, I'm the only one who hasn't seen this footage, and I'm just as speechless. I thought I'd stopped Rajcik by forcing him to detonate the Nova inside the Fortress. I'd been happy to see the station destroyed, but knowing that had been T'Kai's intent all along sucks all the joy out of the event.

I feel sick. The Soldier's Rebellion was rumored to have been started because of an Admin-created virus, the Crowers Croup. People said it got loose and the Admin didn't do enough to control it or to protect the soldiers whose job it was to quarantine its victims. What T'Kai just said proves that those rumors were partly true, but that the whole truth is much, much worse. The virus had come out of Admin labs, and they'd been using it, and probably other biological experiments like it, on soldiers from the very beginning. Vitruzzi's daughter and husband had died because of T'Kai's god complex. Human experimentation, not only on non-cits, the supposed waste and by-products of the species, but the soldiers who *volunteered* their lives for the Admin and the Corps. Used like lab rats, and for what? Did T'Kai hope to achieve some kind of bug-resistant soldier, or was he merely using them for his own demented scientific curiosity? The more I learn of the Admin's schemes, the more I start to believe that even the best in humanity can never hold a candle to the worst in us. Does power make you lose perspective the way T'Kai and those monsters posing as scientists did?

Vitruzzi catches my eye and says, "Now you see why we kept Rajcik close. This is big, bigger than the data we got from the Fortress. This paints the full picture and gives us what we need to settle the score."

I'm not sure if it's the slight catch in her voice or the way her eyes jerk away from me as she says this, but I can see that she doesn't just mean settling the score for the Beachers. She's talking *personally*, settling the score for herself and her dead family. She'll never admit it, but this time, it's about revenge.

And I'm all for it. Working with Rajcik is dangerous and unpredictable, but no more dangerous and unpredictable than letting a murderer like T'Kai, a murderer with the power of the entire government backing him up, run loose. It's gone beyond simply wanting to be left alone. At this point we *have* to do something to try and restore some fairy tale of balance to the social order of the system, at least make T'Kai accountable for what he's done. That, and only that, is the mission.

"What's it going to be Quantum? Is this information *worthy* of your help?" Vitruzzi asks. I can tell she's rattled; it's unusual for Vitruzzi to use sarcasm to make her point.

The wire-rat looks more off center than I've seen yet, but there's also a subtle look of sly contemplation shrink-wrapping his features and pulling his eyes into slits. He's thinking hard about how to play this and about what he can manipulate to his own advantage. Finally, he says, "Is this all you have?"

His flippant dismissal of the video's potential impact surprises me. "All we have? What more could we possibly need? We've got a Ministry director on video admitting to using soldiers for human experimentation and paying off scientists to keep their mouths shut about it." David gives me a look, warning me to calm down, but I ignore him. "He caused the goddamn Soldier's Rebellion for chrissakes! This is enough for the Admin to burn him at the stake!"

Quantum gives me a look of mild contempt. "The Admin will not punish him." He walks toward the back of the room, his shoulders slightly hunched and his head down, as if deep in thought. "They will do nothing except shield him and alter the story for citizens to make this all appear to be nothing but a hoax, a terrorist attempt to launch another rebellion. The Admin will be quick to point out that it was a rogue virus that decimated so many citizens before the Rebellion, that it spread too fast to contain, but that their quick quarantine response saved millions of lives. They will repeat the rhetoric that the soldiers who died were a regrettable loss, but they were good men and women who died for everyone's safety.

"Then they will say that those noble heroes' dignity and honor are being sullied by you malcontents who have bobbed up from the muck of the far-flung backwater Spectras—that you were given a chance at a better life but chose to spit on it." He faces us again, his eyes blazing with dreadful intelligence. "They covered the Rebellion up too perfectly when it occurred, and now they hold that possibility as a threat over the heads of the citizens as a representation of how easily all of our rights and safeties can be taken away if these kinds of antisocial actions are allowed to flourish. They will show that your supposed proof of T'Kai's treason is nothing but a false rendering by deserters that have not yet been caught. And then—then they will find you and squash you until you are nothing but a stain on a lab table."

"Then what, Quantum? You don't think we should blackmail T'Kai?" La Mer asks.

"You'll be wasting your time."

"There's more," Vitruzzi says.

He looks at her, raising one eyebrow.

"We have several drives of data on the experiments they were running. Tests, results, types of viruses, strains of disease—we have the proof to backup his admission. The digital signatures tie it all directly to the Admin."

"And you want to go to T'Kai with it, use it to threaten him into releasing your friends. And then what will you do? Go back to living on the rock you came from?"

She doesn't respond.

"You don't get it. You don't know, do you?" Seeing our confused looks, Quantum shakes his head. "All you Spectres are nothing but ghosts anyway. You're already dead."

TWENTY-SIX

The next half hour is a surreal nightmare of information overload as Quantum launches into an explanation of what the Cabinet of Directorates of the Political and Capital Administration of the Advanced Worlds has been discussing—vehemently and thoroughly—for the last three months.

Quantum wasn't merely theorizing when he said the Admin will have no problem selling the public on the idea that deserters and malcontents are flourishing and threatening everyone's safety; they've kept that message on slow-drip through the media for some time now, every new "catastrophe" instigated by non-cits feeding the public's fears, slowly building their resentment, indifference, and intolerance toward the inhabitants of the Spectras, commonly called Spectres. First the Soldier's Rebellion and now the destruction of the Fortress have rattled the Admin much more than we knew, and their decision to rescind transport contracts and limit travel into and out of Obal airspace is a strategy to serve a more sinister purpose than simply controlling criminal activity.

They plan to completely wipe out the populations of non-cits living on the Spectras.

Quantum's network of wire-rats have had spy-hacking ears and eyes on the Admin since before the Rebellion; he says that it's become clear that the Admin has been prepping for a showdown and just waiting for an excuse for carte blanche freedom to implement total dominion over the system. According to Quantum, their plans focus specifically on the Spectras for the simple reason that non-cits are harder to track and control. Then he brought up something that surprised us all. The Admin has the perfect weapon for the job: the soil amendment compound.

As Quantum lays out the puzzle pieces, I know I'm not the only person in the room whose stomach does flip-flops at his description of the soil compound. The missing piece that Bodie needed would have killed us. Originally called the "C-virus," the compound is a terraforming additive that, indeed, converts marginal soil into a more fecund, life-sustaining earth, but it's first phase is pure poison that kills everything it comes into contact with. It takes between five to ten years for it to become totally inert, during which time the chemical process slowly alters the soil, supercharging it for new growth. The Admin can effectively kill two birds with one stone if they deploy it on the Spectras; clean out the troublesome settlers and provide fertile new grounds for food production and resource development.

Quantum gives us a few minutes to digest all of this, then says, "What if I told you that I know a better way to use this information you acquired from the Fortress?"

"It's our show, Quantum. We just need your transceiver." Vitruzzi's face is an iron mask, inflexible and resolute. Quantum could tell her he is the Messiah in the flesh, but she is finished listening to his stories and machinations. Despite the feeling in my gut that he's not lying, I still try to convince myself he is, and I think she's doing the same thing. He's perceptive enough to realize it and shakes his head slightly, but presses on.

"Can you think of another reason the Admin would be taking a census of Spectra settlements?" He pauses, letting the question taint the air with its obvious implications. "They need to know the numbers they're dealing with, of course. In order to prepare."

I turn to Rob. "You've been working as a contractor for a few years, Rob. Does any of this sound real to you? Have you heard anything about it?"

Rob looks like I feel, sick and angry. "I'm just a contractor, Aly, what could I possibly know?"

Quantum continues, "There are others who want to see an end to this kind of tyranny. If you can truly tie T'Kai to this information, this data, enough people could be convinced of the Administration's duplicity to force the entire regime to its knees. There are many that want this ... revolution."

"You're saying there are people looking for a reason to overthrow the Admin?" David asks.

"Not just a reason. The reasons exist all around us. No, people need proof. Maybe this is the proof."

I'm trying to hold back my bitter laughter at his absurd idea. "Do we have to remind you that they're the ones with most the guns? How can you realistically imagine trying to fight them?" I look at Vitruzzi for confirmation that this guy is nuts, but her expression is surprisingly contemplative. She holds Quantum's eyes with her own, and I get the sense they're communicating on a level I can't quite grasp. "V?"

"How many are there?" she asks.

"Many." He doesn't drop her eyes.

The rest of us are silent, watching this exchange. Hirota, thin and wiry, and the other man, finally identified as Faisal, bigger and mugging like an angry rhino, scan us with busy eyes, though they don't move. "V, you're not seriously—"

"Quiet." She looks at me sideways, speaking sharply. Her attitude *is* serious, as serious as I've ever seen it. It's enough to make me shut up, at least for now. David and I exchange a glance, his expression mirroring my own wary curiosity.

Vitruzzi continues, "Let's say, for the sake of conversation, there was a possibility of starting a rebellion, something substantial, organized, equipped. You say you know of others, but what do you know *about* them? I've seen from the experience here with La Mer that your type wouldn't know each other if you met on the street. With that being the case, how would you mobilize? What would be your plan of attack? How would you initiate this rebellion?"

Before responding, the wire-rat sweeps the room with a paranoid glare. "We can discuss that at another time."

"We don't have time."

"No, Vitruzzi. All you *do* have is time."

Her jaw clenches, but there's no intimidating him. Right now, we have nothing to offer him in exchange. Did we really expect him to give us access to his hardware out of the goodness of his heart? La Mer believed he would, but La Mer's been on the run since the Rebellion, and things have changed for people living outside the Admin's laws. No one who doesn't want next week's newcast to include their obituary would risk what we're asking for the simple satisfaction of making trouble for the Admin. And Quantum has made his price clear.

"We already have a deal. The use of your transceiver for our information. In that order," Vitruzzi says, staring at him with acetone intensity.

Quantum faces her with squared shoulders and an unwavering glare, matching her intensity. Then, for the first time, his lips curl up into a grin that's almost frightening in its ferocity. "As you wish. We have to go to Obal 6." And in a final surreal act, he reaches out to shake hands, sealing a contract that could—if not for the complete insanity of the idea—potentially bring on the downfall of the Admin.

TWENTY-SEVEN

"We're going to have to get a bigger ship." David's voice tickles my ear as his elbow jabs me in the ribs. The half sleep, half daze I've been fading in and out of like a faulty radio transmission for the last six hours comes to an annoying halt. He laughs at my disgusted look and stands up to go to the head.

He's right; this boat is not built for eight people. In the forty-plus hours since we broke through Obal 10's atmosphere and slipped into the general din of interplanetary traders and traffic, I've become more in touch with my kneecaps than I ever really wanted to be. With a hull that is merely a dual row of jumpseats, a toilet, overhead storage cabinets, and a single sleeping bench at the rear of the passenger cabin, moving around isn't an option. The only place tall enough for a person to stand at their full height is the narrow space in the aisle between the overhead lockers that crowd the ceiling. David, Vitruzzi, La Mer, and I, along with Quantum and Hirota, fill up the jumpseats while Rob and Thompson, the only other pilot among us, rotate at the helm. Quantum had left his third man behind, and I almost wish Vitruzzi would have asked me to stay back on Obal 10, too—I've kept my claustrophobia at bay by trying to stay asleep, but a person can only sleep so long. The hop was never intended to support so many people on any kind of lengthy journey, and it's starting to feel like we're attempting to fly to Saturn in an iron maiden.

We have enough water and a solid enough capture-and-recycle system to make it for at least two weeks, provided no one gets attached to the idea of regular showers, but food is tight. We're small enough not to be noticed by most patrol ships in the Obals—being basically nothing but a personal vehicle for jumping between local planets and moons. Usually these types of hops are owned by wealthy travelers jumping between part-time homes or as transports for business stakeholders to get to and from franchise hubs. But if anyone locks on our flight path and does a quick analysis, they'll catch on pretty quickly that we're neither one of those.

Then there's the ship itself. I don't know where Rob picked up such a run-down piece of junk, but I'm a little surprised, and more than a little grateful, that we're still in flight. The interior has been scoured of unnecessary bells and whistles—like seat pads, sound dampeners, or up to code ventilation—making the ride a little like being stuck inside a tin can being flushed through a galactic sewer. The outer hull isn't much better and looks like the ship's been used by a flock of birds as a shithouse for the last three hundred years or so. When we loaded up at the Tunis City docks, the engine housing was so encrusted with grit and droppings that I wasn't sure it would be able to overcome the cross friction gumming up its RPMs enough to break through atmo. Yet, despite its complete derelict façade and torture chamber fuselage, the ship has flown smoothly, and it's obvious Rob has kept this hunk of metal around for a scenario such as this.

Our time aboard has not been wasted. After getting clear of Obal 10, Quantum made it clear that nothing would be sent using his transceiver that wasn't first run by him, so he and La Mer immediately went to work on portable consoles looking for any kinks in La Mer's transmitting worm. After examining it, Quantum came down on him hard for not building redundancy into the signal rerouting piece of the program. Worse, he'd claimed that the transmission's origination source will be easy to find if the satellite administrators are looking. David and Thompson had barely jumped between the two of them in time before La Mer—interpreting the statement as an accusation that he'd been responsible for the Corps coming to Agate Beach and rounding up the settlers—did something we'd all regret.

Why anyone would be looking is the real question. If the worm works the way La Mer built it, no one should know the satellites are being hacked. Besides, it's hardly an issue at this point—we don't plan on staying in one place long enough to give the Admin time to catch up to us. The bigger problem now is managing two-way communication. If we send a message to T'Kai with the expectation that he'll reply, we have to give him a coordinate to reply to, and triangulating our location will be easy from there.

Or so I assume. We're only ten hours out from Obal 6's orbit and Thompson is at the helm, giving Rob time to catch some sleep before the next phase of our mission. Quantum stands up to stretch his legs and Vitruzzi asks, "Why Obal 6? Why not put the transceiver on one of the Spectras?"

"Because Bi Schtum is one of its moons," he responds matter-of-factly, "and home to enough citizen-owned satellites to mask transmissions sent from Obal 6 for a while. We can stay until we hear back from T'Kai. Then we'll have to move."

"What do citizen satellites matter? I thought the whole point of this worm was to use Admin TDRSs," David says from the rear of the fuselage, yelling to be heard over the engines.

Quantum leans back against the wall next to the cockpit hatch, the expression on his face asking, *Why do I have to deal with such morons?* He levels a flat, lizardlike gaze on David for a few seconds before replying. "There are people working from inside—Admin personnel—who are helping us. They forward things that are useful, but for reasons I hope I don't have to illustrate, we cannot let these be sent to us directly. Some of the satellites work as our hubs. They receive and bounce incoming transmissions, but they filter the messages through scramblers that hide their final coordinates. I will contact our allies who have hardware around Bi Schtum and the neighboring planets. Any messages we receive will only be traceable within this quadrant. The Admin may come in and block or destroy the satellites, but unless they are very, very lucky, they will not isolate those that we'll be using right away." He lets this information soak in and then looks around for comprehension. My face reflects the same confusion on everyone else's.

He continues, disdain thick in his voice. "If T'Kai responds, he will use digitally encoded transmissions that cannot be unscrambled by Admin satellite programs. Only Corps and non-Admin satellites will transmit encoded messages, and T'Kai will know—or think he knows—that we don't have a receiver that can pick up Corps transmissions. It is not legal to own receiver codes for those frequencies, and difficult to build one that isn't traceable. Of course, my transceiver *can* pick up Corps transmissions, but that is beside the point." Quantum smiles, pleased with himself. "If he wants to ensure his message will get through, and stay untraceable by any unwelcome Admin ears, he'll have to use alternative satellites. Satellites controlled by *my* allies. With the program Axone has written, he will not be able to figure out where the signal is coming from, but to respond, we will have to point him toward the haystack we are hiding in."

"It sounds like you've been planning something like this for a while," Vitruzzi says.

"We will only have a single opportunity of this nature, and we have been waiting for it. Why would we not be prepared?"

"I'd like to know more about who this 'we' is."

Quantum doesn't respond, but his eyes stray to the opposite side of the fuselage, and after a moment, I realize they've settled on Rob.

QUANTUM'S TRANSCEIVER SITS on the roof of a warehouse inside a pocket of indistinct buildings near the small down of Rej on Obal 6. Like the majority of planets in this quadrant, this one is mainly water with several landmasses, mostly small habitable continents. With the abundance of water, many of the local populace's resources—steel, iron, other metals—are shipped in, and what isn't comes from oceanic drilling. The surplus is stored in these structures and most of the area's activity consists of roving drones used to keep an eye on the place. There aren't many people, and the few we saw as we came in were civilians minding their own business, busy at work.

Quantum directs the hop into a warehouse, which he opens using a remote transmission key. I'm so happy to be out of confinement that I want to run laps around the area just to stretch my legs and move my body again. Instead, we convene inside a cramped com room after being warned to stay inside and keep quiet. It's clear from Quantum's face that I don't have a choice in the matter, but I refuse to sit down a minute longer, broadcasting my decision by leaning grumpily against the wall.

Everyone busies themselves with getting blood back into their limbs while Quantum contacts his resources and arranges for cooperation with the satellite transmissions. Before I'm really prepared, he turns to Vitruzzi.

"Ready to begin your show."

She doesn't hesitate. "Is it on the right channel?"

"Your transmission will be sent directly to the official frequency belonging to T'Kai's office in the Ministry. It will be reviewed and, if you are convincing enough, brought directly to his attention."

She straightens up so that she's poised on the very edge of her seat. The building is deep and long with no windows, making it dark inside, with only dim green LEDs dotting the ceiling and casting a swampy glow over us. As she looks down at the com unit, lines of deadly seriousness create deep, shadowed grooves across her forehead and beside her mouth.

The sound of the mic activating reminds me of a trigger. "This is Captain Eleanor Vitruzzi of the *Sphynx* ISPS, registration ID N295831, formerly a legally contracted arms and cargo transporter for the Ministry of S&E. I'm a resident of the non-citizen settlement known as Agate Beach on the southern hemisphere of Spectra 6. Recently, the majority of the population of our settlement was illegally arrested and one member murdered by Corps soldiers. The remainder were transported to the prisoner colony on Keum Libre without cause. All of these events occurred by order of Director Kurosawa T'Kai. I demand these people be set free and our settlement reestablished with a guarantee of no further Admin or Corps interference.

"I am in a unique position to make these kinds of demands. If you doubt me, I urge you to review the flight logs of the MCACS PCA *Bellerophon*, which was lost en route to the Admin space station known as the Fortress. You'll find the derelict in Beta Delta, where we left it after using it to infiltrate the station and destroy it. You have five hours to respond using the frequency uplink we send." The glowing console of the com unit fades out as she releases the transmit button and hands it back to Quantum to input the freq.

"What if he doesn't respond?" David asks, his question not aimed at anyone in particular.

Unexpectedly, Quantum answers, "Then you give the assets to me and my network. We will take it from there."

I inquire, "And what about our friends on Keum Libre?"

"There are martyrs in every revolution."

It's the flat, uncaring tone in his voice that gets to me. "Fuck that, Quantum. You've helped us out some, but you don't get to decide if our friends live or die."

"I am not deciding. All of you made that decision for them."

His statement smacks me into silence—because it's true. Whatever would have happened, by threatening T'Kai, we're no longer an anonymous annoyance but identified enemies, and our friends are his collateral.

Rob speaks up. "What would be the point of wavecasting the fact that T'Kai is some kind of villain, anyway? What can it possibly achieve?" He sits forward on his seat in the same alert position as Vitruzzi and focuses on each of us in turn. "At best, you'll make a lot of people in the system upset, or angry. But that won't make most of them want to automatically give up their entire way of life. T'Kai's just one man, he doesn't speak for the whole government, who, in case you've all forgotten, wasn't completely aware of what he was up to in the first place."

"But they're just as complicit, Rob," I respond. "Don't you

remember all the shit we did in the Corps? The people, mostly inno-cent people, we were ordered to 'suppress'? That wasn't just a Corps decision; those directives came from the Admin. From the govern-ment. And now, this chemical they have that will wipe out the Spec-tras—" Why is he playing devil's advocate? It's too late for that.

"*Some* of those decisions were Admin, but they had their reasons. They mostly take care of people—healthcare, stability, safe planets for people to live on. And you don't know if this wire-rat is even telling the truth about that soil compound!"

"It's right for people to know," David interjects. "We should tell them what T'Kai is doing anyway. Let people decide for themselves."

"You're just going to introduce instability, and like Quantum says, they'll discount the information as fraudulent the minute it gets out. You'll get nowhere. If T'Kai doesn't cooperate with you, you'll gain nothing by implicating him anonymously."

"Do you think we should just let him get away with it?" I ask.

"That's not what—"

I don't let him finish. "I can't believe I'm saying this, but I agree with Rajcik. T'Kai has to be brought to justice for the things he's done, the people he's hurt."

"But Aly, we're hardly in a position to—"

"*We are in a position.*" Quantum glares at Rob, anger blooming in red stripes along his cheekbones. "You are not listening to me."

"You mean you have enough allies to go to war? With the Admin?" Rob bites the end off his words, his own anger bleeding through. "Then what are you waiting for? If there are that many people who want to overthrow them, there must be a reason. They don't need this information, or *evidence*, that a single member of the Directorate is crooked. If all these people you're talking about want to revolt, they must already believe the Cabinet is corrupt."

"This is the type of evidence citizens should see in order to help them decide which side to take," Quantum responds, eyes spitting defiance.

"I'm with these guys," Thompson chimes in. "Everyone knows the Admin is fucking them over. They just need a reason to do something about it, something to set them off. If knowing the Admin is using its own as bags of test meat doesn't wake people up, let 'em fuckin' die. Let 'em drown in their own rotting guts."

As crude as his words are, no one disagrees, not even Rob. I lean toward him and remind him as gently as I can, "You came with us by choice, Rob. You knew it could come to this."

He holds my eyes for a few seconds, his eyebrows still raised and causing wrinkles to ladder up his forehead. Then he sighs and leans back in his chair. "Yeah, I did, didn't I?"

Vitruzzi reaches for the com unit Quantum still holds. "I want to send a message to the *Sphynx.* Can you give them the same transmission coordinates to respond to?"

AFTER VITRUZZI SENDS word to the *Sphynx,* the rest of us spread out inside the warehouse, killing time as we wait for T'Kai to make his move. We're all edgy and eager to hear back from our crew. Another advantage of Bi Schtum is its proximity to Keum Libre, approximately four flight days away. If there's any such thing as luck, they've already been able to suss out the prison rock and are waiting for us somewhere between here and there. Rob's hop will make it possible to rendezvous with the ship, and we'll be able to execute the next part of the plan as one team again. If I weren't completely mentally and physically wrung out from everything that's happened since the Corps assaulted the Beach, I'd be anxious and uneasy about being back on board the ship with Karl. Only a couple short weeks have passed since things fell apart between us, but they may as well be years, the distance between us galaxies. I don't even know what I'd say to him at this point.

TWENTY-EIGHT

I t's time I tell Rob that I plan on taking him up on his offer.

The warehouse contains orderly stacks of cargo crates almost the size of Rob's hop, and I wander around for a while trying to find him. I don't have any luck, so I nudge David, who's fallen asleep leaning back against a crate. Payback. Irritably, he grunts that Rob's gone back to his ship.

Rob is also probably trying to stockpile some shut-eye, but this is important and I don't know when I'll get another chance to talk to him. The hatch is pulled closed but not latched and I enter quietly, surprised when I don't see him lying on the bench in the fuselage's rear. Except for the light emitting from the cockpit, the interior is dark. The back of his head is just visible over the headrest of the pilot's seat, and I walk up and lean casually against the wall.

"Hi."

He jumps and spins the seat around quickly, his eyes wide. "Jesus! You scared me. How long have you been standing there?"

"I just walked in. What are you doing?"

"Just going through the works, making sure things are all good to go. I don't exactly trust Thompson, so I thought a systems check wouldn't hurt." He runs a finger along the com console control bar to shut it down.

"That's probably a good idea."

"What's up? Have we heard back from anyone?"

"No, not yet." I pause and take a deep breath, as if I'm about to jump in over my head, then let the words tumble out. "I've been thinking about what we talked about, about buying myself a new identity and becoming a citizen, and I want to do it."

The look of relief that springs to his face is oddly surprising. "I'm really happy to hear you say that, Aly. Really happy. I think it's the best choice you could possibly make."

"Yeah. That is, if we live through this."

"We will. I know we will. This deal with T'Kai is insane, and to be honest, I don't know what Vitruzzi thinks will happen. I want to help the Beachers, but I mean it when I say that I'm not going to die for this mission." The laugh lines that groove the edges of his mouth pull down sternly, stretching his lips to thin, bloodless stripes. I'm not sure how to respond. If T'Kai comes after us, dying is the best thing that could happen. Rob must know that.

"Hey," David says, leaning into the fuselage door, out of breath. "We just got word back from Brady. Come on."

We can't get back to the com room fast enough. It's been less than an hour since Vitruzzi sent the transmission to the *Sphynx*. For them to be able to respond so quickly means they must be close, probably in the same quadrant, and able to make use of the higher density of uncontrolled citizen satellites. Nearly shaking with impatience, Vitruzzi waits for everyone to settle, then plays the message.

Patrick is seated at the console in the *Sphynx*'s communication room. He looks tired and worn, with dark circles embedded in the skin under his eyes, but he's smiling. "Your message just came in, and I can't tell you how happy we all are to hear that you're safe. Everyone here is fine. Here's the rundown on what's been going on.

"When we left R'Kadia, we set a direct course to KL with bypasses around Corps security substations between here and there. It worked;

we haven't been in contact with any of their ships so far, and we arrived in KL orbit three days ago. There's no security outside of the moon's atmosphere, so we went down for a better look. The only patrols we've seen are done by remote sentries, all below atmo, and only around the penal colony. They don't seem concerned about anyone showing up here, and Venus has been able to maneuver around all of the drones.

"We were able to do a planet-wide sweep. It's mostly water with five land masses big enough to support a colony or more. The prison island was covered by fog and low clouds when we were in range, so we couldn't get a good look at anything. The climate sensors picked up some weak signs of civilization, but there aren't a lot of people there, that's for sure. The other islands were completely devoid of infrastructure.

"There's an Admin structure, some kind of oceanic command station, with a good-sized landing platform about six klicks from the prisoner's island. From what we saw, it's the only place a ship as big as the *Sphynx* will be able to set down, at least to get access to the prison compound. From what we could pick up from the scanners, the island is just a jungle, either tree-covered or marshy, with no clearings. If it's anything like the other islands we flew over, it'll be a nightmare trying to get in there. Rajcik says it's all changed from when he was a prisoner here, says the place use to be mostly tundra with no forest or jungle, but Venus assures us the scanners are right. So, the Admin platform is the chokepoint. I'll send you the digitals we took after this message so you can see for yourself.

"Nothing we saw could help us confirm the Beachers' status, or if they're even there, but it started getting too risky to stay in KL's airspace. More Corps ships arrived yesterday, flying live patrols over the penal colony. I don't know if there's something going on down there, but we boogied. It's gotten too busy up here for our taste. We're en route to your quadrant now and will wait for word from you there. I don't know what, but we're going to have to come up with a diversion if we're going to get access to that landing platform. We're putting our heads together on it, you do the same. And don't wait long to send word." Brady reaches out toward the screen and gently touches it. "I love you, Eleanor. *Sphynx* out."

The barometer of collective anticipation and anxiety drops for everyone in the room. I draw my first almost-relaxed breath in days, yet we're all still feeling strung out on fear, worry, grief, and fury, the mixture creating a volatile explosive that could ignite at any trigger. Looking around at their faces, I realize the haggardness I saw in Brady's is no different than the rest of us. Rob's the only one who's still cool thanks to the emotional distance he has from the stakes—no one else has that luxury. Quantum and Hirota are the freshest of all of us, still vying for an angle that will bring them out on top. Even so, Quantum has basically claimed that their ultimate goal is something akin to a sparking civil war, and nobody can look forward to something like that without feeling the weight of future destruction trampling them down into their own version of hell.

"T'Kai has under three hours left to reply. Eleanor, we need to make ready to rendezvous with the *Sphynx* if he doesn't. I don't like saying it, but this mission could end right here." Rob's voice is calm, and though no one else likes what he's saying either, we've all been thinking it.

"You seem in a hurry to give up," Quantum replies.

Animosity between the two men sparks like flint and stone. Rob's jaw tightens for a minute as he tries to bite back his words, but it doesn't work. "What do you think is going to happen here? All of you? T'Kai's just going to bend over and take this? He's already shown you how far he'll go to shut up anyone who crosses him. He was willing to blow up an entire goddamn space station. And he's well-enough protected that he got away with it."

Quantum looks him over, derision turning his features stony. Thompson stiffens beside me, and I glance down to see that he's drawn his sidearm, letting it dangle by his thigh. Alarm floods my nerves.

Thompson says, "Quantum's right, Cross. You're pretty eager to give up, and you seem to know a lot about T'Kai."

Rob's seen enough combat to know when things are verging on

the edge of chaos, and his face stretches into a sneer as he responds, "Any moron can tell you exactly the same thing I just did." He looks around at the rest of us. "And if you're implying what I think you are, let me ask this: Can someone tell me what the hell he's doing here anyway? If memory serves, he and his boss already made a deal with T'Kai once. If anyone should know what kind of man T'Kai is, Thompson, it's you."

"Fuck you—" Thompson begins to rise from his seat, bringing his pistol up, but stops with a jerk when he feels the barrel of my Sinbad pressed into his rib cage.

"I think everyone should calm down," I say.

Vitruzzi's face has gone the color of a corpse, but she's not looking at us, her eyes are on the com console, fixed on a green indicator that blinks languidly. A transmission is coming in, and it's live.

"Quantum." Her voice is hushed, almost reverent. She *wants* something to go down with T'Kai, and realizing that makes my arms dimple with goose bumps.

The wire-rat moves toward a selector on the console to play the transmission, but Vitruzzi stops him. "No, open up a video link. I want to see him."

He sets it up and Vitruzzi, still standing, stares into the transmitter's feed and clicks it on. The com monitor is almost as long as my torso and mounted on the wall. T'Kai's face fills the oversized screen.

TWENTY-NINE

" Ah, Dr. Vitruzzi. A pleasure." The image is much better resolution than Rajcik's makeshift recording, and my attention is instantly captured by the man's eyes—one a limpid brown and the other an unsettling, almost cataract blue. He's sitting cross-legged behind a table made of unusual wood that glints with an oily burnish. The room he's in is devoid of any furnishings except a giant warrior mask taking up most of the wall behind him. His business-class suit and the carpet are both a crisp and impeccable white. "We've been keeping an eye on you for a long time. No, don't look so surprised—a mind as talented as yours is not an easy loss for the Administration. There was that . . . unfortunate situation with your family, so we of course understood your decision to leave the Medical Directorate. But don't think that your whereabouts and your activities have gone unnoticed." He smiles a perfect smile, his teeth even and as white as his flawless suit. He speaks to her as if they've known each other for years, maybe shared formal meals at posh restaurants or drank cognac together in a mutual friend's living room. "We did hope you would find your way back to the Administration, but we never expected it to be in this manner."

Vitruzzi stands motionlessly, her face still drained of blood. She opens her mouth to say something, but T'Kai cuts her off. "No, no need to respond. We are quite aware of the accouterments of the lifestyle you and your fellow, ah, villagers have collected. You should know that you have nothing that the Admin would miss overmuch. There are the weapons, of course, but the fact is you could do very little damage with what you've managed to appropriate." He sits rigidly behind the desk, never moving. His hands lie placidly on his knees, and only his gleaming eyes and his mouth give any indication he's not some type of robot or statue. "Despite your Protean personality, Eleanor—if I may—your brilliance in your field has remained almost unmatched. We consider the things you've stolen to be a small severance for your contributions to the advancement of biomedics and engineering. Your husband was a good scientist, not the greatest, but good. Still, his abilities could never compare to yours. It was a blow when you left us. Unfortunately, it's now too late to reconsider."

The rest of us sit at an angle that inhibits T'Kai from seeing us and I'm oddly relieved. There's something so inhuman and cold in his mismatched eyes that I don't want them on me. I can't tell if he's trying to ingratiate himself with Vitruzzi or piss her off. Men like him are so used to speaking obliquely, you wonder if they even know what they're trying to express. In any case, it's clear he's done his research and his patronizing speech is having an effect on Vitruzzi. I haven't seen that look on her face since she asked Karl to kill the captain of the MCACS we'd stolen to break into the Fortress. There's no mercy in that look, no hesitation; it's as stern and set as a tribal chieftain ordering a sacrifice to the slaughter. If T'Kai were here, I'd recommend he start writing his own obituary.

"You know why we contacted you, T'Kai."

"On the contrary. You've placed demands, ones that are so completely outside the realm of reasonable that, if you were still at your post in the Ministry, I would have no choice but to initiate a formal inquiry into your judgment."

"But you're responding, which means you must have found the

Bellerophon. And you know we've been to the Fortress. You can guess what we brought back with us."

Like a shape-shifting necromancer, his friendly smile suddenly morphs into the toothy sneer of a barracuda. "Already I tire of your facile and indirect threats. They annoy me. Tell me something interesting before I regret having let my admiration for the work you've done expose me to petty extortion. If there's anything that I find more pathetic than a shining star that's lost its luster, it's seeing that same star forget its place in the univer—"

"Shut the fuck up and listen, T'Kai. We have proof of what was happening on the Fortress. We could bring you and the entire Ministry of S&E to its knees if we wanted to." Vitruzzi matches his ferocity with icy determination and cold, cold words. "But that's not what we want. My terms were clear in the first transmission you received. Free the Agate Beach settlers, let them return to Spectra 6, and keep the Corps off their backs for good. If you do, Rajcik's footage of your discussion of the Nova and destroying the Fortress, and the data of the biowarf testing being done on non-citizens *and soldiers* will be returned to you. Otherwise, we'll wavecast it to every human being in the system. Your choice."

T'Kai's face has gone the same color as Vitruzzi's and his words are like short, brutal jabs thrown in a bar fight. "János Rajcik was killed during his terrorist activities that resulted in the destruction of that space station. I have never been in contact with that criminal—"

"Shut up," she cuts him off again, her patience for bullshit snuffed. She leans forward and places her hands on the com console, her face centimeters from the monitor. If T'Kai were actually here, she'd be in range to kiss him. "Listen to me, T'Kai, I'm not playing games here. You think you know me? Then you know how determined I am. You know that I'm not going to quit just because you flatter or threaten me. This is how it's going to be. You either do what I ask, set the Beachers free, or I will bring you and every minister in the Cabinet down. Think it over. You have an hour."

She severs the link and the monitor fades into a dull gray that mixes with the green overhead lights, leaving the room as dim as a subterranean tomb.

David says, "What do you think he'll do?"

She's hunched over the console, the ends of her long, curly hair brushing against the controls. She stays there for a minute before answering. "He isn't going to negotiate. I didn't think he would, but I had to see him to find out." She goes silent, not looking at anyone. Finally, she turns around and says, "Quantum, do you have the equipment here to make copies of everything? I'm leaving it with you. The rest of us will rendezvous with the *Sphynx* to try and free the settlers on our own."

"Whoa—hold on," Thompson says. "What are you talking about? You can't leave the footage here with this wire-rat. The deal was to bring T'Kai down."

She ignores him, still speaking to Quantum. "You're our insurance. Give us seven days and then you do whatever you want with that footage. Tell the whole system, I don't care. We're done here."

Thompson jumps up and grabs Vitruzzi by one wrist, towering over her by more than a head, and spins her around to force her to look at him. She's quicker than he expects and faces him with the barrel of one of her pistols pointing into his teeth. "You don't call it, Thompson. *I* call it. You're here because *I* made a deal with Rajcik— now that deal involves him."

Thompson barely breathes, wincing at her like a snake about to strike. Unwilling to carry the confrontation further, she backs away and lowers her weapon. He isn't stupid. He knows the second his hand goes for his gun he'll be target practice for the rest of us. Rage makes his jaw clench and his hollow cheeks flush, but he says nothing.

Vitruzzi looks back at Quantum. "You're prepared to do what you said you'd do?"

He nods.

She looks at Thompson. "Then T'Kai is handled. Now, everyone get out. Take a break. It may be a while before any of us sleep again. I'm calling the *Sphynx*."

"V," I start, but don't get far.

"I'm not arguing. This is not a negotiation. This is done." Her eyes blaze with something that isn't quite anger and isn't quite fear, and I see how close to the edge she is. Something in T'Kai's transmission has hit her deep in the soul, like a pry bar wrenching on the lid of a coffin, and it's hard to say what might be underneath.

THOMPSON SKULKS AWAY into the far corner of the warehouse and throws a crate against the floor, making a lot of harmless noise. Watching him from the corner of my eye, I wait just outside the com room for Vitruzzi and Quantum, who's stayed with her presumably to copy the footage and data. Hirota sits a few meters away on a crate by himself, and La Mer and David keep me company while Rob heads back toward the hop.

David leans against the wall next to the com room door. "What do you think, little sis? Is she going off the deep end?"

I think about it for a minute before answering. "She's definitely closer than I've ever seen her."

"Yeah." He slides down the wall until he's seated and looks out into the dark warehouse. Outside, it's daytime, but the walls block any light from shining in, reinforcing the feeling that we're trapped in a cave. The sound of a distant track vehicle trundling through the area is the only thing breaking the stillness. "You know the chances of us saving the Beachers is just about zero."

Out of the two of us, David is the optimist. It's rare for him to lose heart, and seeing it happening now triggers a primeval fear that tremors up my spine like the aftershocks of an earthquake. "Hey, you forget that we're the same people that destroyed the Admin's most heavily armed space station. If we can do that, saving a few prisoners from a rock that's guarded by nothing but drones won't be hard."

That gets a grin out of him, but it's halfhearted. La Mer and I both sit down beside him and I lean back and close my eyes. It's a futile effort, I know, but there's nothing else I can do for now. No one is talking, and I hear a soft whisper coming from the walls to our left, probably rats or mice looking for nest-building material. After a few minutes, Quantum and Vitruzzi emerge from the com room.

The three of us are on our feet immediately. She looks at us flatly. "Let's get going."

THIRTY

Rob trades off the pilot seat with Thompson and takes a seat next to me on the rear bench. A heavy frown furrows its way down his brow while he stares at the floor distractedly.

"What's the matter?" I ask.

"What?"

"You look like something's wrong." I raise my voice against the engine noise.

"Oh. It's probably not a big deal. There's something wrong with the communication system. I can't transmit. Maybe just a loose circuit board or something."

"Who were you trying to transmit to?"

"Just bouncing some queries around, trying to see who's in the area. I'd like to avoid any Corps ships if we can."

I nod, dropping it. Trying to compete against the hop's rattles and revving is more trouble than it's worth. Everyone else lounges with their eyes closed, probably wishing they could catch some real sleep. The last three days have collapsed together like a waking nightmare, hopping from Tunis City to Obal 6, and now to meet the *Sphynx* on the moon Letum Uti, near Obal 5. From there, Keum Libre is only another day-and-a-half flight time.

We've been in the air thirteen hours with another five to go. Rob has been steadfast at the helm, not taking a break until now. I'm not sure how he's going to hold up once we get aboard the *Sphynx*, but I'm hoping that we'll all be able to take a few hours down time in the relative comfort of the bigger ship. I miss the *Sphynx*. Not just because it has more space to spread out and get some real shut-eye, but because it and the colony of Agate Beach were home to me for the last three months. More home than anyplace has felt in a lot of years, and I've grown attached, despite my own rules against it.

We left Quantum and Hirota behind with basic instructions; give us seven days, then do whatever they want with the footage and data. They have almost no incentive to follow these directions, but Vitruzzi must think they'll comply—or maybe she doesn't see any drawbacks if they don't. Quantum agreed to forward any message that came from T'Kai on to the *Sphynx*, but Vitruzzi made it clear she doesn't expect one. As far as she's concerned, we're on our own and whatever happens to T'Kai is now in the hands of fate.

Based on the intel from Brady, we're gambling on Keum Libre staying minimally guarded. T'Kai may suspect we'll try and rescue the Beachers, but he may not expect our attempt to come so soon. Even though Vitruzzi had given him an hour to respond to her demands, we'd left before he had a chance. He'll expect us to be on the move, so it won't surprise him if we don't have a live-feed link with him next time he tries to contact us. If we have any luck, he'll be able to trace the transmissions to Bi Schtum and look for us there first. Whatever we do, the mission's success hinges on us making our moves before they make theirs.

Which is exactly what Vitruzzi is thinking. I glance at her and realize she's not sleeping. She sits back in the jump seat, her eyes fixed on a spot in the fuselage wall across from her. She's holding something in her hand and every now and then her thumb rubs along the edge of it. A photograph. It doesn't take much guesswork to figure out who it's of. Probably her dead daughter, maybe also her dead husband. Dead because of T'Kai. His experiments, his fault.

David and I were aboard the PCA *Thor's Hammer* patrolling the

Spectras when the Crowers Croup broke out. The Admin kept it quiet for as long as they could after the virus got loose. But soon, word about the Corps being sent in to quarantine masses of citizens in the Obals and rumors that the dead were being burned started to spread. Fast. The Soldier's Rebellion erupted like a gas torch, chaos sweeping through the ranks too swiftly to contain. There was too much happening to be certain of anything, and David and I lost track of distant friends in the Corps who were assigned to the Obals. After the flash fire that launched the Rebellion burned up its fuel, the Admin went to work hunting down those responsible for it, and David and I kept our heads down and kept moving. There was no way to find out if we'd lost any friends, and no point in looking anyway.

For people like Vitruzzi, people who'd shaken hands with the deadly virus and seen their own families destroyed by it, there was no clean break, no easy excuse to forget the past. I can't imagine how much pain she's in, having just been face-to-face with the man who caused the obliteration of her whole world. And who's doing the same thing to her new life a second time. I was closer to completely losing my shit than I care to remember when I thought I'd lost David, but she seems to be staying calm and collected. At least on the surface. If she does lose it, there's no telling what she'll do.

THE HOP DOESN'T HAVE a ship-to-ship airlock seal, so once we arrive in Letum Uti we set it down in a field outside a scratch of a town and wait for the *Sphynx*. The hop's transmitter is still blown, but Vitruzzi had prearranged the pickup with Brady. The shuttle has already arrived by the time we land, and the six of us load up.

Karl is flying the shuttle and turns around with a grin to greet Vitruzzi as we settle into our seats. "It's good to see you again, Captain."

"Same to you."

He nods at La Mer and David, who've taken the seats directly behind the cockpit, and then lets his eyes find mine. "Aly."

"Karl."

"Can we get the fuck out here before some farmer decides to come see why we planted a hop in their field?" Thompson asks.

The ramp door closes and we get airborne.

"Radar picked up two gunships from inside atmo before we left KL, at least that's what we think they were. We couldn't get a positive read, but we didn't want to be IDed, so we kept our distance. We weren't followed." The crew has gathered inside the *Sphynx*'s galley for Brady to lay out what they'd discovered on the prison-rock recon.

"You sure?" Vitruzzi asks from her seat next to him.

"Hundred percent sure, Captain," Venus responds over the intercom from the cockpit.

"Maybe they were bringing in more prisoners," Rob says.

He and Karl stand at opposite ends of the room and do everything in their power to keep from looking in each other's direction. It's been two weeks since I've seen Karl. What will he think of my decision to join Rob and buy back a citizen's life? Am I lying to myself if I think he'll even care?

"We thought of that, and if it's the case, they'll have to drop them on the offshore rig. Maybe it's a failsafe so the prisoners already on the rock can't attempt a takeover or hijack a ship. It's too long to swim to the platform, so we have to assume the only way out of the colony is by boat. The colony itself is spread out along the top of a bluff about three hundred meters above the ocean's surface," Brady continues, outlining the buildings with his index finger on the scans spread across the table. "There's a desalination plant at the cliff's edge that has a pipe dropping down to the sea, and a cargo elevator runs along it, terminating at a dock."

"Which means to get there we'll have to take a boat from the platform," Doug Mason states.

"Right, and first we'll have to disarm whatever security runs it," Brady finishes.

"I can't believe there's *nowhere* to ground a ship on land." I'm seated at one of the galley tables with a plate of food in front of me.

I'm not really hungry, but there's no telling when I'll get another chance for a meal. If you live on the run, you don't hesitate to take advantage of opportunities as soon as they present themselves. "They had to set up at least a temporary building site at some point to even get the platform and desal plant built."

"There used to be," Rajcik announces, his voice a marauding whisper that kills all other sound. "When I got out of there, it was just grass and dirt. No trees, barely even any bushes. There were two landing zones near the colony and half a dozen buildings. "Now"—he stares at the scans—"this. Nothing but jungle."

David and Vitruzzi exchange a glance and he says, "There's something you should know. Something the wire-rat told us."

He gives a brief explanation of the soil compound and its dangers, finishing up with: "It looks like KL may have been one of their original testing grounds for whatever that stuff is. We may even be looking at a dead world." His expression blanches uncertainly for a moment. "I mean, dead in terms of the prison population."

No one likes the sound of that, but Brady says, "No. That isn't the case. We picked up signs of life—of people—when we did the recon. Besides, we all heard the security squad that killed Bodie say they were bringing the settlers here."

The room is silent for a minute as everyone contemplates the possibility that we may be on a wild goose chase. It doesn't go on long before David continues, sounding as if no one is even vaguely entertaining any doubts, "It doesn't look like we could get anything bigger than a shuttle under that canopy, but if we wait for those Corps ships to leave, we can probably access the platform. Do we know what kind of security they have on site?"

"Nothing above decks that we could make out through long-range images," Brady responds. "We couldn't get too close, but the main part of the platform is just open landing tarmac and a small building, probably the command center. Looks like most of the structure is underwater, which makes it that much harder to get to."

"And then there are the drones in the air," Desto adds.

"If we can get the *Sphynx* in range, I think I can neutralize the drones' sentry-net by modifying the trans-worm I built for the satellites. They'll still be out there and they'll still be weaponized, but they won't have the capacity to fire on us," La Mer says.

"How would that work?" Rob asks.

"It's a matter of scrambling their priority matrix." He takes a deep swallow from his cup, obviously secure in his topic, and continues, "Basically, we short-circuit their decision systems; they'll see us, but the AI won't be able to decide on a direct course of action. Their routine patrol programs will stay the same, so they'll move in the right direction, they just won't be able to identify us as a threat."

"This ship has an armed shuttle. Why not just blow them out of the sky?" Thompson asks.

"No, this is better than shutting them down completely because the personnel on the platform will be less suspicious. See, the sentries will still be active, just not reactive. Admin teams won't know they're not doing what they're supposed to."

Finally, something that might actually work in our favor. Heads nod enthusiastically. Brady asks, "You sure you can do it?"

"Yes, definitely. Quantum showed me a few things that will help. I'm not sure how, but he's been inside some of the Admin security programs. He's . . ." He pauses, a look of concern washing over his features, and his eyes shift around the room, then drop to the floor. "I don't know. He's the best wire-rat I've ever seen."

Desto picks up the thread. "Okay, sounds like we've got a way in. Time it so there's no Corps gunships in the area, cut off the drones, get on the platform. There can't be more than a few security personnel. Maybe we don't even have to engage. We just lock them in and shake our asses on over to the colony."

"That's a good idea," Karl says, "but they'll probably have submersibles. We won't even see them coming if they launch."

"The *Sphynx* has enough surprises on board to handle that," Desto responds.

Shaking his head, Karl says, "Yeah, but not if they're firing torpedoes. We'd never know what hit us."

Desto, out of ideas for the moment, gives him a disgusted look.

"So, we'll probably have to neutralize whoever's in the structure," Brady cuts in. "Control them enough to be able to make a trip over to the penal colony and get the settlers out."

"We'll have a better chance if we keep the element of surprise," Karl says.

Rajcik's hasn't said anything in a while and I turn to look at him, not trusting his silence any more than I trust his words. His face is tight with contempt and it sets my teeth on edge. He catches me looking and brings his dark eyes to bear on mine, silently daring me to call him out.

"What do you think, Rajcik?" I ask. "Have you been inside that structure?"

He hesitates before answering. "For inprocessing, yeah. When I was eighteen."

"What can you tell us about it?" Vitruzzi asks.

"Nothing useful, sweetheart." He tries to get off without saying anything, but the weight of a room full of cold stares compels him. "It's been twenty years since I was down there and I only saw one area—where they tag and outfit new prisoners."

"Any suggestions for hobbling their security?"

He sweeps us with a flat, death-mask glare. "Kill everyone you see."

"That's great," Rob replies. "Do you have anything constructive to add?"

He acts like he didn't hear Rob and begins twisting his head, first left than right. His neck bones crack hideously. Finally, he brings his attention back to the room. "You want constructive? Here's my advice —forget about your friends. You'll die trying to infiltrate that rock, and they're most definitely worm food. Your issue—*the* issue—is T'Kai, and from what Thompson tells me, you've let that one slide through your fingers. As far as I'm concerned, I've done what I can to help you people, and every minute I spend listening to your bullshit is a minute wasted."

I lean across the table until my eyes are level with his and seethe.

"No one's stopping you, János. You can walk out of that hold any time you want." Straight into emptiness.

His jaw clenches, but he clamps down on his building fury and leers at me instead. "Your charm, Aly, is that you always say what you're thinking."

"This isn't getting us anywhere," Vitruzzi interrupts. "The fact of the matter is we've done what we can about T'Kai. Quantum will wavecast everything in another couple of days, and it will be up to anyone who sees it to deal with T'Kai. He can't suppress the information once it's out, and we can't attack the entire Admin. This is the only way to help the settlers and bring T'Kai to some kind of justice."

"Justice?" Rajcik says. "I'm a little confused about your idea of justice, Vitruzzi. Leaving to chance what a single bullet could accomplish is a coward's way out. I expected your team to face T'Kai, not run away and let a wire-rat do your work."

"Shut up, Rajcik." My patience is getting close to snapping.

Rajcik knows it and taunts me, "Or what, Aly?"

A dark look from Vitruzzi convinces me to drop it. I glare at Rajcik, daring him to keep going, but he seems content to resume ignoring me. It's Thompson who quietly returns my stare, his eyes eerily similar to the beady, ferocious gaze of a Flat Rat.

"How many levels are there, Rajcik? Do you know anything at all about the structural design?" Vitruzzi presses.

With a final contemptuous grunt, he spills it. "It's basic. Keypad door locks, security screening at all corridor junctions, hermetic seals on all doors. If I had to guess, I'd say three levels, but I've never been below the first. Could be more, could just be the one."

"But if it's underwater, there's only one path of attack. They can't call for backup from outside. That should make it easier to create a bottleneck and hold their security in check," Karl says.

"To keep them in check, we may have to divide into two teams," I insert. "One to hold the platform, the other to get on land."

"Some of the settlers still have their embedded trackers—Zeta, Jade, Fowler, a few others. We can trace them, and they should be able to lead us to the rest," Venus adds over the com.

Everyone puts in his or her piece as we continue constructing the plan. Hearing it spoken aloud helps us feel like we have control, like our actions will bring about the results we expect. A team's faith in a good plan is as important as their ability to carry it out, and we have plenty of both. What we don't have is any guarantee Quantum will transmit the footage, or even live to try.

THIRTY-ONE

S leep is impossible. I lay in my old bunk like a petrified log, every muscle rigid, hypersensitive to the rhythms of the air exchanger and the ship's familiar hums, dings, and creaks. Venus and Bodie take —*took*—care of her better than most parents care for their kids, but she's still older than a lot of the ships that have seen the AUs the *Sphynx* has. My mind races over the plan, looking for holes and alternatives should anything happen that we don't expect—and we can be sure something will. But years in the business of crime and Corps have taught me that you can still prepare for it, even if you can't know what's coming.

After an hour or so of useless tossing and turning, I get up, get dressed, and head for the galley.

"I absolutely think you did the right thing, Jeremy. No question."

Desto is talking to La Mer as I enter, and Karl and David sit around the table they all share.

"What's the right thing?" I ask, returning David and Karl's nods.

"Have a seat, sweet thing," Desto says. His suggestive tone helps calm my frantic thoughts, and it hits me how much I'm going to miss this kind of camaraderie. It's this familiarity and comfort with each other that have made this crew my family and Agate Beach my home. My stomach twists a little. Eventually, I'll have to face the fact that I may never see any of them again.

"What's the matter, babe? You look a little pale," he asks.

I shake it off, not ready to admit my decision to leave. David's eyes follow me as I pull a seat from under the table. "Nothing, just can't sleep. Looks like I'm not the only one."

The chair I take is directly across from Karl. His scrunched brow overshadows his eyes as they bounce from me to the table and back. His naturally stoic composure rarely cracks, and seeing him looking uncertain gives me a momentary, irrational spark of hope. Can he still care about me?

To hide it, I repeat my question, "What did you do, La Mer?"

The way he hesitates before answering has me even more interested, but he eventually spills it. "I shorted the com transmitter on Cross's hop before we left Obal 6."

"What? Why?"

"I just . . . just thought it was a good idea. It seemed better to make sure no one could, uh, inadvertently send any information that could endanger us."

"You mean you don't trust Cross." I don't have to ask; the answer has been clear since the day the *Red Horizon* landed at the Beach. And I have to hand it to him, he's smart and thinks on his feet. Besides, it's done, no point in arguing.

The room is quiet for a few seconds, then David pushes back from the table abruptly. "So Desto, let's you and me walk through the armory. I want to make sure I know what's in stock in case we need it."

"Dave, you know what's in there as well as . . . oh, yeah, sure. Let's go."

La Mer gets up too and follows them out, and like that, Karl and I are alone.

We're strangers again, neither of us knowing what to say to the other. I fumble to come up with something. "What do you think of the plan?"

His eyes settle on me and he responds, sounding relieved to have a neutral topic, "It's thinner than the atmosphere on Nexon, but that's as good as we're going to get. If any team can do it, it'll be us."

Scanning his face as he speaks, I don't really hear his words. I know how thin the plan is, but what I'm really asking is what he feels not what he thinks. He doesn't continue, so I finally respond, trying to dredge up something to keep the conversation going. "Have you talked to Vitruzzi about T'Kai? It seems like he really got to her, the way he brought up her family . . ."

"Why would I?"

He doesn't ask in a confrontational way. He sounds curious, reminding me how clueless he can be when it comes to people's feelings. I almost say something about it, but stop myself. It would only start an argument. Besides, what do I know? Haven't I been just as clueless, made the same mistakes?

"I just mean, you're the only one here who's known her that long. It might help if she had someone to talk to, you know? She seemed upset."

He sighs and looks at the bottle he holds in one hand. "She's strong. She'll cope. Like the rest of us."

"I just thought—"

"So you're going to go back to the life," he cuts me off, finally looking up, his eyes boring into my face.

"How . . . did David tell you that?" It's hard to find my voice, torn between being surprised and defensive. Damn my brother. Doesn't he understand privacy? But I get why he told Karl; he knows I'd never do it on my own. I'd let Karl find out when I was thousands of miles and a new identity away. There's no reason to deny it. "Yeah."

"You may not believe it, Aly." He stands up and walks toward the exit with his shoulders set like iron bands. The tension in them makes his shirt taut, and he takes a deep swallow of his drink before continuing, but his voice is thick anyway as he says, "But I really hope things go well for you."

The words sting in a surprising way. I never would have expected such total and unquestioning acceptance. But what *did* I expect? That he beg me to stay? That he scream at me, or curse at me, or cry? He's a realist, I'll give him that. He knows me well enough to know that when my mind's made up, it's as rigid as his locked shoulders.

I take a deep breath and almost choke on it. "Thanks."

He doesn't look back and leaves the galley, deserting me. Moments later, Rajcik enters through the same door. The hollowness inside me instantly begins to compress as rage wraps itself around my torso like a vice. But this time, it's not about Rajcik.

He pauses and looks me over before coming in, blatantly measuring how much trouble I might be, then walks toward the cupboards.

But talking to Karl has taken the fight out of me. I don't feel like moving, but I can't just sit here and say nothing. "I'm surprised Vitruzzi lets you walk around without a shadow."

He hears the strain in my voice and looks at me again, disquieting interest sparkling in his eyes.

"I guess she trusts her crew to handle me if I do something unwise," he says dismissively, rifling through the cupboards.

He's wearing a thin shirt, the same plain gray color of everything that's been laundered through the cleaning system over and over. The sleeves are tight and ride up on his thick arms as he lifts them to dig past things on the shelf, looking for something edible. I see the scar again, cutting a deep groove between his muscles.

"You almost lost it didn't you?"

He finally grabs a couple of nutrition bricks wrapped in plastic, rips one open with his teeth, and sits across from me in the same seat Karl had just vacated. He knows what I'm talking about, but before responding, he throws the unopened bar on the table and swallows the other in two large bites, then rubs his hands together to shake off any crumbs. My own curiosity keeps my frustration at his stalling at bay. Finished, he leans back and extends his right arm to his side. Once his forearm swings in front of him about half of its full range, it stops, the triceps unable to extend completely.

"I'll never do another push up," he says, looking disgustedly at his arm. "Not unless Vitruzzi decides to work some fancier magic. But she doesn't have the resources she'd need for that. Maybe I'll be able to get them for her once I get the *Temptation* back up and running."

A chuckle escapes me. "That's not likely to happen."

He raises one eyebrow. "You don't think I will?"

"Why would Vitruzzi give you that much freedom? I don't care how much you've tried to help us get the Beachers back; you're still a criminal. And a liar."

He smirks. "Same thing, right? Besides, Vitruzzi still owes me. She helped me by fixing me up. I gave her the video of T'Kai. Now I'm helping you get your friends out of the shank. Don't you think that deserves some payback?"

"She doesn't owe you a damn thing. None of us do. After what you pulled."

"We'll see, Aly. We'll see."

"In any case, you're not much help to us. You said yourself that you don't know the layout or how to infiltrate the platform on KL."

"I'm still a hired gun."

I stand up, no longer able to stomach bandying words with him. "When the shooting starts, Rajcik, we'll see where your gun is pointing. Something tells me you've got other targets besides the Corps in mind. And you can rest assured that theirs won't be the only ones pointing at you. All I need is a reason."

"Sit. Down."

His tone surprises me. He hasn't been my boss in months, but the undeniable command in his voice still gets an automatic reaction out of me. I start to lower myself back into my chair before I even realize it, but catch myself.

"No. You don't get it." I smile grimly. "You're not in charge anymore."

He reaches out and grasps my wrist as quickly as a striking cobra. "There's something I have to explain to you. So sit down."

He doesn't get up, doesn't pull me. He just holds my arm, giving me the chance to decide if I want to listen or not. After hesitating a second, I sit. His grip releases, leaving white bands around my wrist.

"You're smart, Aly, but you're wrong about something. You think

I'm some kind of monster, a big bad wolf. But I'm not the one you have to worry about here."

"Bull—"

He cuts me off. "Just fucking listen. T'Kai is more dangerous than you realize. He's in it for blood. My blood, your blood, your whole crew's blood. The only way to stop him is to kill him. That's why I'm here. That's the only reason I'm here. I don't give a damn about you and your brother."

"And you took a job from him." Acid contempt bubbles in my throat.

"I've been working for him since I was eighteen, three years after they sent me to that shithole on Keum Libre. In fact, you've been working for him, too."

It's as if he's just thrown a bucket of cold water in my face and I nearly gasp. "What are you talking about?"

"How do you think we managed to keep clear of the Corps for so long? After all those jobs?" He has my attention, and he knows how to keep it. "T'Kai's been bankrolling me since I was a prisoner on KL. He picked me to be his personal thief. The first cache of weapons I stole paid for his vote of confidence, and everything after that we split fifty-fifty. When you and your brother were on my crew, nearly every heist we pulled was for T'Kai. We made him rich. It was a perfect arrangement, until he got too greedy."

My mouth opens, but nothing comes out. I'm reeling, not wanting to believe a word, but unable to stop myself. It's so obvious, it has to be true. We were lucky, too lucky, for a long time. The *Temptation* was a wanted ship; we'd seen it come up in plenty of newswave bulletins, and Rajcik's identity has been known throughout the system for almost as long as his reputation has. We were always so careful, so methodical. The truth cuts deeply now, but it never occurred to me that we weren't as good at stealing and selling illegal weapons as I thought we were.

And something else—Rajcik had always handled the arms sales on his own. He kept the crew in the dark, so we didn't know how much he was really making from the deals, and our cuts were always enough to keep us quiet. That and fear of what Rajcik would do to us if he suspected we would turn on him. All that time, half the money had been going back to T'Kai. My skin goes cold as I realize how naïve, how utterly and completely oblivious, I'd been.

"Want to know the best part?" he continues. "Half the shit they blamed on me wasn't even me. That Corps ship I got away in when I escaped from KL, where the crew was slaughtered? I would have gotten out of there without anyone knowing, but T'Kai tipped them off that I was a stowaway. He was testing me, trying to see if I could do the job. I had no choice but to kill them. And New Sweden"—he chuckles coldly—"those stupid colonists were just patsies that T'Kai hired to guard the arms until we got there. They were fine when we left. It was T'Kai who had them wiped out. Now I realize that he was covering his tracks, making sure that anyone who knew I was working for him was gone. Because he wanted *me* gone."

"Why didn't you tell us the truth?"

"Why would I? You all got what you wanted. Don't forget, Aly, you and David were there by your own choice. You could have walked any time you wanted to, but you didn't." His black eyes shine with an evil mirth. He's actually enjoying watching the effect his story is having on me. "I'd already figured out T'Kai was going to try and have me ghosted after the Fortress. In a way, I did you two a favor when I cut you loose. Things might have turned out differently—maybe no one would have escaped."

It's my turn to laugh, and it burns like bile in my throat. "If he wanted you dead, how the hell did you get away?"

He sly smirk makes me want to squirm out of its range. "You're going to like this. You helped. Nothing happened the way it was supposed to on that station. T'Kai didn't have enough security, and the ones he did have weren't prepared for the shitstorm you and your new friends created. When the place blew, the soldiers acted like frightened little ants and scattered. After we launched, only one gunship came after us. That bastard was lucky enough to hit us." He reaches around and rubs the long scar.

I'm scrambling, just trying to keep up with everything he's saying. Through a mouth lined by felt, I ask, "Why didn't it finish you off?"

He arches a speculative eyebrow. "Orders, probably. Their priority must have been to help their distressed comrades." That cold chuckle again. "If T'Kai ever reads that commander's flight logs, I imagine the stupid sap will die choking on his own screams."

My confidence is so badly shaken that it's a long time before I can muster any kind of coherent response. Rajcik has gotten the better of me, far, far beyond what I'd imagined, at every single turn. For the last six years, I thought I had it under control, my life in my own hands, but I'd been wrong. The Corps was everything to me before I woke up to the fact that I was nothing but its puppet, and it had eaten me up inside until I'd escaped. I'd sought out Rajcik as a way of rebelling against the sick corruption of the Admin. But I realize now that I'd merely gone from being a knowing tool of that corruption to an unknowing one of Rajcik's own special variety. I want to scream my lungs out and strangle Rajcik and all his smug contempt to death, but don't. If I'd paid attention, I would have seen the truth a long time ago. Had I wanted to be blind? Is there some terrified, weak part of me that's afraid to be free? Is that what's driving my decision to follow Rob and become a citizen again?

He stands up fluidly, like a coiled spring. "Don't look so surprised. It's just the way they work. And you think I'm evil and corrupt. Now you know the truth. The only reason I haven't killed T'Kai already is because I've never been close enough to him to do it. But that will change, soon. Something tells me that we haven't heard the last from him."

He walks past me out of the galley.

I look down at the table and see the nutrition bar he left behind. Picking it up, I hurl it as hard as I can against the wall, completely unsatisfied by the soft crunch it makes. *Goddammit!* I've never been so gullible, so duped, so deceived. And I swear, it will never happen again.

Does David know about this? I need to talk to him, if only to make the news less difficult to swallow. But first, the com room, find out how far out we are. The sooner this mission is over, the sooner I can put all of it behind me. Forget the past and start completely over from scratch. Nothing has ever sounded so good.

When I get to the com room, La Mer is hunched over the main console that links with the ship's central computer. His long, ropy hair hangs down across his cheeks, and he squints as he types intently on the keyboard. He looks up when I come in, his eyes still far away for a few seconds before focusing on me.

"How's that security program going?" I ask, leaning against the wall beside him.

He looks back at the screen for a few seconds before answering. "If what Quantum told me about their protocols is right, it's basically done. Once we send a signal burst that the drones pick up, they'll analyze it, and that'll be all she wrote. It's like scrambling an egg. All the components in their brains will still be there, but they won't be put together the same way. We'll be able to fly right past. Some of them may retain enough of their programmed protocols to follow us, but that's about all they'll be capable of. It may be a little nerve-racking, but if it gets to be too much, Venus can always shake them. They're intra-atmospheric, so their range will be limited."

His confidence is reassuring, and the conversation helps redirect my scorched thoughts away from Rajcik. "How do you feel about things after we get on the platform?" La Mer is a thinker, not the kind of combat soldier that most of us are. He can hold a gun and point it in the right direction, but his instincts are evasion not engagement.

His eyes shift toward the floor before he answers, the confidence of a moment ago blown away as if on a sudden gust of wind. "I guess I'm just hoping that we won't see much fighting. They aren't prepped like they expect an attack. Why would anyone attack a penal colony guardhouse? Maybe they'll just have a couple of personnel . . ."

"We can hope, right? But just in case, maybe you should stay on ship with Venus. No one else can do what you can. You'll probably be the most help to us on the move and with access to the ship's com equipment."

He looks at me sideways, his large eyes limned with emotion, either gratitude or relief. Or both. Then he says, "About Cross . . ."

"Doesn't matter," I cut in. "You did what made sense to you, and that's a good way to stay not dead. No harm done."

A knock pings against the hatch, and I look over to see Vitruzzi. She opens the door and comments, "We're only ten hours from KL. What's the status on the drone override?"

"I'm there. Just point the transponder in the right direction and give it a boost. Everything within a couple hundred klicks will get zapped. We should try to get as close to the platform as possible in order to hit anything they have on reserve down there. Nothing outside that range should be picking us up anyway, so they'll all continue their normal routines without ever knowing we've been there."

She nods and manages to look almost pleased. "That's excellent. Good job, Jeremy."

"V," La Mer says, "I'm wondering where you want me when you go down into the substructure."

She sees the fear in his eyes and smiles at him softly. "We need you here, on the *Sphynx*. In fact"—she looks at me—"the ship's never going to sit down. We'll take the shuttle in. I've already told Venus to cover us while we make the descent. Once we hit the platform, she'll stay in flight until she hears from me or Brady. We don't know what might happen down there, but if the ship gets locked down, we're all fucked. You two can manage the ship and keep the drones under control from a reasonable distance."

It's a good plan, even though we'll be sitting on each other's laps inside the shuttle until we hit ground. I ask, "How close do we need to be to the colony until you can read the Beachers' tracking implants?"

I don't need to say it aloud, but if none of the devices are transmitting, it's either because the colonists aren't there or their bodies aren't outputting enough energy to keep the devices active. Because they're dead.

"They have a fifty-K range."

I nod. "Any word from Quantum or T'Kai?"

"Nothing," she answers, her voice clipped. She turns back to La Mer. "Do what you have to to make sure that program works, then try and get some sleep. This is it."

This is it.

THIRTY-TWO

"Where the fuck did it come from?!" David yells as Venus forces the ship into a hard left bank and starts to climb.

"I don't know, but it's not a drone," Karl says, his eyes not wavering from the command camera feed linked to his VDU.

I watch mine just as intently as I grip the crisscrossing bars along the armory door a level down from David, my body tensing in anticipation of the next shearing turn. The Corps ship chasing us had come out of nowhere after we broke through KL's atmosphere; our radar never even picked it up. The drone program worked just as La Mer had said it would, and we were minutes outside of reaching the oceanic landing platform, planning on doing a NAP of the earth flyover of the island colony before setting down. Venus began evasive maneuvering the second the *Sphynx*'s secondary sonic pressure wave sensors detected a higher than normal reading coming from above us, but none of us were ready for it.

The ship may have followed us from orbit, or it may have picked us up from somewhere else on the planet. Either way, it came at us so suddenly that no one had a chance to get to the lockdown seats. We'd all been in the cargo bay, getting ready to deploy, when Venus's reflexes thrust the ship into instant pandemonium. As far as I can tell, no one is injured, but we've been thrown around like loose cannonballs. Vitruzzi and Brady made for the cockpit as fast as they could while the rest of us try to get our bearings in the hold.

"Desto, what's going on in the fire control room?" Brady asks, using the onboard com system.

"I'm in position, but I can't get a lock with the way Venus is juggling sky. Can we get on a straight path for a minute?" His voice is calm, almost detached, a freakish counterpoint to the danger.

I look around and see Rob inching for the shuttle's hatch. He has a good idea; we need to be prepared to detach at a moment's notice. The shuttle can't go anywhere while the ship is flying this erratically, but there's a chance Venus can get enough of a lead to let us deploy.

"It's locked on. If I stop for a second, it'll have its chance. Can't let that happen." Venus responds. And then, as an afterthought: "Everyone okay down there?"

Karl lets her know we're all in the green, and the ship goes down in a hard dive that makes my stomach shoot into my mouth and my feet leave the floor.

"Fuck!"

"Get in the shuttle, everyone!" Rob yells. He's at the shuttle airlock but can't activate the hatch without the keycode.

The ship's crazy gyrations halt long enough for me to let go of the armory door and start making my way along the wall toward him, using everything I can get my hands on as a life preserver. David and Karl do the same.

"Desto," I try to warn him, "we're getting inside the shuttle. Can you—?" The target lock siren begins to blare, overriding my voice.

"Brace yourselves! Brace for impact!" Venus screams, and the ship veers sharply.

The missile doesn't impact, but explodes close enough to our port side that I can feel the entire ship suddenly shift laterally through the sky, as if on rails. The alarm continues and the craft shudders violently. I fall flat against the floor and feel every vibration through my skin, rattling my bones, my organs, even my eyeballs. I pull my wrist VDU up against my mouth and try to call for a damage report, but my throat has locked tight against the hammering tremors. My heartbeat is an electric hum inside my chest, and I pray that it doesn't get into lockstep rhythm with the ship and burst through my ribcage.

"Stupid-sons-a-scumbag-bastards, they didn't even hail us! Just started firing. Come here, boys, I'll give you a show you'll never forget." Venus doesn't realize she's broadcasting, but it helps us prepare for another bone-crushing maneuver. The hull's vibrations abruptly fade away, and we start climbing at an impossibly acute right bank. If there is damage, it hasn't hindered the *Sphynx*'s maneuvering capabilities.

The climb goes on and on and my fingers are losing their hold in the deck. The floor starts to slope away steeply over my shoulder. We're moving too erratically for the grav stabilizer to keep up. If my grip fails, I'll slide into the opposite wall, sixty meters away, at a speed that is guaranteed to splinter at least my legs and maybe everything. The angle grows sharper and my full weight hangs on the last joints of my fingers. I can't let go to grab the tie-down anchors that line the walls. My fingers shriek in pain as I crimp them harder, and then the ship suddenly arcs forward and settles into a relatively flat plane. It happens so quickly that my body is momentarily suspended a few centimeters above the floor, the sudden change in direction doing what the climb couldn't and popping my fingers free of the deck. There's still enough angle that I begin to skid anyway, flipping over to try and get my feet in front of me. My hand is suddenly grabbed, and Karl pulls me up off the floor to the safety of the wall.

"You okay?" he yells into my ear, his voice echoing the chaos around us.

After a pause to catch my breath, I reply, "Yeah, I'm okay." His arm circles my waist and he holds me tightly against him. I turn my head, and our faces are centimeters apart. His eyes drill into mine, and the feelings I thought he'd lost spill out as if his soul had cracked apart.

"I'm okay, you can let me go," I whisper.

Instead, his grip tightens for a moment. "I'll never let you go, Aly. Not again. I'm going to make sure you're safe." Then he releases his hold and staggers toward the shuttle's airlock.

"Where are you going?" I ask, getting a death grip on the wall as Venus makes another sudden evasion.

Karl white knuckles a pipe running next to the airlock and opens the hatch. "I'm going to get rid of them. This is the only way." He opens all channels on his VDU. "Desto, I'm taking the shuttle. Give me some cover. Venus, get us level for a few seconds. I'll release and draw him off. Climb out of range and drop down behind him. Then blow that motherfucker to pieces. Do you copy?"

Without waiting for an answer, he pushes by Rob and jumps into the shuttle. The hatch closes before anyone can move to help him, or stop him.

Vitruzzi's voice comes over the com: "Karl, don't be crazy. We need the shuttle."

"It won't do anyone any good if we all go down. If I can divert him off our tail, you'll be able to get some distance and surprise him. I'll have a better chance of evading him in the shuttle, and we can rendezvous at the platform after you punch his ticket. Venus, try to keep her flat for release—in five . . . four . . . three . . . two . . . release."

I let go of the wall as he breaks free and let the ship's momentum carry me to the cargo deck porthole. Pressing my forehead against it, I catch sight of the shuttle as it drops back. Karl engages the forward thrusters and elevates directly into the path of the ship chasing us. It's a Corps skiff, used for high-speed stealth reconnaissance. They aren't often deployed for enemy engagement, so its weapons payload will be minimal. They move fast and cover a lot of ground, making them unlikely to be seen on radar. But this one's seen us, and now we have to deal with the likelihood that reinforcements have been called. How long until they get here?

Venus glides the *Sphynx* up into another steep climb, letting Karl pass below us. I'm pushed against the rear hatch with what feels like the weight of an elephant on my back, but not before seeing the skiff take the bait. As far as it knows, we're not armed, and if we're hiding something, we'd likely have jettisoned it in our shuttle. I lose sight of them quickly as the *Sphynx* rises above the clouds, levels off, and decelerates.

"Venus, get back down there! Follow him!" I yell through my VDU. I should be trying to stay calm, but gut-wrenching helplessness turns my voice into a strained warble.

She doesn't respond, but the ship begins to slide smoothly through the air in a controlled descent. "Desto, get ready. You're on," Venus says. The command feed coming through my VDU is scratchy with interference from the skiff's backdraft.

"Missile released," Desto says.

Flames engulf the VDU screen in a high intensity wash of red, yellow, and green, and Desto shouts in victory. Venus rocks the ship carefully, skimming around debris, then comes back to bear on the same trajectory the shuttle had taken. I hold my breath waiting for Karl to transmit his status. In a second, we catch his tail, but something is drastically wrong. The shuttle cants at a dangerous left angle, the thrusters spurting erratic jets of fire. I can't tell if he was fragged by the skiff's wreckage or took a hit. As we approach, the shuttle begins descending in a steep arc straight for the unforgiving surface of the ocean.

Scrambling for the hold's transmitter, I say, "Karl, pull up, you're coming in too hot. The shuttle can't maintain that rate of descent. Do you read?" If he keeps diving like that, there won't be time for the reverse thrusters to slow him down enough to avoid a catastrophic collision. I don't let myself think about the possibility that he might have no control over the thrusters anyway.

There's no response and no change in the shuttle's course. Venus starts to ease the *Sphynx* off for the same reason Karl should be slowing the shuttle. The *Sphynx* will need more time to decelerate, and in a few more seconds we'll lose visual contact. I try again. "Karl, do you read? You need to pull back. Over."

Still nothing. Panic sinks ice cold fangs into my heart. "Strahan! Goddammit, acknowledge. Slow your rate of descent. At least try!" The ship melts into a cloudbank and disappears with no sign of a course change. Frantic, I yell, "Venus, keep on his ass! Do not lose him!"

"Aly, we can't—" Rob says as he comes up beside me.

I cut him off. "I know we have to pull back, but we can keep him in range. I want to know where he hits."

The *Sphynx* floats through the clouds, Venus gradually cutting her speed until we're only about a klick above deck. We come out of the cloudbank looking into a grayish-green expanse of water, small whitecaps dotting the horizon to the edge of my sight. A speck that can only be the shuttle is a short distance away, still hurtling toward the water like a dart. In no time, its silhouette blends into the spray below it.

"Strahan! Karl! Acknowledge!" I'm screaming into the transmitter.

We approach out of the north and are greeted by a thick cloud of curdled steam being greedily snatched up by a crosswind where the shuttle went down. My mouth dries up. Venus drops us into a slow glide. Everything around me seems to freeze solid, even the passage of time. Finally, she brings us in range, and I see what I most feared. The ship fell hard, slamming into the water and fracturing into debris on impact. Sheered metal and parts scatter over the surface, sinking fast. Jets of fire can be seen underwater, components still exploding inside the wreck.

Through a fog, I hear Vitruzzi over the VDU. "Pull us up closer and skim slowly over the surface in the immediate area. We need a better look."

"Vitruzzi, if you plan on doing anything else today, it would be wise to get to the platform ASAP." Rajcik says over the intercom. "That skiff made us. It's only a matter of time before more Corps arrive. Besides, your shuttle looks like a total loss."

I feel my body in motion before any conscious thought happens. We're hovering about five meters over the wreck and the metal hull is still visible suspended beneath the surface. Swinging my carbine strap over my back, I reach out and grasp the hatch's handle, torque it open hard, and hurl myself out. Instead of falling, I'm grabbed by my equipment belt, yanked backward, and shoved against the wall.

"Aly! Don't be insane! You can't do anything for him." Rob, his eyes wide and alarmed, uses his weight to keep me pinned.

"Let go of me! We have to help!" I struggle with him, but he holds my arms rigidly against my body in a bear hug.

Burning, chemical-tasting air rushes into the cargo hold. "Someone get the door!" he yells, and the sharp reek is choked off as Mason pulls the hatch to.

I struggle against Rob, straining to get free, but the ship suddenly banks hard. Gravity shifts direction, pulling us to the floor while Mason grasps whatever's nearest to avoid being thrown through the hold.

"Venus is taking us back to the platform. There's nothing we can do for him." Vitruzzi's voice comes through the com system, defeated and dead sounding.

I yank an arm free and scream into my VDU, "No! What does his tracker say?"

There's a pause, long enough to give me hope. Then: "There's nothing."

Disbelief pummels me in the stomach, making me nauseous and shaky.

Rob pulls himself into a sitting position and lets go of me. "You'll get yourself killed too if you jump out there. You know he couldn't have survived that impact." He pauses, gauging the effect hearing the hard truth will have on me. When I don't flinch, he continues, "I'm sorry, Aly. I'm really sorry."

My eyes fall closed, as if darkness will hide the despair scrabbling through my soul.

THIRTY-THREE

A quick aerial sweep of the area confirms that we're alone for now, and Venus sets us down on the platform. Three drones locked on us after the skiff was destroyed, but none followed for more than a couple kilometers, their programming irrevocably scrambled. It's only a matter of a few hours, maybe less, before Corps ships arrive. Every second counts.

The ramp lowers and we move out in sweep positions, running in formation for the platform's only building, which must serve as an access point to the underwater structure. La Mer and Venus wait for us to get inside. They'll relaunch and stay airborne while we take care of business on the station, the plan unchanged except for the loss of the shuttle. I take right flank and run hunkered low, my mind blank and shut down to anything that's not going to keep me alive. Desto and Mason take right and left rear and David takes point with Rob near his right shoulder. Vitruzzi and Brady spread out in front of Mason, and Thompson and Rajcik are in front of me.

Gritty wisps of sea spray blow over the edges of the platform, cold against my bare cheeks. We're at least ten meters above the ocean's surface and the platform is stable against heavy seas and storms. The platform spreads north to south about the same length as the main cavern of Agate Beach's mine, and east to west about twice that distance. Venus landed within a short run from the access hut, and we're able to get out of the open quickly.

David reaches the entryway first, where a small alcove protects the door from the wind. The stock of his rifle remains planted against his shoulder as he takes a quick look around the corner, scanning for guards. When he determines it's all clear, he gives the signal to take a knee while he runs a keypad bypass to get us inside. I'm more than a little nervous about all of us being stuck on the same elevator to get below the surface, and I know I'm not the only one. But from what we can see, it's the only way in or out. If the elevator is destroyed, the station would be cut off from the surface for who knows how long, possibly even at risk of being breached by the relentless ocean. Knowing T'Kai's history of sacrificing whatever is necessary for his own benefit, the hope that anyone not wanting us here wouldn't dare destroy the elevator seems empty.

It's been too long. What's the hold up? As soon as I start to get up to find out, David leans back and waves us up. It only takes seconds for the crew to reach the entrance and pile through to the room inside, leaving Mason to stay back and keep a visual on the platform. No guards are in the access room, and David and I exchange a worried look. Where is everyone?

The room is large and utilitarian. One wall is lined with communication consoles and monitors, all dark and powered down, and a thick steel sub-bay gate above the elevator shaft covers a wide section of the floor. The gate looks strong enough to resist anything from a small nuclear explosion to a minor volcanic eruption—probably designed to guard against an accident or explosion below the surface from traveling up the shaft and decimating the control room. David and Brady immediately get busy on the consoles figuring out how to operate the elevator.

Outwardly, I'm nervous and unsettled, but something worse than mission anxiety looms just behind it. Something frightening and deadly that's creeping up on me like a tsunami on the distant ocean, a huge wave that's traveling too fast to run from. *Karl's dead.* I haven't allowed the thought to creep into my consciousness, but it lies in wait within that wave. When it reaches me, I'll be crushed and I'll drown.

I glance toward Rob. He stands by the entryway keeping an eye on the outside with Mason until we can get the elevator running. For a split second, a barely containable urge to aim my carbine at his skull and blow it off surges through me. Jesus, what's wrong with me? Nothing that's happened is his fault. The only one I can blame is me.

"What's the problem?" Thompson asks David, his tone tight and abrupt. Judging from the rising level of tension in the room, the lid could blow off any minute. Why isn't there any security? Everyone's eyes are lit up with hot intensity. Death and danger are nothing new to us, and no one has any false illusions about the probable outcome of this mission. The deaths of both Karl and Bodie just bring everyone that much closer to bursting apart at the seams.

There's a clicking sound followed by a deep vibrating hum beneath our feet that makes me jump.

"It's on its way," David informs us.

We take firing positions, bracing for a security crew to greet us. Hydraulic safety bars open around the gate perimeter, coming to rest vertically like teeth. Finally, the humming stops and yellow lights begin flashing on the corners of the railing surrounding the gate as it slides open. We're looking down at the roof of the elevator, thick and solid. When it's clear, the elevator rises all the way and comes to rest at floor level. There's no sound inside the control room.

"Open it," Brady directs.

David activates something on the console and the doors slide open. Exposing emptiness.

I glance at David again and we both shrug at the same time.

"What the fuck is going on?" Thompson asks no one in particular.

"Maybe they have it rigged to gas us when we get inside," Desto offers, and I throw him a dark look.

"Rajcik, any ideas?" Vitruzzi asks.

He turns toward her, his face expressionless, and shakes his head slowly. Vitruzzi hesitates and exchanges a look with Brady. None of us are in a hurry to get inside. It's nothing but a box with no way out once it starts to descend.

"Shit," Brady mutters. "Okay, everyone inside except Mason and Thompson. You two keep watch. Monitor topside coms, and get down there if we call you."

"I'm not staying up here," Thompson says.

He glares at him. "Yes. You are."

Thompson scowls and looks toward Rajcik, who gestures for him to sit tight. He hunches out toward the entrance and joins Mason.

"Let's go," Vitruzzi says and steps aboard.

It's hot inside the elevator, but there's more than enough room for all of us and we spread out. A touch screen is mounted on one wall, and David steps up and slides his fingers along the activation bar. The doors close and a basic structural schematic showing three levels flashes onto the screen. The first is labeled "Vessel Dock," the next is "In-processing," and the final is labeled "Research." A shudder runs through me. A lab, here, at a penal colony. I don't have to wonder what that means.

"Take us to the bottom," Brady says, his voice thick with either rage or something close to derangement as he reacts to the schematic.

David swipes the screen and a female voice says, "Enter the security clearance code."

He turns around, eyes wide and uncertain. "I'm not sure how to override this. I thought I had it at the control console."

Vitruzzi activates her VDU. "La Mer, do you copy?"

A few seconds later, La Mer's voice comes through, but it's choppy. " . . . here . . . every . . . okay . . . over."

"Must be distance," Desto says.

Vitruzzi grimaces and tries another tactic, this time using the elevator intercom. "Doug, come in."

Mason responds immediately, "Mason here."

"Get in touch with La Mer. Ask him if Quantum gave him anything that might be an elevator control code."

"Roger. Wait one."

The seven of us wait tensely as the minutes pass by, pressure building with all the force of tectonic plates in a subduction zone. The schematic fades from the screen after a few seconds, but it might as well be burned onto my retinas. Desto stands in front of me and sweat begins to bead up on his thick neck and run down between his shoulders beneath his heavy body armor. I wipe my hands against my pant leg; I don't want them to be slippery if shooting starts. The wind outside blew my hair helter-skelter and I brush the tangles out of my eyes, feeling bits of damp spray still clinging to them. The waiting becomes interminable.

"V, do you copy?" Mason, finally.

"Go ahead."

"He said he found a master security code, but he's not sure it'll work for the elevator."

"We'll take it."

"Okay, here it is." As he reads it off, David reengages the touch screen and repeats the string of numbers and letters into the voice console. I pull a marker out of my equipment vest and hastily write the code on the inside of my wrist. When he's done, he asks Vitruzzi, "Which level?"

Before anyone answers, Mason clicks back on. "Hey!" His voice is more excited than I've ever heard it. "Venus says she picked up active tracker feeds."

"Hallel-goddamn-ujah," Desto says. "That kid is a genius."

Breathlessly, Vitruzzi cries, "How many?"

"She says it looks like everyone. All of them."

"Take us to the docks. Now," Brady orders.

Finally, some good news. David makes the pick and the clicking sound we'd heard earlier repeats, this time much louder. The lift starts down.

In less than a minute, we come to a smooth stop. Before David opens the doors, Vitruzzi says, "Okay. Keep low, move fast. Don't make yourself a target. We can't get locked down in here. Aly and Rajcik, take point."

Suddenly I remember something. "Wait, don't open it yet."

David's nerves sizzle almost audibly, and he responds with a short, "What?"

I reach into another pouch on my vest and show them what I have.

"What the . . . Aly, did you take that from the *'Rize*?" Rob knows immediately what's in my hand.

I don't look directly at him, feeling a touch of embarrassment at my thievery, but it turns out it was a good idea. "This is a holographic imager," I explain to the others. "It can hide us behind a fake projection of the inside of the elevator when the doors open. Whoever's in there won't be able to see us through the image, and we can get a fix on the room. Then surprise them."

Rob is annoyed, but the others are quick to adopt the plan and we set up the cloak.

When it's ready, Rajcik and I move up against the opposite side of the doors, our actions coordinated from long practice. As much as we've come to hate each other, we still retain the survival instincts that once made us a good team. Before he tried to kill me. For a second, he looks me in the eye as the doors slide open: *Are you ready*? I nod.

The doors stop. And—nothing. Just more silence. Simultaneously, we lean out to get a snapshot of what lies outside.

We've arrived at a belowdecks boathouse underneath the main platform. A dock extends directly from the elevator over placid water, one side flanked by a squat, flat, open-top cargo carrier with a covered steering booth and not much else. The other side of the dock is empty.

The rest of the bay is dark, but there are no other visible structures or watercraft. "Looks clear," I comment, stepping forward.

The rest file out, Rob hesitating long enough to pocket his projector. The local personnel must use the cargo ships to transport people to and from land. Thick walls drop from the edges of the platform overhead and disappear below the surface of the water at some depth we can't make out. The entire space is barely illuminated; the only light coming from inset lighting tracks that extend to the end of the dock and from within the elevator itself. I move at a jog to the end of the pier to get a better idea of what there is and Rob follows at an interval behind me. We arrive at the end without incident, no spotlights flashing on or gunfire breaking the silence. The boat bay is just as uninhabited as topside. Brady and Rajcik climb cautiously aboard the carrier and do a quick pass. They locate the hold controls and open it up. No one's below.

Confused, nervous, and ready for a more complete picture of the space, I turn on my scope light and sweep it around.

"Hey, Rob. A submersible." I wave my light over the craft's sleek hull where it floats at the dock's terminus, its hatch a few steps down a short ladder.

He gives it a quick look and says, "No, too small. Looks like a recon or scout sub. We couldn't get everyone aboard."

"True, but—"

Before I finish the thought, Vitruzzi uses the elevator intercom to call Mason and ask him to find the controls to open the launch-bay doors, then grab Thompson and meet us down here. We need them on the island more than guarding the platform. Within a minute, the giant bay doors rumble open and suffuse the chamber with outside light. The elevator disappears, returning with Thompson and Mason.

As we wait, Brady tells the rest of us, "We'll take the carrier to the penal colony. We should be able to find the settlers quickly and get back here and off this rock."

"Did they evacuate the whole complex because they saw us coming?" Thompson wonders aloud. "That could mean they're waiting for us on land. Or, who knows, maybe they went over there to pick up some fresh meat." He must have read the levels schematic, too.

"We'll know soon enough," David says.

Rajcik had sketched out what else he knew about the prisoner colony on our way from Letum Uti. When he was here, there were two main housing barracks, each six stories tall with plumbing and electricity. They desalination plant also fed a turbine generator that provided power. The prisoners mostly stayed within the complex, but with almost no security oversight or controls, many had ranged afield and set up pseudo-tribal factions that vied against each other for whatever they could get. There had been around six hundred other inmates on the island, the most hardened and violent men and women the system had produced. Problem is, like Rajcik said, it's been twenty years since he was a prisoner here. The hard truth is, we have no idea how many people besides the Beachers we can expect to encounter on the rock. The more of us there are, and the more hardware we bring, the less interference we should encounter while we search.

But there is something else I have to do.

As the crew loads aboard the carrier, I lag behind. Rob, sensing my hesitation, turns to me, his eyebrows steepled questioningly. "We better get going," he says.

"I'm not coming."

He snorts with a tinge of irritation. "What do you mean?"

The others turn to look at me, surprised.

"It's only been forty-five minutes since the shuttle went down. He could still be out there. I have to know," I try to explain, but I can see that I don't have to. Not to them.

Rob walks back onto the dock, his deep brown eyes filled with concern. "Aly, look. I get it. You were in love with him"—he puts a hand on my elbow, exerting the slightest pull—"but there's no way he survived."

I take a small step back and let his hand slide off my arm. "You're right, Rob. I did love him. And I still do. I'm taking the sub. Please, just let me go."

His mouth curls downward in a frown, and he glances back over his shoulder at the others. Then he moves closer to me, speaking in a whisper that only I can hear, "Aly, if you go out there, I may not be able to help you."

He's so sincere that I feel like I must be misunderstanding something. Does he mean that if I choose Karl, there's no life for me as a citizen? The choice is easier than I would have expected. "It's okay. I understand."

David starts to walk toward us, and I put up a hand to stop him. "It's all right. It shouldn't take me long. I'll meet you at the colony dock."

"Can we get the hell out of here?" Thompson asks.

Rob doesn't say another word, but I see the dark flames of anger burning behind his eyes. He turns around and steps aboard the carrier.

THIRTY-FOUR

As the engine powers up, I load the shuttle's crash coordinates into the sub's nav-system. The sub cycles through a maintenance and safety checklist and prompts me to activate detachment when all readouts are green. There are no portholes to see into the water outside, but the front half of the cockpit is embedded with screens video-linked to exterior cameras, every image enhanced to achieve perfect clarity. After diving a short distance, it begins to propel backward toward the crash site, its design negating any need to turn around.

Sub training is part of every Academy student's routine, but it's been at least ten years since I'd been in one and I'd forgotten the feeling of being underwater in a tiny tin can. Human perceptions aren't developed enough to detect the difference between pressurized, climate-controlled interstellar versus underwater crafts, yet my senses are alight with anxiety, my innate fear of tight places making even my skin feel as if it's shrinking over my muscles, choking me. I'd rather not know it, but even the smallest breach of the hull will quickly lead to an implosion, letting billions of gallons of crushing water obliterate me. Something about that sounds much worse than having my blood boil out of my pores in the middle of space.

The sub moves as soundlessly and smoothly as a ray and I arrive at the wreckage site in under twenty minutes. The video-link shows nothing but black empty water. I raise it above deck and activate the long-range radar, searching the area for anything still above water, hoping Karl was able to get free of the shuttle and find something to float on while waiting for a rescue. The scan shows nothing. I force the craft into a steep dive until the pressure gauge blinks a warning and auto-adjusts the speed to keep me from descending too fast. Within moments, it comes to a stop and a voice from the console tells me I'll have to don the onboard pressure-control suit if I want to continue. Frustrated, I quickly slide into the suit. It's stiff and much too bulky to allow optimal freedom of movement, and I won't be able to grasp my carbine—not that I'd want to shoot anything down here.

Another three thousand meters and the video-link scans the ocean floor, but I'm no longer looking. Karl is dead. There's no sign of the wreckage; underwater currents must have swept it away. It's useless to search. Even if he survived the crash but was stuck inside, he'd have died long before he got this deep. Tears burn my eyes and slide down my cheeks, a flood of pain and anguished guilt. Why had I been so stubborn? Why hadn't I ever told him how I felt? What the fuck is wrong with me?

Staring unseeing at the control panel, I cry until my eyes feel like overheated ball bearings, until they go dry and rub my sockets raw. The suit holds me erect, keeping my sagging body from spilling bonelessly onto the floor. Time passes, I don't know how long, and I consider what would happen to me if I took the suit off and let the sub resurface. The agony of nitrous bubbles stabbing through my blood, skin, and bones would almost be welcome as long as it could overcome the torment I feel in my soul. What had Karl felt? Was he still conscious when he hit the water? God, I hope it had been quick.

But I'm not ready to die. There are people here who can maybe still be helped. David would never forgive me. And there's T'Kai. Above all else, he's behind everything, the reason everything has gone to shit. I finally understand Rajcik's rage, and like him, it makes me want to live long enough to see T'Kai squashed and bleeding like an insect beneath my boot heel. Quantum should be transmitting in another day, if he hasn't already, and I plan to convince Vitruzzi to go back to Obal 10 and watch the Admin deconstruct from the inside.

Pulling it together, I reengage the sub's controls, letting it rise to a shallower elevation and deadhead toward the island. On the way, I set one of the console arrays to cycle through feeds from the multiple scanners installed throughout the platform and sub-complex, wanting to be warned if watercraft or aircraft arrive. It shouldn't take more than half an hour to get there, and I begin playing with the sub's transmitter to try and notify the crew I'm on my way. An image flashing on the scanner console catches my eye and makes my lungs lock around my breath. There's another ship landing on the platform, and it looks familiar. It's the *Red Horizon*.

Confused, alert, and prepared for anything, I alter course to pass closer to the platform. What the hell is the *'Rize* doing here?

Anxiously, I watch the bioreadouts on the pressure suit, itching to get out of it and back in control. As soon as I have the green light, I shed it and jack the sub's speed up a few knots, all the while keeping my eyes locked on the cycling video feed. The ship sits quietly, none of the hatches opening. And then the feed shows something else unexpected: the *Sphynx* is coming in to land, too.

What's going on? Did they find the settlers already? The fire racing through my nerve endings warns me that isn't it. I try the com console again but nothing happens. It's either broken or being jammed, and I can't pick up or send anything. I'm only a minute or two from the platform and I have to make a blind decision—get to land or find out why Venus and the *'Rize* have docked.

I reach the docking bay and kill the sub. If Venus and La Mer are in trouble, right now I might the only one who can help. Steering the sub to its magnetic anchor point, I scramble out and onto the pier. The elevator is still where we left it. Saying the code I'd written on my arm, I bring my carbine up to firing position and prepare for the doors to open topside. Fleetingly, I wish I'd taken the cloaking projector back from Rob, then let the thought fade into oblivion. It doesn't matter what I wish.

The lift comes to a stop and I open the doors. The control room is just as we'd left it. Empty. Carefully, I make my way toward the exit, listening for the sound of footsteps or a ramp opening, but I can't hear anything over the wind. A quick look outside shows both ships still sealed. Backing up into the alcove, I try to contact Venus through my VDU. Nothing but silence from her end, so I try Vitruzzi. Same issue.

Seconds tick by as I try to imagine what could be happening. There's only one reason Venus would have landed; someone from the crew hailed her. Yet, my gut and the unexpected presence of the 'Rize tell me something else is going on, something not part of the plan. Something wrong.

The longer I hesitate, the worse the scenarios I imagine become. It comes almost as a relief when the cargo ramp on the 'Rize opens and four sets of legs begin to descend. A second later, they're in full view standing at the bottom of the ramp.

With another glance around the edge of the alcove's protective wall, I recognize T'Kai immediately though he's shorter than I'd pictured, barely a few centimeters taller than me. He stands in front of Venus and La Mer, both standing with their hands linked behind their heads, eyes cast down. Rob's crewmember, Baker, is a few steps behind, a carbine pointing at their kidneys.

T'Kai looks in the direction of the control room and calls, his voice malicious and all business. "Come out where I can see you, Ms. Erikson. You're friends should also be along shortly."

I don't believe it. Thompson had been right. Rob's crew is Admin. We've been betrayed.

"I've got a bead on you, T'Kai. Let them go or you'll take one in the heart. I won't miss at this range."

His expression doesn't change. "Your pilot and wire-rat deserter friend will be next. You don't want to cause their deaths, do you? No, of course not. Now, I'll give you five seconds to come here. And be smart. Keep your weapons in a neutral position."

Too enraged to even speak, all I can do is what I'm told, not doubting for a second that the bitch Baker will happily fill Venus and

La Mer with holes if I give her a reason. I approach holding my AK-80 and Sinbad by their barrels at arm's length.

"Very good. Soldier, take those from her," T'Kai orders Baker.

For a moment, I consider ending everything right here. All I have to do is raise the 'Bad, pull the trigger, and T'Kai is done. Then, so are my friends and I.

I reach the group and stand stiffly in front of Baker. She sneers at me, a look that reflects my own loathing for her, and motions for me to drop my weapons. I do it. She pushes them back toward the ramp with her feet without taking her eyes from mine.

T'Kai walks to my Sinbad, picking it up and turning it over in his hands thoughtfully, noting the disabled ID reader. Putting it into the waist of his pants, he leans toward me and speaks close to my ear. "You see. It's people like you that make the work I do necessary." He steps away and nods at Baker.

She demands, "Everyone, on your knees. Hands stay up."

I get down and tilt my head to Venus. Her eyes are wide and scared, but she seems to be staying calm. "Are you two okay?"

She nods.

"How did they get the *Sphynx*?"

Baker shoves her carbine's barrel sharply into my cheek. "Shut the fuck up."

Rage surges through my veins, and I have to clench my fists into tight balls and dig my nails into my palms to keep from jumping up and strangling her.

"Ah, here they come," T'Kai says.

The rest of my crew is filing out of the control room, their weapons held in the same manner as mine. No one is with them forcing them to surrender, but they know if they don't, Venus, La Mer, and I are dead. As they approach, I hear footsteps coming down the *'Rize*'s ramp behind me. Montoya and Sims?

T'Kai continues talking. "Come, join your comrades. That's right, down on your knees."

"What kind of rotten fuck salad is this?" Desto asks as he drops down beside me.

I catch David's eyes. He doesn't have to say anything; I know what he's thinking. There are only three of them, plus T'Kai. How many more on the *Sphynx*?

We're forced into a semicircle at T'Kai's feet, but Rajcik refuses to kneel. He stands a little in front of us, towering over the director, his bulkiness shielding the smaller man almost completely from sight. The muscles in Rajcik's shoulders bulge through his shirt, tension and rage making him seem even larger.

"Here I am, T'Kai."

The director's eyes crease into slits, Rajcik's insolence and complete lack of fear souring his brute disdain. It only lasts for a moment. Then he smiles, his lips splitting apart grotesquely, like the skin of an overripe tomato.

"Yes. So clever of you to have evaded me this long, János." He takes a sliding step backward, and Sims moves up beside him with his gun leveled at Rajcik's stomach. "I've been very curious how you figured out that I would no longer be needing your services."

"You mean how I figured out you were going to kill me?" Rajcik grunts derisively. "It's what I would have done."

T'Kai blows air through his nose in an expression that suggests he laments having to speak to a simpleton. "You've wasted a great deal of my time, Rajcik. Can you possibly not understand that the resources at my disposal are *unlimited*? I *am* the Admin, or all of it that matters. And you—nothing but a speck of dust. *You* betrayed *me* when you stole the Nova, and the punishment you're about to receive is justly deserved."

The inside of my throat turns to sand at T'Kai's words. Did he say Rajcik had stolen the Nova? Stricken disbelief causes me to blurt without thinking, "The Nova's been destroyed. Rajcik detonated it inside the Fortress and blew the whole place apart."

The director nods at Montoya, who stands to the side of the group. He walks up and jams the butt of his rifle into the back of Rajcik's right thigh. The smuggler's leg buckles, sending him to one knee with a snarl.

T'Kai's eyes shift to me, their strange colors unnerving. "The remains of the space station showed only nuclear residue. I've no doubt you detonated something"—they slide back to Rajcik—"but it was not the Nova. You covered your tracks very, very well. However, it was your former crewmember, Ms. Erikson, that led me straight to you at R'Kadia, and I was able to recover the weapon."

Rajcik looks to where I kneel, his lips drawn back in a predatory grimace, but I return the stare with nothing but confusion. "I don't know what you're talking about," I say. "I didn't even know he was alive."

"You didn't have to know to still be of use. Our mutual friend brought us all together. And that, Ms. Erikson, is how you led me to Rajcik." His leathery skin wrinkles around his mouth and eyes in a reptilian smile, but I'm no longer paying attention to him. The only mutual "friend" he could be talking about...

My body jerks around, looking for Rob, but he's no longer seated behind me. He stands next to Montoya, a pistol in his right hand. From the corner of my eye, I see David's face contort into a kind of anguished spasm. It was *him* who had betrayed us. It was Rob all along. The word *sonofabitch* drop from David's lips like a blood spatter.

"Rob?" My throat contracts and turns my voice into a squeak. "What the hell is going on?"

His eyes barely meet mine before skittering away again and he says, "C'mon, Aly. You know I only gamble on winners."

"You motherfuck—" Thompson begins, rising from his knees, but the flat of Montoya's rifle butt against his teeth ends it.

I'm stunned, shaking with anger and something else, a deep, writhing feeling in the pit of my stomach. I wouldn't, *couldn't*, have ever believed he'd be capable of this. I whisper, "You turned us in," needing to hear it aloud for confirmation,

Bored with the spectacle, T'Kai turns and waves at the cockpit of the *Sphynx*. Shortly afterward, two more men walk down the ramp and join the others. Rob walks around and stands next to the director. The carefree grin he's always worn is scoured from his face, replaced with carefully crafted neutrality, like an automaton.

Rajcik spits, disgusted, but also amused. "Even I'm impressed, Cross. You had everyone fooled. I can see Aly being blinded by her own gullibility, but I don't know how you sold her brother on your bullshit. Bravo."

"I'm happy you're so impressed. Now shut the hell up."

"Right, or you'll shoot me, is that it?" The two men lock eyes, neither flinching.

For the first time, Vitruzzi speaks: "T'Kai, you have us. Arrest us, do what you want. But the settlers having nothing to do with any of this. Just let them go."

"Dr. Vitruzzi, surely you realize by now that there is nowhere left for them *to* go." He stares at her quietly for a moment, waiting for a comeback, but Vitruzzi falls silent.

"Where do you want them?" Baker asks.

T'Kai nods in the direction of the platform's edge. "Over there. Let them fall into the water and the tides will clean up. Mr. Cross"—he turns to face the Judas—"please prep your ship for takeoff. We'll be returning to Tunis. And notify my private dock of our estimated arrival on"—he looks at a display on his wrist—"Wednesday."

Rob climbs the *'Rize*'s ramp. Before he reaches the top, I yell, "You made the biggest mistake of your life, Rob! You'll pay for this!"

He stops for a second but doesn't turn around, then disappears inside.

"Get up," Baker grunts, jerking me by the collar and trying to push me toward the edge. I don't budge, and she jams her rifle butt into my kidney. The pain is sharp and immediate, helping to redirect my fury back to the here and now.

We're prodded and jostled and finally lined up along the edge of the platform. There is no railing. I glance down into the water before being spun around to face our captors. It's far, probably far enough to break my neck. Is a bullet preferable?

In a tone that's nearly pleasant, as if she's explaining a minor surgical procedure to a patient, Vitruzzi says, "T'Kai, you may kill us, but you'll still go down."

He and the five shooters are lined up in front of us, the salty wind whipping everyone's hair and clothes. "You're referring to those wire-rats, aren't you? Cross filled us in, and we wiped that slate clean a couple of days ago. Such wasted talent. But then, the damage sending that information to the public would have caused—it might have had a highly negative impact on the Administration. Dr. Vitruzzi, you have no idea how important the work I do is. One would think that a scientist of your caliber . . . but I understand. Some minds are simply not capable of thinking beyond a very narrow set of parameters."

They'd gotten to Quantum. Just like that, my last bit of strength collapses, a desperate sense of defeat pushing my heart to the verge of quitting. The last hope we'd had, smashed in a firestorm by a maniacal psychopath with a God complex. I look down into the water and imagine how it will feel. A burst of pain, freezing cold; then, thank Christ, it will be all over.

Rajcik takes a slow step forward from the line until he's standing directly in front of T'Kai. Three guns swivel toward him instantly but have no effect on his smug grin. He levels his gleaming black eyes on the director.

Without turning around, he says, "Vitruzzi, my business with your crew is finished."

So quickly no one has a chance to react, he lunges toward T'Kai— and the world fills with the sound of gunfire. I drop down and hurl myself forward toward Baker, the will to survive still ruling me. She jumps back and I yank free my Mini-Derg—they hadn't searched us —firing at her, but she's too fast and I miss. Movement erupts in every direction; Mason and David charge Montoya. while Rajcik grapples with T'Kai, and Vitruzzi and Brady hurtle toward Sims and one of the other men from the *Sphynx.* Venus sinks her teeth into a soldier's arm, and La Mer is punching another one in the face furi-ously, trying to keep the man from aiming his carbine.

Baker lunges away and trips, landing on her back. I pounce, reaching for her weapon and getting a grip on its strap. I yank as hard as I can, but she's already lost her hold and it comes away much too freely, flying off over the platform's side and into the water. She jumps to her feet, dashing frantically toward the *'Rize.* I fire the Derg, missing her again. It's out of juice and useless now, and I throw it after her carbine in disgust.

As I push myself to my feet, something solid connects with my ear, and I immediately fall back. My eyes blur with water, a distant ringing beginning in my head. Pain radiates down my face, into my teeth, and deep into my jaw as I roll to my side. In the panicked melee, I can't tell who hit me. I put a hand down to get some purchase to push myself up again, and it slides through a wet, warm puddle, the coppery smell of blood bursting into my nostrils. A cavalcade of pistol shots ring out so close that I have to cover my ears. Then, it's quiet.

"Hey, Aly, you okay?" I look up into David's face as he reaches down and grabs my shirt, pulling me to my feet. He's bleeding from his bottom lip, and a dark red bruise sweeps across one cheekbone.

"Yeah. Okay. Baker took off, she's heading toward the *'Rize.*" I pull myself to my feet and look around. Montoya is definitely dead. He's down on his stomach with his neck twisted at an angle that isn't natural. Two other soldiers also lie prone, with Desto standing above them holding his own recovered rifle. There's blood splashed around us like a slaughterhouse. But it's Rajcik that draws my attention.

He stands over T'Kai's still frame, his back to everyone. A thin trail of blood leaks into his shirt from a gash on his neck. The wound looks superficial, but the pool of blood growing beneath his feet tells a different story. He must have been struck by at least three or four bullets when he'd jumped T'Kai. He can't last long with the amount of blood he's losing.

I glance down at T'Kai's body, quickly looking away as my stomach does a nauseating flip. There is nothing left of his face but shredded bits of bone and oozing brain matter sticking out of his shirt collar. Rajcik had grabbed my 'Bad from T'Kai's belt and shot him over and over in the face, no doubt getting exactly the kind of revenge he'd planned and imagined. For better or worse, T'Kai has ceased to be an issue for us.

"Baker and Sims ran back to the *'Rize,*" David says, his breathing quick. "Rob's in there, too. We have to stop them from taking off."

Vitruzzi waves her arms at the two wounded soldiers. "Mason, tie them up. Watch them. Everyone else, let's go." She takes a step forward and then stops suddenly, bending over and gripping her side.

"Eleanor!" Brady grabs her gently, his face terror-filled.

She sucks air through her teeth. "It's okay, went through. Just hurts like a sonofabitch. Hand me my bag."

I bend down and pick it up. "What do you need?"

"You go get Cross. Venus, help me with this."

I exchange a look with Brady; it's clear that he's not leaving her side, so I nod at Mason, who joins the rest of us as we start a cautious ascent into the 'Rize's hold, picking up weapons as we go. Desto and Mason take a flight of stairs for the upper deck while David, Thompson, and I split up to cover the larger lower deck. I take a look back before going in and see Rajcik still standing like a gravestone over T'Kai's body. He doesn't budge.

THIRTY-FIVE

My first sweep takes me through an outer corridor that runs along the ship's left flank, serving mainly as a service tunnel for the engines and life-support components. As I cover the distance, I pass three or four narrow doorways and several service panels that are big enough for a person to fit inside. Cautiously, I flip open every one, listening for movement or breathing to verify if they're empty. When I find no one, I'm not surprised; Baker doesn't seem like the type who'll hide.

The corridor dead ends at a ladder leading to a ceiling hatch near the bow. I decide to turn back toward the hold instead of climbing it, hoping to meet up with another one of my crew. Whatever T'Kai's people had done to jam our VDU's, it's still in effect. The jammer must be aboard the *'Rize,* probably somewhere on the flight control deck. Except for my footsteps, it's completely silent. Rob hasn't been able to start the engines yet. He must have heard the firefight outside and is lying low, setting up an ambush, planning to pick us off one by one instead of en masse.

My guts tighten up more each time the thought of his betrayal fires through my brain. How could he do this? He'd never been deceptive or malicious, never been the kind of person who'd sell his soul for profit or make a compromise that would fuck over his friends. He and David had practically been brothers. And he and I . . . I'd believed he cared about me. There had to be something, T'Kai must have threatened him . . . I don't know. And it doesn't matter, the results are the same. Rob betrayed me, betrayed *us*. There's only one way to resolve it.

I reach the door to the hold. Closed. I thought I'd left it open. Using the activation keypad, I try to open it, but nothing happens. I hit the button again and again, frustrated by its failure to cooperate, and finally give up. Shouldering my '80 on its strap, I grab the manual crank and begin pulling with all of my strength. The thing's locked up tighter than a hangman's noose. Grunting with the effort, it still doesn't move, and I begin to think I'll have to go back down to the ceiling hatch, when out of nowhere, it starts spinning. I jerk my hands out of the way just in time to keep them from getting ripped off inside the mechanism. The hatch opens and I careen off balance into the hold like a drunk, catching myself just before hitting the floor. Quickly sweeping my carbine off my shoulder, I try to look into every corner and angle at once.

A rustling noise makes me jerk my head left just in time for a fist to land squarely on my cheek. As my head bounces back, my attacker strikes my right arm hard, just above the elbow, making it fall momentarily numb. My carbine sling slips from my shoulder, and the gun drops from my grasp. I hadn't seen the attacker, but reflex takes over and I close the gap between us in one quick lunge.

Water pours from my eye again—the same goddamn side as last time—but I can see fine from the other. Baker stands near the wall, poised and ready to fight. She feints to her right and then jumps forward with a flat hand aimed at my throat. Barely in time, I block her arm and let the momentum spin me into a roundhouse kick that catches her in the ribcage and sends her sprawling sideways. Lightning fast, she's back on her feet before I can close in and finish the job. She lunges in low, blocking the next kick, and sending me backward off balance. She follows through—*so fucking fast*—and lands a kick of her own directly into my side. Air explodes out of my lungs and I crumple sideways, my back exposed for another kick, which I know instinctively is coming. Instead of giving her space for a windup, I roll back toward her and scrabble to grab her booted foot as it swings toward me. I catch it as she tries to jump over me and send her smashing into the wall. I have no breath and struggle to unlock my lungs as I roll away this time, blinking and trying to get to my feet. She spins around, blood dripping from a cut above her right eye where she'd hit the wall.

"I'm going to fucking kill you, Erickson."

"Try it," I wheeze, finally pulling in snatches of oxygen as my chest opens up.

We circle, both looking for an opportunity to tear the other to shreds. I'd felt her animosity like a walking cancer since the first time our paths had crossed, even before my crew had become the Admin's target. The friction between us was destined to turn into flames and we're both prepared to fight this out to the death.

She snarls and picks the moment to dart forward and reach for my carbine, still lying on the floor a meter away. I leap toward her, using my body to push her past the gun, but she grabs me and pulls me over. Moving with the dexterity of a snake, she somehow gets on top of me and grabs my throat. I buck furiously and twist onto my side underneath her, forcing her hands to release. But she grabs my hair instead and jerks my head up, then slams it down against the hard floor.

Sparks erupt behind my eyes and she does it again. A warm sensation spreads down the side of my face and the sparks start to dim, as if a shade is being pulled down on the inside of my eyes. I flip my body back to flat beneath her trying to get my arms up to make her release my hair, but she's ready and smashes her fist into my nose. Ferocious, mind-splitting pain erupts inside my head, my brain stutter-stepping in a dance of agony like a hive of angry bees. I taste the blood pouring down the back of my throat, and suddenly the pain no longer matters because I'm choking on it. Gasping, coughing, gagging, I spray her with blood while I struggle to breathe.

She jumps up, her weight mercifully gone, and I'm able to roll over and get to my knees. I cough hard, nearly vomiting as I clear the blood from my throat and lungs. My vision has narrowed to two small chinks of light directly in front of my eyes. All I see is the floor beneath me and the spatters of blood from my struggle to breathe, like delicate drips of bright red paint.

"I told you I was going to kill you."

I look up and see her knees a few centimeters in front of my face and realize she's pointing my own weapon at my head. The sound of a gunshot—

Her body buckles and tumbles over backward, lolling in an unnatural sprawl as blood begins coating the floor beneath her. Nearly in shock, I spin over into a sitting position to see who's behind me and where the shot came from.

Rob stands there, his weapon lowered, and his hand reaches out to help me up. "I'm sorry, Aly. I didn't want it to go like this."

I hitch air into my lungs and stay sprawled on the floor, unable to react.

"Come on, we can still get—"

Then he's tumbling forward as a giant red flower explodes from his chest, landing on top of me. I writhe out from beneath him, pushing his body over in the effort. One of his hands clenches around my wrist and I look into his face. The pain and sorrow I see in his eyes rips at me like daggers. Then his hand grows slack and he's gone.

I turn around and find David standing a few meters away. Our eyes meet, and his aquamarine irises are as hard as obsidian, as cold as a glacier. I pull myself to my feet, unable to look back at Rob's body, and start walking toward my brother. The sound of footsteps on the ramp draws our attention.

La Mer runs up, out of breath. "Venus is on the *Sphynx* and picked up two Corps ships in the area, coming directly for us. We've got to get the hell out of here, now!"

"Desto, Mason?" I wheeze, still short of breath, my nose swollen and clogged.

"I'll get them, you just go," David says, running back into the corridor toward the bow.

Galvanized, La Mer and I run outside and board the *Sphynx*. A glance toward T'Kai's captured soldiers shows them still tied up and lying where the crew left them, alive. I'm momentarily surprised, but then, with the way things have unraveled, what difference does it make at this point if they're dead or alive? Both the Corps and the Admin know who we are; there's nothing these soldiers can tell them that isn't known already. Vitruzzi isn't bloodthirsty; she knows their deaths would be futile.

The ship's engines are already cycling up and Brady waits for us in the hold. "Where are the others?" he asks.

"David's gone to get Mason and Desto. What about the settlers?"

Brady's expression is desperate, but he merely gives his head a short, definitive shake. "We'll have to try and come back." He looks haggard and angry, but there's the same solid determination in his face that epitomizes his approach to everything.

"We'll get them, Brady. Soon." I try to be encouraging, these are his friends and family, but deep inside, I feel the bottom dropping out.

In a minute David, Desto, and Mason sprint up the ramp, Mason slamming the control and closing the hatch. Brady's on the com telling Venus to go, go, *GO!*

She launches and arcs into a steep climb, everyone in the hold grabbing onto something. We're all here except for Vitruzzi, who's in the cockpit with Venus, and—

"Where's Rajcik?" My eyes dart around, searching for him.

"He's . . ." Brady starts and trails off.

"David, did you see him on the *'Rize*?" I ask.

Instead of responding, he slams a fist into the wall. "Shit!"

Realization dawns on all of us: both Thompson and Rajcik are missing.

"T'Kai said the Nova was on that ship." My words come out flat and dull, wasted. "He was bleeding. He can't get anywhere."

Brady says, "Eleanor slowed the bleeding and gave him an IV. That ship's got to have a med-station, maybe some supplies. It's hard to say how long he'll last."

Venus's voice comes through the com: "I think we'll shake them, we've got enough lead—" She's cut off by ear-splitting feedback and then the ship starts to dive, hard, cutting through the sky like a plunging eagle chasing its prey.

"Ohfuckohfuckohfuck." I'm looking directly at La Mer as he whispers what will probably be his last words in a prayerlike litany.

The pressure changes inside the ship as we descend, and my grip on the hold's railing grows so desperate I feel as if the bones in my hand will crack. It's the only thing I can do.

Suddenly the *Sphynx* bucks hard, throwing everyone forward, and a small explosion emanates through the hold from somewhere near the belly. Mason's body hits the wall like a piece of stout furniture, and he slides to the floor unconscious and bleeding from the back of his head. Our rate of descent begins to decrease. The explosion may have been Venus engaging the reverse thrusters before our speed was slow enough, effectively destroying them, but maybe, just maybe, keeping us from hitting the deck so hard that the ship breaks into a million pieces. Maybe giving us a chance.

As soon as I have the thought, the floor beneath me begins to bounce and vibrate furiously, knocking me to my knees. Then I hear things crashing into the ship outside, banging off the hull and snapping, like we're going through trees. Venus got us over land, at least. Clenching my teeth and preparing to be flattened or blown up, I curl my body into a tight ball against the floor, one hand still clutching the rail as, finally, the ship starts to slow and drop, almost gently, to the ground.

I open my eyes, first to unexpected stillness and then frantic movement as the crew starts to pick themselves up. I hear engines outside, at least two ships buzzing us, and know that the shit is just beginning.

"David?"

"Yeah, I'm good. You?"

I hardly believe it, but aside from some bruises, I'm not hurt. "Good. Desto? Brady? La Mer?" Mason is still unconscious, but it doesn't look like he's bleeding too bad.

Brady doesn't bother to respond, but immediately takes off running for the cockpit to check on Venus and Vitruzzi. La Mer stands up shakily and follows.

"We can't stay here, we gotta move out," Desto says, grabbing Mason under one arm. "Give me a hand."

David runs over and the two of them lift up Mason's limp body. I reach into my vest and pull out a vial of chemical salts, snapping them under his nose. He groans and twists his head, then, with surprising vitality, regains his feet, yelling loudly.

"Hey, man, it's all right. We got you," Desto says.

Mason's cloudy eyes slowly focus and he asks, "Did we go down?"

"Yeah. There're still Corps ships in the area. We need to move. Can you walk?"

He nods.

"What about the others?" I ask, knowing we can't wait for them.

David says, "Let's figure out how to get out, then get a bead on things from outside."

The cargo ramp is buckled, useless, which means we won't be able to get the Rover out. The three of them start working on the man-door while I run into the armory and gather more ammunition, passing it out to them once I've collected as much as I can carry. The door is jammed and Desto melts a hole through it with the last of the ship's E-10 wax. With a short drop to the earth, we're free of the ship and in the middle of a jungle.

THIRTY-SIX

The air hits my nostrils in a frontal assault, the stench of wetness, putrescence, and rot. The entire atmosphere is hot and heavy, almost syrupy, and I have a hard time buying Rajcik's assertion it had once been arid. The ground squishes as I step across it, each footprint instantly filling with seepage that is the same greenish color as everything around me. The ship is infested with vines and foliage that broke from the canopy during our descent and were pasted against the hull like camouflage. Despite the cover, Corps ships will still spot the wreckage easily.

David holds his carbine at the ready, surveying the area around us as we all hustle toward the bow. There's a service door for the electronics bay directly underneath the communications room, the closest exit to the cockpit. It isn't open when we reach it, and Desto, the tallest of us, stretches up to bang on it, hoping to attract Brady or La Mer's attention. In a minute, we hear Brady's voice.

"Desto?"

"Yeah, is everyone okay?"

"No." There's a noise, like someone's stomping on the door, then it flies open and Brady leans out. "Venus is hurt, pretty bad. I'm going to hand her down. Grab her."

Desto and Mason position themselves below the door as David and I keep watch. I look back over my shoulder and see Venus's limp body being lowered. There's no blood or obvious injuries. Internal? Her eyes flutter as Brady releases her, but she spills into their grasp almost lifelessly. La Mer jumps down immediately and takes her, cradling her in his arms like a child.

"Where can we take her?" His eyes are wide and desperate. No one answers, and I have to turn away before he sees in my expression what we're all thinking—she probably won't make it.

As I look back toward the swathe of wreckage the ship's landing caused, I see another ship coming in low, following the broken tree line.

"Time to move!" I shout.

I turn back around to make sure they're reading me as Brady helps Vitruzzi down. She's carrying her heavy med-bag, and her face is twisted in pain. She only puts weight on one leg as she hits the deck, reaching out for help, and fresh blood that had begun to crust on her shirt from where she was shot seeps through. Brady supports her with her arm over his shoulders and we all begin running, as best we can, toward the nearest patch of heavy overgrowth. The trees are thick with ropy plants climbing them, and the ground sucks at our feet, keeping our progress slow and laborious. We make it a few dozen meters as the Corps ship sweeps overhead, dropping a stun bomb directly onto the *Sphynx*. The heavy *whoomph* sound of the payload detonating reverberates in our ears. If anyone had still been inside, they'd be down for hours.

"They didn't blow the ship. They must want to capture us alive," David remarks, fighting with the stalk of a leafy plant that's somehow become wrapped around his leg. I walk over and cut through it with my NKT bolo. Exasperated, he says, "We need to try and find the colony. They've got to have some kind of barracks or buildings. At least somewhere we can help Venus."

Vitruzzi says, "We came over it during the escape. We're probably about ten klicks away, back toward the east." Her jaw is set, cords standing out on her neck from pain.

Ten kilometers might as well be a hundred in this undergrowth, but we can't just stand here and wait to die. We have at least fifteen weapons between the eight of us, and enough ammunition to fend off or assault a small force should we encounter any. We should be all right against any hostile prisoners we come up against. The key is to move steadily, stay alert, and keep under the canopy in case the Corps comes back.

Desto and Mason make a quick run to the ship, returning with some food, water packs and purifying tablets, and a stretcher to carry Venus. Her skin, always pale, has gone the color of watery cream, the network of her veins clearly visible beneath the skin. Vitruzzi works on her briefly, trying to keep her stable and out of shock, but we don't know the extent of her injuries. After donning an inflatable splint, Vitruzzi lets us know she's ready to move out. David and Desto take the stretcher poles, and the rest of us span into a line, keeping our weapons at the ready.

The drudge is interminable, the sticky jungle floor and tangling plants making every step a battle. Trying to conserve water in the stifling humidity is a lesson in defeat as our skin seems to instantly convert every sip we take into sweat. My nose and head ache from the fight with Baker. Anti-inflammatories help curb the swelling, but the thick air still makes me feel like I'm breathing through a wet towel. The nasal filters we all wear are flexible, almost like a low-density sponge, so Baker's punch had not dislodged mine. There's no telling what else is in this atmosphere thanks to T'Kai's monstrous science experiments. Lethal pollens come to mind.

Three hours pass and eventually the ground around us begins to show signs of activity. Trees have been cut and undergrowth has been trampled or ripped away, allowing us to walk faster. We cross a wide path containing tread marks that extends to the west as far as we can see. It must serve as the main artery for this region, but we don't know where it goes. Our better judgment tells us not to follow the road, but after trudging through the odious undergrowth we can't resist the easier going it affords. Besides, we'll be able to make much better time, which is what Venus desperately needs.

About an hour into the march, we'd witnessed two Corps ships overhead, their flight paths so close it seemed as if one had been in pursuit of the other. It struck us all as unusual, but what had been stranger was the sound of an aerial explosion far south of us just after we'd lost sight of the ships. Whatever was happening is of little consequence to us now. Once they land on the ocean platform and figure out that the bloody mess lying there had been T'Kai, we're certain to see more activity out here when they come searching for us. In the meantime, all we can do is try to help Venus and continue the original mission of finding the Beachers.

A hedge of low-slung stone buildings emerges from the line of trees directly in front of us, looking derelict and abandoned. The group stays put while David and I move into the doorway of the nearest in order to find out what, or who, is inside. The door is made of iron and wood and swings inward heavily, the hinges reluctant. The walls are completely windowless, and it's pitch black in the interior. There's no sound. I flip the scope light of my carbine on and scan the room. There are about fifty bunk beds lining both sides of the walls, like a barracks, all with sheets and blankets that appear to be in reasonably good shape. There *are* people living here. The room takes up the entire floor of the building, and there's another door at the far end. David explores it and says it's a latrine and shower. Nobody's home. Cautiously, I signal to the others, and they join us inside.

Brady finds a panel on the wall and hits a switch. Naked overhead lights ping to life, showing more of the room. It's definitely lived in. Every bunk has a locker at the foot and to the side for the inmates here to keep personal belongings. It's a lot more orderly than I'd expected to see.

"Put her down over there," Vitruzzi tells La Mer and Brady, who've taken over the stretcher.

Venus's breathing is ragged and shallow, but she's holding on. La Mer kneels beside her, holding her hand and whispering something into her ear too quietly for anyone else to hear.

Vitruzzi leans against the wall next to the bunk they'd laid Venus on and says to the rest of us, keeping her voice down, "She has at least three broken ribs that have probably punctured a lung. If I open her up here, she'll get an infection, and I don't have what I need anyway. The only thing we can do is keep her completely still so the tear doesn't get worse. But she's bleeding into the pleural cavity and developing a pneumothorax, so time is getting short." She's angry, almost spitting the words out, knowing that she could save Venus if the situation was different. "Patrick, we have what I need on the *Sphynx*."

"Eleanor, we can't go back."

She stands completely still for a minute, her eyes focused hard on the wall, then hurls her med-bag against the floor. "Goddammit! Goddamn those bastards!" She lets her head fall forward, her hair obscuring her face, but not before I see the tears spilling down her cheeks. Brady puts his arms around her and they stand together in an embrace.

I turn to David and Desto, the need to keep moving making me jittery and volatile. "Let's sweep the rest of the buildings and then head to the desal plant. There may be someone who can help." I feel like an idiot for saying it, but their eyes show they're on board. Anything is better than standing here watching our friend die.

Mason elects to stay behind and help keep watch with Brady, so we move out. Four other buildings stand in the immediate vicinity, all of them squat, built of the same brown stone. Two of them are also barracks and one is a dining facility. We don't find anyone. The fifth building is newer and bigger than the rest. Like the others, there are no windows, but this one is two stories tall. Along with a standard man-door, an articulating track door rises up the wall. It's a warehouse, probably where they store all the supplies, and locked up tightly.

I turn to David. "Where do you think everyone is?"

He shrugs. "Maybe they're all at the desal plant. Or hiding. Corps ships in the area may make people antsy."

"Or maybe there's nobody here at all. Maybe they just killed everyone," Desto comments, his eyes sweeping the surrounding jungle suspiciously.

"No, that's not possible. Those barracks have been used. The DFAC's stoves are still warm."

"Well, whatever it is, it's going to be dark in another hour or so," David says. "We should make a quick run over to the plant, then head back to Brady and the rest."

We can see a silo or smokestack rising from the plant, and the road continues past the warehouse straight toward it, about fifteen hundred meters distant. Keeping close to the trees, we extend into a wide line to reduce the chance that any shooters can hit all three of us with one burst. David takes lead, I'm in the middle, and Desto is behind. The brush and trees have been hacked away to nothing several meters around the plant's perimeter, leaving a wide-open area that makes the last of my spit dry up.

When we reach the edge of the cleared area, David takes a knee and looks back at the two of us, giving us a tiny nod. I move up into a closer position to cover him as he makes the dash forward. When I'm ready, he stands up, leans forward for the sprint, and—

Someone grabs him by the collar and yanks him hard into the trees. David lets out a grunt of surprise and I see him and whoever had grabbed him rolling down a short berm, bodies entangled. I'm on my feet instantly, jumping down the berm after them. I arrive as David gets on top of his attacker and plants a knee in his chest, simultaneously pulling a pistol and pointing it into the attacker's face. His bright, wide eyes gleam through a layer of dirt, and blood leaks from his lips. Desto hurdles over the edge of the ditch and lands heavily beside me.

"Got it, it's under control," David hisses, his eyes not leaving the attacker's face. "Who the fuck are you?"

Desto hunkers down beside me, his eyes cutting back and forth between the trees and the guy on the ground, ready for more people to jump out of the bushes.

"I'm a prisoner, just a prisoner. Don't shoot me, man!"

"Why did you jump me?"

"Look, there's about thirty Corps soldiers in the plant. If you go in there, they'll cut you down." The man's breathing starts to slow, and a look comes over his face that reminds me of a rat that has just escaped a trap. "You got guns, right? How many you got? I saw your ship go down. Can you get me outta here?" Then, in a peevish voice, he asks, "Can you get offa me? I'm not gonna do nothin'."

"David," I whisper, "don't." But he doesn't need my advice.

"Shut up and listen. You're really goddamn lucky that I didn't kill you for that. Here's what's going to happen. I'm going to ask you a few questions, and I better like your answers or a busted lip is going to be the least of your worries. You get me?"

The man on the ground nods miserably.

"What are you up to out here, and where are the rest of the prisoners?"

He sucks at his lip, reluctant to give up any information. So David gives him incentive by deliberately pointing his pistol straight into the man's eyes, letting him get a good look down the barrel.

He decides to talk. "They're locked up in the plant. The Corps came in early this morning and rounded everyone up, just like they do right before they bring in a new group." He adds ominously, "Or before they take some away."

"Why didn't they round you up?"

"Not all of us live in the barracks. Some of us have been here awhile. Since before . . . before the big die off. So they don't know we're out there."

"How many?"

He starts to squirm. "Man, I told you what you want to know. Can't you just get off me?"

David grasps him by the chin and forces him to keep still. "How many?"

"Ten, man, there's ten of us."

"Okay, good. One more question. Were some new prisoners brought in a couple of weeks ago? About a hundred of them?"

"You mean those miners from Spectra 6. Yeah, they're here."

I glance over and catch the excitement on Desto's face. The settlers are here, probably still alive. Only thirty soldiers—and the entire Admin and Corps—between them and us.

"All right look," David says, "I'll let you up, but I want you to take us to your group and show us the weak spots in the plant, help us figure out how to get in there and neutralize the soldiers. Then, if we work together, we can help you and your friends get off this rock."

"You want to take on those soldiers? There's only three of you!"

David stands, keeping his pistol at the ready. "There are others, and we've got the advantage of surprise. With your group, we'll have more than enough."

I glare at David, not liking his plan at all, but I keep my mouth shut. Giving guns to a bunch of murderers and thieves is like giving them to a pack of rabid monkeys, but maybe there's enough incentive for them to help, and not turn on us, if they think we can get them out of here.

The prisoner brushes himself off exaggeratedly, though the filth ingrained in his clothing isn't coming clean without the aid of a fire hose, or possibly a fire, and then moves into the jungle without another word. We follow closely, struggling to match his pace. He's used to walking through the grasping, clinging undergrowth and adopts a dipping and diving method that is almost completely silent. We try to move with equal stealth but can't help making a little noise just trying to keep him within sight. Finally, David demands that he slow down so we don't expose ourselves. He complies, obviously disgusted, but it gives me the time I need to dig a food bar out of my pack. I don't remember the last time I ate anything and some extra energy is sorely needed. My mouth is too dry to do much more than break the material into small enough chunks to swallow, but it helps keep me going.

"Duchamp, what are you doing bringing strays out here?"

The voice comes from somewhere close by but I can't see anyone. The man called Duchamp freezes and says, "Found them trying to get into the plant. They're the ones from the ship we saw, not Corps."

Like an apparition materializing from inside the tree, a man steps into our midst. He's dirty like Duchamp, bald, and missing most of his left ear, creased shrapnel scars covering that side of his face and neck. He carries a thick, straight branch that's been sharpened to a wicked point. "Why are you people here?"

There's a rustling around us almost like a breeze, and suddenly there are several more of them. Standing in trees, under tall plants, in front and behind, all of them carrying some variation of club or spear. Desto and I close ranks and point our weapons at the nearest figures.

David thumbs his pistol to auto-fire but keeps his tone conversational. "We came to try and rescue the settlers who were brought here from Spectra 6."

"Does your ship still fly?"

"No, but with your help, we can overrun the Corps team and get out of here on one of their ships. We've been to the platform, we know their security, and we have enough weapons to do the job." David's taking a huge risk, but then, they don't know what's really going on.

The man turns his back to us and walks a few paces away, thinking. Then he spins back and says, "Let's go somewhere we can talk."

David glances toward us and I ask, keeping my voice low, "Don't you think we should try and get word to Vitruzzi and Brady?"

"We can't afford to get separated."

I tap my VDU, more out of frustration than hope, but it's still black. Nodding reluctantly, I fall in behind Desto, and the group begins walking deeper into the jungle. There's a noise by my ear, a *whzzzngg* sound that resembles a mosquito's buzz or hummingbird's wings, and the man leading the group suddenly begins clutching at his back frantically, like he's been stung. Then something metallic clicks loudly behind us. Everyone begins to run.

THIRTY-SEVEN

Rubble lies on all sides of me: broken rocks, shards of glass, bits of steel and lathe. It creates a cradle of debris that I sit amid like an invalid on a sick bed. When the occasional Corps craft does a low pass overhead, the broken roof of the building I'm in vibrates, shaking loose more dust and debris, which rains down on me. The humid air saturates the fine particles quickly, leaving me in a sticky sheet of dirt. It's easy to imagine the foliage creeping in and swallowing me completely in a short time, the jungle life around me as potent and teeming as I am drained and wretched.

I don't know where the others are, or even how many are left. The Corps assault had hit too fast and hard for me to keep track of everyone, all of us scattering to keep from getting mowed down. At first, they'd only been shooting tranquilizers, trying to round us up, but switched to live rounds as soon as they realized we were firing back. I've been lying in this ruin for the last two hours trying to decide what to do next while the prisoner I'd followed through the jungle bleeds to death beside me. The last thing he'd told me was his name, Slobadan Zand, apparently arrested twenty years ago for nothing but stealing supplies from Admin warehouses. Delirious at the end, he'd pleaded with me to find his family on Eruo Pium if I make it out of here and tell them what had happened to him. Despite the three bullets he had taken in the back, he managed to lead me to this decrepit ruin after the attack, part of the original complex built sixty years ago and long abandoned. There was nothing I could do but give him something to dull the pain as his life drained out on the ground around us. Another good person dead. I'm almost surprised I still have the energy to care.

My ears start to hum and the wall I lean on begins a slow vibration. I press into it in a primitive impulse to try and make myself smaller and less conspicuous as another ship flies over. Their passes are getting closer together as they close their search grid. An explosion echoed through the jungle some time ago, reverberating like thunder. They must have decided to blow the *Sphynx* to make sure no one could get out of here. I'm going to have to do something soon or they'll find me, but it doesn't seem worth the effort. In reality, I'm too tired, too spent, too far beyond caring anymore to move. It's over. We failed. The Admin is too strong and we're too weak. It's a simple matter of evolution. If this is what our species has become, I'll go ahead and die now.

"ALY ERICKSON. Do you copy? Come in."

I scramble upright, realizing simultaneously that I'd fallen asleep and my carbine is missing. Running my hand along the ground beside me, my fingers encounter the familiar cold metal, and I take a relieved breath as I pick it up.

"Erikson. Come in. Are you there?"

It's clear that I'm starting to lose my grip. The voice can't possibly be who it sounds like, but my VDU is working again, at least the receiver. The screen is destroyed, so I can't see who's calling me, but the transmitter button is still intact.

The light faded while I slept, the blackness so dense it's an almost physical presence. How long have I been here? It's strange to be on solid ground and have a real night; I'd grown so used to the short darkness of Spectra 6. In space, it's always night, but it's different. It's an artificial, disjointed night, not in touch with natural Circadian rhythms. But here, the darkness seems prolonged; it feels like days since I've seen the sun. My bone-tired weariness blocks every other consideration out and ignoring the voice coming through my com seems like a rational choice. When have I ever been this tired?

"Do you read me? Come in, Erikson. Aly Erikson. This is Karl Strahan. Do you copy?"

I jerk fully awake again. What the fuck is going on? Karl is dead. And in a short time, I will be too. Is this some kind of joke? Does the Admin have our names? Of course they do; Rob had given them everything.

Strangely, I'm annoyed. What's the point of this game? Am I really a threat to the Admin anymore? What do they care? My crew is wiped out, probably dead, and the settlers don't have anyone else to come for them, so they'll be dead soon, too. Can't they just leave us alone, leave *me* alone, instead of playing this sick charade?

"Aly, are you out there?"

But that voice. It *sounds* like Karl, and there's an edge of desperation in it. Not an easy tone to fake. I think for a few minutes. If I'm going to die anyway, does it hurt to satisfy this last touch of curiosity?

It's hard to stand; my legs have gone to sleep and I'm dehydrated. Jamming my hands into chinks in the wall's crumbling surface, I use it to pull myself up, like scaling a rock face. The silhouette of the doorway is a lighter shade of black than the room, and I begin to stumble toward it, tripping over chunks of concrete and roots that have broken through the floor. I switch on my carbine's light, and my legs begin to tingle as the blood starts moving through them, making my steps even more faltering. Finally, I reach the doorway and lean outside, taking a deep breath of the thick, moist air. It's less stagnant at night, a cool wisp of breeze stirring it around. Almost pleasant.

The breeze picks up, whipping through the dark forest like a swath. No, not a breeze, someone is coming, several someones, moving toward me in the dark. My light is a target, and I turn it off automatically, knowing it's probably too late to do anything.

"Aly?"

The movement has stopped. I don't respond, can't respond. There's no way I can mistake that voice.

"Aly, it's Karl."

It's as if my throat has closed to the width of a pinhead, but I force a whisper, "Karl?"

A form materializes less than two meters in front of me as the dull green glow of a nightstick slowly powers up. A man stands there. It could be him, but I don't move. Finally, he pulls the night vision goggles off and I see him. Karl. Alive. I'm forced to grip the doorjamb as my legs threaten to collapse. Then he's standing beside me, holding me up, his breath blowing through my dirt- and blood-matted hair.

"Are you hurt?"

I shake my head, unable to believe what I'm seeing. "Karl, what . . .?"

"Come on. Let's get you out of here. I'll explain when we're airborne."

THIRTY-EIGHT

A doctor comes in and takes the vitals for Vitruzzi and Venus, ignoring me. He's used to me by now. His Corps uniform still makes me feel edgy and slightly unreal, like some part of me that lives in the future is looking back at the past but is unable to warn me. I want to run like hell whenever I see him or an orderly, but where could I go anyway? The ship is fleet, as Corps as his uniform, and even though I know the personnel *aren't* Corps, not anymore, I still can't shake the feeling that they're going to arrest me.

Vitruzzi and Venus are both awake listening to Karl explain what had happened between the moments we watched his shuttle go down and several hours later when he'd used our embedded trackers to locate everyone. He's already gone through the series of events twice, but even now, most of me is still in too much shock to really believe it.

The patroller that had picked up the *Sphynx* and shot Karl out of the sky had been on advance recon for T'Kai, just waiting for us to show up. After it had blown out his flight controls, Karl was able to coax just enough auxiliary power out of the shuttle to pull the nose out of its dive and cut the engines just before hitting the water, alleviating the impact enough to keep from killing him. Bruised but whole, he'd swum out and been carried more than a kilometer from the impact site by the current. Over an hour passed before a Corps drop-ship had flown over. Figuring his ticket was already punched and preferring to die dry, he'd flicked on a strobe and they'd spotted him. When they fished him out, he'd prepared a story about being aboard a cargo hauler with a malfunctioning nav-system that went down on Keum Libre, just to see how much time he could buy. Turned out, he never had to launch into the story at all. The drop-ship's captain had taken him to a long-range fleet cruiser where he met the commander, General Medina, and her associate—a wire-rat named Quantum.

Even though Vitruzzi and I have heard the story, this is the first time Venus has been awake since coming out of surgery, and Karl continues to explain. "Quantum didn't wait. He copied the information we got from Rajcik and the Fortress and sent it to a dozen other wire-rats and contacts he had in the Corps. They started lightwaving it just a few hours after you left Obal 6. Apparently, they've been planning another rebellion since the last one was squashed, and planning better. This ship's commander, Medina, is one of the, I guess you'd say, leaders. They've got seven other carrier commanders, or at least their ships, and most of the troops on Obal 5, 7, and 8 behind them. This is bigger than it was last time. They're planning a coup on the Directorate within the week."

"Quantum is alive? T'Kai said they'd killed him before the transmission was sent," Venus says. Her feet bob to-and-fro under the blanket as if she's pedaling a tiny bicycle, causing the IV tubes tangling from almost every limb to dance and jitter around her. Her voice is barely a whisper.

"T'Kai either had bad intel or he was bluffing. Quantum wasn't lying when he said they were ready for this. He's here, been on this ship since the transmission was sent. He and General Medina have been working together since the beginning. Don't ask me how a Corps fleet commander can hide the fact that she's planning a mutiny, but that just goes to show you how widespread this is."

La Mer asks, "Why did Quantum bring them to Keum Libre?"

It's a good question. Quantum never hid the fact that he didn't give a damn about us or the settlers. It was always about over-throwing the Admin.

Karl continues, "Two reasons: he knew Cross was working for the Admin, and he knew enough about what had happened between Rajcik and T'Kai to expect T'Kai to come for him. Where better for T'Kai to erase both us and Rajcik than KL? But after they picked up Rajcik on the *'Rize* and interrogated the soldiers you'd left on the platform, Medina decided to try and help, if it wasn't too late. I think she's a little more humane than Quantum."

"What's the other?" I ask.

"The other reason? It's a good place to lay low. Keum Libre is outside the normal flight patterns for Corps assault and enforcement crafts. Medina can stay relatively obscure in this zone and launch battalion gunships from here to mop up Corps holdouts throughout the rest of the quadrant."

Karl puts a warm, rough hand on my neck, rubbing the skin gently. I'm sitting on a chair at the foot of Venus's bed with him beside me, and my body floods with a deluge of emotions, almost too many to manage. I feel like I might burst. Relief, fear, guilt, gratitude, shame, hope. And the deepest, most powerful, love. I sit still, letting them wash through me, not trusting myself to say anything, or even look at Karl. Not yet.

After Rajcik's suicide move on T'Kai, only one of the ships that had chased the *Sphynx* from the platform had been hostile. The other two were part of Medina's battalion, the one that had picked up Karl, and the third that had gone after the *Red Horizon*. Rajcik launched just after the *Sphynx,* knowing that he wouldn't be a target for the Corps drop-ship since the *'Rize* was supposed to be trans-porting T'Kai. To his extreme surprise, Medina also knew T'Kai was supposed to be aboard Rajcik's hijacked ship and had curtailed the escape with a ship-net, incapacitating the engine, and allowing Medi-na's carrier to bring the *'Rize* in. They'd questioned him and Thomp-son, learning what had happened to T'Kai and about the *Sphynx*'s dire situation, prompting Medina to send three gunships to neutralize the Corps ship looking for us, destroying it, which must

have been the two ships we'd seen flying over us as we'd been hiking
Venus to the colony. Finally, when things were under control, Karl led
a company of new rebel soldiers to land, overtaking the detachment
guarding the plant, rescuing the settlers, and then taking a search-
and-rescue squad to track down the rest of his crew.

A RABBLE OF VOICES comes from the main benches of the locker room
as I push through the door. All I want right now is a shower, some
clean clothes, and food. I highly doubt a Corps ship has any good
hooch in the galley, but I'm betting I can track down a handful of
soldiers—make that *ex*-soldiers—who'll have a stash somewhere. I'll
leave that for when I have more energy.

The smell of gun oil and aftershave hits me in a wave. Karl is
seated on a bench with Desto and David, who turn their heads as I
enter.

"Desto, you look like you were in a fight with a wildcat," I
comment. The scratches covering most of his face, neck, arms, and
hands from running through the jungle when the Corps attacked
have finally started to fade. David looks only a little better, having
been right behind Desto, who broke through most of the brush.

"Honey, I'm looking at the only wildcat I ever want to tangle
with."

I can't help but laugh.

Moving past them to the shower stalls, I drop my clothes on the
bench outside. The water is hot and abundant, and I linger for a
while beneath it. I forgot how good this feels—one of the perks of
being a soldier on a fleet cruiser my subconscious had conveniently
stifled. If not for these little things, mutiny would be a much more
common occurrence among the fleet. Or would have been, until the
events of late.

After a few blissful minutes, I can't steal any more time or any
more water from the ship's tanks and turn off the tap. All of the
Beachers have been given an assigned locker and extra clothing from
the ship's requisitions. I stand in front of locker 1127 and pull the

familiar pieces of uniform on once more. The Corps fatigues and undershirt are soft and loose, probably a batch salvaged from recycling, and I'm grateful for their comfortable intimacy.

By the time I've slipped the shirt over my bra, pulled on the cargo pants, and cinched up my boots, the dry air of the ship has sapped most of the moisture from my hair, which is getting long and unruly. I look into the mirror hanging from the locker door as I pull it back from my face and wrap it up in an elastic band. The bruises from my fight with Baker are already faded, and my nose just has a small cut on the bridge, the swelling completely gone.

I pop the door closed and notice Karl standing at the end of the line of benches, the muted lights in the room casting a shadow over his face. I can't see his expression, but I can see the sparkle of his amber eyes.

"Aly, we need to talk."

The locker room is full of metal, but his husky voice doesn't echo. It carries to my ears like a balm made from cherished, yet painful, memories. We've been airborne for just over a week, enough time for me to catch up on my sleep and listen to the unbelievable story again and again, waiting for it to feel real. We still haven't spent much time together, and the moments we have were awkward, neither us capable of saying what we're really thinking.

"Sure. What's on your mind?" I turn back toward the locker to hang my wet towel on the protruding hook, hoping he doesn't notice the way my hand tremors.

After a pause, he comes closer and stands resolutely beside me, centimeters away. I turn to look at him, and his face is fully illuminated by the overheads. I'm almost knocked to the bench by the depths of both sorrow and hope I see in his eyes.

"Look, I know I was wrong. I owe you an apology."

"Forget it," I say quickly, my voice too thick, betraying me.

"Aly, I shouldn't have said the things I said. I . . . I fucked up. The way I treated you was—you didn't deserve that. I was just so afraid I was losing you. I didn't know what to do."

"It's all right, Karl. It's over. I'm not worried about it, okay?" I don't know how much longer I can take him standing there staring at me like that before I break down. If I let him in again, will it hurt as much as last time? Am I strong enough to try?

He doesn't say anything for a few seconds, then puts a hand on my wrist. Its warmth spreads up to my elbow like a burning brand. He takes a deep breath, searching my face, as if what he's about to say is something heavy that will take all of his strength to utter. "I'm trying to say I'm sorry. When I thought I'd lost you, it felt like someone had ripped me open. I was so afraid of what life would be like without you. For the first time, I realized what you mean to me. Aly, you're the reason I keep going. You're the only thing that makes all this shit that's happening worth it. When I thought I'd never see you again, I realized how I've failed you—"

Overwhelming emotion suddenly wells up in my throat and threatens to choke me. I raise a hand to try and put it over his mouth, but he grabs it between both of his and wraps it away like a tiny, fragile gift that he treasures too much to even chance a look. "I realized what you needed from me wasn't just for me to be around. You needed to know that I love you. I love you. I love you so much."

Salty water slips from my eyes to my lips, left, right, left, like disciplined soldiers on the march. His blazing eyes search my face for a response. Gently, I pull on my hand and he lets it slide out of his grasp. Swiping at my face, I say nothing and reach out to grab the sleeve of his jacket and lead him to my bunk.

"DON'T FORGET, MEDINA wants us all to meet her in the command center at 1700," Karl says as he straps on his boots. His shirt is still off, and my eyes trail along the muscles of his back, his wide shoulders, strong traps, long lats. The familiar pattern of scars on his skin is a roadmap for me in the dark, all I need to find my way to complete happiness. As he pulls his shirt over his head, I make a silent promise to myself that I'll never lose him again, never fail him again. Or myself.

"I'll be there."

He leans down and kisses me once more, then heads out the door to help Mason and Brady sort through the rest of the salvage from the *Sphynx*. Just before stepping out, he picks up his jacket from where he'd thrown it on a chair, and a scowl crosses his features. He reaches for an inside pocket and pulls out a small box.

Hesitantly, he comes back beside the bed and extends it toward me. "We found this with Cross's stuff on the *Sphynx*."

I take it from him uncertainly, not understanding why he's giving it to me until I see my name written along the top. "Thanks."

His eyes linger on my face for a second. "I love you, Aly."

I smile widely, surprised that those words can penetrate so deeply into my heart. "You too."

Once he's gone, I get dressed, leaving the box lying on the bed. Cross's betrayal had been so unexpected that I still haven't wanted to examine the full extent of the damage he'd caused. More of me wants to forget about it and never think of it again than deal with it. David hasn't spoken a word of the situation to me, and I know that he's feeling just as betrayed and hurt as I am. Cross must have known I'd never have taken him up on his offer to buy a new identity and false citizenship if I'd known what he was up to, but how could he have believed he could hide the fact that he was working for T'Kai?

The box sits there, tugging at me like a tiny black hole, its weight on my thoughts a physical burden. I break down and clean both my Sinbad and then my AK-80 before I finally give in and open it. Inside lays a small recording projector. Not completely sure I want to hear whatever Rob had wanted to tell me, I position it on the edge of the bunk with the lens pointing toward the blank wall across from me and turn it on.

The first image I see is a hand moving away from me, presumably having just turned on the device. As it recedes, I'm looking at the black-shirted chest, and finally, the face of Cross. He sits down—by brain notes that he's sitting in his cabin aboard the *Red Horizon*—and looks directly into the lens for several seconds before saying anything. The image is so sharp that he could actually be sitting there in the flesh. Goosebumps ripple up my arms.

"Well, Aly, if you're watching this, I must be dead." He almost smiles, the statement evoking some kind of cynical humor that he'd rarely displayed in life. There's a long pause, and it doesn't look like he has any idea of what he's going to say. I almost turn off the device. The man had nearly been responsible for getting everyone I know killed. But somehow, even worse, he had betrayed me. I'd been stabbed in the back by others, like Rajcik, but no double-cross could have ever surprised me, or hurt me, more than Rob's.

"Aly, I want you to understand what happened. I'm sure you believe I betrayed you, and Vitruzzi and the crew, but I never in a million years wanted that to happen." He takes a deep breath and continues, "I was busted by Admin security five months ago. They knew about my smuggling. Jesus, I thought I was so smart, but they knew everything." He runs a hand through his hair, creases appearing around his eyes and forehead as if he's in pain. Even through the medium of the image, I can see the turmoil writhing just behind his dark eyes. I want to hate him. He deserves nothing but my loathing and contempt, dead or not. But I can't.

"They offered me a deal. Keep doing what I was doing and lead them to the more dangerous procurers—the people that actually posed a threat to them, not just random non-cits looking for backup parts for rusted out derelicts. The Admin knows there are a lot of people like that out there, but they don't care about them. So I did what they wanted, informed on the people I delivered to, people like Rajcik, and I got to keep my ship and stay out of prison.

"But you and Vitruzzi's crew hit them hard when you blew up the Fortress. T'Kai fed them Rajcik as the most likely culprit. Of course, he knew it was him anyway, but it was a good way of redirecting the inquiries. T'Kai's back was against the wall. He was responsible for the Fortress's security and operations, and the Admin lost billions from the station's destruction. The only reason he wasn't held accountable was because he had enough evidence to convince them that it was Rajcik. He had security scans from the outpost on Obal 3, from when your team stole the station's disc. Goddammit, Aly, he even had scans of you and David."

I suck in a quick breath. T'Kai had been telling the truth about knowing we were part of Rajcik's team.

"After that, T'Kai changed the game. He wanted me to keep my eyes out for Rajcik and his team, gather intel from around the system, and he showed me the scans. At first, I couldn't believe it. See, I didn't know about the research they were doing on the Fortress. I just thought you and David had been part of some massive weapons-smuggling op that turned into a . . . a mistake. Back when we were in the Corps, you'd always thought the Admin was corrupt; blowing up that space station seemed like just the kind of thing you'd have done if you had the chance. And T'Kai had proof. If I'd known what he was trying to cover up . . . but I didn't. What was I supposed to do?

"I only wanted to find Rajcik. But when I landed on Spectra 6 with Vitruzzi's transceiver parts, you can't know how shocked I was to find you and David there. That was the last thing I ever expected. It wouldn't have mattered, I would never have turned you in after you led me to Rajcik, but my crew—Sims, Baker, Montoya—they're Admin, they're not mine. They were assigned to me to make sure I did my job and kept my mouth shut. I just wanted to bring Rajcik in, but now T'Kai knows about the footage and the data."

He looks at something away from the screen and his vision goes distant for a few seconds. Are there tears in his eyes? The skin of his face is tight and shiny with torment. When he made this recording, he already knew there was no way he was going to get out of this, but I can see he's still wishing he could. Still not wanting to betray anyone.

"I don't know what's going to happen, but if it goes bad, you have to know how sorry I am. If it were just me, I'd have taken the bullet for you already. But it's not. My crew . . . they know almost everything, and they're not going to stop, even if they have to kill me to carry out T'Kai's orders. The only thing I can do is try and find an angle that gets the least amount of people hurt. But shit"—that cynical smile again—"like I said: if you're seeing this . . . well, you know.

"Remember this, Aly, whatever happens, I'm not the bad guy. I never wanted to involve you or David in this. Vitruzzi, Brady, Desto, they're all my friends. It's just the way of the worlds. It's a fucking mess and the best we can do is try to survive." He leans forward and his hand approaches the recorder, preparing to turn it off. Before he does, he adds one more thing. "I'm sorry for whatever trouble I may have caused between you and Strahan, but I never met another woman like you after the Corps. You should know, Aly, I'm going to do—or I did—everything I could to keep you safe."

And he shuts it off.

I don't know how long I've been sitting on my bunk staring at the blank wall when someone knocks.

"It's open."

David comes in, gets ready to say something and then pauses, looking at me closely. "Everything okay?"

I nod, lacking any certitude that everything will ever really be okay again.

"Yeah, well this shouldn't upset you too much then—Rajcik and Thompson killed the dock control crew guarding the *Red Horizon*. They took the ship."

THIRTY-NINE

We've been gathered on the carrier's flight deck for forty-five minutes watching the reports coming in from all over the system: citizen and non-citizen station casts, Admin-controlled newswaves, even some Corps ships who are still under the Admin's control. Rajcik flew the *Red Horizon* directly to Obal 10. When we warned Medina about the Nova being on board the ship and how deeply Rajcik's anti-Admin motivations were rooted, she'd had other things on her mind and never secured it. There is no way to set up a search-and-destroy mission with the amount of fighting going on throughout the quadrant. Rajcik had slipped through all the nets, sliding by rebel ships who had more important issues to deal with than a harmless transporter, and aided by those still loyal to the Admin for being known to be contracted by, possibly even carrying, T'Kai. He'd breached Obal 10 airspace an hour ago, using the ship's transceiver to send one final message to the Admin.

A communications tech sergeant put his broadcast on one screen set to loop, and I haven't been able to look at anything else since the first viewing. Rajcik stands in the 'Rize's cockpit, staring into the lens of a handheld recording device just like the one Rob had used. His opalescent teeth gleam as he talks, telling the Admin that the time has come for them to reap what they'd sown for so long. Tunis City can be seen through the ship's viewscreens as the *'Rize* approaches it in a full-tilt dive. Rajcik pans the device over the sleek body of the Nova as he explains what it is and what he's about to do with it. There's a loud explosion, and the recording jolts violently as a gunship in the area begins pursuing him, someone out there realizing he's on a collision course with the system's capital city, even if they don't know he's about to annihilate it. But the dive can't be stopped. The last thing Rajcik does before short-circuiting the ship's electrical systems and causing an electromagnetic pulse that detonates the Nova is smile his deadly, yet somehow completely sane, smile.

Tunis City is destroyed. Obal 10's atmosphere is destabilized. Millions are dead. The real war has begun.

AFTERWORD

Follow Aly and David on their vendetta against the Admin in the next book in the Spectras Arise Series, CONTRACT OF WAR.

Thank you for reading! If you enjoyed this story and like to sing the praises of authors who entertained you, you would have my boundless gratitude if you were to write a review on the retailer of your choice.

ALSO BY TAMMY SALYER

SPECTRAS ARISE SERIES

When all other options run out, never let go of your gun.

In a few hundred years, the Algol system becomes humanity's new home. The question is: Is it a better one?

THE SHACKLED VERITIES SERIES

In a Cosmos-wide war between celestials, humans are as expendable as pawns. Until Ulfric Aldinhuus, leader of the Knights Corporealis, uses the celestials' weapons to fight back.

OTHERWORLD OUTLAWS SERIES

A sawbones fae with a supernatural-sized grudge, a necromancer gnome obsessed with pixie dust, and a hoodoo cowgirl with a Sharps buffalo rifle and damn good aim—the Tuatha Dé Danann will never know what hit 'em.

COLLECTIONS

A Scorpion's Heart: Four Twisted Tales of Love and Lust

SHORT STORIES

Artificial Fate * Creepers * No Suede Soles in Hell

Visit my website to see if anything new has been released since this publication.

www.tammysalyer.com

ABOUT THE AUTHOR

Tammy is an inveterate verbarian, who spends her days surrounded by the written word, both hers and others'. As an ex-paratrooper with the 82nd Airborne Division, her stories are often as gritty as a grunt's pile of three-week-old field gear. Her military science fiction Spectras Arise series debuted to acclaim in 2012, and her epic fantasy adventure series The Shackled Verities was launched in 2020. She's currently five books deep in a Weird West series called Otherworld Outlaws, featuring half-fae sawbones, a necromancer gnome, and a hoodoo cowgirl galavanting into mischief in the Old West.

When not hunched like a Morlock over her writing desk, Tammy runs and bikes silly miles with her super-cool weirdo partner in the Pacific Northwest playground and spends an inappropriate amount of time watching Henry Rollins videos on YouTube. Contrary to whatever ideas her last name might conjure, she's never really been much of a Slayer fan.

Fantasy, space opera, satire, and snark fans will feel right at home with Tammy. Learn more about her and her books by visiting www.tammysalyer.com. She hopes you enjoy reading her works and welcomes your reviews.